SOMEDAY AWAY

A PACIFIC NORTHWEST BOYS NOVEL

BOOK ONE

SARA ELISABETH

Paperback ISBN: 979-8-218-35549-4

Published by Woodchuckery Publishing

Printed in the United States of America

First US Edition: January 2024

Edited by Caroline Acebo

Cover Design by Kate Farlow at Y'all.That Graphic.

For Ramses "xLore" Lopez, who inspired me to write this book when we were just 16 years old. I wish you were still here to read it, my friend.

And for all my readers—life is too short so love who you want, haters be damned.

Playlist

"Someday Away" - Overshot
"Mean to Me" - Tonic
"Fall for You" - Secondhand Serenade
"If I Am" - Nine Days
"Someday" - Rob Thomas
"Vindicated" - Dashboard Confessional
"Shimmer" - Fuel
"Fix You" - Coldplay
"Whatever It Takes" - Lifehouse
"The Middle" - Jimmy Eat World
"Hunger" - Ross Copperman
"Broken" - Lifehouse
"The World I Know" - Collective Soul
"Be Yourself" - Audioslave
"How Do You Love" - Collective Soul
"Become" - The Goo Goo Dolls
"bad decisions" - Bad Omens
"Unwell" - Matchbox Twenty
"Inn Town" - Whiskeytown What
"What About Now" - Daughtry
"Black and Blue" - Counting Crows
"Let Love In" - The Goo Goo Dolls
"Hand Me Down" - Matchbox Twenty
"February Stars" - Foo Fighters
"Collide" - Howie Day
"Life on a Rope" - Overshot

Listen to the playlist on <u>Spotify</u> or <u>Apple Music</u>.

PREFACE

Someday Away is an adult dark MFM college romance with a healthy mix of enemies-to-lovers and spice and some LGBTQAI+ representation. It features an introverted heroine and two best friends–a golden boy and a broody bad boy–who know how to hate and love in equal measure. This book is a stand alone in an interconnected series and ends with a happy ever after.

Trigger warnings include drug and alcohol use, addiction, parental abandonment, suicide, eating disorders, abuse, and sexual assault/rape.

CONTENTS

Chapter 1	1
Chapter 2	4
Chapter 3	12
Chapter 4	17
Chapter 5	21
Chapter 6	24
Chapter 7	30
Chapter 8	34
Chapter 9	46
Chapter 10	49
Chapter 11	55
Chapter 12	59
Chapter 13	68
Chapter 14	74
Chapter 15	84
Chapter 16	91
Chapter 17	97
Chapter 18	105
Chapter 19	113
Chapter 20	123
Chapter 21	128
Chapter 22	142
Chapter 23	149
Chapter 24	161
Chapter 25	169
Chapter 26	177
Chapter 27	183
Chapter 28	193
Chapter 29	197
Chapter 30	205
Chapter 31	220
Chapter 32	230
Chapter 33	234

Chapter 34   239
Chapter 35   247
Chapter 36   259
Chapter 37   270
Chapter 38   286
Chapter 39   296
Chapter 40   302
Chapter 41   310
Chapter 42   330
Chapter 43   340
Chapter 44   350
Chapter 45   359
Chapter 46   370
Chapter 47   382
Chapter 48   388
Chapter 49   397
Chapter 50   410

Acknowledgments   421
About the Author   423

CHAPTER ONE

CHARLIE

$\mathcal{I}$ stare at the gray cathedral-like buildings of Whitmore University, the most prestigious private school in the Pacific Northwest. Anxiety blooms in my stomach, but I swallow down the unwanted nausea and sling my backpack over my shoulder. I don't have much with me, just a few books, some clothes, and the laptop my mom gave me.

Today is "Washington stormy," a constant state of gloom and misty drizzle. I could have gone to a fancy school in California, but I'm not really a fan of hot weather. And while the East Coast has a lot of Big Ten schools, the thought of moving that far away from Sebastian and Marcus, my stepbrothers, after my mom's recent death was unthinkable. I had already deferred college a year to recover from the loss, but the wound is still there, a constant, raw burn in my chest that feels like it's melting away my heart like some sort of flesh-eating bacteria.

I walk through the wrought-iron gate, looking for some indication of where to find my dorm room assignment. Students bustle around the expansive quad, chatting and toting their belongings into various buildings. You can tell who's local and who isn't. People running for shelter, sporting bright-

1

colored jackets and umbrellas? They're definitely out-of-town-ers. Most Washingtonians are thick-skinned and wear black jackets if they even own a coat at all. In general, we walk at a casual pace with nothing more than a sweatshirt to protect us from the incessant mist.

I tuck my long, wavy brown hair further back into my hood and head for the closest person with a clipboard. Unfortunately, that person doesn't look very friendly. She studies me as I approach her tent and flips her intricately braided blonde hair over one shoulder. Her name tag reads "Serenity Smith."

Perfect.

"Hi." I give my best polite smile. "I'm looking for my dorm assignment."

She grimaces as her eyes assess me, and I tense up. She reminds me of the mean girls from my high school. I'm dressed casually in ripped jeans, a hoodie, and Converse, which are already thoroughly soaked. By contrast, Serenity looks like Lumberjack Barbie—and I don't mean that in a bad way—but she's trying a bit too hard to fit into the Pacific Northwest motif with her dark skinny jeans, calf-high rain boots, and designer flannel shirt.

"Name?" Serenity asks.

"Charlie—I mean Charlotte—Bennett."

She raises a perfectly manicured eyebrow at me, but doesn't say anything.

"Charlie's short for Charlotte," I repeat lamely, trying to ease the weird heaviness weighing on my chest. I used to be better at "peopling," but after months of limited human interaction, my skills feel disjointed and rusty, like I'm the Tin Man from *The Wizard of Oz*, desperate for some social oil.

She makes a noise under her breath that's something between a snort and a snicker. "Oookay," she murmurs.

She flips through the pages on her clipboard before turning to a boy standing to her right. He's chatting with a group of students who're hauling over what looks like grocery bags of marshmallows, chocolate bars, and graham crackers.

"Brantley, do you have a Charlotte Bennett on your list? Her name isn't on my roster."

He turns and walks over to us, scanning his list. He looks up at me with warm hazel eyes.

"Well, well, I do, in fact, have Miss Bennett on my list. You're in the Raven Building in"—he raises his eyebrows—"a private suite? How'd you pull that off?"

I shrug, feeling self-conscious. "It was part of my scholarship, I guess."

Serenity frowns. "You got one of the private suites? I've been on the waiting list for two years. Typical that they would just give it to a charity case."

I bristle at her remark, clutching my backpack straps tightly. I'm about to tell her where to shove her sparkly pink pen, but Brantley steps in first.

"Stop being a cunt, Seren," he says, watching me with interest.

Serenity scowls at him.

He winks and hands me an envelope with my name and room number on the back. "The Raven Building is the last one on your left," says Brantley. "It has a raven statue out front, so you can't miss it."

CHAPTER TWO

CHARLIE

*D*espite being a single "suite," my dorm room is pretty small, but that suits me just fine. The walls are a calming shade of blue, and it has one window overlooking the woods behind the school. Being on the sixteenth floor, I can't complain about the view. In the distance, through a break in the heavy clouds, I can see the snowy peak of Mt. Baker blushing pink in the light of the sunset.

My room has a twin bed adorned with a fluffy gray duvet (another scholarship perk, apparently), a simple oak desk in one corner, and a closet with more than enough space to house my meager collection of clothing.

After I unpack, I walk out into the hallway, exploring the communal bathrooms and laundry facilities. Everything is close and clean. No complaints here.

After returning to my room, I sit down, wondering what I should do next. There's a knock at my door. Puzzled, I walk over and open it. A girl stands in the doorway. She has beautiful long auburn hair, flawless, pale skin, and adorable freckles peppered across her petite nose. Her green eyes light up as she takes me in, and she smiles widely.

"I'm Fiona Flowers!" she gushes. "We're neighbors."

I smile cautiously. "Hi. I'm Charlotte Bennett—Charlie for short."

She peeks around me. "Can I see your room? I've never seen a single suite before."

"Uh, sure," I say, moving to the side.

"Wow! This is pretty nice," Fiona says. "Not that there's anything wrong with my roommate, but the privacy would be nice." She glances up at the clock above the door. "Are you going down to the bonfire? I think they're about to light it up."

"Bonfire?" That would explain the s'more fixings I saw earlier.

"At the start of every year they light the fire pit in the center of the quad, and everyone goes down to mingle and drink and eat s'mores. Were you not here last year? You look like you're older than a freshman."

"Actually, I had to defer a year for personal reasons, so technically I'm a year behind," I explain.

"Oh! Well it's super fun. You don't want to miss it."

I like that she doesn't pry into my past.

"Okay," I say, smiling. I don't normally immediately take to strangers, but this girl has something in her upbeat demeanor that sets me at ease.

"Great!" She beams. "Let's go!"

Fiona loops my arm through hers, and we walk to the elevators, riding down together. When the bronze doors open, I'm struck by the beauty of the foyer. I'd already passed through once on my way to unpack, but fully taking in its vaulted ceilings and flickering chandeliers is impressive to say the least.

"It's pretty, right?" exclaims Fiona, also admiring the stone archways curving above us. "Walking through here feels like living in a fantasy novel. It never gets old." She smiles dreamily before pulling me toward the front door.

We walk out onto the quad. The rain has stopped, but the

air is still chilly and damp, and it smells like earth, pine, and smoke. I shiver as we approach the fire, and Fiona and I huddle together for warmth as I take in the festivities around me.

Fiona chatters away, pointing out different groups of students, and I smile and nod. Suddenly, I feel a chill that has nothing to do with the night air.

I'm being watched.

I scan the crowd until I lock eyes with a boy across the dancing firelight. Something about him is familiar, but I can't place where I would have seen him before. To say he's hot is an understatement. Tousled, almost black hair frames his sharp features. He has full lips, which are pulled into a slight frown. His eyebrows are drawn down, making the expression on his perfect face almost angry, and I turn to look behind me, thinking his ire must be directed at someone else. But there's no one there.

Frowning, I glance back over at him, but his attention has moved on. He's standing with a group of boys who're also ridiculously gorgeous. I recognize Brantley from earlier. One guy throws his arm around the dark-haired boy's broad shoulders and says something, causing Mr. Attitude to smirk, while the others erupt in laughter.

"Who're they?" I ask Fiona, nodding my head at the group.

Fiona looks across the quad. "Oh," she lowers her voice, "Brantley Michaels is super annoying, but he's one of our hockey centers. The super-hot broody one is Lincoln Evans, and the funny golden boy is his best friend, Trey Walker. They're both seniors." She gives me a knowing look. "I'd avoid those guys though, if I were you. They're hot, but they're also conceited assholes, so not exactly relationship material." She taps her chin thoughtfully. "In fact, I don't think they've ever dated anyone. They're kind of slutty."

We both giggle at her comment.

"I'd be a slut, too, if I looked like them," I say, glancing back over at Lincoln.

"Right?" says Fiona. "Girls throw themselves at them constantly." She rolls her eyes. "They probably have the personalties of wet paper bags, but it's hard to tell with all the bad-boy moodiness and drunken shenanigans."

"Speaking of girls," I say. I watch as Serenity swaggers over to their group. "Does Serenity always walk like that? Like she's about to do a strip tease?"

Fiona snickers. "She does when she's pursuing Lincoln. That girl has been after him for an entire year."

I look at her in disbelief. "He's not interested? A girl like that with her shiny hair and perfect thigh gap?"

Fiona shrugs. "I thought they were going to date last year, but then the rumor was it was just a fling. But Serenity has been throwing herself at him ever since." Fiona smirks. "I don't think she's used to rejection."

I grin and glance back across the fire. Once again, Lincoln's acrid gaze collides with mine. My smile falters, and I glare back.

What is this guy's problem?

"Let's get a drink," Fiona says.

Turning away, I follow her to a tent sheltering a table stacked with boxes of graham crackers and bags of marshmallows. A girl—a freshman by the look of her baby face—waves as we approach, but before she can greet us, a boy walks up next to the table, dumping a pile of sticks onto an already sizable heap.

"I'm done with stick duty," he snarks angrily before stomping off.

Fiona and I glance at each other and hold in a laugh.

The girl smiles apologetically. "Do you want to make a s'more?" she asks brightly. "Or there's drinks in those coolers." She indicates two large red Colemans sitting in the grass to her left.

"Just drinks," I say. "Thanks."

7

We walk over and open one of the chests, and I scrunch my nose when Fiona pulls out two Rainier beers.

"Not a beer fan, huh? Me either, but it's all we get for free on campus."

"Honestly, I'm surprised you can drink so freely. Aren't we breaking open container laws or something?"

Fiona snickers. "Totally, but Whitmore U is full of entitled trust fund babies. Campus security gets paid a lot of money to look the other way during these little events."

"Right." I crack open the beer and take a swig, wincing as the bitter taste assaults my tongue. But as the night wears on, the beers seem to go down easier, and I suspect it has to do with my level of inebriation.

It's been a while since I really allowed myself to relax and have fun, but despite the panic that always sits restlessly in the back of my consciousness, I feel relatively safe following Fiona like a lost drunk puppy, and she doesn't seem to mind.

After polishing off my third drink, I crush the can in my hand and wander over to one of the overflowing recycling bins. I toss the can from a few feet away, missing my target entirely. It ricochets off into the surrounding darkness.

"Shit," I mutter, squinting as I step past the firelight and trip over something hard. I fall backward and land with a wet thud on the rain-soaked grass. I stare daggers at the tree root that caught my foot, and spot my discarded can next to the tree's trunk a few feet away. Sighing I crawl over, grab the can, and sit a moment, my eyes sinking closed.

I need water, I think as I breathe in the cool, damp air.

"Did you recognize the new scholarship girl?" Serenity's voice reaches my ears, and I open my eyes, watching as she approaches the recycle bin and carefully sets her can on the already precariously stacked pile. "Charlie or whatever?"

"Yeah, Seren, what about her?"

I tense up at the smooth, deep voice and peer around the bin to get a better view of the speaker. Lincoln and Trey are standing next to her smoking a joint. Lincoln takes a long pull and inhales before passing it to Trey.

"She's from Brighton like us," Serenity says.

"Is she?" Lincoln asks disinterestedly as he blows out the smoke.

Of course I would run into Brighton townies. Lucky me.

"Yes," Serenity continues, "and I have a friend who went to Brighton Prep who told me that Charlie's mom was the socialite who committed suicide last year."

My heart rate escalates and the air squeezes from my lungs.

Lincoln stiffens. "No one actually confirmed that it was suicide."

Serenity shrugs. "Just what I heard."

"Why do you care?" Trey asks.

"I'm just surprised she's here on a scholarship. Her family obviously has money."

"Wait, which girl are we talking about?" Trey asks. "The hot little number with the Converse? I saw her and Link sharing a smoldering look across the fire."

My cheeks heat with embarrassment.

Lincoln's face darkens, and he shoves Trey, who stumbles away with a chuckle. "She's pretty average if you ask me—looks like every other rich bitch at this college."

Lincoln's words sting, and anger sparks in my veins, which is only exacerbated when Serenity responds with a sly smirk.

I'm not sure why I do it—probably the alcohol—but I stand and march toward them.

They all look over in surprise as I stomp into the light, wiping dirt and grass from my backside. "And I suppose next you'll say I'm tolerable?" I snark at Lincoln, stepping into his space. He smells faintly of beer and weed with a potent dose of musky sandalwood.

"Well, well, what's this?" Lincoln's tone is cold and condescending, and his eyes are practically black as I stare up at him in the flickering firelight. "Are you living out your own *Pride and Prejudice* fantasies eavesdropping in the darkness?"

I raise my eyebrows, surprised that he understood my reference. "Please," I scoff, "you're hardly comparable to Mr. Darcy."

Which is a lie. He's just as hot—if not hotter—with an attitude to match.

Lincoln glances around with a cocky grin. "I suspect most of the girls on this campus would disagree."

He looks at Trey and reaches for the joint, takes another puff, then blows the smoke in my face.

I step back, wrinkling my nose at the skunky scent. "Yeah, you're right." I seethe. "You're arrogant, conceited, and self-centered, so I guess the attitude fits."

I turn on my heel and stalk away, grinding my teeth when I hear their laughter behind me.

As the adrenaline from the encounter drains from my body, I feel perspiration trickling down my back. I walk over to the drink table and snatch a bottle of water, twisting at the cap angrily when it slips against my sweaty, shaking hands.

"Let me help."

I tense in surprise, looking up to find Trey standing next to me, his hand outstretched in askance. I narrow my eyes at him but hand over the water bottle. Our fingers graze, lingering a bit too long, and a spark of warmth flutters over my skin from the contact.

Trey opens the bottle and hands it back to me.

I take a sip, studying him. Trey's even more stunning up close, his hair a mess of blond highlights, and his eyes warm, caramel brown. He smells faintly of apples and cinnamon, and when his full, pink lips curve in a roguish smile, I feel my stomach flip.

"Don't let Link get to you," Trey says. "He's been through some shit."

"We've all been through some shit," I retort. "But some of us still have manners. We're not all self-righteous assholes."

Trey smiles widely. "Fair enough." He runs his thumb along his bottom lip. "What's your name again?"

I hesitate before I answer, eyeing him. Fiona said I shouldn't trust Trey, but he puts me at ease for some reason—though I can't for the life of me understand why this beautiful, charming guy is friends with Lincoln. "My friends call me Charlie," I say finally. "My full name is Charlotte Bennett."

"Bennett? Like Elizabeth Bennett? You do have her sass."

I shake my head with a small smile. "How do you guys know so much about *Pride and Prejudice*? Are you English majors or something?"

"Nope, but we've watched a lot of movies. Link is double majoring in theater and film."

I nod, somewhat relieved that Lincoln won't turn up in any of my English classes. What a nightmare that would be.

I glance longingly at my dorm. I'm tired. "I think I'm done for tonight. It was nice to meet you, Trey."

"See you around, Bennett," he says with a wink, and my stomach does that weird flip as I walk back across the quad.

CHAPTER THREE

CHARLIE

*T*he clouds still hang heavy in the late September sky, but the rain isn't in full swing yet, so it's perfect fall weather. Whitmore's campus is adorned with clusters of Japanese maples that light up like fire as the season starts to turn.

The start of my first week has been hectic, but I'm easing into the feeling of going to school again. My stepbrothers have been calling me a lot to check in—or rather my youngest older stepbrother, Sebastian, has FaceTimed while Marcus ignores me in the background. I try not to be hurt by Marcus's indifference. He still blames me for my mom's death and my stepfather—their father—leaving. The guilt and anger are constant weights on my chest. Sometimes, I can't breathe.

I think Seb is afraid that I'm going to let the anxiety overwhelm me, and I get it. He was the one who found me sobbing on the bathroom floor the day my mother died. But I eventually learned to control the panic attacks. As long as I felt in control, I could act normal, be normal.

The clocktower bell echoes across the quad, and I shake off

my dark thoughts. Today is the first day of my advanced English class, and I'm beyond excited to get back to writing. I had to get special permission to even enroll in a junior-level course, but I'm hoping that I'll be able to churn out some portfolio pieces to submit to a summer publishing internship in New York with Rosewood Publishing. More than anything, I want to be a book editor and an author, and the opportunity would be a huge step toward that dream.

I enter the humanities building, which naturally also houses the library. The smell of books assailing my nostrils is delicious. It's a rare smell these days with everyone (myself included) reading on their iPads and Kindles. I can only get my fix sitting in a library or a Barnes & Noble, sniffing the air like a crack addict.

I walk into the lecture hall, choosing a seat a few rows from the back. I don't like unwanted attention, so I tend to avoid sitting in the front. My high school English teacher Mr. Shockley always insisted I was such a talented writer because I'm quiet—good at blending and observing.

I pull out my MacBook, preparing to take notes as my new professor strolls into class. He's fairly young, maybe in his late thirties or early forties. He flashes a friendly smile as he drops his briefcase on the floor and perches on the edge of the desk.

"Hello, everyone," he says. "I'm Dr. Jackson. Welcome to English 305 and Film 311, Fiction and Screenplays."

Did he say film?

I frown and glance around. It's a pretty large group for a junior-level class. In some stereotypical ways, you can pick out the English majors from the thespians and film geeks. A boy in front of me leans back, passing me the stack of syllabi going around the room.

"If you're an English major, you may be confused right now." Dr. Jackson gives a knowing smile when some students start looking around the room. "Our theater and film department lost a professor suddenly, so the university made an adjustment and combined the fiction and screenplay classes together. It's a bit unorthodox, yes, but in the future, you'll spend your careers working with people from other backgrounds—designers, programmers, marketers, producers, and so on—so take this as an opportunity to mirror the real world."

I vaguely hear the door opening behind me, and then, I can smell him—spicy, earthy, and crisp. Sweater weather in a scent.

Don't sit next to me.

The chair to my left scrapes against the floor, and I glance over at Lincoln freaking Evans sitting next to me in all his broody glory.

Dammit.

I turn back to the professor, trying my best to concentrate. Lincoln reclines in his chair, and his knee brushes my leg with a zap of heat. I jump.

He chuckles darkly. "If it isn't Elizabeth Bennett's plain doppelgänger."

I glare at him from the corner of my eye.

"Such a ray of sunshine," he whispers. "Still just as uptight and self-righteous, I see."

"Do you mind?" I snap. "I'm trying to listen."

He frowns, probably unaccustomed to someone deflecting his bullshit.

Entitled asshole.

"Hello, folks in the back. Am I interrupting your conversation?"

My stomach bottoms out, and blood rushes to my cheeks. "No, Dr. Jackson. I'm so sorry."

So much for not drawing attention.

"That blush looks good on you," Lincoln murmurs, and I kick him under the table.

"What're your names?" Dr. Jackson asks pointedly.

"Charlie Bennett."

Lincoln smirks. "Lincoln Evans."

"Ah, Mr. Evans. A family legend around here, aren't you? Perhaps you would like to start off the partnering process with Miss Bennett."

I feel the color drain from my face. *No, no, no...*

"Sure," he says. He seems almost gleeful about this horrible turn of events.

"Great," Dr. Jackson says, and he starts pairing off film majors with English majors.

I cross my arms over my chest, glowering at Lincoln.

"What?" he asks, grinning. It's an evil grin, like he's enjoying my misery, and it makes me hate him even more.

"Now that everyone has a partner, this class will culminate in the spring with a final project," Dr. Jackson announces. "The owner of Lakeside Cinema on Main Street has graciously agreed to show a collection of short films written and performed by Whitmore U students. English students will write the screenplays and film students will be directing." He takes a deep breath and smiles. "Whitmore U's drama department will be performing the pieces, and we'll have some help from the technical theater majors as well." His dark eyes scan the class-room. "This is a big deal, folks—it will be seventy-five percent of your grade and a great portfolio piece for a future employer, so I suggest you take it seriously."

I try to swallow the sinking sensation in my stomach as I glance at Lincoln. He's completely tuned out, texting on his phone.

This is going to be a disaster.

The rest of class passes quickly, and thankfully, Lincoln doesn't cause me any more grief.

As we get up to leave, Dr. Jackson raises his hand. "One more thing," he calls over the din of laptops closing and backpack zippers. "Lakeside is hiring, so if anyone is interested, stop by the theater and ask for John."

That gets my attention. I could definitely use the extra cash.

I look over as I finish packing up, thinking that I probably need to grab Lincoln's number, but he's already gone.

CHAPTER FOUR

CHARLIE

*T*he next morning, I wake to relentless knocking on my door. I sit up, pushing the tangle of long hair from my bleary eyes. I glance at my phone. It's seven.

Fuck. Who wakes up this early?

I pull on a pair of yoga pants to answer the door. Fiona stands in the doorway practically bouncing on her toes.

I stare at her. "You do realize it's 7 a.m., right?"

"And that's why I brought you coffee." She raises a tray of four steaming cups with a hopeful smile on her face. The smell is heavenly. "I'm not normally a morning person either, but coffee fixes everything, right?" She stares at the drinks. "I wasn't sure what kind of coffee you like, so I brought you a latte, a mocha, and an Americano."

"Always a mocha," I say, grinning. I grab the mocha, then narrow my eyes at her. "But why are you bribing me this morning?"

"Well," she says, "I thought we could get an early start and get to the theater before our classes this morning."

Yesterday, I told Fiona about the theater job, thinking she might want in on it, too.

17

"Yeah, I suppose that's a good idea," I say around a yawn.

"I did some research last night, and apparently Lakeside was bought up a few years ago by one of the university's rich donors, and he's finally gotten around to revamping it," says Fiona with a shrug. "I heard they are reopening it to show older movies with student pricing."

"That sounds awesome."

"I thought we could get breakfast and then walk over. What do you think?"

I gnaw on my bottom lip. "I don't really have any interview clothes."

"Oh, I have plenty." Fiona claps her hands with excitement, and she gestures for me to follow.

I do so reluctantly, sipping my coffee and wondering if I'm going to regret this. I have a lot on my plate with schoolwork since I'm taking one class over the recommended number in order to play catch-up. But my savings are running low, so I definitely need to find a source of income.

An hour later, we walk into the little three-plex that immediately feels like home. The floors are covered with worn, garish red, blue, and gold carpet except for the burnt orange ceramic tiles lining the concession stand, which houses a large popcorn popper, two registers, and a glass countertop case that was probably used to display candy. The box office is a literal box in the corner of the foyer. The place is in need of some cleaning; a grayish layer of dust coats every surface. The walls facing the street are all windows, and I can see dust motes sparkling lazily in the morning sunlight.

Even though I'm certain that the popper hasn't been used in a while, I can still smell a hint of stale popcorn in the air, tickling my senses like a buttery, salted memory.

Growing up, movies were a huge part of my life. My parents were kids of the eighties and nineties, and they loved to show me classics like *The Princess Bride, Back to the Future, Die Hard,* anything directed by John Hughes—I could go on. It was part of the reason I became a writer in the first place. Films are a form of storytelling, and storytelling starts with writing.

Fiona and I stand in the lobby talking quietly until a man enters from a side door. He's walking backward, juggling a large box while making his way through the doorway awkwardly. Finally, he turns and drops the box onto the gaudy carpet.

He looks up, eyeing Fiona and me with raised eyebrows. He's older, maybe in his fifties, and very handsome. He has dark eyes and dark hair with a few gray streaks at his temples. He looks familiar.

"Can I help you?" he asks, his deep voice slightly breathless from exertion.

"I'm Fiona Flowers, and this is Charlotte Bennett. Dr. Jackson mentioned that you were hiring."

"Oh yes." There's a hint of recognition in his gaze when he looks at me. "He's right about that. Are you film students?"

"I'm an English major, but I'm one of Dr. Jackson's students," I say with a shy smile.

"And I'm undecided, but I could really use a job," Fiona quips.

"I'm John." The man extends his hand, and we both shake it in turn. "Charlotte Bennett," John says with a wide grin. "You're Martin Conner's daughter."

My expression falters, but I catch it before it falls. "Stepdaughter, yes—how do you know Martin?"

"He was a business partner of mine," John says, his expression unreadable. "He actually sold me this place a while back."

Of course he did, I think. My stepfather is a wealthy property investor and a workaholic.

"It just took me a while to start updating it," John says with an apologetic lilt to his voice. "Anyway"—he claps his hands together in a back-to-business way—"the work is a bit of a smorgasbord. This is a small theater, so I want the staff to be able to run everything—concessions, the ticket booth, the projectors. You would also clean theaters, help with inventory, and build movies when they come in."

"Build movies?" I ask frowning.

He chuckles, his eyes crinkling at the corners. "Don't worry. These are things I would train you on. We have to purchase our movies from special vendors because the projectors are so old. We still use Mylar film and have to cut and tape the movies together. They normally come in four smaller reels of film that we build into one large reel with a building table."

Fiona and I exchange confused looks.

John laughs. "It's easier than it sounds."

"So are you a big cinephile?" I ask politely.

"I am to some extent, but this place is actually a bit of a pet project for my son, who loves movies as well. He'll open the place as general manager once we finish up some renovations."

The back door bursts open, and a dark-haired boy with thick black glasses peeks around the lobby, pausing when he spots John.

"Sorry, John," he says haltingly, his voice edged with panic. He's sweating profusely. "There's a guy here with soda syrup, but he only brought Diet Pepsi and Dr. Pepper. Everything else is missing, and I'm not really sure what to do."

"It's fine, Damon. We're just wrapping up." John glances at us. "Why don't you write down your numbers, and I'll call you with the details on when you can start."

"Are you sure you don't need to formally interview us?" I ask.

John shakes his head. "You have Dr. Jackson's recommendation in my eyes, and that's enough for me. I'll be in touch soon."

He gives us a cordial nod and follows Damon through the door.

CHAPTER FIVE

CHARLIE

*F*iona and I leave the theater just as it starts to rain in earnest. We glance at each other and break into a run, heading for the closest coffee shop. I'm soaking wet by the time we enter, my boots squeaking on the tile floor as I run into someone very tall and firm. The person's arms fly wide, attempting to save his hot coffee from sloshing onto the floor. His scent, a subtle mix of sandalwood and pine, envelops me, and I shake my head, trying to think straight. I look up into a pair of stunning gray eyes, dark and turbulent like an incoming storm.

Lincoln.

"I'm so sorry." I step back and glance at his coffee cup. The liquid drips down his wrist and onto the sleeve of his pristine white shirt.

His gaze hardens when he recognizes me. "Maybe you should watch where you're going." His voice would be a deep, sexy timbre if not for the snobby undertone.

Wait, what? Not sexy. What's the opposite of sexy?

Fiona quickly hands him some napkins from the nearby dispenser, her green eyes wide.

SARA ELISABETH

I frown. "You don't have to be rude," I say, putting my hands on my hips. "It was clearly an accident."

He raises an eyebrow, and I fight to swallow the sudden unexpected rush of nerves rippling through my body. My heart is hammering so hard that I'm sure he can hear it. He snatches the napkins from Fiona and wipes coffee from his skin, sneering at me the entire time.

The nerve of this guy. As if I set out to ruin his day when he clearly just wants to ruin every experience I have at this damn university.

"I said I was sorry," I fume.

"Of course you are," he says coldly, shoving the used napkins into Fiona's face, which just ignites my anger further. "Just like you're sorry you eavesdropped on my private conversation about your insignificance in my life."

"Wrong." I huff. "I'm not sorry about that at all now that I know what a stuck-up rich boy you are. But I am sorry I met you."

"Burn," Fiona whispers.

Lincoln glances at her darkly before those stupid beautiful eyes return to mine. We glower at each other, standing so close together that I can feel his minty breath brushing across my cheeks. Finally, Lincoln concedes, pushing roughly past me and walking out the door into the downpour. My shoulder tingles where our bodies touched.

I stare after him. "Well, isn't he a treat?"

Fiona snorts with laughter. "A delicious treat. I want to eat and swallow him whole." She waggles her eyebrows suggestively.

I giggle. "God, you're so crude." I walk up to the counter to browse the menu.

"Like you weren't thinking the same thing while you eye-fucked him," Fiona says with a smirk.

"I definitely *did not* eye-fuck him," I protest, but my face flushes.

I certainly don't like him, but she's right—he's easy on the eyes.

CHAPTER SIX

LINCOLN

I run to the red Mustang and throw open the door, jumping inside before I get too wet.

When the fuck did it start raining like this?

Trey glances over at me from the driver's side and does a double take. "The fuck happened to you?" he asks, noting my grim expression and then looking down at my stained sleeve.

"That chick from the bonfire ran into me," I snap.

"Charlie Bennett? The hot brunette?"

"Was she hot though?" *Yes, unfortunately.* "Not really my type."

Trey chuckles. "I mean, who *is* your type? You've never really been picky." He puts on his blinker and pulls into traffic.

I grind my teeth instead of arguing with him. I haven't really been interested in anyone for a long time, so it seems like I'm indiscriminate. I use girls. I'm not really proud of it, but I also have needs that I let consume me because I want to feel something—anything—even shame and disgust with myself.

Until yesterday.

Every muscle in my body tensed when I saw her again, as if

bracing for impact. I know who she is, but I don't think she recognized me, which just enraged me further.

This is my school, and she shouldn't be here. I left her behind when I came here.

But then our eyes locked, and she stared at me with a quiet intensity that made my heart beat again for the first time since *that* night. She looked confused, and then just as angry as I was. She was fire, and with one heated look, I was burning alive.

After we first locked eyes, I watched her off and on throughout the night, obsessing over her long chestnut hair that swayed over her back, her skinny jeans that hugged her tight ass and curves in all the right places, and her full lips that often fell into a distrustful pout when she caught me staring.

Then she opened that perfect little mouth, standing up for herself, showing me a sassy side of her that I'd only suspected existed.

I hate her.

And today, I learned she has eyes the color of pine in a dark forest—alluring and wild. I'd had to resist the urge to wrap her hair around my fist.

It was a foreign feeling and so visceral.

"Link?"

"Huh?" I look over at Trey.

"What the hell are you thinking about?"

I shrug.

Trey pulls into the school's student parking lot, and we both get out. He spares his Mustang a loving glance before looking at me with narrowed eyes.

"What?" I ask, annoyed.

"You want to fuck her, don't you?"

I stay quiet. He knows me, so he already knows the answer to that. And he starts laughing.

"I don't blame you, but she strikes me as a good girl. She's probably not going to fall for a deviant like you."

I smirk at him as we walk onto the quad. "No, probably not. But maybe she doesn't have a choice."

When we get to the Wolf Building, we step into the elevator and take it up to the twentieth floor, which is pretty much the penthouse of dorm rooms. Trey and I live up here together, and we have a ridiculous amount of space. The place has two bedrooms with en suite bathrooms, a large modern kitchen trimmed with marble and stainless steel, and a generous living room. It's not very personal, but it's comfortable, and it's the perfect space for the epic parties we host every year.

I drop onto the couch with a heavy sigh, thinking about how to resolve my anger issues with Charlotte Bennett.

Trey tosses his backpack onto the floor and walks into the kitchen, opening the fridge and considering its contents before grabbing an apple and biting into it. The noise makes my skin crawl, and he stops, smiling widely when he notices my irritability.

"I know that look," he says. "You're plotting."

"I'm not plotting." I look over at him. "Charlie just keeps popping up everywhere. It's like the universe hates me. She's in my film class."

Trey takes another bite of his apple, talking around the mouthful. "So fuck her out of your system. That's how you've gotten rid of other girls."

I do generally get bored after I sleep with a girl. But I don't want to just hurt her pride when I ghost her—that seems too easy—I want her to burn, too.

Trey is watching me closely. "Yep. You're definitely plotting. Your face has that Hans Gruber look, all calculating and cold, like a German terrorist."

I chuckle. Even after all this time, he makes me laugh when I take myself too seriously.

"*Die Hard* references aside, tell me why this girl bothers you so much."

I sigh. "She's the daughter of Ellen and Martin Conner."

"Whoa," Trey replies. "That's heavy. How did I not know Sebastian and Marcus Conner have a hot sister?"

I roll my eyes. "Because you were sky high at all of the Conners' investment parties."

Trey grins. "I did love hot boxing in their pool house." He frowns. "Wait. Why is Charlie's last name different?"

"Martin isn't her real father. I think she took Ellen's maiden name."

He raises his eyebrows. "Was she involved in whatever shit went down the night your mom left? Are you finally going to tell me what actually happened?"

"No," I say. "Not a chance. But I am going to make her life miserable."

Trey knows the Conners had something to do with the change in my family dynamic two years ago—he's been pretty much living with us since he was ten, after all. But Trey doesn't know the whole truth. He knows my mom, Allie, left abruptly for a job in New York, that my dad, John, became an emotionally detached asshole (like father, like son, I suppose), and that the Conners were somehow involved. Trey also knows what the media reported later that same year: Ellen, the wife of Martin Conner, one of Brighton's wealthiest property investors, died. Charlie's mom's cause of death was kept private. Which is unfortunate since that bitch deserved to have her name dragged through the mud. But enough money will keep anything a secret —even a suicide.

Trey shrugs, completely accepting of my irrational thought process. Then he smiles broadly. "Okay, but can I tap that? Because honestly, Charlie's stunning no matter what her parents did. And she's a natural beauty, not a painted fake mess like Seren and her friends."

I wave my hand dismissively. "Do whatever you want with her, I guess."

But a strange pang shoots through my stomach at the thought of Trey kissing her. Touching her. Fucking her.

I shake my head, pushing the feeling aside.

Why do I care? He'll probably lose interest if he fucks her, too.

We're both emotionally damaged like that.

THE NEXT MORNING, after an early workout session, Trey and I stroll into the dining hall around nine. The place is cavernous with row after row of long oak tables and a wall of tall cathedral-esque windows to the right, which allow the gray morning light to filter in.

We walk over to the food line, and I pick up a tray and start carb loading. I feel a cold hand on my arm and glance down at Serenity.

I sigh inwardly and turn to her. "What do you want, Seren?"

She pouts. "I just came to say good morning," she says in a syrupy sweet voice.

I grunt in acknowledgment. And then suddenly I can feel a familiar gaze on me.

How am I so aware of that girl?

I look up, meeting Charlie's dark green eyes. She's sitting across the dining hall at one of the long tables. Her expression is curious but stoic as she watches me, picking at her yogurt with a spoon. Her eyes widen when she realizes she's staring, and she quickly looks back at her laptop.

I smirk.

"Am I right?" Serenity interrupts my thoughts.

"Sorry, what?" I ask, looking back at her, distracted. Her eyebrows drop. She turns to see where my attention has been and scowls.

"Homeboy was checking out Little Miss Sunshine over there," Trey says with a suggestive grin.

I elbow him in the ribs, but the nickname echoes the one I used at the bonfire, and it fits. The girl has frowns for days.

"Yeah," Serenity remarks smugly. "She has a resting bitchface for sure."

I meet her eyes, amused. "What's your problem with her?"

"She goes by Charlie, first off."

"So?" I say, confused.

"It's a stupid boy's name," she says. "Plus, she's here on a scholarship." Serenity wrinkles her nose like she's smelling garbage.

I shake my head, knowing her comments probably aren't personal. She's a deeply insecure person through no fault of her own.

"Damn, Seren," Trey says. "You're cold."

Serenity's comment does intrigue me though. I look back at Charlie, wondering why she doesn't use her family's money. I finish my walk through the line and tap my phone to pay.

As I sit down at our table, I study her again. She's typing something on her laptop, her brow furrowed in concentration and her long hair making a protective veil around her heart-shaped face.

Instead of joining us, Serenity bends down, brushing her breasts against my arm. I shudder, and she smiles, probably mistaking my reaction for lust.

"Watch this," she whispers in my ear with an evil smirk. And she walks over to Charlie's table.

CHAPTER SEVEN

CHARLIE

I refuse to look at Lincoln again. Instead, I focus on enjoying my yogurt, but it's just sad and white. I wish they had sprinkles, and I make a note to buy some from the grocery store. My heart rate slowly returns to normal.

The clack of expensive heels interrupts my meal, and I watch as Serenity approaches my table. Her makeup is flawless, and her blonde hair is tied into schoolgirl pigtails a la Britney Spears in the "...Baby, One More Time" video. Her blue eyes are ice cold as she stares at me.

"You're sitting in my seat."

I glance around at literally dozens of empty tables.

This bitch, I think, looking up at her with a bored expression.

After allowing Serenity to make me feel so small with her snobby attitude during our last encounter, I'd decided I wouldn't let her intimidate me again. Or I wasn't going to show it, at least.

I wave my arm expansively. "Well, I'm sitting here, so why don't you walk your fake ass somewhere else and find another seat. It's a big fucking dining hall."

I hear several students gasp, and I gauge her reaction. Her face is definitely turning a blotchy shade of red.

"Listen, you little whore," she says through pinched glossy lips. "I'm not kidding. Move."

I roll my eyes and return to my homework. I hear her annoyed huff, and for a moment, I think she's given up on this ridiculous high school-esque show of dominance.

But then everything seems to happen in slow motion. Out of the corner of my eye, I see Fiona enter the room, and I wave at her. She starts to wave back but stops suddenly, her eyes going wide. Serenity lurches forward in a tripping motion, her tray of food—waffles with syrup, fruit, and a large cup of milk—spilling directly onto the keyboard of my laptop.

I jump away from the table, trying to avoid the worst of the breakfast mess, and watch in horror as my laptop teeters at the edge of the table, then clatters to the floor, a crack splitting the screen.

The dining hall falls eerily silent, but covert snickering starts as I drop to my knees.

My laptop. The laptop that my mom gave me.

Hot tears blur my vision, and I stare up at Serenity, angrily shaking food from the damaged computer.

"Oops," she says, smiling sweetly. "Maybe next time you'll move."

I stand, shoving the MacBook into my backpack, my face red hot with embarrassment. Everyone is staring. Trey has a hand over his mouth, though I can't tell if he's hiding a laugh or shock. Lincoln isn't smiling, but the message in his stormy eyes is clear.

You deserved that, it seems to say.

I glare at him, and look back at Serenity, rage burning through my veins like acid. Without thinking, I make a fist just like Seb taught me when I was being bullied in middle school, and I swing. Hard.

Serenity's eyes widen in alarm before my punch connects with her face, and this time the loud crack comes from the breaking bones in her nose. She screeches, her hands flying to her face to stop the torrent of blood following the hit. She collapses to her knees dramatically.

I stare down at her a moment as she cries and whimpers in agony on the now crimson dining hall floor.

It's just a laptop, I repeat over and over, breathless as I try to hold off the inevitable panic attack.

I picture my mom's face as she handed me the laptop, saying I could use it to become a famous writer one day. Pride shone in her green eyes.

My green eyes.

And now there's so much blood.

But the worst part is that I let Serenity get to me again, and this time, she actually won.

I run to the exit, pushing through the double doors. I can't let anyone see me cry, especially him.

I fast walk across the quad toward the Raven Building, my vision swimming with tears. I only slow when I hear Fiona calling me from behind.

"Charlie! Wait!"

I stop just before entering the building, clenching and unclenching my fists as I pace, allowing the cool autumn air to slow my racing heart.

Fiona catches up to me, breathless and concerned. I quickly wipe the tears away. I don't want her to see me as a poor charity case, so I stare at the ground.

"I don't need your pity," I mutter, my tone brittle.

"I don't pity you, but what that bitch did was totally heartless," she says, her voice soft like I'm a wild animal that might bolt at any minute. "We're friends now, so I'm making sure my friend is okay."

I look up at her, my gaze softening, and she smiles shyly. I'm suddenly grateful she's here—someone I think I can trust. Fiona grabs my hand, and we walk inside and take the elevator up to my dorm room. I throw my backpack on the bed and gingerly remove the ruined laptop.

"What do I do now?" I ask, looking at it miserably.

"It's just a laptop," Fiona says quietly. "You can check out a laptop for the semester in the library until you get a new one."

"It's not just a laptop." My voice breaks as fresh tears fill my eyes. "My mom gave it to me. She's... " I take a deep breath to steady myself. "She's dead."

Our eyes meet as Fiona sits heavily on the bed with a hand over her mouth, at a loss for words. Finally, she releases a sigh.

"Well, we'll still get you another laptop," Fiona says, smiling tentatively. "But now I have to say I'm twice as happy that you punched Serenity in the face."

I wince before giving her a tearful grin. "There was a lot of blood...," I say, biting my bottom lip.

Did I do the right thing?

"And she deserved to have it spilled," Fiona finishes for me as if reading my mind, her voice resolute.

CHAPTER EIGHT

CHARLIE

I'm sitting in my dorm room on a Friday afternoon, typing class notes from the past week into my new library-issued laptop. It took the school a while to track one down since I didn't reserve it before the semester started. It's not as nice as my MacBook, but it'll do as a replacement for now. Thank God all my documents were backed up to my iCloud.

It's been a week since the incident with Serenity, and I've avoided the dining hall ever since, still feeling self-conscious about the whole thing. And people definitely know who I am now. So much for living my best life as a college introvert.

I've caught a few glimpses of Serenity, sporting a cast on her nose and two black eyes that even her heavy foundation can't hide. Visceral hatred pours off her whenever she notices me, but I've been choosing to ignore her for now, hiding out in my dorm room more often than not. I'm paranoid she'll rain revenge on me when I'm least expecting it.

I've noticed Lincoln and Trey around campus a few times. Okay, I've actually been stalking them like a creep. Though I don't think they've noticed me lurking under trees or sitting against tall stone buildings while I scribble in my notebook.

They're an unlikely pair. Trey, the beautiful golden boy with smiles for days, and Lincoln the mysterious, broody bad boy. I don't understand their friendship dynamic, which is what makes them so interesting to me.

Of course, class is the only normal place I can casually interact with Lincoln, and he hasn't said a word to me all week. He still sits next to me, his body pressed unnecessarily close to mine, so I have to believe it's intentional considering there's a sea of empty seats around us. I've spent the last two classes engulfed in his scent while trying desperately to concentrate.

I don't know why he hates me so much, but I can certainly feel his animosity with every tick of his jaw and intentional glare. He makes me feel small, and I hate it.

Yesterday before class, I tried to speak to Dr. Jackson about trading partners with someone, but he told me rather dismissively that this wasn't high school. "We're all adults now, Ms. Bennett. If you can't handle this type of assignment, you're welcome to take a freshman-level class."

Feeling self-conscious, I mumbled an apology and turned just in time to catch Lincoln's angry glare, and it cut me to ribbons. Knowing he may have heard added another level of shame to my embarrassment because while I do hate him, I'm not a monster.

So, yeah, I'm stuck with him as my partner for the long haul.

"I guess, give me your number so we can coordinate writing sessions?" I said as we started to pack up our belongings after class. It came out sounding like a question, and my voice was all high and squeaky.

Lovely.

His gray eyes were empty as he snatched the phone from my outstretched hand and quickly entered his number. Then he texted himself and saved my info. As he slid the phone back to me, his fingers brushed mine. The touch was brief but it sent a jolt of heat straight to my core.

For a moment, the air seemed to crackle between us. He raised his hand as if to touch my face, but then he abruptly grabbed his backpack and practically fled from the classroom.

My whole body tingles as I remember the moment our fingers touched. I still don't know why it happened. Lincoln Evans is infuriating, and I hate the way my body responds as if it can't get on the same page as my brain.

There's a knock at my door, and I jump up in anticipation, closing my laptop and sliding it under my pillow. Sebastian texted me this morning telling me he was coming to Whitmore U for a quick visit on his way to Seattle. I asked about Marcus—they often make these business trips together—but Seb said he was too busy to come this time. I try to ignore the ache in my chest. I know Seb is just being nice, and Marcus really just didn't want to see me.

"Hey, little sis," Seb says with a wide smile when I open the door. He's dressed in dark jeans and a blue and green button-up flannel.

I grin back and step into one of his signature bone-crushing bear hugs.

He pulls back, looking around my room, his arm still resting heavily on my shoulders. "This place is cool. Dad really set you up nicely in this suite."

I feel a stab of guilt. Seb doesn't know I'm here on a scholarship. The reasons behind it would make him angry and hurt his relationship with his dad. "Yeah, it's a cozy space, and I like having a room to myself."

"Can I meet your friends?" he asks.

"Well, my friend from down the hall, Fiona, is in class, so I don't think you'll get to meet her," I say lamely.

Seb frowns. "Just one friend?"

"School's only been going on a few weeks, Seb," I say quietly. "And you know me—introverted to the end."

He accepts my answer with a nod, his expression softening, and I'm grateful that he doesn't push the subject. When I was younger, Seb and Marcus were always nagging me about making more friends outside of my boyfriend, Matt, but I was shy and awkward, and it's hard to step out of your comfort zone when your two beautiful, extroverted stepbrothers are the most popular guys in school. Half of the time, girls would try to be my friend just to get close to Seb, which pissed me off to no end. The rest of the time, I was just invisible.

"So, what's on the agenda?" Seb asks, interrupting my thoughts.

"Well, I thought we could grab a coffee, and I'll give you a campus tour," I say, pulling on a hoodie.

"That sounds great." He smiles widely and opens the door for me to lead the way.

The sky is overcast with a thick layer of clouds, but it's thankfully not particularly cold as we walk across campus. The oak leaves are starting to turn, hinting at bright shades of orange and yellow that pop against the gray stone buildings.

I take Seb over to the coffee cart in front of the hockey arena first.

"This place is a trip," he says, admiring the gothic architecture. Seb whistles when we enter the building and pauses in the stands surrounding the chilly rink. "Wow, this is amazing."

His eyes scan the expanse of stadium seating. Whitmore U's logo—an angry-looking otter sporting ice skates and a helmet and wielding a hockey stick—adorns the center of the rink.

Seb snickers. "An otter?"

"Don't knock it. Otters can be very vicious despite their cuteness. And didn't you already know our logo, Mr. Hockey Fanatic?"

Seb shrugs. "I follow the NHL, but college hockey? Not so

much. But..." He taps his finger on his chin. "I might start following it more if you can get us into a few games."

I smile widely. "I'll see what I can do."

"I think Marcus would love it."

I frown at the mention of our older brother. That ache from earlier returns even stronger.

Seb notices the change in my expression, and he quickly places his hands on my shoulders and steers me toward the exit.

"Show me more. This place has to have a grumpy groundskeeper with a scruffy cat."

I giggle, and we walk out into the hallway.

Just as we're leaving the arena, I almost run headfirst into Brantley. He's leaving the locker room, his hair still damp from a shower. He stops as I skid to a halt in front of him.

"Well, if it isn't Charlie Bennett," he says with a wide grin, his hand reaching out to steady me.

"Sorry, I didn't see you, Brantley." I glance at the equipment bag slung over his shoulder. "Just finishing practice?"

"Sure am. And we're going to be on fire this year." He gives me a smug smile. "We've been training with a new forward who just transferred from the University of Washington—Matt Johnson. The guy is a machine—totally untouchable."

I stiffen, my body vibrating with shock. Despite the common name, there probably aren't that many Matt Johnsons who play college-level hockey. It has to be him.

But why is he here?

I glance at Sebastian, noting the angry set of his jaw as he eyes Brantley before sliding his gaze to mine.

"Cool," I say with a tight smile, trying to mask the panic rising in my chest. "I'm just showing my brother around campus, so I'll see you around."

"Yeah, see you around, Charlie," Brantley says with a coy wink, walking in the other direction.

Seb blows out a slow breath. "Did you know he was here?"

I shake my head. "I had no idea." I can tell my overprotective brother is watching my reaction closely, and I put on my best show of nonchalance. "But who cares? He's a hockey jock, so we probably won't even run in the same circles."

Seb looks dubious but lets it go. My phone buzzes, and I glance down, seeing a text from Fiona.

FIONA:

> Party toniiiiiiight! I'm coming right now to convince your sorry ass to go.

I sigh.

"What is it?" Seb asks.

"My friend wants me to go with her to a party."

"Oh, you should definitely go." He pushes his shoulder into mine playfully.

"But aren't you staying for dinner?"

"Actually, it's fine," he says, running his fingers through his hair. "I'd rather try to get into Seattle before rush-hour traffic snarls up I-5."

The thought of a party has my anxiety spiking. I text Fiona back.

> Hard pass.

FIONA

> Nope. Unacceptable. See you in five.

I text her several angry emojis.

> I have a visitor. Give me five minutes to say goodbye.

FIONA

> What visitor?? Is it a he?!

I roll my eyes.

It's my brother.

FIONA

I want to meet him!!

Too late. He's leaving now. See you in ten.

FIONA

Ugh, fine.

I glance up to find Seb watching me. "What?" I ask, sticking my hands in my hoodie pouch self-consciously.

"You're sure you're doing okay here?" he asks, his tone low and serious.

I put on my best little sister smile—the one I've been wearing since my mom died. "I'm good, Seb. I promise."

"Pinky swear?"

"I'm not going to pinky swear with you. We're not twelve," I snark.

"I'm not leaving until you pinky swear, Charlie." He holds out his hand with his pinky extended.

"Fine," I grumble, fighting a genuine smile. I lock my finger around his. "Pinky swear."

Seb seems satisfied after that, and I walk him back to the visitor lot. I can't help but feel the sting of sadness in my chest as he drives away, but I push it down and head back to my dorm to wait for Fiona.

A few minutes later, she barges into my room with several dresses draped over one arm and what looks like a damn suitcase of makeup and hair products.

"No," I say, staring at her deadpan. "I'm not a Barbie doll."

"You've been hiding all week. Don't let Serenity think she's won."

I press my fingertips to my eyes in frustration. "But she *has* won. I hate even walking across the quad now. I have to listen to everyone whisper and giggle behind their hands."

"If they're talking about you anyway, why not give them something better to talk about?" She lays the dresses out. "This one is perfect."

I eye the scrap of crimson fabric she's holding. My eyes widen. "That will hardly cover my ass."

"I'm not seeing the problem." Fiona grins. "Plus, it's the same color as the blood that poured from Serenity's nose," she continues in a sinister tone.

"Jesus, Fi, that's dark," I say, suppressing a laugh.

An hour later, we walk across campus, and I feel completely out of my element. Thankfully because I'm so short, the dress isn't as scandalous as I originally thought it would be. It has a plunging neckline that showcases my ample breasts, and it cinches at my waist before flaring out, so it accentuates my curves nicely. After an argument about my shoes, we compromised with my favorite pair of calf-high brown leather boots.

Fi gave my hair some messy waves, and she fussed over my makeup. I have to say, I look pretty hot.

I slow when we come to the Wolf Building. "Wait, whose party is this?"

Fiona glances away sheepishly. "Lincoln and Trey's."

I stop.

"Don't be mad," she gushes, grabbing my hand tightly. "They throw like every campus party worth going to."

"It's fine," I say haltingly before throwing her a smirk. "At least I look hot."

"Damn straight," she says, pulling me toward the doorway.

When we step out of the elevator, I'm completely caught off guard. The huge chandelier makes the space look like a fancy hotel foyer. I'm still gawking at the extravagant entryway when we walk through the front door.

This isn't a normal dorm room—it's a fucking penthouse.

The living room is huge with towering glass windows that

face the dark silhouettes of the distant mountains. It would be beautiful if it weren't for the sound of blaring rap music.

"Is that Eminem?" I yell, just as the chorus to "The Real Slim Shady" warbles from the speakers. Scantily clad people are grinding against each other to the rhythm. Couples make out on the couch while they clutch red Solo cups. In the kitchen, a crowd is cheering over a lively game of beer pong. There's a keg in the corner.

"God, I feel like I just stepped into a teen movie from the nineties," I say, looking around with raised eyebrows.

"And what do you have against nineties teen flicks?" asks a deep voice from behind me.

I turn to find Trey leaning against the wall. His blond hair falls haphazardly over his warm brown eyes framed by long, thick lashes. He's beautiful, and he looks delicious in dark jeans and a button-up black shirt that stretches across his wide chest. His shirt sleeves are rolled up, showing off tanned forearms crisscrossed with veins that end with his large hands.

He snaps his fingers at me. "Hey Bennett, eyes up here. I'm not a piece of meat, you know."

My eyes bounce back up to his face, and I feel my neck and cheeks flush. "I wasn't checking you out, if that's what you're implying," I stammer, even though I definitely was. "And there are very few teen movies from the nineties worth watching."

He steps closer, bringing our mouths only inches apart. The scent of fresh apples with a hint of cinnamon fills the air. Something about him makes me feel calm, like I've known him forever, even though this is only the second time we've spoken.

"Uh-huh," he says. "What about *10 Things I Hate About You* or *Clueless?*"

"They don't count." I breathe him in. "They have an unfair advantage because they're based on literature."

"Loosely based," he replies huskily, staring at my mouth.

I lick my lips. The sudden attraction I feel for him is heady and intoxicating.

Fiona clears her throat, looking between us. "Um, I'm going to get a drink." She starts walking toward the bar. "Do you want something?"

I step back from Trey to calm my racing heart. "A whisky and Diet Pepsi, please."

Trey laughs. "Whisky Diet? I pegged you for a daiquiri girl."

"Why?" I ask, feeling defensive. "Because it's a girly drink?"

"Hardly," he says with a smirk. "You're a writer, right? Wasn't that Hemingway's drink of choice?"

His comment gives me pause.

"Actually, I read in an interview that Hemingway's drink of choice was scotch and soda," I say quietly. "So maybe my drink isn't so far off base."

Trey's eyes fall to my lips as I speak, and everything below my belly button starts to tingle as he presses closer to me. I stare up at him in shock when I feel his erection hard against my thigh. He doesn't even try to hide it.

"I see," he whispers. "You're kind of a smarty-pants, huh?" Trey's free hand falls to my waist and then runs down my leg before reaching under my dress. His rich brown eyes watch me closely as if daring me to stop him.

I should ask him to stop, right?

"Is that a problem?" I breathe. His rough fingers dance over my skin, leaving prickling trails of heat in their wake. "I heard from my friend that you're not particularly picky when it comes to hookups."

Trey looks amused.

My brain is screaming at me in protest. I mean, I don't know this guy at all.

"What're you doing?" I ask, but my voice comes out all low and breathy. I try to reinstate some of my sanity by pulling back from his touch.

"Welcoming you to campus?" he quips.

I smile faintly. "So you do this with all the new students?"

"Can't say that I do, actually." His hand slides higher up my leg tracing lazy circles that are beyond distracting.

And then my body completely takes over.

I close my eyes as his fingers reach my panties and my legs spread farther apart, giving him better access. I'm beyond wet already.

What the fuck is wrong with me?

His eyes widen. "You're completely soaked," Trey whispers as he skims my pussy through the thin material gently.

We're standing in the middle of a party with people mingling all around us. I should be mortified, but I'm not. Nope. Instead, I've never been so aroused. My restraint is being seriously tested. I'm desperate to grind against his hand.

"Open your eyes," Trey demands, his voice a deep rumble in my ear that causes my core to clench. "I'm going to touch you now."

I look up at him through my lashes just as he slides my panties to the side and eases two thick fingers into my aching pussy, moving them in slow thrusts.

My breath hitches. "Holy shit," I breathe when his thumb grazes my clit lightly, rolling over it and then quickly releasing the pressure. "You're a tease," I challenge, glaring at him darkly.

"And?" he responds with a cocky smirk.

Our eyes lock while he continues to edge me, both of us panting but also trying to look natural, like we're just having a casual but intimate conversation.

I stare at his full lips, smelling a hint of weed and vodka on his breath.

Finally, he adds a third finger and uses an embarrassing amount of my own arousal to circle his thumb more firmly over my clit. The sensations that follow are completely unexpected and too much at the same time, and I detonate. There's no other word to describe it. The orgasm is so intense, I almost collapse. I moan loudly, but the sound is lost over the pounding hip-hop music as I come all over his hand.

His hooded gaze holds mine, and I nearly come again when he withdraws his fingers and brings them, still glistening with my arousal, to his mouth, dragging his middle finger slowly across his bottom lip before sucking them clean.

Why is that so hot?

I'm still lightheaded from my release, my hands clutching Trey's biceps as I stare up at him, my lips parted in shock. His ember eyes seem to soften with an almost tender look.

Then, my breath catches when I see past Trey's shoulder to where Lincoln is standing in the corner. He normally has such a commanding presence, but I hadn't even noticed him, which probably means he was intentionally watching us.

Did he just see everything?

His gray gaze is intense, and a strange mix of emotions war in his eyes.

Fiona returns and hands me a drink, and I quickly pull away from Trey. I take a steadying breath, but I can feel wetness dripping down one of my thighs.

Awesome.

"Let's dance," Fiona says, pulling me toward the swaying bodies. I follow her, happy to escape whatever the fuck just happened.

CHAPTER NINE

TREY

I watch Charlie walk away with Flowers, who looks back at me with what can only be described as murderous intent. I raise my hands placatingly with my best panty-melting smile, but I know she's just looking out for her friend. My reputation as the campus slut precedes me, though about half of the rumors are just that—rumors and nothing more.

I've honestly never done that to a girl so publicly, and I'm not sure what happened. This campus is crawling with fuckable rich kids, most of them insecure and damaged in some way—and I say "kids" because I'm into everyone—guys, girls—the package is hardly important. I don't really have a type—preppy, gothic, skinny, curvy, whatever—it's never really mattered. Some are closeted, some play hard-to-get, and some are pathetically easy.

But Charlie doesn't act like the typical rich brat. She doesn't plaster on fake smiles. In fact, her emotions were as plain as day on her face tonight—she was nervous and uncomfortable. No. She's clearly not a party girl. Not to mention she punched Serenity in the face. So feisty.

Who does that, and why was it so hot?

I had to touch her tonight. The words that spill from her mouth fascinate me to no end—she's not out to impress anyone, and that seems to be a turn-on for me. Who knew? And suddenly I didn't know if I wanted to friend-zone her or fuck her. Because somehow I wanted both. But I'm not friends with girls, so that's off the table—fuck buddy, it is.

Lincoln's been raging about Charlie for days, and I want to know why.

What makes her so special?

I'm trying to get him to admit that he's into her, even if it's just for a quickie or a blow job. I'd back off if I thought he was actually interested, but when has that ever happened? Plus, I like fucking with his head, and maybe he'd be open to a group sesh. It wouldn't be our first. The thought has my dick hardening again.

"Walker." Lincoln's voice interrupts my thoughts.

Shit. I wince and adjust myself.

Lincoln never calls me by my last name unless he's pissed. I'm guessing he watched us—I think that's one of his secret kinks.

I turn to Link with a shit-eating grin and rub my fingers together in his face like an asshole. They're still sticky and smell like her sex.

"What's up, Link?"

His gaze darkens. "The fuck is wrong with you?" Lincoln slaps my hand down.

I smirk. "What? You said you didn't care what I did with her," I say. "But if you're into her, I can back off."

"I'm not into Little Miss Sunshine," he snaps. "But you could be a little more subtle about it. Is exhibitionism your new kink?"

I shrug.

His eyes narrow. "How drunk are you? Or are you high?"

"Relax, buddy. I'm not on a binge," I say with a wink.

47

Link studies my face before he visibly relaxes.

I've had my fair share of trouble with substance abuse in the past, and me falling off the wagon? Well, that's a hard line for Lincoln. I have no doubt he'd thoroughly kick my ass if he caught me in a full relapse.

Link takes a deep breath, and his signature "no fucks given" expression slides into place.

I smile. "Better. Now, this is a party, so we should probably be having fun."

Lincoln rolls his eyes. "It looks like you were doing that for the both of us."

I laugh out loud. "You have no idea. That was unexpected and—"

"Hot," Link finishes for me.

We both turn and stare at Charlie Bennett swaying to the music, her hips grinding against Fiona's ass, and shake our heads.

CHAPTER TEN

CHARLIE

*L*incoln cradles Serenity in his arms and carries her down the hallway to what I assume is one of the bedrooms in this ridiculous suite. She'd been hitting on him all night before she finally passed out, though to be honest, he didn't seem particularly responsive to her, which still confuses me. I catch him watching me a lot. It's weird.

Why is he always staring?

And then there's Trey, sprawled out with his legs wide in that sexy way only guys can pull off, his arm thrown over the back of the couch. I glance at his hands—the same hands that gave me an earth-shattering orgasm a couple of hours ago. I shudder and press my thighs together.

Just then, a large body blocks my view, and I look up, annoyed.

"For the love of..." I take a step back when I recognize the tall, dark, and handsome boy standing in front of me. My insides turn to ice as my gaze meets his. He looks a little older— stubble darkening his jaw—but he still has that possessive glint in his eyes that he could barely hide when we were together.

"Hey Char," my ex-boyfriend, Matthew Johnson, says with a cocky smile.

His voice triggers all kinds of emotions in me—anger, betrayal, heartbreak, and shame. I resist the urge to bolt from the room. He seems to sense my thoughts and steps closer.

Suddenly, I can't breathe and my heart is pounding. I think I'm going to have a panic attack.

Just before my mom's suicide, Matt and I were ridiculously in love—childhood friends to lovers—though looking back, there were a lot of red flags.

But one night when my parents threw a party, I caught him fucking another girl in my bedroom. I can still remember walking in, the smell of sex heavy in the air, and seeing his bare ass pounding this girl into my mattress. I was paralyzed in the doorway at first. It felt like he was clawing my heart out of my chest with each pump of his dick. But what really scared me was the unhinged look in his eyes when they met mine.

I didn't bother to find out which skank from the party was fucking my boyfriend. I just fled. I ran into the woods behind my parents' house and hid Bella-from-*New Moon*-style until Seb found me hours later.

Matt's blatant lack of humanity that night was the start of my panic attacks, and they only got worse with my mom's death a month later. The whole situation messed up Seb, too. Evidently, he saw me running from the room and went to investigate, and saw the whole thing as well. Matt was Seb's best friend, so I suspect his heart broke that day, too—though I doubt he'd admit it.

I try not to mentally return to the scene, but it's hard looking at him without recalling the memory with alarming clarity.

I clench my fists to keep my hands from shaking. "Hi, Matt." Somehow my voice doesn't tremble. "What're you doing here?"

He shrugs. "We always said we'd go to college together after high school."

I look at him deadpan, swallowing the panic that threatens to choke me. "Yeah, that was before you fucked some party skank," I say, giving my best eat-shit smile. But my confidence is all fake. Next to me, Fiona giggle-snorts, nearly spraying alcohol all over the counter.

Matt gives her a dark look before returning his attention to me. "I deserve that."

"You deserve worse, Matt." I sigh. "Why are you really here?"

"Didn't you hear? I'm Whitmore U's star hockey center."

"I did hear, actually." I grimace. "You're here *just* for hockey?" I ask doubtfully, though other than me, hockey was his favorite childhood obsession.

"Look," he says, raising his hands, "I just want to talk."

My heart rate kicks up again.

Fiona watches us as if trying to determine whether to defuse the situation.

Breathe.

Matt reaches for me, and I flinch as his fingers graze my cheek and push a strand of hair behind my ear. I feel sweaty and nauseous. I step back, trying to escape his reach, but my knees are weak like hot Jell-o, and I stumble.

Someone grabs my wrist, steadying my balance and yanking me backward at the same time. To my surprise, Lincoln is hovering over me. My panic attack stalls as I stare at him.

"Don't fucking touch her," Lincoln growls.

I thought he hated me, but he stares at Matt with murder in his pitch-black eyes. Lincoln pulls me roughly behind him, then pushes my ex with his other hand. Matt stumbles back, surprise etched on his face.

Lincoln is shaking with rage; I can feel his hard muscles tense against my body, and his grip on me is borderline painful.

A more gentle hand clasps my free one, and I look back to see Trey, his expression equally livid.

Lincoln drops my hand and stands in front of Trey and me.

Matt recovers quickly, shoving him back. Lincoln doesn't even move.

"The fuck is your problem?" Matt demands, stepping into Lincoln's space. Big mistake there. Fiona senses the mood and moves around the counter to stand next to Trey.

"Are you with him or something?" Matt asks, trying to catch my eye around an enraged Lincoln.

Before I can think to respond, Lincoln hits Matt in the mouth, and he falls ass-first onto the ground, blood pouring from a split lip.

"You don't get to even look at her. Do you know who I am?" Lincoln asks coldly.

"Yeah," Matt replies, standing back up and spitting blood onto the floor. "I know who you are, Evans, and I'm not fucking scared of you, pretty rich boy." Matt starts laughing. His lips and teeth are red, giving him a slightly unhinged look—like Heath Ledger's Joker personified. "You can't do shit to me," he says, his grin widening. "Your daddy might own buildings at this school, but I'm fucking hockey royalty."

Lincoln stares him down, muscles bulging, the tendons in his neck taut. "Don't touch what's mine."

Wait, what?

"And get the fuck out," Lincoln rumbles.

Matt's eyes flash with rage. "She's yours, huh? We'll see."

I shiver, and Trey looks at me sideways, his hand tightening slightly. Then Matt shoulders his way through the small crowd and stalks to the door.

I can breathe again.

Lincoln is still staring after Matt like he's in a trance. I reach out, touching his arm gently, and he flinches, goosebumps rising on his forearm. He looks back at me, his dark gaze intense, but at least his anger seems to have dissipated.

His eyes are the perfect stormy gray color, and I'm lost in

them. I smell Lincoln's cool, woodsy scent, and it mixes perfectly with Trey's warm, spicy smell. I realize I feel safe, the panic attack long forgotten.

With Matt gone, the party seems to pick up where it left off, though we're getting a lot of sideways looks. Fiona hands me my drink from the counter, which I gladly accept, taking a long pull. I'm suddenly aware that my hand is still interlocked with Trey's, and I unwind my fingers from his, clearing my throat.

"I was okay," I say finally, needing to break the silence. "You didn't have to step in caveman style. And I'm definitely not *yours.*"

Lincoln looks down at me, his eyebrows dropping in annoyance. "Do you ever stop talking?"

This asshole.

"How about next time, I just let the creep hit on you?" he grinds out.

"I didn't ask for your help," I snarl.

Then he pinches my chin in his grasp, forcing my gaze to his. I lick my lips, and his eyes track the movement. He's so close we could kiss. My entire body heats with his exhale.

"I wasn't helping you, Sunshine. I was marking you. Believe me when I say that no one at the school will ever touch you," Lincoln snarls menacingly, which does nothing but ignite my annoyance into full-blown anger.

"Why?" I challenge. "Because *you* want me? Because let me tell you—your attitude sucks." I jerk my chin from his hold and fold my arms under my chest, which causes my boobs to nearly burst out of my dress. I watch as Lincoln and Trey's eyes fall to my breasts, and I cover myself with a sigh. "Really?"

Their eyes snap back to mine. Fiona snickers.

"No." The muscles in Lincoln's sharp jaw twitch. "Because I want to be the one to ruin you."

I hear Trey chuckle darkly behind me.

Lincoln's words cause a rush of heat through my entire body, but it's different from the familiar heat of panic. This rush is a mix of unwanted lust and a warning that seems to tug at my heart.

CHAPTER ELEVEN

CHARLIE

*F*iona and I left the party pretty quickly. We're walking arm in arm back to the Raven Building, which isn't a long distance, but feels much longer when you're fighting the damp autumn air in skimpy clothing.

"Well, that was an interesting party," Fiona says, her teeth chattering as the cold breeze whips through the quad.

"Yeah" is all I can manage as my brain short-circuits when I realize Matt knows I'm here.

Did he know all along?

Fiona glances at me. "Do you want to tell me about him?"

I shake my head. "Not really, but I'm guessing you won't let me sleep tonight until I do."

A gust of wind blows brown and yellow leaves around our feet and whips my hair into a tangled mess. We pick up our pace, practically sprinting across the quad, and we both let out a sigh of relief when we burst through the doors of our dorm building.

Fiona and I stay quiet on the elevator ride up, and I immediately grab pajamas and head down the hall for the bathroom the second I enter my room. It's past 2 a.m., and I feel my eyelids trying to force their way closed.

Fiona is sitting on my bed expectantly when I return.

I groan. "Really? We can't chat about it over coffee tomorrow?"

She smiles sweetly and pats the bed next to her.

"Ugh, for fuck's sake." I plop down dramatically. "He's my ex-boyfriend, okay?"

"That much I gathered from the interaction," she says quietly. "What happened, though? You put on a good show, but I can spot the start of a panic attack a mile away."

"Really?" I raise my eyebrows. "I thought I was pretty good at hiding it."

"You are, but I've spent my entire childhood hiding my mother's anxiety from the rest of the world, so I'm kind of an expert," she says with a wink.

"Oh gosh, Fi. I'm sorry. That sounds—"

Fiona raises her hand, stopping me mid sentence. "We can talk about my fucked-up mommy issues later." She gives me a pointed look. "Right now, I want to hear how this douchebag broke your heart."

I look away, chewing my lip. "Well, Matt and I were together for a long time. There was a park about halfway between his house and mine—when we were kids, it was our sanctuary. He was kind of an odd little boy when I met him. He always seemed sad, and I suspected that he was being abused. At first, I think I just wanted to protect him."

Fiona looks sad but keeps quiet.

"By the time we were fifteen, we started dating, and we were together all through high school and were practically engaged just before senior year. He never actually proposed, but it was kind of implied." I pick at my fingernails. "I guess looking back, I should have seen the signs. As we got older, something about him changed. He was under a lot of pressure from his dad to take over the family business. He always seemed off, like his mind wasn't really like everyone else's."

Fiona frowns. "What do you mean?"

I flush, suddenly not sure if I'm ready to share, but I swallow, forcing myself to continue.

"He was a little rough when we fooled around, and I don't mean like playful spanking or bites. Honestly, I kind of like things a bit rough."

"I would not have pegged you for a kinky bitch," Fiona says, smirking.

I flip her off, laughing. "Well, not like *Fifty Shades of Grey*-type BDSM or anything, but anyway. When Matt and I did stuff, I always felt uneasy, like he wanted to actually hurt me. Like he got off on my pain and his control over me. Once when I was sixteen, I actually asked him to stop."

I take a deep breath at the memory. Fiona puts her hand in mine, nodding encouragingly.

"Only he wouldn't stop. He pulled my hair so hard I could feel the strands pull from my scalp. And then he started choking me. Before I blacked out, I could see this euphoric look on his face."

I don't realize I'm crying until Fiona wipes a tear from my cheek.

"Charlie, did he rape you? You asked him to stop, and he didn't."

I shake my head. "No, we never had sex. At least I don't think we did. I guess I don't know for sure since I blacked out," I say quietly. "But I...checked...myself afterward, and everything seemed normal. I was so ashamed after it happened, but I was also young and in love at the time, and I thought I just didn't know how to enjoy foreplay."

"You're lucky he didn't kill you," Fiona murmurs. "What happened after that?"

"Well, most of the time, I thought we were happy. But one

night during my senior year, my stepfather threw my mom a birthday party at our house. I went to get something in my bedroom." I take a shaky breath. "When I walked in, he was fucking some girl in my bed."

"What?! What a fuck-bucket," Fiona says, her nose scrunching in disgust.

"The worst part is that he saw me. He looked like he was getting off on the pain he saw on my face. And then the asshole came inside her, still staring me right in the eyes and still grinning like a crazy person."

"Whoa!" Fiona exclaims. "Stage-five creeper. That's gross."

"I was heartbroken," I say. "But looking back, I guess I lucked out. I certainly wouldn't be here."

I stifle a yawn with my hand, and Fiona follows suit, talking around her own yawn. "You're right, you wouldn't be here fending off the two hottest guys at this university."

"Ha ha," I say sarcastically. "I am *not* fending them off. They're just fucking around with me like all their other conquests."

"I dunno, Charlie," Fiona says with a shrug. "Say what you will, but they were both throwing around a lot of big dick energy tonight. I've never seen either of them go all alpha male about anyone, let alone the same girl."

"Whatever." I'm too tired to overthink it.

"Wait, so you never had sex with Matt? He wasn't your first? But you're not a virgin?"

"Nope," I say. "Someone else took my virginity." I smirk. "But that's a story for another night. With lots of alcohol."

CHAPTER TWELVE

CHARLIE

"So what're you going to be for Halloween this year?" Fiona asks as we walk toward the elevator.

After a couple weeks of training with John, Fiona and I have our first shift at the movie theater today. We spent the past weekend shopping because he requested the dress code be slacks and button-ups, but I own mostly street clothes.

"A hard-working college student?" I quip.

I nervously smooth invisible wrinkles from my white dress shirt. I hate ponytails, so I tied my hair into a loose fishtail braid that trails down my back. I went with natural makeup with slightly heavier eyeliner to look a bit more professional.

She rolls her eyes. "How about a *slutty* hard-working college student?"

"Okay, yeah, sure," I laugh, pushing her shoulder. "Is Halloween a big deal around here?"

"Oh yeah." Fiona nods. "Have you seen that cemetery at the end of Main Street?"

I stop and turn to look at her. "You guys party on Halloween in an *actual* cemetery?"

She grins widely.

"That's creepy as fuck," I exclaim, though I'm actually a bit excited at the prospect.

Growing up, I loved Halloween, and as I got older, I became a self-proclaimed basic bitch. Every year on the first day of October, I put on my boots and a cozy hoodie and helped my mom decorate our house from top to bottom, and I loved pumpkin everything—even the overhyped Pumpkin Spice Latte.

I still love all those things. But the last couple of years have been rough. My mom passed in late September just after my senior year started, and by the time Halloween rolled around that year, I was dealing with the fallout of my stepdad leaving. The next Halloween, I was completely alone. So instead of enjoying the fall leaves and apple cider, during the last two autumns, I listened to the never-ending rain hammering on the roof of our garage while I tried to drown out my own dark thoughts with the constant white noise.

Maybe this Halloween will be better. Famous last words.

The morning is clear (for once) and chilly as we make our way down Main Street to the theater. Lakeside, Washington, is an isolated town that was built around Whitmore U when it opened in the 1800s so that the students had resources nearby. The closest big cities are Seattle, which is two hours south, and Vancouver, British Columbia, which is just over an hour north, across the Canadian border. I'm from Brighton, a small town about an hour-long drive from campus, and Lakeside gives me similar small-town vibes. Everything you'd ever need that isn't on campus is on Main Street: coffee shops, bars, a grocery store, and now the reopened Lakeside Cinema.

The building was constructed with classic red brick, and John cleaned up the white marquis, which currently reads *Halloween*, *The Shining*, and *Pet Sematary*. I guess the new manager liked the idea of the theater featuring horror movies with the grand opening being in October. And speaking of the new manager, we still haven't met him.

We enter the lobby, reveling in the rush of warmth, but I stop short when I see Lincoln and Trey leaning against the concession stand bar, talking in hushed tones. Fiona runs straight into my back, and I stumble forward, dropping my phone, which bounces across the garish carpet and slides to a stop in front of Lincoln's shiny black shoes.

"Sorry," Fi mumbles. "I wasn't paying attention."

Link and Trey stop talking, and Link watches as I step forward and bend to retrieve my phone.

When I stand, we're practically toe-to-toe—way too close for comfort. My breath stutters.

Lincoln is dressed to perfection in a black button-up shirt with a gray tie—the same shade as his steel eyes—and dark slacks. His expression is cold, and his jawline and eyebrows are all angles except for the curve of his full lips. His hair falls in a sexy, haphazard way across his forehead—the only part of his carefully controlled appearance that seems chaotic.

A chill runs through me as our eyes meet. Lincoln gives me a cruel smirk, and I frown in confusion.

What the heck is he doing here?

"If you want to actually work here, I hope you're going to drop the Wednesday Addams attitude for the customers, Sunshine," he says, standing up to his full height.

This guy.

"You're one to talk," I snap back. "You're about as broody as a *Twilight* vamp. Don't tell me you work here, too."

His lips curve up in response.

Fiona snickers behind me, and Trey covers his mouth to hide a laugh but his shaking shoulders give him away.

"Hey, Bennett," Trey drawls, winking at me.

As usual, Trey is somehow the complete opposite of Lincoln. He sports a slightly wrinkled blue button-up, which is rolled up at the sleeves, showcasing his ridiculously hot forearms. His navy tie is thrown back over one shoulder, and his messy blond hair is practically glowing under the warm concession lighting. He looks like some sort of golden god—though despite looking like Thor, his personality is more akin to a trickster like Loki.

"Ah, I see you met my son," John says, walking into the lobby carrying a stack of drink cups. "Lincoln is going to be running the theater."

Son?

The world tilts as the realization hits that he's my boss, and I consider immediately quitting. I'm not sure I can stand any more forced proximity with Lincoln Evans and his mood swings. But, dammit, I really need this job.

I vaguely remember John from my stepdad's elbow-rubbing functions, but I don't remember Lincoln at all—probably because I always stuck close to the adults like the goodie-two-shoes I was.

Was he there?

I watch them, feeling numb, as Lincoln and his dad walk over to the manager's station to exchange a few quiet words.

Their rapport is strange. Lincoln's expression is closed off, as usual, but John's shifts between sad and hopeful, as if whatever he's saying is meant to elicit some sort of emotional response from his son. Finally, he claps Link gently on the back and turns back to us.

"You're in good hands," he says with a wave before he leaves.

I grit my teeth because I'm entirely sure that's not true, but I take a deep breath and attempt to play nice.

"So you're John's son, huh? Our parents did business together. I suppose that means you've been to a few of my step-dad's parties?" I ask, raising my eyebrows in question.

Lincoln's expression darkens, but he doesn't answer me.

What did I do now? He's so confusing.

Finally, he says, "I have the perfect job for you today,

Sunshine." His tone suggests that unlike me, he has no intention of playing nice.

I roll my eyes. "Can you just call me Charlie?"

"Nah," he says, running his thumb over his bottom lip.

I'm distracted by the gesture, despite feeling infuriated by his response. He steps closer to me, and I'm assaulted by his earthy scent. But I refuse to back down. I look up at him to keep eye contact.

"And I suggest you drop the attitude. Now." His voice drops to a low growl. "As soon as you walk through that door, I'm your *boss*."

I narrow my eyes at him. I hate that he's right. So much.

I'd never think to sass anyone else in a position of authority, but him flaunting it makes my blood boil. I hold back a sarcastic comment and force a smile.

"What job, *boss*?" I bite off the last bitter-tasting word.

He stares down at me, and I swear I see the corner of his lips twitch with amusement before he nods at the box office.

"You're going to work in the box. You can come out for bathroom breaks."

I stifle a groan before grabbing my coat and purse.

Working in the box office sucks. It's cold because of the opening at the bottom of the ticket window. John let us leave often during training, but Lincoln is being an asshole by keeping me in his version of ticket purgatory.

Just as I move toward the entryway, resigned to my fate, a warm hand on my forearm stops me. I swear I feel electricity shoot directly to my core at the contact.

"No personal items," he says, his voice cold.

"Not even my coat?" I protest. "It's freezing in there!"

He raises his eyebrows as if to ask if I'm questioning him. "Your coat isn't part of your uniform," he says with a tight smile. "It's not a request."

Yanking my arm free, I turn to Fiona and hand her my stuff

before storming to the box office. I pull the door shut with a slam, refusing to look back into the lobby, and go to work booting up the computer and ticket machine and setting up my till.

The first few hours of my shift pass slowly. I hate it. I can hear Fiona and Trey in the lobby chatting and laughing, and Link's running the concession stand with a perfect view of my misery. A cold gust of autumn wind whistles through the little hole in the window, and my teeth chatter.

I jump when there's a knock at the door. I spin in my chair and open it to find Trey, a smiling tugging at his lips.

"Can I come in?"

I look to see if Lincoln's watching. "Are you allowed to?"

Trey laughs, the sound stirring a flutter in my stomach. "It's cute that you think Link has any say in what I do."

I glance around the small space doubtfully but shift to the side and let him enter. His body presses close to mine, and I start to warm up.

"Relax, Bennett," he says with a smirk when he sees me lean back awkwardly against the ticket machine. "It's not like this is the first time we've been this close."

A blush creeps up my neck as I recall the way he touched me at the party, but he has a point. Trey reaches for my sad, red hands and rubs them with his. I close my eyes at the contact. His skin is callused and so warm, and his larger hands engulf mine perfectly as he massages feeling into my aching fingers. I moan involuntarily, and Trey chuckles.

I open my eyes to find his bronze eyes looking back, his pupils dilated. His breath picks up and mine follows suit as we stare at each other, our faces inches apart. I can see the dusting of freckles across his nose and a little scar running above his mouth that stops just at the pink of his upper lip.

The box office door swings open, and I startle.

Lincoln looks between us and then his eyes drop to where

our hands connect, but he doesn't seem angry. He gives Trey an exasperated look, then points a finger at me. "Out," he commands. Now, he sounds angry.

"I thought I had to stay out here...," I start.

"Do you *want* to stay out here?"

"Well, no."

"Then go inside," he grits out as if I'm annoying him.

I glare at him. He's giving me whiplash. First he goes all alpha male in my defense at his party, and now he's back to being a bully.

Pick a lane.

I push past his shoulder, hating the way my skin zips with the contact even with two layers of clothing between us. Trey follows us into the lobby, and I give Fiona a tired smile when she gives me a sympathetic wave. But as I walk toward her, Link's voice stops me.

"This isn't a social hour," he sneers as I turn to face him. "There's film Mylar all over the floor upstairs—it needs to be cleaned up."

John taught us early on in training that if you let the end of a reel slap against the metal of the projector when a movie is finished rewinding, it makes a mess. It's one of the downfalls of having old-school projectors—they have a lot of upkeep.

"Oh, that was my fault...," Trey starts, but Lincoln raises his hand, his eyes never leaving mine, and Trey falls quiet, his gaze curious. "Sunshine, here, was cold, and I think this task will warm her up."

"Sure," I clip, walking to the supply closet and wrestling out the ancient vacuum. I eye the frayed cord. Damn thing is a fire hazard.

"No," Lincoln interrupts as I start to haul it toward the stairs.

"What?"

"You can't use that—it'll make too much noise."

I blink at him in confusion, and he rolls his eyes.

"Use the broom."

"But that'll take forever. Can't I just wait until the movies are out and vacuum then?"

"I need it done now." His stare is steady, as if daring me to challenge him further, but I don't take the bait. I practically throw the vacuum back into the closet and snatch the broom, walking upstairs before he can make this task even more miserable.

He wasn't wrong about it warming me up. I'm sweating bullets as I sweep aggressively, the bits of Mylar either sticking to the old carpet or jumping around with each brush of the broom bristles.

It takes me over an hour to clean around all three projectors, and my shift is almost over by the time I trudge downstairs, trying to tuck loose hair back into my disheveled braid.

Through the large lobby windows, the sun is just starting to set, the light fading to a dusky orange over the treetops. I sigh in relief when I don't see Lincoln anywhere.

I walk into the back room where Fiona is already putting on her coat.

"Are you okay?" she asks.

I nod. "Nothing a coffee or a shot of whisky won't fix."

"That was pretty brutal of him," Fiona says. "You look like hell. Let me help." She uses a gentle touch on my shoulders and turns me around, untying my hair. She runs her hands through the sweat-damp strands and quickly rebraids them, smoothing away any flyaways. "Much better."

"Thank you," I murmur, feeling a bit more human again.

A throat clears behind us, and I look over to see Trey and Lincoln standing in the doorway. Lincoln's lips are pinched as though he wants to say something. I'm hoping an apology is about to fall from his stupid mouth, but I'm not holding my breath. After a few moments of uncomfortable silence, I sigh in frustration, put on my coat, and grab my purse.

My first day was draining and humiliating, and I feel so defeated. The fact that I was looking forward to working at the theater only magnifies that feeling. Tears prick the backs of my eyes, and I blink them away before anyone notices.

Fiona and I turn to head to the lobby, but I pause when Trey steps up to my side. His presence is instantly calming. I take a deep breath and look away, afraid he'll see the vulnerability in my eyes, but Trey tips his finger under my chin, forcing me to look up at him. Something in my face makes his expression soften.

"Don't feed into his bullshit, Charlie. Keep that fire. Lincoln wants to break you. Don't let him," he says quietly. My first name on his lips sends butterflies spiraling in my stomach, but his words leave a bitter taste in my mouth.

I give him a skeptical look. "What's your angle, Trey? Your best friend spent the better part of my shift bullying me, and you were completely complicit. Now you want to play the neutral party?" My tone reeks of resentment, but I can't help feeling like Trey's words are some sort of ploy to get in my pants.

I point at Lincoln, who's been watching us with a neutral expression. "You two deserve each other."

Fiona shuffles her feet to break the tension and nods to the door. I push past both of them, refusing to look at Lincoln.

"Sunshine?" Lincoln calls just as I'm stepping out into the cold.

I stiffen at the nickname and glare at him over my shoulder. "Yeah, boss?"

"Have a nice night."

I resist the urge to flip him off.

CHAPTER THIRTEEN

CHARLIE

I'm reluctantly waiting for Lincoln at a table in the coffee shop. Surprisingly, he agreed to meet so I could give him my screenplay draft since our class was canceled this week, but now I'm not completely sure he's coming.

I glance at my phone.

Fifteen minutes late and no texts. Typical.

Just then, he strolls in, commanding the attention of every girl in the room.

I roll my eyes.

He looks like he just came from the gym, dressed in a hoodie and gray sweats, but despite his messy hair and casual appearance, he's still unfairly hot, and I hate that I notice. He glances around before his gray eyes fall to where I sit at a table by the window. As he approaches, he pulls out a chair, its legs scraping the floor loudly, as if he isn't drawing enough attention with his presence alone.

"Aren't you going to order something?" I ask, irritated.

He smirks but doesn't answer, instead unzipping his backpack and pulling out a piece of paper.

I stare at it in confusion. "What's this?"

"Well, I'm the director." His voice carries an air of superiority that has my hackles rising. "I'm giving you a list of tired tropes that I hate—I'd avoid them if you want us to play nice." He literally sounds like he's threatening me.

"Lincoln, you're *directing* theater students who will be acting out *my* script. You're hardly *my* director."

He gives me a hard look. "Semantics."

Just then, the barista walks over and places a steaming mug in front of Lincoln. "Extra hot," she chirps.

He winks, and she flutters her eyelashes at him. *Gag.* Apparently, this is Lincoln's world, and we're all just living in it.

"You couldn't give me your notes *before* I started writing my screenplay?" Not that I would have taken them into consideration.

He just shrugs and takes a tentative sip of his drink. "I didn't have time to write them up before. I'm really busy."

"For fuck's sake." I mutter.

I straighten the papers in front of me before placing them flat and sliding them across the table. I write to rein in my anxiety. My ideas for this project are very personal, and I hate that he's the one who will read it first—and, no doubt, judge it based on the list he just shoved down my throat.

Lincoln ignores the stack of papers and blows on his drink as if he has all the time in the world. But my irritation stalls when I look down at the mug, puzzled.

"Is that black tea?" I ask, peering at the little tag on the end of the string.

"Yes," he says, wrapping his long fingers around the cup. "Why are you staring at it?"

"Well first, you strike me as a coffee drinker."

"I like both," he interrupts defensively.

"And second," I say with a wide grin, "is that Earl Grey? Like Picard's drink from *Star Trek*?"

His eyebrows rise. "Are you making fun of me?"

"Yes," I quip. "You deserve it."

He glares at me and taps his nails against the mug pensively. "What do *you* know about *Star Trek?*"

"I'm no Trekkie but I've seen *Star Trek, Next Gen*," I say. "I suppose I don't look like the typical demographic though. But neither do you."

"Fair enough," he says.

Then his eyes lose focus and he smiles.

Actually smiles.

And I almost stop breathing. It's the most beautiful thing I've ever seen. Under the table, his leg grazes mine. My heart rate kicks up at the contact.

But you hate him. He's a jerk.

I stare at him, my throat feeling sticky and dry as I swallow. Something about this moment is different, like our conversation triggered a memory. I take a large gulp of my coffee, then sputter when the hot liquid scalds my throat.

Smooth.

Lincoln looks amused.

"I used to watch it with my mom as a kid," he says, shrugging. "I idolized Picard—he was such a hard-ass, and so calm under pressure, but always loyal to a fault—so I even started drinking his tea of choice."

My eyes widen. "Did you just disclose something personal?"

He grimaces. "Did you just use the word 'disclose' in casual conversation?"

I grin. "So I guess it didn't work out then, huh?"

"What?" Lincoln asks, his gray eyes intense. They're a lighter gray today, like an overcast sky.

"Well, you're no Picard," I say. "You're definitely a little too morally gray for a noble Starfleet captain."

Lincoln stares at me like he's trying to figure something out. I start to squirm under his gaze.

"A bit judgy, aren't you? You don't really know anything

about me," he says, a finger running back and forth over his bottom lip. Finally, he shrugs and puts my screenplay into his bag. "But you're not wrong, I guess." Then he stands abruptly, swinging his bag over his shoulder.

"Are you leaving?"

Whatever rapport we just had seems to dissolve with his cruel smirk. "Places to be. Women to fuck, you know," he says with a wink.

"There it is," I mutter.

He walks over to the counter, taking a to-go cup and pouring his tea into it. When he glances back at me, his usual broody expression is firmly in place again, but there's something else there, too. Confusion? Regret? Then he walks out the door.

I realize then that he just shared something personal with me for the first time, and I ruined it with one insensitive comment. But I suppose it's a dose of his own medicine, right? For some reason, shame tugs at my throat anyway, but I swallow it down and pull out my journal.

LINCOLN

I leave the coffee shop and head back toward the school, kicking through the leaves on the sidewalk.

I'm disgusted with myself.

Was I flirting with her?

The more separation I try to force between us, the more she crawls under my skin. I'm attracted to her, sure. I always have been, though it took years for me to figure that out. But that's just me thinking with my dick. It's Charlie's personality that's got me off my game. Unfortunately, her stubborn instinct to fight back and her fiery comebacks give me a hard-on just as much as her body. But she's Ellen Conner's daughter, and every time I look at her, I picture my family's destruction.

The thought makes me see red as I push through the gate and storm across campus.

I still want to hurt her. I want Charlie to feel what I felt when my mother and I walked in on that whore half naked after fucking my father.

The rage. The betrayal. The humiliation.

Everyone seems to sense my dark mood, so I don't attract my usual entourage of fan bros and girls along my way to the Wolf Building. Despite outward appearances to the contrary, I actually hate the attention my looks and money bring. No one is really interested in me as a person—they want wealth and power and connections. Except for Trey.

Speaking of Trey, he's waiting for me when I enter our dorm room, lounging on the couch, surrounded by open, discarded textbooks. Instead of studying, he's watching a *Friends* rerun.

I take off my shoes and drop my backpack with a sigh.

"How was your date with Bennett?" he asks, without looking away from the TV screen.

"You know it wasn't a date, asshole."

"Right, right," he says dismissively, taking a swig from a tall can of Rainier. I eye his beer and note that it's eleven-thirty in the morning, and there's an empty on the side table.

"Already two deep, huh?"

"Don't judge—math stresses me out. I'm too dumb for this shit."

I drop onto the couch beside him and glance over, meeting his brown eyes briefly. "You're not dumb. You just need to ask for help, Trey." I give him a gentle shove. "I bet there's a lot of hot, smart girls—and guys for that matter—who would kill to tutor you."

"Yeah, I suppose."

I decide to drop the issue for now. Well, multiple issues if you count the drinking, too.

"You ready for Halloween?" I ask, changing the subject.

He nods with a wide grin, turning toward me. "I'm going after Charlie. If I don't get to fuck her, I at least want a blowie."

I stay quiet. His words make me uneasy for some reason.

"You can join in if you want, buddy," he says, waggling his eyebrows suggestively. "You were watching us at the party, and she and I both knew it. I think she might be down with a bit of sharing."

"No," I say quickly. "Do whatever you want."

"C'mon man. It'll be like that time with—"

"I said I'm not interested," I say firmly, giving him a glare.

The truth is, the idea does appeal to me, but as much as I want to claim her body, I want to keep my distance. She hates me, and I hate her, and that's the way it should be. That being said...

"But just you—no one else touches her."

Trey rolls his eyes. "Whatever. You're such a possessive weirdo. I hope you change your mind."

"Not happening, Walker," I snark.

But I can feel myself getting weaker every time I see her—every time she speaks—and I'm not sure what'll happen when my hate for her isn't enough.

CHAPTER FOURTEEN

CHARLIE

I walk out into the chilly night air. It's almost eleven on Halloween night, so the streets are pretty empty, and almost everything is closed except the coffee shop and the pub. Somehow, it's not raining, so that's lucky, considering the night's festivities.

I hold up my phone, swipe up, and text Fiona.

> I'm just leaving the theater. Meet me there?

FIONA

> Already here! Two drinks deep. Hurry up! This party is the GOAT.

I smile and roll my eyes. Fiona is so much cooler than me. I had to Google what GOAT meant after she used it for the third time.

> We'll see.

I pause when I'm done texting, wondering where to put my

phone before I unzip the top of my skeleton onesie and shove it between my breasts.

The cemetery is far from the brightly lit part of Main Street, and as I get closer, the street gets darker. I shiver. I probably should have worn something warmer, but I didn't have money for anything new, so I settled for my Dia de los Muertos costume and some colorful face paint.

I get the odd feeling that someone's watching me, and I stop and look around.

The wrought-iron graveyard gates rise before me like skeletal fingers reaching for the inky sky. The ground is littered with damp leaves, and the trees sway with each windy sigh.

I wrap my arms around myself and pick up my pace, pushing through the open graveyard gate toward the sound of laughter mingling with Michael Jackson's "Thriller."

Cresting a hill, I'm impressed by the scene below. Purple and orange lights have been draped between the trees, creating a twinkling canopy above the party. There's a large table with mixed drinks and a keg, and another where a DJ bobs her head, her blue hair swaying. Students clutching orange or black Solo cups mingle between the gravestones, and everyone is wearing with some sort of glow stick or bracelet.

I spot Fiona in her bright red devil costume and head toward her, but stop short when a tall, dark figure steps out from behind a tree right into my path.

My skin prickles and my hand flies to my chest. "God! You scared me!"

I glare at the imposing figure. He's wearing all black and one of those masks like the killer from *Scream*, and he doesn't say anything—just stares at me.

"Oookay, creeper," I say.

I stare a moment longer before giving him a wide berth. I can still feel his eyes on me, and I glance back with a frown. But he's gone. Feeling creeped out, I pick up my pace, my Converse squishing through the damp grass.

"You're *here!*" Fiona squeals, running—more like stumbling—up to me. Her devil horns and matching red eye shadow glitter under the lights.

I smile. "You look hot—no pun intended."

"Damn, girl. You do, too." Her eyes rake up and down my body. "You've got some killer curves in that thing." She gives me an impish grin.

I flush at the compliment. "I need a drink."

I head to the bar. where I pour myself a whisky and Diet Pepsi, careful not to add too much alcohol after I spilled so much personal information to Fiona at the bonfire.

Drunk Charlie cannot be trusted, I think, taking a small sip.

Fiona leans in close and throws an arm around me. She smells like cherries and vodka.

"You're drunk," I say, giving her a playful push.

"No," she says, winking. "But I'm close. I'm keeping an eye on your boys." She points over my shoulder, and I turn around. Lincoln, Trey, and Brantley are leaning against some rocks, drinking and talking.

Serenity is sitting off to one side in what looks like a baby-pink prom dress, and there's a dark red slit across her throat.

"What's Serenity supposed to be?" I ask, smirking. "The horror movie blonde who dies first?"

Fiona snickers. "She's been hanging out with the guys ever since I got here, but she doesn't seem like her bitchy self."

"I'm sure that'll change when she sees I'm here," I say with a sigh.

She's been giving me dirty looks and whispering to her friends whenever we cross paths, but I'm trying to ignore her, hoping she'll lose interest.

I look at her again. She does seem to lack her usual spunk.

While her friends are giggling and drinking, she's staring off into space.

Except not into space.

She's staring at Lincoln.

I realize then that she's probably in love with him, and he treats her with indifference at best.

"I bet that hurts," I murmur, my empathy bleeding through despite how awful the girl has been to me.

"What?" Fi leans closer.

I'm about to tell her my theory when I look closer at the guys. Brantley's hockey gear is obvious, but Lincoln and Trey are just wearing normal clothes.

Lincoln is dressed in a blue button-up shirt and a leather jacket with dark jeans and brown boots. His hair, which usually falls over his forehead, is spiked up in a fauxhawk.

Trey's wearing a flannel shirt with a brown jacket, bootcut jeans, and also brown boots. His blond hair, which is longer than Lincoln's, is parted down the middle.

I smile when he tries to tuck the shorter strands behind his ears with little success.

As if sensing my gaze, Trey looks over, and he smiles back, raising his drink in my direction.

Feeling brave, I walk over.

Lincoln looks up as I approach, his eyes ironically gravestone gray in the dim light. He nods, his face its usual apathetic mask. I keep hoping flirty Lincoln from the coffee shop will resurface, but he's been his normal standoffish self ever since.

Brantley whistles. "Looking hot, ladies!"

Fiona rolls her eyes. She acts like she barely tolerates him, but I suspect there's more to their relationship.

Lincoln shoves him. "Don't be a dickhead." But he glances at me from the corner of his eye as if he made a mistake coming to our defense.

"Takes one to know one, boss," I snark.

Lincoln glares and takes a drink, licking a drop of alcohol from his full lips.

"How was closing shift?" Trey asks. I still don't trust him, but I like the way he's looking at me like he could eat me up.

"Slow," I say. "Apparently, everyone is here instead of watching old-school horror flicks." I gesture with my drink. "Are you guys even dressed up? You look like...you."

Lincoln pulls a plastic machete swimming with fake blood from his belt and hoists it over one shoulder. "We're the Winchesters"

"Like, from *Supernatural?*" I ask. "That explains the weird hair."

Brantley bursts out laughing. "It totally does look weird."

Serenity, who's been eyeing us with a sneer, hops off the rock she was sitting on. "Oh, is that your costume, Link?" She steps into Lincoln's space, and he looks down at her. For some reason, I have the urge to pull her away from him by her shiny hair. "I thought you were both just dressed as super-hot college guys." She bats her perfect eyelashes.

Fiona and I glance at each other and roll our eyes, but I frown, when Serenity places both of her hands on Lincoln's chest and rises on her tiptoes to whisper something in his ear. A smile tugs at his lips. I feel my hand tighten into a fist, but I catch myself before I throw the punch, even as jealousy curls in my stomach.

The guy is insufferable, yet I'm jealous? What's wrong with me?

"Okay," Fiona says quickly, noticing the tension in my stance. "Time to party."

She leads me into the thick crowd of swaying bodies. We dance together the way only girlfriends can, grinding our asses against each other. We're so close that I can feel her tits grazing my back, and we both look at each other and laugh every time it happens.

Suddenly, someone grips my waist, pulling me in a different

direction. I gasp in shock as the hands tug me close to a large, hard chest that sways with my body in perfect sync.

Before I even look back into his eyes, I recognize Trey's heady scent. I relax completely in his arms, my body melting against his warmth. His fingers graze my neck as he pushes my hair over one shoulder, and the feeling travels all the way to my toes. Then his lips brush against the shell of my ear and his breath flutters against my skin. The smell of whisky causes a rush of heat, and my panties start to dampen.

"Did I mention you look unbelievably hot tonight, Bennett," he whispers. "Once again, nothing like the good girl you pretend to be. You put on a good show."

His other hand slides up my body and cups the side of my breast, and I can't stop the moan that escapes my lips. I lose my train of thought. All the reason and control that I normally cling to dissipates with every touch of Trey's hands. Just like the last time we were together.

"What can I say," I reply. "You bring out my naughty side, I guess."

His dick is rock hard against my back, and I grind against it. I smirk when Trey groans loudly, one hand tightening on my waist while the other blatantly grabs my breast. I turn in his embrace, still swaying to music, and I look up into his warm brown eyes. The lust I see there is almost feral, and it mirrors my own. It's the same feeling that overwhelmed me back at Link and Trey's party—this undeniable, irresistible attraction I can't shake.

As if reading my mind, Trey turns, grabs my hand in a firm grip, and pulls me through the crowd of people. I mumble multiple apologies, bumping into strangers as I stumble after him, his long legs eating up the ground toward a dark copse of trees.

We barely reach the shadows before he picks me up, turns, and slams my back against the rough bark of the closest tree.

My legs wrap around his slim waist, and I feel his cock pressing heavily into my stomach, grinding into my clit through the thin material of my onesie. My arms encircle his neck, and my hands run through his silky hair. Our faces are inches apart, our breaths short and needy.

"I don't know why I'm doing this." I lick my lips nervously. Trey's eyes follow the movement before coming back up to stare into mine. "I swear I'm not normally this easy."

He looks away for a moment, and I bring my hand up to his cheek, pulling his gaze back.

"What?" I ask.

"I'm not normally this monogamous." His voice is deep. Just listening to him makes me wet. So. Wet. But his comment makes me snort out a laugh.

"Monogamous? We've fooled around one other time."

"Right," he says, his fingers trailing along my spine. "I should be tired of you by now."

His words send a little thrill through my chest, but I ignore it. "So are we gonna fuck, or what?"

"Ugh," he groans. "It's so hot when your pretty little mouth says 'fuck.'"

I hesitate for a moment before I lean forward and brush my lips against his. He pulls back slightly, his eyes bouncing between mine.

"Is something wrong?" I ask.

"I just don't kiss many people," he murmurs. "I don't normally want to. But I want to really fucking badly—with you."

My stomach somersaults, and I lean forward again. I swallow Trey's groan as my tongue slides tentatively into his mouth, running along the seam of his velvety lips. His grip on my ass tightens.

"Shit," he says against my mouth. And then he slams his mouth to mine with bruising force. The kiss is urgent and needy and the fire it lights inside me is insatiable and wild, and I submit to it completely.

He releases my ass, lowering my needy body to the ground. His large hands slide up my sides before he grasps my zipper and pulls it down to my belly button.

I shiver when the cold air hits my heated skin, throwing my head back as he kisses my collarbone, just above my aching breasts. I shrug out of the onesie sleeves, internally cursing myself for not wearing a dress—though I didn't really plan on Trey mauling me against a tree like some sort of horny wood nymph.

Trey's other hand snakes around my back and releases my bra clasp, spilling my breasts free. We both pause as my phone falls to the dirty ground. Trey smiles apologetically, and I shrug, grabbing his face and hauling his lips back to mine. He slips his tongue inside my mouth before pulling away.

He puts a hand on the rough bark of the tree, pressing his face into my neck for a moment as if to catch his breath. Then, he looks down at my breasts.

"They're fucking perfect," he breathes, rolling one of my nipples between his fingers.

I moan in response, pushing my chest further into his grip. I can hardly stand the tension between my legs as I grind against him shamelessly.

"I want you," I whisper.

"Not yet," Trey says with a smirk.

He bows his head, pulling my tight nipple into his warm mouth, sucking and licking. I practically combust. He releases me with an evil grin, and I feel the loss potently, whimpering in response.

Trey pulls my zipper all the way down and attempts to strip the onesie from my body, but the damn thing is pretty snug, so there's a lot of grunting (him) and giggling (me) before he manages to shimmy it past my thighs. I teeter and grab Trey's shoulders with a startled laugh while he peels the fabric past my knees, finally dropping it to the ground. Somehow, I manage to kick it the rest of the way off, and I pause, feeling ridiculous as I stand there completely naked except for my black Chucks.

"Well, that was a workout," Trey snarks.

Despite the wet leaves and pine needles at our feet, he kneels. His fingers slide slowly up the insides of my thighs, and my self-conscious thoughts are quickly forgotten.

"No panties?" he says with a raised brow.

I shrug. "Panty lines are a fashion faux pas."

"You do seem very fashion conscious," he says with a sarcastic lilt, and I smile. Then he moves his face closer to my throbbing cunt, inhaling the scent. "God damn, you smell good." I push my pelvis toward him until I can feel his hot breath against my clit. "And so responsive."

He slides his hot wet tongue over my clit before taking it in his mouth and sucking. Hard.

Electricity shoots through my blood, the sensation euphoric. I arch my spine, throwing my head back, but he stops.

I look down at him, panting.

"Eyes on me, Bennett," he says darkly. "I want to see you come apart."

Then he dives in, his mouth on me with renewed fervor. I tangle my hands into his hair, tugging him closer. His thick fingers circle my entrance before thrusting inside me, and his tongue laps my clit eagerly.

I look down at Trey and movement catches my eye.

In the darkness, I catch sight of Lincoln leaning against a tree. His eyes are straight fire. His jeans are unzipped, and his hand is in his pants, moving against his obviously hard cock as he watches us.

Again.

Creeper, I think.

But I don't care. If anything, Link watching, his eyes

branding me while he touches himself, only heightens the pleasure already threatening to drown me.

Trey's hot mouth closes over my clit repeatedly, and I bite my lip in a poor attempt to keep quiet. At least we're not in the middle of a crowd this time, but it's still a public place.

And then everything hits me at once. Pleasure rips through my body with unexpected ferocity. I fall off the edge. I plummet.

"Trey," I moan loudly, twisting his hair between my fingers. He continues to lap at my clit as he teases out my orgasm with his tongue.

My knees give out, but Trey's grip on my thighs keeps me steady. When my climax finally dissipates, I glance up, searching the darkness, but Lincoln is gone.

CHAPTER FIFTEEN

TREY

I stare up at Charlie, my face still wet from her arousal. She lets me steady her when I stand, placing my hands on her hips.

I glance around, but we're still alone. I kiss her deep and slide my fingers between her dripping folds.

Holy shit. She's so wet. For me.

I hum against her lips in appreciation.

I know I won't be able to take much more foreplay. My cock is already straining painfully against my jeans.

She looks at me with eyes as dark and green as the forest to her back. Her fingers fumble with the buttons on my shirt, and she pushes it off my shoulders, sliding her hands over my sweaty skin while tracing the edges of my muscles.

"I'm on the pill," Charlie breathes, her gaze still bright with lust. She grips my biceps, and her nails dig into my skin.

It's all the encouragement I need.

She smells like vanilla and whisky and sex, and the scent is completely intoxicating. I unzip my pants and pull my aching cock free. "I'm clean. I get tested weekly."

I fist my dick while I memorize her delicate features, fascinated by the untamed hunger in her hooded gaze. I step forward and tease her entrance with the head of my cock, and I hesitate a moment, searching her eyes, giving her the chance to stop me.

"Please," she begs, her possessive grip dropping to my forearms.

I ease inside her, sliding in inch by torturous inch.

"Fuck, Trey." Her voice is breathy and needy, and it hits me like heroin.

Charlie's legs wrap around my waist, her heels digging into my bare ass, which only pushes me deeper into her pussy. An obscene moan leaves my mouth. My restraint starts to unravel when I pull out, and I can't hold back.

I thrust inside her roughly with a sharp grunt, and her heat drives me crazy but I hold back, pulling out before thrusting in again.

She's tight. So tight.

Charlie clings to me, whimpering as she meets my movements, one hand wrapped around the back of my neck, her fingers weaving into my hair.

The sensation is too intimate, too raw.

I never fuck bare like this. What the fuck is wrong with me?

The unfiltered bliss ripples through my veins, the intensity so unexpected that I can't slow down. My thrusts are needy, wild, desperate. I've never felt this out of control with anyone, the pleasure almost painfully potent, and the thought startles me.

Then I come with a grunt as I feel Charlie's pussy spasm around me with her second orgasm, milking me dry. I still against her body, my breaths ragged. I can feel her breasts pressing into my chest with every gasp.

"I'm sorry," she says finally. "I don't normally...I mean, I hardly know you."

She pulls back, and I release her. She reaches for her

discarded onesie, trying her best to wrestle it right-side out. Her movements are quick and disjointed, and if it weren't for her makeup—which is still in surprisingly good condition, all things considered—I have no doubt she'd be blushing with embarrassment.

I look away, tucking myself back into my jeans, and sigh as I button my shirt.

This was a mistake.

For the first time in forever, I feel ashamed.

What if she wants something from me? Some form of reassurance that this was more than a quick fuck?

But was it?

It felt different. But that's not me. I don't let girls get inside my head. I'm a selfish prick. That's my MO. I fuck for my own pleasure.

Comforted by my own bullshit, I lock away any pesky feelings that might have been bleeding out.

"Enjoy the party, Bennett," I say, my tone dismissive.

Her head snaps up, her eyes flashing with anger. "So that's it, huh?" Her is voice pure venom.

"Did you think we were making love?" I ask with a wide smile.

I know. I'm an asshole.

"No," Charlie says, pulling up her zipper. "I just thought you might want round two, but I guess the rumors are true—you're just a one-and-done guy."

I know she means the words to offend, but I can't help it. I burst out laughing. "Are you propositioning me for more sex? Even though I was just a dick?"

"Not anymore." She crosses her arms over her chest.

I half expect her to stamp her foot like a petulant child. I feel my cock perk up, definitely ready for more.

"You're cute when you're pissed," I say.

"Whatever," she huffs, turning to walk away. "I need to get back to my friend."

I grab her elbow, but she yanks it from my grip, her gaze flashing up to mine.

I raise my hands in surrender and let her go, watching as she stomps off, the sway of her hips taunting me as she walks away.

CHARLIE

I walk back to the party pleased with myself. Don't get me wrong, I'm angry that he was so cold, but I like that I threw him off his game. I think he expected me to beg for his attention, but fuck that.

Do I want more sex? Yes, absolutely. Whatever happened between us was positively euphoric.

But if he feels the same way, he's going to have to work for it. That boy is a player, so I trust him as far as I can throw him.

As I leave the privacy of the trees, I spot Fiona refilling her drink. I take baby steps down the small slope, but my right foot still manages to skid through a patch of mud, throwing me off balance.

"Whoa, careful, Sunshine," Link's deep voice rumbles as he catches the back of my onesie like he's holding a cat by the scruff.

I freeze, trying to right myself as elegantly as possible in this position. I narrow my eyes at Lincoln. He still has a firm grip near my collar and an amused smile on his dumb, handsome face.

"Are you following me?" I ask.

I recall his hooded gaze and the way his hand pulled at his

cock as he watched me and Trey moments ago. I shiver at the memory.

He releases his grip and I straighten. "Actually, I was out there taking a leak. Is that allowed?"

His tone rubs me the wrong way, but what else is new. What is it with these guys pissing me off? Either way, I'm over them tonight. I don't answer him, step away dismissively, and continue back down the hill, waving at Fiona when she spots me.

She grins and hands me her drink, then grabs the bottle of vodka, free pouring a generous amount into a second clean Solo cup and adding a splash of Cherry Coke.

"Let's dance some more!" she shouts over the crowd, and I nod.

I feel like we dance for hours. The alcohol flows warmly through my veins, and I let go, swaying to the music. Fi grabs my hand, twirling me around, and we stumble into a couple too busy grinding on each other to care about the intrusion.

I can feel Lincoln and Trey watching me. I'm hyperaware of them for some reason, and every once in a while, I catch a glimpse of them standing on the outskirts of the party, like a pair of stoic gargoyles.

I finally pull Fiona from the crowd, and we plop onto a bench, panting. "I can't dance anymore, dude. I'm dead."

Fiona giggles. "That was a good pun."

"Bennett."

I look up as Trey approaches me. I try to give him a stern glare, but fail miserably because he's too damn beautiful.

Fuck, I've already forgiven him.

He glances at Fiona but doesn't ask her to leave, which I like. "So maybe you were right—I'm normally that one-and-done guy." He drops his gaze for a minute before raising it back to mine. "But maybe tonight is different."

"What?" I ask.

He steps closer and skims his fingers along my jaw. "Come back to my place."

I close my eyes at the contact. When I glance sideways at Fiona, she gives me an encouraging nod.

"Okay." I take his hand, anticipation swimming in my veins, as he leads me back through the graveyard.

TREY

I unlock the door to my dorm suite. "After you, Bennett," I say, gesturing for her to enter.

She rolls her eyes. "Don't act like you're a gentleman now." She steps into the space but pauses awkwardly in the kitchen, looking around as if she's suddenly not sure what she's doing here with me. Honestly, I'm not sure why she's here either. I don't normally bring girls back to my bed for round two.

I step forward and take Charlie's hand, leading her to my room. She looks around with interest. Her wavy hair falls messily around her shoulders and across her forehead as she steps up to my bookcase, examining my collection.

"It's mostly Manga," I say.

"I see that." She pulls out one of the books to look at the cover, then frowns, her green eyes flashing with sadness.

"What?" I ask.

"It's nothing," she murmurs, putting the book back.

"Bullshit," I say, smiling. "I saw that look. Tell me."

She glances at my collection again and then looks over at me. "My mom used to buy me Manga."

"And..."

"And she died."

"Shit, right, I'm sorry." I internally curse myself for bringing up her dead mom.

Real smooth.

She waves her hand dismissively. "It's okay. I told her they inspired my writing, so she pretty much bought me my whole collection, but I don't think she realized they were so deviant," she says with a small smile.

I laugh. "What are you in to?"

She bites her lip, then gives me a stern look.

A-fucking-dorable.

"If I tell you, you can't judge me."

"Sure." I give her a wide grin while my fingers cross an X over my heart like we're making some sort of middle school pact. "Promise."

Her eyes narrow as if she's assessing whether to trust me, but she finally takes a breath, looking away. "My collection is a mix of reverse harem and male-male." She frowns, looking almost offended. "People always think since I'm into English that I should like the classics, but I'm a sucker for smut—Manga, romance books, you name it. Male-male stuff is especially hot."

I raise my eyebrows, fighting back a shocked chuckle. "You're just full of surprises, Bennett. You come across as this innocent, introverted little thing, but your taste in books and the way you fuck says otherwise."

She seems flustered by the compliment, her gaze dropping to the floor.

I reach out to cup her chin and run my thumb along her bottom lip. "Speaking of fucking..."

Charlie squeals as I grab her hand and pull her to my bed, pinning her soft body beneath mine.

CHAPTER SIXTEEN

CHARLIE

I smooth my hands down my black satin dress and glance around the party.

Where is he?

I haven't seen Matt in over an hour. I spot Sebastian mingling with Mr. and Mrs. Farthing, some of my stepdad's investors, no doubt. Seb has a polite smile on his face, but his eyes meet mine with a silent plea.

I grin, walk over, and place my hand on his shoulder. "Excuse me, but I need a word with my brother," I say, smiling at the couple. Mrs. Farthing looks distraught and Mr. Farthing, who looks as though he wants to crawl under a table, nods in relief.

"Of course," he says, pulling his wife away.

"Thank you," Seb says. "They weren't even talking about Dad's business. Apparently, Mrs. Farthing's son just came out, and after a few glasses of wine, she'll share anything, including her homophobic opinions."

"Yikes," I say, frowning.

"Yikes, indeed," Seb agrees. "The whole conversation was making me uncomfortable." He brushes his dark brown hair from his forehead. "How're you doing?"

SARA ELISABETH

"I was looking for Matt," I say, glancing around again. "I want him to pretend to be a doting boyfriend. You know how creepy some of Dad's business people can be. Ever since I hit puberty, they hang around and stare at me." I make a gag face.

Sebastian grimaces. "I haven't seen him, but I think it's almost toast time." He nods toward the mic being set up at the front of the room.

"Oh crap!" I say. "I have cue cards. I think they're in my room."

"Of course you made cue cards," Seb says. "Always prepared, little sis."

"Damn straight."

I do my most ladylike fast walk out of the dining room and rush up the stairs, trying not to twist an ankle in my heels. I open the door to my room, pausing when I see movement on the bed.

My brain misfires when I squint into the darkness.

Is that...

My eyes adjust. Someone is fucking on my bed.

Not just someone.

Matt.

His head snaps up, and our eyes meet. I'm frozen in place, bile rising in my throat.

Sweat plasters his silky black hair to his forehead. His sharp features don't show guilt or remorse. In fact, he looks almost...bored. And he keeps his rhythm, pounding his dick into this girl over and over. I can't see her face, but I hear her whimpering. His grin turns sinister, baring sharp, unnatural teeth and his eyes light up, glowing red. Burning embers in the darkness.

A wave of panic rips through my body.

I turn to run, but the door is gone. And then I hear Matt's guttural moan as he comes and the slap of flesh on flesh stops.

I claw at the wall in front of me, desperately wanting to escape. But then I feel his grip on my throat and his hot breath on my neck.

"Your turn," he growls in my ear.

I WAKE WITH A JERK, my skin damp with sweat and my heart pounding in my ears.

I look around the dark room in panic, searching for those red eyes. But then I feel a strong arm around my waist tighten, and my muscles relax as I inhale Trey's heady, familiar scent.

Right. I'm in his bedroom.

Looking around, I see my skeleton onesie balled up with my phone on the floor beside the bed.

I carefully turn under Trey's arm so that I'm facing him and smile when I see my black lipstick smeared all over his plump lips. He's naked from the waist down, the navy sheets barely covering the v-shaped cut of his lower abs. I chuckle to myself when I also see my lipstick on his biceps, pecs, and stomach.

Clearly, we had a good time last night.

Careful not to wake him, I wiggle from beneath Trey's grasp, and pull on my clothes, then slip into his bathroom and do my best to wash the smeared makeup from my face. When I'm finished, I walk back into the bedroom and pick up my phone.

It's 5 a.m. I have four missed texts from Fiona and a missed FaceTime from Seb. He knows I have a hard time at Halloween and probably expected me to be in bed sulking.

I look back at Trey for a moment before I leave. A strange, sad feeling pulls at my chest, but I push it away because I'm not naïve. Trey Walker is a lot of things, but a girl's boyfriend isn't one of them. I know our moment together was just that: a moment. And no doubt a meaningless one. So it's time for me to go.

I close his door softly and tiptoe down the hallway. When I reach the kitchen, I remember the bottled waters the guys passed out to drunk friends at their last party. I smile at the memory, thinking it was actually a thoughtful gesture. I walk to the fridge and open it.

"Bingo." I grab a water from the top shelf, twist off the cap, and take a large swig. I turn around, closing the fridge door with my hip, and immediately slam into Lincoln's warm, hard, *naked* chest. My hand instinctively squeezes the water bottle, causing the contents to erupt between us like a geyser, soaking his abs and the front of my onesie.

"Oh my God, I'm so sorry, Link!"

I spot a dish towel by the sink and grab it, using it to wipe water off his stomach and the front of his shorts. Then I realize what I'm doing and stop, my face flaming. I can see the outline of his sizable dick beneath the thin material. And it twitches when I touch it.

Fuck. Me.

Now I'm horny *and* mortified.

Lincoln hasn't moved or spoken. I close my eyes and take a deep breath before looking up at him. He's staring down at me, his eyes completely unreadable, and I step back, putting space between us.

The silence is too much.

"What're you doing up?" I ask.

"I like to workout in the mornings. It's *normally* very peaceful." He eyes the water puddled at his feet. His socks look...wet. He looks back at me, his eyes narrowing. "What're you doing here?"

"I, uhhh..."

Suddenly, I don't want to tell him why I'm here.

Would he even care? He has to already know, anyway. He watched Trey and me fuck last night, didn't he?

"She was having a sleepover," Trey's deep voice rumbles from behind me.

My whole body prickles with surprise. I turn my head to

94

look at him, and then I glance back at Lincoln. His eyes darken for a minute as he stares at Trey. Trey gives him a knowing smile that almost says "I told you so." Then he raises his eyebrows in question, and Link rolls his eyes.

What kind of fucking pantomime is this?

Link directs his attention back to me. "Is she about to pull a smash-and-dash on you? I thought that was your move, Trey."

Trey laughs and rubs his chin. "That *is* my usual move." His eyes track over my body. "The walk of shame looks pretty good on you, Bennett."

My hand self-consciously goes to my hair to flatten what's probably a horrifying case of bedhead.

Lincoln looks between us for a moment, and his shoulders start shaking with repressed laughter. "Is that black lipstick smeared all over you?"

It's the first time I've ever heard him laugh, and it's equal parts beautiful and irritating.

Trey's hand goes to his lips and then he glances down as if noticing the dark smears for the first time. "Oh yeah," he says, grinning widely. He reaches for the waistband of his shorts. "You should see how much is on my—"

"Enough!" My voice rises to a squeaky, uneven pitch. "I need to go."

I duck around Lincoln, then run for the door, rip it open, and slam it shut behind me. I lean against it for a moment while I try to slow the adrenaline coursing through my body.

The guys' laughter sounds from inside, and I grind my teeth in frustration.

Assholes.

Just then, the door opens, and I fall backward against Lincoln's damp skin. He's still chuckling.

"For fuck's sake," I mutter in panic while I try to regain my balance and turn toward him.

He dangles my black Converse in front of my face. "You forgot your shoes."

I snatch them with an embarrassed huff, then I try to look casual as I speed walk barefooted down the hall.

CHAPTER SEVENTEEN

CHARLIE

*M*y life has morphed into a ridiculous balancing act between school, the movie theater, and avoiding the two most popular guys on campus who show their stupid, hot faces every-damn-where.

My English/film class has taken on a vampiric quality, sucking every last drop of creativity from my body at an alarming rate. Dr. Jackson has us writing short story after short story, and each one is more emotionally draining than the last–though admittedly that's my own fault. My topic choices tend to be dark in nature. And that doesn't include working on our final projects. Lincoln hasn't given me any feedback on my screenplay so far, so I have have no idea if I'm even headed in a good direction. Plus, I downloaded the application for the summer publishing internship in New York, trying to get a jump on it before the winter deadline.

I'm huddled under an oak tree, grateful for a break in the rain, scribbling in my journal, when I hear a familiar voice.

"Hey Charlie," Matt says, approaching me with caution like I might grab my stuff and bolt.

My mouth dries as I take in his messy dark hair and pale blue eyes. He's wearing black sweats and a Whitmore U hockey hoodie and carrying a large duffel bag.

I glance around.

Conveniently Lincoln and Trey are nowhere in sight. The last thing I need is another altercation between them.

Matt stops a few feet away. "Can I sit for a few minutes?"

I take a deep breath, feeling more in control than I did when he surprised me at the party, and despite the creepy vibe I still get from him, we're in public, so he won't do anything to hurt me.

I smile politely. "Sure, Matt."

He sits and gives me a small smile back, tilting his head so that his hair falls over his forehead. I used to find that familiar gesture hot, but now it just seems predatory.

"I saw you at the Halloween party. Still like that skeleton costume, huh?"

My head snaps up. "You were there?"

"Uh, yeah," he says haltingly. "I was the *Scream* guy—ghost face."

My blood runs cold. He was so close to me, and I didn't even realize it.

"Sorry, I didn't say anything." He shrugs. "I guess I got scared you'd run or something because of what happened at the party, so I froze."

"It's fine, Matt." I fidget with my pen, tapping it on my knee while I wait for him to say something. He stares at me with a calculating look as if trying to memorize my face.

"I see you're still forever the writer," he says finally, nodding toward my journal.

"I am," I reply tightly. I point to his equipment bag. "And I see you're still killing it in the ice rink."

His grin is a bit too smug. "First line, of course. Coach recruited me personally at the end of last semester where I was racking up the stats at U Dub." Then his voice drops lower. "I'm untouchable at this school."

Chills rake over my skin as I stare into his cold eyes. The simple statement feels like a threat, but Matt covers it with another cocky smirk. "Though I do spend a lot of time in the sin bin."

"You always were good at bullying people," I quip, rolling my eyes.

Matt ignores my jab, craning his neck to look at my notes.

I slam the book closed, glaring at him. "What do you want, Matt?"

His expression turns serious. "I need to apologize for...everything."

I grimace. "You really don't have to." I swallow the unwanted feelings of anger and betrayal that float to the top of my consciousness. "It's been more than a year, and I'm over it."

Matt raises his eyebrows, his gaze steady. "We were best friends for eight years and lovers for another two, and you're just over it?" His hand tightens into a white-knuckled fist.

I sigh. "I don't want to talk about this with you." I start to stand, but he reaches for my arm, grabbing my wrist. His touch burns like acid, and I pull away. "You ripped out my fucking heart, okay? Is that what you want to hear? I was hurt, but then other shit happened, and it turns out the world didn't revolve around you and what we had. So, yes, I got over it. End. Of. Story."

He narrows his eyes as I speak but doesn't interrupt.

"Are you looking for forgiveness? Fine. I forgive you. But I'm not going to forget it. We're not friends anymore, and I don't think we ever will be again."

Matt's quiet for a moment while I stare down at him, my chest heaving like I've just run a marathon. Then he smiles. He fucking smiles.

"Did you just cuss?" he asks, grinning more broadly.

"That's what you took from what I just said?"

He shrugs. "I'll take your forgiveness in whatever form you'll give it. And we'll be friends again, maybe more. Just you wait." He stands and gives me his signature wink again.

The chills resurface as I watch him saunter away.

LINCOLN

I watch Matt the Prick walk away from Charlie with barely checked rage slithering through my veins.

I don't get the guy's appeal—never have.

"Stupid hockey players," I seethe as I turn on my heel and stalk back across the grass.

The weather is, dare I say, perfect—crisp and clear but not too cold.

I hate it.

I can't wait for the gloomy mornings and rainy afternoons. Sunny days remind me of my mom, so they're always tainted with resentment. She loved the sun and spent every second she could basking in its light. In the summer, we went to the beach (albeit a rocky Washington beach), and if the skies cleared on winter days, she'd walk the path along the harbor, no matter how cold it was.

But now, instead of my mom, the sun just reminds me of *her*. And I don't want to think of her all the damn time.

Sunshine.

It's why I ran after that night two years ago. Being in her orbit is an emotional minefield.

When I get to the Wolf Building, I realize I don't really want to go up and sulk in my dorm, and I have an hour before my next class, so I sit down on a bench and stew about the interaction I saw between Matt and Charlie instead. Which is super healthy, I get it, but I know enough about Matt fucking Johnson to know Charlie deserves better.

I clench my fist and grimace when I feel my nails bite into the skin of my palm.

My eyes wander. I can still see Charlie across the quad, scribbling in her notebook with her brows pinched together in concentration.

Why am I obsessing about this? It's infuriating. I hate her. Maybe if I just fucked her like the others...

My body seems to agree as I feel my cock stir against my jeans.

"What's got your panties in a twist?" Trey snarks from behind me, pulling my dark thoughts out of the gutter. "Or should I ask who?"

No point in lying to the guy. "Matt and Charlie were chatting earlier."

Trey gives me a pleading look. "Look, I don't like him either, but you can't exactly tell her who not to talk to."

"Well, technically I can," I grumble. "It just makes me look like an obsessed crazy person."

"You are obsessed." Trey sits down beside me and tosses his backpack onto the ground. "It's part of your charm." He gives me an appraising look. " I saw you giving poor Damon an earful for flirting with Charlie the other day—don't deny it."

I give him a dark look. "I tried to sweet-talk Chancellor Edwards into kicking Matt out of here."

"Really?" Trey says with a knowing smile. "And why would you do that? Are you trying to protect her? So sweet."

"Absolutely not." I grimace. "I just don't like the guy on my turf. He gives me the creeps."

Trey frowns. "You and me both. So what did the chancellor say?"

"She basically told me to pound sand."

Trey's hand goes to his chest in mock shock. "What? An Evans who didn't get his way?"

"Fuck off," I growl, my mood darkening by the minute. "Johnson is one of our hockey centers, and you know how this damn school feels about its hockey team."

Trey whistles. "He probably knew he was invincible, otherwise he wouldn't have intentionally pissed you off."

"Or the dude is a damn sociopath," I say. "Basically, we have to catch him doing something pretty fucked-up to get him expelled."

Trey rubs his stubble thoughtfully. "I wonder if Brantley has any dirt on the guy—maybe he takes 'roids or something."

"Worth asking," I agree. "But Brantley is going to be disappointed. My guess is that Johnson is the key to some serious wins, and Brantley needs those under his belt this season to help with his NHL recruitment."

Trey nods. "So I take it we're also going to keep our own tabs on the fucker, then?"

"Bingo," I say, glad that my friend is on the same page. "I just hate that Charlie's so damn nice to that asshole."

"She's a nice girl, Link. She's nice to everyone."

"She's sassy as hell to me."

Trey stares at me, deadpan. "Evans, you've been nothing but rude to her since that first night on the quad."

"Beside the point," I huff.

"Someone's a Bitter Bert."

"That's not even a thing." I look back over at her still sitting under the oak trees looking perfectly fucking innocent like she doesn't have my balls in a vice. "She's been avoiding us since Halloween."

Trey shrugs. "We fucked, and it probably freaked her out. Sex makes things weird."

"How would you know?" Link asks, amused. "You don't normally talk to girls afterward. Maybe *you* make it weird."

"Fine, maybe." He shoves me. "But you're not exactly a ray of sunshine around her—in fact, you're straight-up cruel most days. Maybe you should ease up."

I choose to ignore his suggestion, but my mind drifts back to Trey's expression when I caught Charlie leaving our apartment the morning after the Halloween party. "Was she just another one-night stand? Because you realize you've never brought *anyone* home before."

Trey rubs the back of his neck. "I'm just...comfortable with her."

I study him. "Explain."

He doesn't meet my eyes. "She seems to care about little things. She didn't come back to my room and immediately want to fuck. We talked about my Manga collection and her mom." Trey leans back against the bench, focusing on Charlie in the distance. "My usual hook-ups tell me I'm hot and funny, but they don't see anything else. She does, and it makes me feel like she might actually like me as a person."

A strange feeling flutters in my gut. Trey looks over at me apologetically. "I can back off..."

I hold up a dismissive hand. "I don't care what you do. I'm not interested."

Trey eyes me like he doesn't believe my bullshit. "Could've fooled me," he says. "You know you don't have to hide shit from me, Link. I'm not going to judge you for wanting her and hating her at the same time." He puts a hand on my shoulder. "I trust that you have a right and a reason to feel both."

His touch is comforting, but his words scare me, and not much does that these days. Since my mom left, anger has had a permanent foothold in my personality. But fear? Not so much.

"I need to get to class," I say, jumping to my feet. "Catch you later?"

Trey nods, and I walk away.

I still hate Charlie but for the first time in a while, I wish I didn't.

CHAPTER EIGHTEEN

CHARLIE

*T*he movie theater is the one place I can't avoid Trey and Lincoln. I hardly see John anymore as Link has fully embraced his role as general manager of the joint. It's strange seeing him passionate about something; he gets lost in the moment talking about movies, whether he hates them or loves them, and I can see something spark in his eyes beyond his usual indifference.

Not that he has these conversations with me. Normally, I overhear him and Trey geeking out like a couple of little kids, and it's honestly kind of cute. Their favorite hot take is which film out of a trilogy is superior, and I'm always pleasantly surprised by Lincoln's choices.

"He's a third movie guy," Trey says with a dramatic eye roll as he winks at me. I glance at Lincoln, who's standing next to me eating a handful of popcorn, and I smile as I finish wiping up a small puddle of Coke from the concession stand counter.

"Even *Back to the Future*?" I toss the paper towel into the trash.

Lincoln grins and shrugs.

"Really?" I ask. "The Western one?"

Trey leans back against the counter across from us and folds his arms over his chest. "You should see him when Marty's zapped to 1885. You know the scene: he's chased by the cavalry and a bear before he's knocked unconscious. Link dies laughing. Every. Time."

Lincoln tosses a kernel of popcorn at Trey's face, but Trey just catches it in his mouth, which is stupidly hot for some reason.

"I can't help that Michael J. Fox's scream is hilarious," Lincoln says. "Besides, you like all the trilogy movies that everyone likes—the first *Back to the Future*, *The Empire Strikes Back*, *Raiders of the Lost Ark*. I could go on."

"Nothing wrong with liking what other people like, is there, Link?" Trey asks, his tone playful as he raises his eyebrows suggestively.

Link gives him a steady look but doesn't take the bait. "I'll be in the office doing payroll," he says, walking across the lobby toward the upstairs door.

Just then, Fiona comes skipping from the bathroom, a broom swinging from her fingers. "The bathrooms are all clean," she says brightly, opening the storage room to put the broom away before joining us.

I glance at Trey, worrying my lip while I consider my words. "Hey Trey, why won't Link let me screen any movies?"

Lincoln's been pretty intent on making my life hell while I'm working, and I'm trying not to take it personally. I've been asking him to let me screen a movie, but he's refused so far even though I know he lets Trey and his other meathead buddies watch—I've even seen Serenity attend a few.

Trey gives me an apologetic shrug. "What can I say? He's an asshole."

"Just to me, it seems," I mutter to Fiona.

She smiles, her emerald eyes crinkling at the corners. "You do get on his bad side for some reason."

I frown. "*Is it just me?*"

"I don't know where all his sexy hate for you comes from," she says, shrugging. "Honestly, it's like he spews some sort of vitriol and then looks at you like he wants to eat you when your back is turned."

Trey barks a laugh at her comment.

"What?!" I whisper yell at her. I glance at Trey as my cheeks flush. "He does *not* do that." Fi just gives me a look that screams, *If you say so.*

While it's true that Lincoln still seems intent on nagging me to do menial tasks around the theater—last week he made me reorganize the movie posters alphabetically *and* by genre—his cold exterior has cracked some over the past couple weeks. But then again, I've been avoiding him and Trey after embarrassing myself on Halloween, so maybe he just hasn't had a chance to aim his usual hate my way.

"Whatever," I say doubtfully. "I'm going to avoid Link and grab the new marquee letters from upstairs."

It's Thursday night, so the movies change over before we open tomorrow, and I have the *super-fun* job of updating the signage outside. Note the sarcasm.

I stare at the chaotic sway of the trees as I walk by the large glass windows. November in Washington is definitely what I like to call "box of chocolates" weather—you never know what the fuck you're going to get. The other day, the drizzle changed to sleet and then it was sunny for twenty minutes before it started snowing. Now, it's a mix of wind and sideways rain.

I trudge up the stairs and stop when I reach the first projector. "Shit," I say, shaking my head. On the ground, shiny, jagged pieces of film Mylar litter the floor, winking up at me in the flickering light. "Trey strikes again, but I'm sure Lincoln will tell *me* to clean that up later."

I walk to the manager's office. The door is closed, but next week's movie docket is taped on it. I stare at the list: *The Lord of the Rings: The Fellowship of the Ring, The Lord of the Rings: The Two Towers, The Lord of the Rings: The Return of the King.*

"For fuck's sake."

Do we even have that many letters?

I turn away, cursing Lincoln for his movie choices and J.R.R. Tolkien for his lengthy book titles. Then I remember something John said a couple of weeks ago about showing *The Hobbit* trilogy first.

"Better double-check," I mutter to myself and ease open the office door.

Lincoln's sitting at the manager's desk, the room illuminated by a table lamp instead of the usual overhead fluorescents. He's slouched in the rickety rolling chair, his sleeves pushed up and his tie loosened. Next to a pile of discarded papers, Link's laptop sits open, and I recognize a scene from Baz Lurhmann's *Romeo + Juliet* playing.

I realize that I probably should have knocked, and I'm just about to back out of the room when I hear him sniff. I pause and study him more closely. He has a hand over his mouth, his elbow resting on the table, and I catch his eyes shining with each flicker of action on the screen. He sniffs again and raises his thumb to his cheek.

He's crying.

It's so unexpected that I just stare, watching the emotions run across his normally cold, vacant features. And while he's obviously sad, there's a hint of anger in the set of his brows— but it's not like the hatred he throws my way—this anger looks like betrayal. Someone hurt him.

But he doesn't care about my feelings, so why should I care about his?

But I do.

I decide to follow my initial instinct and leave, but the office door creaks as I start to pull the handle, and Link's head turns, his eyes snapping to mine.

He slams his laptop closed with one hand and scrubs his fist across his cheek with the other.

"Don't you know how to knock?" he snaps with barely veiled rage.

"I-I'm sorry." I take a few steps back.

"What do you want?" he snaps, rolling across the room to flick on the overhead lights.

I squint at the sudden brightness. "I was just wondering if the movie list for next week is right. I thought your dad said we were showing *The Hobbit* trilogy first," I try to look everywhere but his face.

"Yeah, I vetoed that garbage. *The Hobbit* movies are mediocre at best."

"Right," I agree. "Okay then."

I turn on my heel and flee down the hall to the supply room, then close the door behind me.

I'm SITTING criss-cross applesauce on the floor surrounded by stacks of letters when Fiona peeks around the door. "What the heck are you doing?" she asks, trying to hide a smile when I look up at her.

"Link thought it would be a fun idea to showcase *The Lord of the Rings* movies next week." I gesture to the piles of letters I've made. Pieces of my hair have escaped my braid and are now stuck to my sweaty forehead. I grimace, tucking the damp strands behind my ears. "And it's hot as hell in here."

"The movies are getting out soon. Do you want some help carrying these down?" Fi asks, eyeing the mess. I nod. Between the two of us, we manage to carry everything downstairs, entering the lobby with the stacks of letters teetering like a stack of books in a cartoon.

"No, no, it's okay," I sneer at Lincoln and Trey, who glance up from their clipboards and watch us with repressed amusement as we stumble toward the back room. "No need to help us. We totally got it."

Fiona giggles behind me. I nudge open the door with my foot, and we place the letters carefully in the corner.

I turn on my heel and walk back into the lobby. Link looks up when I enter, his eyes narrowing dangerously. I know that look—he's angry about earlier. I caught him in a private moment, and it embarrassed him.

"Hey Sunshine," he says with a cruel smile. "After this set of movies, I need you to go upstairs and sweep up the Mylar around the projectors."

I'd normally just take the punishment, but I'm sweaty and tired and over this day, so instead, my brain misfires. "Are you serious right now?"

I take a deep breath, giving him a chance to take the task back and not be the dickhead I know he is. Here, in this space, Lincoln is my manager, so I know I should take his abuse like a good little employee. I've been doing that since Halloween. But fuck that.

"Here it comes…" Fi mutters, and she steps back as if to escape my wrath.

Lincoln's eyes darken as he takes in my stiff, defiant stance. "It's probably something you should have taken care of earlier."

He glances at Trey for support, though for once, Trey seems unamused.

My patience detonates like a bomb, and rage courses through my limbs, making my hands shake. "Why should *I* clean it up?" I shoot back, my voice rising. "*I'm* not the one who lets the film slap for twenty minutes."

I glare at Trey accusingly, but he can't meet my eyes.

Something about Lincoln rubs me raw without fail, and tonight, I've reached my limit. "I have been cleaning up this shithole for months, and I can never meet your impossible standards, *boss*. I can't do a damn thing right. And you never ask anyone else to do anything beyond their fucking jobs. Why me? Why do you hate *me* so much, goddammit?" My voice cracks, and it makes my anger simmer hotter. I refuse to show him weakness. I swallow hard, trying to blink away unwanted, frustrated tears.

Lincoln steps into my space, crowding me.

I reach out, placing my hand on his bicep. My intent was to push him back, but my traitorous body responds to his proximity, and instead, a spark rips through me at the contact.

Lincoln pulls his arm away, his eyes flashing. "You ruin everything," he hisses. I recoil at the venom in his voice, my brows drawing together in confusion. I'm forced to look up at him, but I don't see hate swirling in his stormy eyes.

There's just pain.

Agony.

What did I do to cause this?

The rage burning hot under my skin, starts to dissipate. This isn't an argument between a manager and his employee. This is something else. Something deeper.

I have no idea what to say, but I know if I stare into the cloudy abyss of his eyes much longer, I'll lose myself completely.

Or I'll hit him.

Auditorium three's doors burst open, and patrons start streaming out, laughing and chatting happily. I flinch and look away from Link as people walk around us, completely oblivious to the tension in the room.

I look over at Fiona, who's been watching our standoff in stunned silence with Trey, my eyes pleading, and she gives me an encouraging nod—she'll cover for me.

I walk to the back room to get my coat and backpack and reenter the lobby refusing to look at either of them.

"I wouldn't just leave if I were you," Link says coldly.

I stiffen at the threat. "Or what?" I challenge as I turn to face him. His jaw tightens.

Then, I do just that—I leave.

CHAPTER NINETEEN

LINCOLN

*Y*ou need to tell me why you're being such a hardcore asshole," Trey demands. "I know it has to do with her parents. I want to hear the whole fucking story. Now."

After Charlie left the theater, we closed it up in silence. Trey was fuming by the time we got home.

"What? Now you're fucking her, so you suddenly care about her feelings?" I say, sitting down on the couch and putting my face in my hands. I know I've been a dick. I know I was pushing her on purpose. Given her fiery nature, I should have expected she'd push back.

"Don't do that," Trey says.

I look back up at him, gritting my teeth. "Do what?"

"Pretend like you don't give a shit," he says angrily. "You soften around her. I've seen it. And you've been giving her hell ever since Halloween. Why are you punishing her but not me? If you're jealous, just say so. Punch me in the face or something."

"I'm not jealous," I snap.

That's the truth. But I still want her despite fighting the feeling. Everything about Charlie draws me in, and it's fucking infuriating. Her quiet nature and her ferocity constantly challenge me. What pisses me off most is when I look at her, I see what we could've been if the past had been different. But then I see her mother, and my hate wars with this underlying need that's always been there to connect with her.

I finally sigh, looking up at Trey. "I get it. I fucked up tonight." I pause, smirking slightly. "But really, I'm kind of not sorry because that was..."

"Hot as hell," Trey finishes for me..

"Yep," I say, popping the "p" with emphasis. "Agreed."

Our eyes meet for a beat, and I wonder if it's weird that the thought of us being turned on together in the same room with her isn't weird at all.

"So now that you've admitted that, I need you to tell me why you're intent on torturing her."

I lean back on the couch, rubbing my eyes. I'm suddenly exhausted. "Her mom fucked my dad, okay?" I say quietly. "Ellen's the reason my mom left."

"What?" His eyebrows furrow. "I thought your mom took a job in New York."

"She did, but she took the job after the affair." I swallow the emotion threatening to choke me. "Mom and I caught them in the act, and it broke her." I look over at Trey.

"You do realize none of your damage is Charlie's fault, right?" Trey says. "Your dad was half of that affair and, therefore, half the problem. Not to mention, Ellen tore Charlie's family apart, too."

"And then she killed herself."

Trey flinches at the way I say it so calmly. "Shit. She just told me that her mom died," he says, frowning. "I didn't realize it was a suicide. I guess the rumor Seren was talking about at the bonfire was true."

I sigh. "After I found out about the affair, I was so angry. I made it my prerogative to get revenge, but then Ellen took the easy way out. Charlie was her only daughter, and that hate just naturally transferred over."

Trey gives me a pointed look.

I sigh. "Look, I know it was irrational, but it just happened. My dad was a mess without my mom, and he was so guilt-ridden that he shut down." I grimace. "You were there for the shit he pulled. He didn't show up to my graduation. He didn't say goodbye when I left for college. He only bought the movie theater and let me run it because he felt bad about pretty much abandoning his only son for more than two damn years."

I look over at Trey expecting to see pity, but I don't—just empathy as he absorbs my pain.

"My mom hasn't spoken to either of us since it happened. She's just...gone. I mean shit, Trey, she left you, too."

Trey drops down next to me, his face uncharacteristically stoic. "I know, man, and it felt shitty, but it wasn't Charlie's fault. You've got to let it go."

"Trey, Charlie's mom didn't just fuck my dad," I growl. "She fucked my whole life. It's been two years, and I don't know how to shake this anger."

"Two years? But you only started talking to Charlie this semester," Trey says, shaking his head in confusion.

I look over at Trey. "There was one time the summer after graduation, when this really all started, but it didn't go like I planned...."

TWO YEARS AGO...

I lean against the wall in a dark corner of the room, watching Charlotte Bennett mingle. She looks uncomfortable. Vulnerable. Perfect.

Brighton is a pretty tight-knit community, so I fucked around with some of the gossip girls in town and had no trouble digging up her life story. Last I remember, Charlotte was a good girl, dating Matt Johnson, Brighton Prep's hockey jock, but not anymore. She was recently dumped, but even more interesting, they never fucked. She's a virgin.

I crack my knuckles as I stare at her. Really, she's a pretty girl—petite but curvy with long, wavy brown hair. She's wearing ripped skinny jeans, a tight black T-shirt, and Converse. Her simple style makes her even more stunning.

I run my index finger over my bottom lip pensively as I watch her. I honestly don't know why she's at this Washington Prep party. She hasn't been drinking or dancing or even talking. Whereas most people are socializing with their fake-ass smiles, she just stands at the edge of each group, observing.

She looks fragile, and I'll break her tonight. Just like her mother broke my family.

I'll fuck her. She'll beg for more. I'll promise her everything.

And then I'll leave.

Like my mother left.

Like my dad left.

Like her mother left.

Everyone leaves.

Maybe breaking her will finally make me feel normal again.

I take a sip of my whisky, feeling the amber liquid burn down my throat. I swirl my drink around in what's probably a very expensive crystal glass. Rich kids are strange. Instead of kegs full of cheap beer, these teenage dirtbags are drinking pricey liquor and champagne.

The air suddenly seems too warm. I turn away from my vantage point, and head down the hallway. This is my buddy Jason's house, so I know all the doors in this wing belong to a bedroom. I enter one of the rooms, which is surprisingly empty. The music muffles as I close the door softly. I don't bother to turn on the lights. I walk past the bed to a set of French doors that open onto a balcony. I step out into the cool summer air and place both hands against the railing, taking a deep breath.

All I can make out are tall evergreen trees silhouetted in the darkness, and the distant glow of Vancouver's city lights illuminating the skyline to the north.

I don't know how long I've been standing there when I hear the door open. I glance back, about to tell some horny couple to fuck off, but it's just one person—a girl based on her small frame. She steps into the room and looks around but doesn't seem to notice me. I step closer to the balcony door, which still stands ajar, and squint into the darkness. As my eyes adjust, I notice the white toes of her sneakers—Converse.

Well, isn't this perfect, *I think.*

I watch as Charlotte sits at the foot of the bed and draws her knees up to her chest. She rests her forehead on her arms, and her shoulders shake.

She's crying.

I step into the room slowly and clear my throat so I don't startle her too much.

Her head shoots up, and she looks around the darkness.

"Who's there?" she asks, standing quickly. She doesn't sound scared like I expect. No, her voice is confident and strong. It's the first time I've heard it in a long time, and it stirs something in my chest.

"I was getting some air on the balcony," I say. "I'm sorry if I scared you."

"You didn't." She rubs her cheeks, probably to hide tears. "I just didn't know anyone was in here, and I needed a break."

I move closer, crowding her space. The smell of vanilla and whisky overwhelms me for a moment, and I take a deep breath, trying to clear my head. I reach out and gently place one of my hands on her forearm.

Her skin is warm beneath my fingers. Her breath picks up when I touch her, and I smile cruelly, knowing that if she could see me, she would run. I half expect her to pull away, but for some reason she stays, looking up at me.

"What're you doing?" she asks. Her voice sounds thick as a strange tension builds between us.

"Just seeing if you're okay," I say. "You sounded sad."

"I was sad, but just for a moment."

I'm shocked when her fingers tentatively graze the front of my shirt.

"Why?" I ask, closing my eyes. Her touch makes my cock harden.

"Some asshole broke my heart," she whispers. "The usual."

I chuckle. When I open my eyes, I run my hands down her arms and toward her hips, pulling her closer. I'm positive she can feel my dick straining against my jeans. She moans quietly.

I'm starting to wonder if the virgin rumors were true. The way she's responding to me, a stranger, violating her space makes me think she's probably been having revenge sex since her breakup, or at least revenge foreplay.

"Do you normally come on to strange men in dark rooms?" I ask. "I could be hideous. Or worse, dangerous." There's a warning in my voice, as if part of me wants her to flee before I ruin her.

She shivers. Then her fingers slide under my T-shirt, her nails skimming over the ridges of my abs and hovering in the hair just above my waistband. I want to grab her and tear the clothes from her body. I want to wrap my hand around her pretty neck and squeeze. But I hold back.

"No," she says. "I've never done this before. But I want to. With you. I need to. Now."

Her words are clipped and needy. They do something to my insides. I feel like my heart cracks open. Blood rushes through my body, sending confusion and rage and uncontrollable lust burning through my veins.

"Sorry, that was forward of me," she murmurs, sounding a little unsure when I don't immediately respond.

All that escapes my mouth is an animalistic growl, and that's all the confirmation she needs. Charlotte's nails bite into my skin as she pulls herself against my cock. I moan and tug her shirt over her head with one motion, then toss it aside. My hands force their way under her bra, roughly cupping her breasts. I revel at the mewling sounds coming out of Charlotte Bennett's mouth.

This isn't right. I should be in control, *I think as I feel that numbness sliding through fingers.*

She unclasps her bra with one hand, and her breasts spring free. I take a pebbled nipple between my lips, sucking and biting. I stop a moment to tear my shirt over my head as her fingers claw at the button on my jeans. I kick them off and toss them on the bed.

I push her back and peel her pants off, leaving her in nothing but panties. I can't see her face in the darkness, but as I drag my body over hers, I feel the rapid rise and fall of her chest.

Something in my brain tells me that this was supposed to be slow. It was supposed to feel like lovemaking. It was supposed to break her. But somehow, she's breaking me.

My hand runs down her flat stomach and under her panties, brushing over her clit and sliding between the folds of her pussy. She's wet. Holy fuck, she's wet.

She bucks against my hand.

"Please," she begs.

I hesitate, thinking she's about to shut me down and come to her senses.

"Don't stop," she whimpers instead. "I need more."

I fucking lose myself. I can't think. I can't even remember why I'm here. I just know I need to bury myself deep inside her. I don't just want to fuck her. I want to claim her. Mark her as mine.

Her hands grab the back of my head, and I can't stop it. Our lips crash together with bruising force. Her tongue is everywhere, and when she bites, I bite back harder. The metallic taste of blood spurs me on. She's just as rough as I am, her nails raking the back of my neck.

My hand is still in her panties as I finger-fuck her. The scent of her arousal permeates the room, and it smells fucking delicious. Then her body tenses against mine as her orgasm builds, and I rub my thumb hard against her clit. She comes apart all over my hand, her legs quaking. She cries out loudly, and her release drips through my fingers, and it's the hottest goddamn thing I've ever felt.

I hear the tear of fabric as I rip her panties off. I pull down my boxers, my cock springing free to press against her soaking-wet pussy. I close my eyes, savoring the skin-on-skin contact before I pause a moment to grab the condom from my jeans pocket. I rip it open with my teeth, then roll it on.

I lower myself back on top of her small frame. We're both sweating, and our slippery bodies are pure, lust-driven heat.

I grab her throat with one hand and bring my mouth to the shell of her ear. "I'm going to fuck you now," I say darkly. "And I'm not going to be gentle." I wait for her to stiffen in fear—to tell me no.

But I feel her nod. "I want you," she breathes back. "Please fuck me." Her voice sounds small and innocent, but her hands grab my ass, pulling me closer, driving me crazy.

She's fucking fearless is my only thought before I drive my cock into her virgin pussy in one go.

TREY IS SITTING NEXT to me, his lips parted in shock. "You hate-fucked away Charlie's virginity?" he asks, raising his eyebrows in disbelief.

"That's the problem. It wasn't a hate-fuck. It wasn't just mindless sex," I stand and run my hands through my hair as I start to pace. "I lost control. We were the same person. It was..."

"Mind-blowing," Trey finishes. "It's the only way to describe sex with Charlotte Bennett."

I sit back down.

"So she doesn't know it was you?" he asks.

"No," I say softly. "When it was over, she fell asleep pretty quick, and I bounced in a panic." I sigh. "I had this whole plan to lead her on and break her heart. I wanted to ruin her. But that night I left feeling even more empty without her, and I hated that even more. But now..."

"Now, what?" Trey asks.

"Maybe you're right. I've spent the past two years so angry with Ellen, with my mom, with my dad, with Charlie." I lean back, staring up at the ceiling. "I don't want to feel this way anymore. It's exhausting."

"Time to forgive and forget then?" Trey says, sounding unconvinced.

"I'm not saying my feelings will change overnight, but I hope I'll get there."

Trey sighs. "So, what now?"

"I dunno. She's got us both by the balls and she doesn't even know it."

He shrugs and gives me a small smile. "So assuming Charlie's on board, are you done fighting this?"

I bite my lip pensively. "You don't think three's a crowd?"

"We've shared before."

"This is different, and you know it."

"Yeah, it is," he says simply.

I clear my throat. "Uh, and is this like the previous situation, or are we going to...cross swords?"

Trey snorts a laugh. "Do you *want* to cross swords?"

"I don't know." I flush and scratch the back of my neck. "I'm just figuring out some ground rules."

"Well, you know I'm comfortable with whatever, so the ball is in your court."

"I'll think about it." I rub my eyes. "I need a drink." As I walk over to the bar, my mind wanders back to that late summer night.

I may have omitted a detail or two in my retelling. I didn't just leave. Charlie fell asleep, and I lost my shit. I curled myself against her warm body, listening to the sound of her steady heartbeat, and I cried. I hardly ever cry, but that night I really cried, biting back sobs. I cried because I missed my happy life and my mom. And I cried because Charlie had given me all those feelings back when my intent had been to hurt her all along. So I gave myself twenty minutes of self-loathing, buried in her smell and her warmth, and I prayed that someday I'd forgive myself for what I'd done to her.

CHAPTER TWENTY

CHARLIE

*I*t's late morning, and Fi and I are headed to Seattle. Last night, after I got home from the theater, I packed a quick weekend bag, determined to get the hell off campus, and I figured visiting my stepbrothers in Vancouver would be the perfect distraction.

But Fiona convinced me I shouldn't rage drive and dragged me back to her dorm room for an evening of *Pride and Prejudice* —the 2005 version, of course—and Twizzlers. Then she hyped up having a girl's weekend in Seattle instead, so here we are. We're headed down I-5 toward Mt. Vernon, driving through a corridor of picturesque farmlands.

I glance over at Fiona. She's humming along with the music. Her auburn hair falls in loose curls just below her shoulders, and she's wearing a chunky cream sweater and dark skinny jeans with boots.

My mind drifts as I focus on the ribbon of highway and Michael Bublé's breathy voice floating from the speakers. I'm a little sad that I won't see Sebastian and Marcus like I had planned, but they probably have a lot going on at the pub leading up to the holidays. They do well for themselves, but it certainly helps that my stepdad, Martin, has ensured his sons are well-funded.

Marcus is five years older than Seb and six years older than me. He graduated *magna cum laude* from business school while we were still in high school. With money as no object, Marcus opened the pub in Vancouver, and it's been pretty successful so far. Seb, on the other hand, had no interest in college, so he left for Vancouver right after high school to work as the head chef in Marcus's place. They've always made a good team.

I was close to both of my stepbrothers growing up, so I missed them when they finally left, but I was a naïve high school senior distracted by her boyfriend. Then I caught my mom cheating, and I wrecked everything.

I overheard her phone call. I didn't find out who it was or why it happened. I only knew that I felt hurt and betrayed, and I couldn't keep such a poisonous secret to myself. My step-brothers were shocked as well, and we all watched in horror as our parents' marriage fell apart, my mom committed suicide, and my stepfather left six months after her death. He emails my brothers sometimes, but we have no idea where he is, and Marcus and Seb still don't know that he left me with nothing— and I'm not just talking about money. He left me all alone in that big, empty house.

Those months were pretty bleak. Every room triggered some sort of childhood memory.

Biological child or not, Martin raised me, and his abandon-ment was the final knife in my already fractured heart. I still had my car and some cash in my personal bank account— enough to feed myself and keep my phone active—but that's about it. Like Marcus, I know Martin blames me for my mom's suicide. I was the one who told him about the affair, after all. I unconsciously rub the ache in my chest. It never truly goes away.

TWO YEARS EARLIER...

I skipped school again because I'm having a hard time caring about something that seems so trivial now, but at least I got through the day without crying for once. I walk up to the front door, pulling out my key, but to my surprise, it's unlocked. I frown and open the door, stepping into the entryway cautiously.

"Dad?" I call out.

He should be home working, but the house is deathly quiet. When I walk into the living room, a jolt of shock vibrates through my entire body. It's...empty. All the furniture is gone.

I drop my keys and purse onto the floor and run from room to room to room.

Empty. Empty. Empty.

I run upstairs, bursting into my father's office and whirling around. Everything is gone. His oak desk. The little basketball hoop over the trash can. His books. Family photos. The artwork my brothers and I made when we were little.

My heart is racing impossibly fast, and my limbs start trembling. I drop to my knees, trying to breathe.

I can't breathe.

My hands are slick with sweat. My stomach rolls with nausea. Bile rises in my throat.

I dig my fingers into the hardwood floor, needing to feel something solid and real, and I start counting backward, trying to rein in the panic attack.

"one-hundred...ninety-nine...ninety-eight...ninety-seven..." My vision is going black at the edges, and I think I might pass out. "Ninety-one...ninety..."

Finally my heart starts to slow.

I lean back against the wall, taking deep breaths. I shake as the adrenaline leaves my system.

Breathe. Just fucking breathe.

Outside, rain starts to fall, tapping insistently on the window. I stare out into the oncoming storm. Everything looks cold and gray. Desolate.

I am all alone.

Hot tears slide down my cheeks

So much for not crying today.

"You're going to love Lola's apartment—it's down the street from some pretty swanky bars." Fiona interrupts my thoughts, and I glance at her.

"You know I'm not normally a bar hopping girl, right?"

She waves her hand dismissively. "Make an exception this weekend. You can go back to being cute little studious Charlie on Monday."

I give her a doubtful look. Crowds of sweaty people drinking in small spaces sounds awful, but it's better than being on campus where I can run into Lincoln, I suppose.

Fi takes a breath like she wants to say something but then pauses.

"What?" I ask. "Spit it out."

"It's just, we haven't really talked about what happened yesterday." Fi glances over at me. "Are you okay?"

"Yes and no. I know I shouldn't have blown up at Lincoln like that—"

"Except the prick totally deserved it," Fi interrupts, raising an eyebrow.

"Agreed," I say. "But something else is going on there. I want to find out what."

"Maybe it had something to do with you sleeping with his best friend?" Fiona says pointedly.

Could Lincoln be jealous?

I flush. "I dunno. Maybe. Lincoln just doesn't seem like the jealous type. I even heard a rumor the other day about how they shared some chick."

"What?!" Fi practically screams.

My hands slip on the wheel, and I almost swerve into the shoulder. "For the love of Christ! Don't scare me like that."

"Sorry," she says, her hand resting over her heart. "I might have to do some digging into that rumor." Her fingers tap against her collarbone before she gives me a saucy smile. "But lucky girl, am I right?"

"I'm sure it's just a rumor," I say, pointedly ignoring her question.

"Honestly, though Charlie, you need to guard your heart around those two." She gives me a serious look. "They're hot as sin, but neither one of them has a reputation for being the good guy. Though I will say they act differently around you some-times—Lincoln especially, like he's fighting with some sort of emotional shit in his head."

I make a face. "Let's not talk about them anymore. Let's just have a fun weekend so I can forget that there are two confusing assholes and a shitload of schoolwork waiting for me when I get back."

Fiona smiles. "You got it, babe."

CHAPTER TWENTY-ONE

TREY

I've been feeling antsy ever since Link and I talked yesterday about sharing Charlie. Not because I don't want it to happen, but because I do. I'm actually kind of nervous about it, and it's starting to freak me out.

So I've turned to alcohol.

I'm already six beers deep, and I'm switching to liquor to speed up the process.

I place the whisky bottle back on the coffee table and tuck my legs under my body. Then, I pull a blanket over my shoulders like a cape and take a large gulp of the liquid.

I sigh when it burns down my throat.

Perfect.

The way I've been thinking about Charlie is new. I've never been attached to anyone but Lincoln since I was a toddler. But something's pulling me to her.

So why am I so scared?

I take another sip from my favorite coffee mug and squint into it, surprised that it's empty.

I did fill it, right?

I lick my lips, definitely tasting whisky.

I jump in surprise when the lock clicks, and Lincoln walks through the door. I almost drop my cup, but catch it between my knees. I smirk at my Spider-Man-like reflexes.

I watch Link toe off his shoes and hang his coat by the door. I think he looks tired, but it's hard to tell in the dim light of the living room.

He stops, taking in my appearance with narrowed eyes. "Fucking hell," he mutters when he notices the empty beers and the bottle of whisky. "It's early, Trey," he says, his voice disapproving.

Staying clean hasn't been easy over the years.

If it weren't for Lincoln, I probably wouldn't be at Whitmore U. He's beaten the shit out of me more than once when I've slipped back into my old habits, but this anxious feeling made me want to use, which is out of the question, so I chose alcohol instead.

I wave my hand. "It's five o'clock somewhere," I mutter, grabbing the handle and pouring more into the mug still balanced between my thighs.

Link walks over and reaches for my drink. "You've had enough."

I frown but let him take it. "I'm sorry. I don't mean to worry you, Link. I just needed a little extra help today."

When I was sixteen, I almost died from a cocaine overdose, and after that, I found other ways to manage my mental health. That's when I started sleeping with my friend Jeremy in between fucking just about every cheerleader and closeted football player at our high school.

He sits down next to me, concern coloring his gray eyes. "What's going on? It's been a while since I've seen you this bad."

"I just had a few drinks."

"You're slurring your words, Trey. Please talk to me."

I stare at my index finger running absently over the soft

material of my Marvel sleep pants. "Do you think Charlie will let us share?"

Link's posture stiffens, and he sighs. "I dunno. Are you worried she won't?"

"I just—I want her to want us both, you know? She's a good person. We need more good people in our lives."

I glance up at him when he huffs a laugh, his hand falling to my wrist. It's warm. He looks happy for once, and it makes my insides fuzzy.

"Trey Walker," he says, smiling wider. "Do you have your first real crush?"

I flush, rubbing my stubbled cheeks. "Maybe? I don't know. Being with her feels different, and it scares me. Doesn't it scare you?"

Lincoln shrugs but doesn't answer. He smells good, musky like leaves and pine. Without thinking, I place my hand on his thigh.

"Trey..." His voice has a warning note to it.

I ignore him and inch my fingers higher, enjoying the roughness of his jeans against my skin. He catches my hand just as I slide it over his crotch. I freeze when I feel his cock hardening behind his zipper.

"We talked about this," Link says, his grip on my hand tightening. "You can't grab my junk without consent."

"Can I?" I ask hopefully as my own cock stirs to life.

We've never actually done anything—I think Link is pretty damn straight—but I get handsy when I drink too much.

"No, Trey, you're drunk."

"I really am," I say with a resigned sigh, but then I give him a wicked smile and press my hand against his dick, watching in satisfaction as Link's breath catches and his eyes flutter closed for a moment. Then he clears his throat and gives me a hard stare.

"Save it for Charlie, okay?"

I nod and reluctantly move my hand.

Lincoln leans forward to grab the remote. "What should we watch?"

I shrug. "*Ironman?*"

Link chuckles. "You've only seen it like a hundred times."

"I know, but—"

"It's your favorite movie," he finishes for me. Then he starts it up, and we sit shoulder-to-shoulder, until I finally fall into a dreamless sleep.

CHARLIE

I'm not a fan of Lola's scratchy couch. After spending a few hours club-hopping with Fiona and her friend, I was happy to make it back to the tiny apartment in one piece. I'm a bit drunk. Fi, the lucky bitch, is sharing Lola's bed, though from the heavy snoring I hear through the door, maybe she isn't so lucky.

I sigh, rubbing my eyes as I try to force myself to relax. I miss my bed.

My phone buzzes, vibrating loudly on the hardwood floor. I reach down, snatching it up, hoping the noise didn't wake anyone. I'm about to silence my texts altogether when I see Lincoln's name light up the screen.

> **LINCOLN**
>
> Hey Sunshine, you up?

I stare at the message for a beat, knowing I shouldn't respond. I'm definitely too drunk and should wait until morning.

"Fuck it," I mutter.

> Asshole. Did you seriously text me like some sort of horny teenager?

LINCOLN

Yes. And?

> And, it's weird. If you're looking for a booty call, try Serenity.

LINCOLN

Nah, tried that. Not really my type.

> And I am?

My heart is pounding, I watch the three dots appear and disappear several times before he replies.

LINCOLN

I never said that. Where are you?

> In bed.

LINCOLN

Liar. I'm at your dorm. You're not here.

"The fuck...?" I breathe.

> What? Why are you at my dorm?

LINCOLN

Why aren't you here?

> Answer my question first.

LINCOLN

I came over to talk.

> I'm in Seattle with Fiona.

LINCOLN

Do you always run from your problems?

I'm glad you admit you're a problem.

LINCOLN

Touché. But can we cut the shit? Come
back. Now.

I can't.

LINCOLN

Why not?

Because I have freewill, and I don't want to.

Also, I'm drunk.

LINCOLN

Fun night?

Hardly. I say stupid shit when I drink.

LINCOLN

Come drink with me.

Fat chance.

LINCOLN

When will you be back?

None of your business.

LINCOLN

You are my business.

You better not be hooking up with any Seattle
hippies.

My stomach flutters involuntarily as I stare at the message.
What is happening?

The night is young.

We can talk tomorrow. Goodnight Link.

Then I power off my phone with a smirk, knowing the abrupt way I ended our text exchange will probably piss him off.

Take that, asshole.

I sit back, closing my eyes, but sleep won't come, and I lie awake for a long time thinking about Trey and Lincoln, and I hate that I can't stop.

IT'S ALMOST midafternoon before we roll back into the student lot at Whitmore University. We tried to sleep in, but being hung over in a strange place makes it difficult. So we finally gave up and took the bus to Pike Place Market for the morning before driving back to campus.

Lincoln has been texting me off and on all day, but I haven't answered him since last night. His sudden desire to talk has my stomach churning, but I'm scheduled to work at the theater tonight, so I can't really avoid him much longer.

Thick gray clouds rolled in overnight, but the wind is still icy, plucking at our hair and clothing. Campus has already started its transformation from autumn to winter, the maple trees looking skeletal against a rich backdrop of evergreens.

"Are you working tonight, too?" I ask Fiona as we walk, our feet kicking and crunching through the crisp leaves littering the pathway.

"Not tonight," she says. "I have a ton of studying to do before tomorrow, so I traded off my shift to Damon."

"Oh, okay," I say, biting my lip.

Fi sighs, probably sensing the anxiety in my tone. "You can't just avoid him, especially at work." She holds open the heavy door to the Raven Building, and I relish the sudden rush of warm air that heats my skin as we walk to the elevator.

"What if we have another fight? The last one was pretty bad," I say as the bronze doors ding open.

"Just be cautious but open-minded." She gives me a reassuring smile. "And don't back down if he's a dick. You're a fucking badass woman, and you deserve better than to take shit from narcissistic alpha males like Lincoln Evans."

"Right," I say, trying to channel Fiona's confidence.

"Oh, and tell me everything," she says with a wink as she steps into the hallway and heads to her room.

I continue down to my dorm room.

I glance at my phone, realizing I only have about twenty minutes to get to work. I change and twist my hair into a loose braid before throwing on my coat and heading back out. The last thing I need is to be late and give Lincoln another reason to jump down my throat.

Huddled against the cold, I run back across campus and down Main Street, my eyes tearing as I skip over icy puddles on the pavement until I'm standing in front of the theater.

I shift anxiously from foot to foot as I stare into the lobby. Damon seems to be running the concession counter alone. He's a quiet guy with dark hair and thick black glasses, and he smiles and waves when he notices me loitering on the sidewalk.

I walk inside, looking around. As always, the buttery scent of popcorn immediately assaults my senses, salty on my tongue as I inhale. "Hey, Damon. Where is everyone?"

"Trey is here somewhere," he says with a shrug. "I think he's cleaning one of the auditoriums. And Lincoln was here, but he left. He got a call that seemed important. I'm not sure where he went."

"Oh," I say, disappointment and annoyance evident in my voice.

All those stupid texts, and he's not even here to talk to me?

"You guys must be pretty slow tonight if Link just left."

"Yeah," Damon says. "I think everyone is cramming for all their tests before Thanksgiving break."

Just then, Trey strolls out of Auditorium One whistling, a broom in one hand and a dustbin in the other.

"Hey, Bennett," he says, giving my shoulder a gentle bump as he comes to stand beside me. His tie is thrown over one shoulder, and his hair is a tousled golden mess. His warm cinnamon scent tickles my nose, and his arm brushes mine, raising goosebumps along the back of my neck.

"Where've you been?" he asks, placing the broom and dustbin against the wall. "Link's been extra broody since the proverbial fireworks display on Friday."

"Fi and I had a girls' night in Seattle." I cross my arms over my chest to hide my hardening nipples. Seriously. My body's reaction to this man is ridiculous.

"Sounds fun," he replies.

"Trey, can I ask you something?" I ask, chewing my lower lip.

"Sure thing," he says, leaning against the concession counter and crossing his long legs. I take a breath and try to focus, looking into his autumn eyes.

"I know you're both from Brighton, and John said he did business with my stepdad. Did you and Link know me before I came here? I don't ever remember seeing either of you at our investor parties."

Trey's hands tighten on the edge of the counter, and something akin to guilt flickers in his eyes. But he blinks, and it's gone. "Probably. We went to a lot of parties over the years. Lincoln's parents were always looking for their next big property."

"Lincoln's parents? Not yours?"

"Nah, my parents checked out when I was a kid," he says with a shrug. "My mom is a stage actress, and she and my father travel around the UK. Link's parents pretty much adopted me after they left."

"I'm sorry, Trey," My heart squeezes with empathy. "That's sad."

"It is, but I hide my trauma behind a façade of crude humor and sexual escapades," he says with a wink.

Damon clears his throat. "I'm just gonna go clean two and three," he says, indicating the other two auditoriums.

"Anyway," Trey says, changing the subject, "to answer your original question, I don't know. But we did smoke a lot of weed back then, so I may not remember. Maybe you should ask Link."

"Where is he, anyway?"

Trey pushes off the counter and walks over to the popper to start a new batch of popcorn. "Serenity called him about an hour ago, and he left saying he needed to take care of something."

"Serenity?" A pang of unwanted jealousy stabs through my chest.

"Yeah" Trey watches me closely. I look away in a poor attempt at nonchalance. He clears his throat, and my eyes snap up to his. "Here's the thing with those two," he explains. "They've been friends since they were kids and have spent most of their lives bailing each other out of bad situations. I'm sure Seren has just gotten herself into some trouble."

"I guess I didn't realize they've known each other for so long." I look down at my hands, picking at the black polish on my fingernails as the irrational jealous feeling sharpens.

Trey steps close to me, his large, warm hand wrapping around my chin, and when I look up, our lips are inches apart. "Hey," he says softly. "You don't have to worry about Serenity. She's not his type. That ship sailed and sank. Spectacularly." His minty breath fans over my cheeks, and my heartbeat kicks up a notch.

"So I've heard," I croak, licking my lips nervously. Trey's eyes follow the movement. "Not that I care who Lincoln is fucking," I say quickly.

Trey smiles, his thumb running along my jawline. I close my eyes, the sensation entirely too sensual. The only sound is our breathing and the crackle of popping popcorn. "I think you care very much," he says, his voice low and husky. He releases me and steps away, and I open my eyes, watching him as he walks over to the ticket booth. He glances back at me with a knowing smirk. "And as much as he fights it, Link cares, too."

DAMON WAS RIGHT; the night is slow. Only a few patrons trickle in with each showing, and I'm bored out of my mind by the time I head upstairs to start up the last movie of the evening.

I thread the film for *The Lord of the Rings: The Return of the King* through the old projector, double-checking my work before turning the machine on. It roars to life, light flickering through the lens as the film winds its way off of the top reel through the projector and onto the bottom reel.

I watch the movie for a while, happy to hide in the darkness.

"'Death is just another path, one that we all must all take.'" Gandalf's words reverberate through my body.

I picture my mom's face. From this perspective, it seems ironic now that she was the one who read Tolkien to me when I was a kid. The clack from the film fills the space like quiet laughter, mocking me.

I hear soft footsteps. I assume it's Trey until I catch a hint of Link's cool earthy scent. I look back, and our eyes meet. He motions with his head for me to follow, and I do, my hands clenching and unclenching.

I enter the manager's office, squinting at the harsh fluorescent lights flooding the space. It feels like the dull brown walls are smothering me, and my heart pounds uncomfortably against my ribs as I stand there in awkward silence, looking down at my black Converse.

"We can't do this," Lincoln says, his tone caustic and clipped.

"What?" I ask. My voice sounds so small, and I hate the way I feel right now—helpless, anxious, and completely confused about how to act around him.

You're a badass bitch. Fiona's words come back to me, and I feel a thread of confidence take root.

"We can't just explode at each other," he replies. I stay quiet, unsure of what to say, and he sighs heavily. "Please, look at me."

I comply, raising my gaze to his.

"It's just, when we're here, I'm your superior. We need to act professionally around one another."

My eyes widen in disbelief. "Act professionally? Are you serious right now?" I ask, my voice tight with repressed anger. "You have been everything *but* professional to me since we started working together."

He raises his hands, which I'm sure is meant to be a placating gesture, but it just infuriates me further. "I know I've been kind of a dick—"

"Kind of?" I almost shriek.

"*And…*," he interrupts, cutting off my tirade, "I'm sorry. I'll do better."

My mouth drops open in shock, and the rage drains from my body like he just opened a wound. I stare at him, searching for something sinister in his eyes. But Link's not channeling his usual cruelty or indifference—just a sincerity I haven't seen since that day in the coffee shop when he talked about his mom.

Did Lincoln Evans just apologize to me?

Regardless, disappointment twists inside me when I realize this conversation was always just about work and nothing more.

"Thanks," I say, lowering my eyes. The silence between us stretches on, and my cheeks heat with embarrassment. "I guess I'll get back to it."

I turn on my heel and leave the office before he can react. I don't want him to know I wanted more from him. I don't even know what I wanted. At least with Trey, our attraction is tangible—undeniable—but Link is so damn confusing, and it's like I'm always being pulled in two directions—I either hate his guts or I feel like a stupid little girl with a one-sided crush. My eyes fill with unwanted tears, and I blink them back.

I'm such a naïve idiot.

"Wait, Charlie."

I hear Link's footfalls, and I stop just before I reach one of the projectors, my arms wrapping around my body in a vain attempt to keep my turbulent emotions in check. "Hey," he says quietly, coming up to stand behind me.

Why does he smell so fucking good?

I turn. He's much closer than I expect, and I have to tilt my head back to meet his steady gaze. He looks conflicted, his dark eyebrows drawn together and his full lips pressed into a hard line.

A traitorous tear trickles down my cheek.

My stomach flutters as I wait for him to say something, but he just stares at me like I'm some sort of problem to solve. He's too damn beautiful with his messy, dark hair falling over his steely eyes. I can't stand it.

I reach out hesitantly before I take a brave, shaky breath and brush away the silky strands with my fingertips. I half expect him to pull away, but he allows my fingers to graze the rough stubble on his face before my hand falls back to my side. In the flickering darkness, I see Link's pupils dilate with...lust? I frown in confusion, my eyes searching his face, certain I'm reading him wrong.

"Sunshine," he breathes.

For once, his nickname for me doesn't mock. Instead it sends chills through my entire body. He raises his thumb, and my breath catches as he runs it over my lips, his remaining fingers cupping my chin. "What're you thinking about? Tell me," he demands, his voice husky.

"I..."

A million dirty thoughts fly through my brain. I try to pull away, but his grip is ironclad, holding me in place, and I finally stop fighting.

"You, okay, Link? It's always you." I don't bother hiding the note of defeat in my voice because at that moment, despite all the terrible things he's done to me, all I can see is him.

CHAPTER TWENTY-TWO

LINCOLN

*C*harlie's hand falls back to her side, but I can still feel the trail of heat from her fingers searing my cheek. She stares back at me, her forest-green eyes glassy in the dim light. My body is practically vibrating with the strength it takes to resist giving in to everything I feel and want.

And what I want to do is kiss her, touch her, *make her mine.*

I tried to keep her at arm's length with the whole bullshit workplace conversation. It's not the conversation I wanted to have. But I know Trey feels something for her, and I've seen the way he watches her. She's more than a quick fuck to him now.

And I get it. I wanted to hate her.

As fucked-up as it was, I wanted to unload all my anger and frustration before I exploded.

But Trey was right: Charlie is not Ellen, the woman who took a wrecking ball to our otherwise mundane, happy childhoods. Ellen's actions destroyed two families and triggered my deep-seated, misplaced resentment that has made my tumultuous relationship with Charlie a toxic mess.

And here we are.

I take her cheeks in my hands and pull her lips to mine. She stiffens in surprise, but as my tongue teases the seam of her soft lips, she relaxes, returning the kiss. Her movements are tentative at first before she growls—literally growls into my mouth—and lets go.

Holy shit, does she let go.

Our kiss becomes needy and desperate and messy. Our teeth clash. Our tongues collide. I bite her lower lip, pulling it into my mouth and sucking it with fervor. Charlie moans, and my dick twitches, thickening against the zipper of my pants.

She presses her hands against my chest, and first I think she's going to push me away, but instead, she fists the fabric of my shirt, pulling us closer. Her breasts press against my pecs, and despite the barrier of our clothing, I can feel her heated skin and the rapid flutter of her heart.

My hands skim down her body, landing on her firm ass. I squeeze eagerly and then lift her into my arms. Charlie's sexy-as-fuck legs wrap around my waist and her arms circle my neck as she buries her fingers in my hair, tugging roughly.

Our lips are still locked together as we fight for dominance, and fuck me, kissing her is better than I remember. Charlotte Bennett is not shy or submissive. She kisses the way I do with rage and anger, lust and need, and some deeper emotion I don't understand. It's animalistic and intoxicating, and I never want it to stop.

Shit.

I turn, barely avoiding the projector, and set her down on the nearest table, stepping between her legs and pressing my rock-hard cock against her center. We both moan loudly at the contact, and I swear I almost come right there. A stack of film trailers falls to the floor with a clatter, and they roll away into the shadows.

My fingers pull her shirt open, buttons coming apart. She pushes her breasts into my waiting hands, and I pinch her hardened nipples through the thin fabric of her bra. Charlie whimpers, and the sound goes straight to my aching dick. I reach down, my hand sliding under the waistband of her pants and into her panties to cup her pussy.

"Jesus, you're soaking," I say, my long fingers sliding between her folds.

"Don't stop," she whimpers, spreading her legs wider for me. Her cheeks are flushed, and a sheen of sweat covers her skin. Her braid is a haphazard mess, and loose strands stick to her forehead as she stares at me, her chest heaving. I've never seen her look so fucking beautiful.

I drop to my knees, flicking open the button on her pants and pulling them to her ankles. I push her panties to the side and press my lips against her clit, sucking it gently into my mouth.

"Holy shit," she groans, bucking against my face as my tongue flicks out, sinking into her pussy. She's sweet and tangy —fucking delicious—and can't stop myself from burying my face in her heat and eating her out–ravishing her.

Charlie's fingers run through my hair, grabbing a handful in a painful grip and pulling me closer as she fucks my face. I'm starved for her, and she absolutely knows it. She claps a hand to her mouth as her breathy moans become louder. The move is somehow both adorable and sexy.

"Link, you asshole, did you forget to—" Trey's voice stutters to a stop.

Charlie and I freeze, turning to stare at him.

Trey's eyes dilate as he takes in the scene: Charlie spread eagle on the building table and me on my knees, face inches from her pussy.

I clear my throat, but my voice still comes out like gravel. "Did I forget to what?"

His eyebrows raise with interest. "Invite me to the party."

I glance back at Charlie, who's turning fifty shades of red, her lips parted. Her hand is still tangled in my hair, and her dark green eyes dart between us. To my surprise, I find myself hoping against hope that we didn't just fuck up this whole sharing idea before it even got started.

But instead of panicking as I expected, Charlie brings her hooded gaze back to mine, and she has the audacity to look annoyed.

"Why did you stop?" she asks, her fingers tightening against my scalp.

"I…," I start, dumbfounded. "Well, okay then."

I lower my head, sucking her clit into my mouth, and this time, she doesn't muffle the obscene sounds that fall from her lips. I bring my hand from where it rests on her thigh and ease my index finger into her tight hole.

I hear Trey's purposeful footsteps behind me and then he sits on the table next to Charlie. I pull back to watch their exchange, fascinated by their dynamic. Trey cups her face, pulling her mouth to his, and she doesn't hesitate to reciprocate, her other hand gripping the back of his neck with greedy fingers. So greedy in fact, that Trey has to catch himself on the wall before he loses his balance. He chuckles into her mouth.

I pull out my finger, wet with her arousal, and rub it in circles over her clit as I watch Trey feather his hands down her neck. When he pushes his hand beneath her bra and pinches her nipple, my cock aches at the sight, a quiet moan escaping my throat because, fucking hell, this is way hotter than I thought it would be.

I lower my mouth again, savoring her taste while also aware that my face is a foot away from the erection straining against Trey's khakis. While he continues to kiss Charlie, the filthy sounds almost lost over the clicking of the projectors, Trey drops a hand to his crotch, rubbing himself through the rough fabric, and I up my game, pushing two fingers inside her pussy while I bite and pull at her clit.

"Fuck, Link," she says, pulling back from Trey momentarily.

Her grip on my hair tightens to the point of pain—not that I mind a bit. "I'm not going to last."

"Then come for me, baby. Now," I say, like the bossy asshole I am.

I suck her clit hard, swirling my tongue around. Charlie pushes herself forcefully against my mouth. Her eyes roll back in her head, and her whole body quakes as she falls apart. Trey takes her mouth again, swallowing her moans.

Watching her lose her mind is beyond erotic. My control teeters, slips, and like a goddamn teenager, I come in my boxers —hard—pleasure rocketing through my veins with so much force that I have to clutch Charlie's thigh with one shaky hand to stay upright.

Holy fucking shit.

I continue to lick as her arousal soaks my face, and watch as her hand, which now rests over Trey's larger one, rubs his cock hungrily. He grunts and groans loudly against her lips, his other hand fisting her hair in a white-knuckled grip, and I smile to myself knowing he also came like a prepubescent kid.

We're all breathing hard when I finally push her panties back into place and pull her pants back up to her knees. She stands on unsteady legs, blushing, and I'm not sure if it's the afterglow of her orgasm or her introverted nature resurfacing.

I stand as well, adjusting my semi-hard cock, and thank God that the wet cum stain won't be noticeable through my black trousers. Her eyes follow my movements, and holy shit if she doesn't lick her lips while staring at me palm my dick. I glance at the wet spot on Trey's khakis.

"You should've worn black." I snicker.

"Laugh it up, asshole. Next time, I'll come prepared for a quickie behind the projectors."

Charlie raises an eyebrow. "Next time?"

Her words plant a seed of doubt. I know this is over, for now anyway. I certainly shouldn't be fucking her at work—neither of us should.

Should we even be fucking her at all?

Now that my head is clearing from the lust-driven haze, I'm starting to feel uneasy about the situation. I'm not some sex-starved kid, and yet, I just blew my load from eating her pussy while my best friend rubbed one out.

One, I don't normally share, and two, I'm not normally a giver, if you catch my meaning, so what the fuck?

"That was very...unprofessional," Charlie says, directing a smug smirk my way.

The comment is so unexpected, I can't stop my laugh. Her smile grows wider, laughing with me. After all the tension and angst between us from the instant we locked eyes across the bonfire, it's a rare, light-hearted moment, and fuck if it isn't everything.

"I don't get it," Trey says, looking between us, which just makes us laugh harder. His eyes narrow, and then he clears his throat meaningfully, his gaze falling to one full perky breast that still peeks from the top of Charlie's bra.

"Fuck!" Charlie exclaims, fumbling to cover herself and button her shirt.

Being that she's clearly mortified, Trey and I look away, but neither of us can stop grinning.

"Guess that was some talk you guys had, huh?" Trey murmurs with a wink. "Good thing Damon didn't walk up here. Poor kid would have shit himself."

I bark out a laugh before looking back at Charlie, who's fidgeting with the hem of her shirt. She glances between us, and the realization of what just happened slides across her face. The moment of levity is gone. Her uncertainty is contagious, and I feel my emotional walls creeping back up.

I sigh inwardly, wishing I were a different person—a better

person. "Right, well, we have enough people to close up this place, so why don't you head out, Sunshine." Despite the soft smile I give her, my tone sounds dismissive. I know it does. But I need to get my head on straight and figure out what the fuck this means.

Trey frowns at me, and Charlie's steady gaze meets mine, a hint of hurt and confusion in her eyes, but she heads downstairs.

"So what was that, exactly?" Trey says once the lobby door clicks closed.

"I wish I knew."

But whatever it was, it wasn't enough.

CHAPTER TWENTY-THREE

LINCOLN

I skipped my last class, hoping for a few hours of peace before Trey or my parents get home, but no such luck. When I pull up to the house, my mom's silver Tesla is parked in the garage.

I can hear her when I walk in; she's in the kitchen humming and her blue-gray gaze meets mine when I enter and toss my backpack onto one of the bar stools.

I'll always remember her that afternoon. It was the last day she was...herself, I guess. Or my version of her, at least. Her eyes are soft and kind, and her long dirty-blonde hair is tucked neatly behind her ears. When she smiles, her one dimple pops and her face crinkles in certain places. She's so beautiful.

Mom raises an eyebrow. "Hey, kiddo. What're you doing home? You're not sick, are you?"

I shrug. "No, I just needed a break from school. Had a bad day. Why are you home?"

She gives me a small smile. "Same. I just got here as well." She starts moving around the kitchen, opening the fridge. "Do you want a snack?"

I grin. "Mom, I'm not a little kid. You don't have to make me a snack like I'm five."

She moves close, the scent of vanilla and lilac—her favorite perfume—enveloping me like a warm hug. "You're always going to be that five-year-old little boy to me, Lincoln," she says, patting my cheek fondly.

Her words make me feel loved, but I still roll my eyes. I nod toward the cheese and crackers she's assembled on the counter. "That looks good."

A noise from upstairs makes us both turn and then we glance at each other in confusion. It sounds like muffled laughter.

"Is Dad home?" I ask, my brow furrowing.

She shrugs.

We both leave the kitchen, our snack forgotten, and walk up the stairs, following the source of the noise. It sounds like two people are talking now. One voice is definitely my father's, but I didn't remember seeing his car when I got home.

I approach the office. The door is ajar, and I can hear his conversation.

"You're being unreasonable," my father says. "You haven't given me enough time."

"But I love you," a woman's voice responds. My blood turns to ice in my veins. "I'm ready for us to move on and start our lives together." I toe open the door to see a woman sitting on my father's desk. Her legs are wide, allowing my father to stand between them. Her clothes are in disarray—one strap on her dress hanging from her left shoulder, the top barely covering her full breasts. Her black bra is on the floor next to the trash can. Both of them have mussed, just-fucked hair.

My stomach bottoms out, reacting like I'm riding some sort of fucked-up roller coaster, and I hear the woman's gasp when her eyes meet mine over my father's shoulder.

My father whirls around. His face pales and he steps away from the woman as if distance will absolve him of guilt.

I turn in panic when I hear my mom's breath hitch. I'm not sure what I expect to see on her face—tears, shock, betrayal, rage, some sort of violent emotional response. But the light in her gray-blue eyes dims and fades to nothing. It's just blank, like she died.

"Allie, Link...," my father stammers.

The shock coursing through my body starts running hot. Rage floods my system, clogging my throat, choking every rational thought from my brain.

The woman jumps from the desk, scrambling to rearrange her dress and grab her bra. She just stands there cowering in the corner like a caged animal when she realizes the only way out is through us.

I turn my gaze on her. "Get. The. Fuck. Out," I growl, my hands shaking uncontrollably.

She nods sadly and pushes her way through the doorway, shrinking away so as not to touch me when she passes and disappears down the hall.

I turn to my father. "What the fuck, Dad?" I scream, hating that my voice cracks.

He just stares at me, his eyes wide. "Link, you're too young to understand," he starts, raising his hands as if to soothe some sort of beast.

And that's what it feels like—I want to tear him limb from limb. How dare he break this family?

"The fuck I am," I say, gritting my teeth so hard it feels like my molars might crack. "How could you do this? To Mom? To me and Trey?"

I want to hit something.

I've never felt this out of control, this helpless, this raw. It's suffocating me. I clench my shaking fist, the urge to punch my father overwhelmingly strong.

"Lincoln," my mom says quietly, her hand landing on my forearm before I can throw the hit. "Go to your room. I can handle this."

I jerk away from her and stare, my eyes bouncing between them.

Her expression is cold and calculating. It sends chills rippling through my body. She doesn't look like my mother.

"How are you so fucking calm? Aren't you angry or hurt? You can't send me to my room like a goddamn child."

"Go, Lincoln. Now. This isn't about you." Her tone is firm, leaving no room for argument.

"Fuck this." I storm into the hallway.

But I don't go to my room. Instead, I walk to my car in the garage. I open the door, slamming it angrily. Then, because I'm sitting there all alone, I break.

I slam my hands against the steering wheel over and over, screams shredding my throat like broken glass.

My cheeks are wet.

I let everything I'm feeling consume me, all the hurt and anguish my father's betrayal has caused seeping out of every pore in my body, filling the car, fogging the windows until I can barely breathe.

I. Can't. Breathe.

Please don't leave again. I'll be good. Just stay.

I startle awake.

I stare wildly at my surroundings while my heart rate slows. Muted gray light filters through my thin curtains. I roll onto my back, staring up at the ceiling, and wipe sweat from my upper lip.

I haven't dreamed about that day in a while. Right after my mom left, I had it a lot. I think the nightmares scared the hell out of my dad because he shut down after they started happening.

I'm not sure what I would have done if Trey hadn't been there. The first time it happened, he found my dad standing in the doorway to my bedroom, frozen in panic, while I sobbed and screamed into my pillow, unable to tell the difference between the dream and reality. Trey climbed into bed with me and told me that I wasn't alone—that he loved me.

I don't remember that moment exactly, but I remember the feelings. He was warm, his presence calming, and I curled into his side, the nightmare finally retreating.

After that, every time I woke up in a panic, he was always there.

Honestly, if not for Trey, I would've lost my humanity a long time ago. Even with his constant support, I still don't recognize myself anymore. I think the old Lincoln is in there somewhere, trying to claw his way out, but when I look for him, all I see are distant memories reflected back through a broken mirror. Nothing and no one can put me back together—I'm sure of it.

I heave a sigh and climb out of bed. I walk to the bathroom, start the shower, and sit down on the closed toilet lid while I wait for the water to warm up. I put my head in my hands, closing my eyes. My mind drifts to that unexpected event yesterday: *Me. Trey. Charlie. Hooking up.*

I still don't know what to make of the situation. I definitely liked it, and I *think* she did, too. And Trey? No question that he did. I suspect he's been scheming about some variation of that scenario since the start of the school year.

The logistics of all of us together are spot on. Trey's always been an affectionate guy. It's just the way he is (and even more so when he drinks), and it's never really bothered me. And, yes, I'm starting to doubt that my hate for Charlie was ever justified. And Charlie seems at least attracted to both of us. So then why do I have so many doubts about this?

I stand, step into the shower, and let the nearly scalding water wash the stress from my aching muscles. When I finish, I scrub the moisture from my hair and get dressed in jeans and a black T-shirt. My next class isn't for a couple of hours, so my plan is to sit in the living room and do some homework until then.

But just as I'm opening my laptop to start on my film history paper, there's an insistent knock at the door. I frown, set my computer on the coffee table, and walk to the door. I peer through the peephole like the suspicious bastard I am and see Serenity bouncing on her toes in the entryway. I roll my eyes.

"Hey, Seren," I say, opening the door and standing aside so she can enter. Her blonde hair is in a high ponytail, and she's wearing an oversized off-the-shoulder crewneck. Her hot-pink dance tights are painted on her shapely legs and are paired with neon-yellow leg warmers. Give her a headband, and she could star in *Flashdance*.

"It's like thirty-five degrees. Aren't you cold?"

She waves her hand dismissively and skips into my living room. "The dance auditorium is practically next door, and I didn't want to change before I came to talk to you."

I raise my eyebrows with interest, and we both sit on the couch.

Serenity turns to face me. Her fingers tap restlessly against her thighs.

"Just spit it out."

"You're always so cranky."

"I'm impatient."

"Fine."

Serenity has been like a sister to me for most of my life. At one time, we did everything together. She's a dancer, and I've been to more productions of *The Nutcracker* than I care to admit. As we got older, her feelings changed, but mine never did, and only recently has she started to understand that our sibling-like relationship is all I can give her. A lot of people see her as the mean girl, and she does wear that persona well, but I see past it, just like she knows I wasn't always a broody asshole.

"Did you hear how well our hockey team has been doing thanks to Matt Johnson? Brantley told me that the guy is unstoppable."

I stiffen. "What do you know about Matt Johnson? You should stay away from him."

"Did you know he's from Brighton?"

"Actually, I did."

She pouts as if she's upset that I knew something before her. "Well, did you know that he used to date Charlie Bennett?"

Charlie's name rolls off her tongue with a pretentious lilt I don't like, and I give her a dark look.

When I don't respond right away, her eyes widen. "Dang, I'm zero for two. How did you know?"

I still don't answer. I could lie and tell her that I found out at the party when I punched Matt in his stupid face, but she can read me well, so it's safer to stay silent.

The truth is I've known Charlie a lot longer than most people realize—or known of her at least.

Serenity plays the dumb blonde well, but the girl is smart, and she looks at me with narrowed, calculating eyes.

"Oh my God." Her eyes light up. "She's the cat girl."

Her statement catches me off guard. "What?"

NINE YEARS AGO...

Something's wrong. I can feel it when I look at her. She's not colorful tonight. She's wearing a black satin dress, black tights, and shiny black Mary Janes. Even her face is colorless, the rosy tint gone from her pale cheeks.

I frown.

"You coming?" Sebastian pulls at my sleeve, and I nod absently. "Trey's been in there twenty minutes, and he's already blitzed."

I pause, and even though my brain screams that it's a bad idea, I ask anyway because I have to know for some reason. "What's wrong with your sister?"

Sebastian glances over to where she stands with Matt, glumly toeing the floor. He gives me a steady look, and I know he's probably wondering why I care.

Why do I care?

"Our cat's missing," he says, his eyes flashing with empathy. "She's worried."

"Ah" is my only response, and then I follow him to the pool room without another thought.

But later that night, as I sprawl on one of the pool loungers, lazily blowing smoke into the cool night air, I hear raised voices. I stub out my cigarette and walk over to the French doors leading into the main part of the house, pausing just within earshot of the argument.

"Charlotte, it was just a cat," the young male voice huffs. I assume it's Matt when I hear Charlotte's stricken voice.

"But she was sleeping in my room. How did she get out? I swear I heard something."

"What?" he scoffs. "You think someone catnapped her? You're being ridiculous."

My heart squeezes when I hear Charlotte sniffle, obviously upset.

"She's dead," he continues, and I stiffen at his words. "I mean, she's probably dead—hit by a car or something."

"Someone hurt her," Charlotte says quietly. "I know it."

He grabs her elbow to pull her back inside. "Just go back to the party, and stop embarrassing me."

Anger sparks in my chest, and I take a step toward the patio, but Charlotte beats me to it. She jerks her arm, and when he doesn't release his grip, she stomps down on his foot. She's clearly not a helpless little girl.

Matt grunts and drops her arm.

I step back into the shadows as Charlotte scurries by me, running into the garden. Her silhouette fades into the darkness, and then I turn to watch Matt storm back into the house.

I hate him. She deserves better.

The next day, I walk over to Serenity's house because I don't want to share my idea with Trey or my mom, and I have no other girl friends. I find Seren swinging on her backyard swing set, her scrawny legs pumping back and forth. She's not eating again—I can tell by the way her bones seem to stick out of her body and the dark smudges under her eyes.

"Hey, Seren," I say hesitantly, and she drags her feet on the ground, coming to a halt. She smiles at me, and I return it. "Will you help me with something?"

A few minutes later, we put on our bike helmets and head to the only toy store in downtown Brighton.

"Do we have to ride our bikes?" she whines over the rushing wind as we pedal up the sidewalk. "Why can't my driver just take us?"

I give her a hard look. "I told you. I don't want anyone to know. And you better not tell anyone either."

I jump my bike off the curb.

"Fine," she huffs.

We drop our bikes next to the door, a bell jingling as we enter the toy store. I glance around and spot what I want almost immediately: a floppy black stuffed cat.

I pick it up, running my fingers through the soft fur. I look doubtfully at Seren. "Girls like stuffed animals, right?"

Serenity looks at me like I'm stupid. "Little girls?"

"Like, maybe a couple years younger than us—twelve."

She shrugs. "I always liked dolls myself, but yeah, some girls like stuffies."

I give her a grateful smile and pay for the cat with some cash that Trey gave me to buy his weed. I could use my dad's credit card, but I don't want him to ask about this. It feels private. I don't even like that Serenity knows, but I know she'll keep my secret.

The next time we go to a party at the Conners', I leave the toy on Charlotte's bed, staring at it with a frown. I've never really done something special for anyone but Trey until now. All I know is that

157

Charlotte was sad, and it made me sad, and maybe this gesture will fix it.

I slip back downstairs and out the backdoor to smoke in the pool room.

I NEVER SAW Charlie's reaction, and no matter how many times I tried to catch her gaze from across the room after that, she never really saw me. Worse, despite Matt's obvious disregard for her feelings, she was still always with him. It left a bad taste in my mouth.

"The little stuffed cat," she continues with a smirk. "You told me that day that it was for a girl from the other side of town. You told me her name was Charlotte."

"I also told you not to talk about it ever again," I say pointedly, and her smile widens.

"I knew you knew her that night at the bonfire. I thought it was just because she was from Brighton, but you actually *knew* her."

"I never knew her. I never even talked to her. My dad just dragged us to her stepdad's business parties."

"Don't bullshit me, Lincoln. You can pretend you hate her all you want, but your eyes tell a different story. You want her."

"Just because I want to fuck her doesn't mean I don't hate her."

She covers her mouth with her hand dramatically. "You've never *wanted* to fuck anyone."

I refuse to meet her eyes. "What do you mean? I fuck people all the time."

"But you don't *want* to. You choose sex to manage your damage." She drops her hand, and her eyes look glassy and sad. "You actually want her," she repeats quietly.

I don't really know what to say. I'm not about to tell her she's right. And while the realization is hurting her, there's nothing I can do to change it. I'll never want Serenity like that.

I change the subject. "Do you want to grab a coffee or something?"

"I can't," she says with a sigh. "But I did mean to ask you how you're doing."

"I'm fine. Why?"

"Your mom's birthday just passed, Link." Her blue eyes crinkle with concern.

I swallow, a tendril of anger still curling in my stomach when I remember how I yelled at Charlie that day. "It was extra terrible, actually."

Seren frowns. "What happened?"

"Charlie walked in on me watching *Romeo + Juliet*, and I lost my shit. We had a pretty nasty fight."

Given her and Charlie's animosity, I expect Serenity to act smug, but she surprises me when she gives me a pointed look. "Did you apologize and tell her what happened?"

"Err, no. Well, I mean, I sort of apologized?"

Seren looks exasperated. "You're such a guy sometimes." She stands. "I need to go, but there's one more thing I heard the other day."

I motion for her to continue, knowing gossip is her love language.

"So I learned this from Melanie, Monica's girlfriend." I stare at her blankly. I don't know who the fuck that is. She rolls her eyes. "Anyway, Monica said her cousin's boyfriend is on the hockey team. And *he* heard that one of the regular puck bunnies hooked up with Matt."

"Jesus, this is like one of Luis's stories from *Ant-Man*."

She gives me a confused look before continuing. "Apparently, the girl came forward a couple days ago and accused Matt of raping her. And the school board dismissed her claim."

A chill runs through my body. "What?"

"I don't know the girl's name, but if it's true, how despicable is that? Typical untouchable college jock."

I frown because she's right. If Matt really raped a girl and got away scot-free, it would take nothing short of murder to get the guy off campus.

My instincts about him are spot on: Matt Johnson is bad news.

CHAPTER TWENTY-FOUR

CHARLIE

*I*t's late, and I'm tucked into a table at the library, studying for a European history test. At least it's interesting, learning about the rise and fall of empires. It makes my problems feel small, like maybe I'm blowing everything out of proportion.

I sigh, my concentration wearing thin as my mind returns for the hundredth time to the encounter I had with Lincoln and Trey yesterday. I was a romantic before Matt ruined me, and sometimes I wish I still were. Now, I'm a cynic with serious trust issues. But I guess letting those two give me orgasms has nothing to do with trust.

I glance at my laptop screen. My internship application sits open, the cursor blinking in one of the white answer fields. I've been filling out bits and pieces and saving it, but the process has been slow. I can't submit it until I have some polished writing samples, and I need to take their editing test, but every time I try to get ahead and fill out the application, my mind goes blank.

I hear a whisper of clothing as someone approaches my table, and in the dim light, I'm surprised to see Serenity walking toward me. She's wearing yoga pants, a sequined pink pullover, and little makeup with her shiny blonde hair pulled into a pony-tail. It's the first time I've seen her look, well, normal—if there is such a thing.

I glance around at the empty space, realizing it's just her and me. "You're not here to murder me and hide my body in the stacks, are you? Because I'm not in the mood for a bitch fight."

"Relax," she says, folding her arms over her chest with a conceited smirk. "I didn't come to start shit."

I lean back in my chair, regarding her a moment before I decide she seems truthful. "Okay, so what do you want?"

She kicks her Ugg boot at some invisible rock on the worn brown carpet. "I just want to know why you chose him."

"Who? Lincoln? I didn't choose him," I say with a frown. "He aggressively inserted himself into my otherwise peaceful life. I didn't ask for his attention, and I'm not entirely sure I want it."

She raises her ice blue eyes to mine, and I see the hurt simmering beneath her mean girl façade. "Well, I've wanted him my whole life. He was my best friend once. We were raised on the same street, and we used to do everything together. He came to my birthday parties and my dance recitals and..." She hesitates as if she's not sure she should continue.

"Look, we're not buddies—we're not even frenemies—so you don't have to share this."

She schools her expression and smiles at me. "You're right. But I wanted to tell you that I'm leaving Whitmore after this year."

"Really?" I won't lie, a guilty sense of relief floods my limbs at the thought of being rid of her.

"Yeah, I wanted to tell Link first, so I called him at work yesterday." Some little part of me that was wound tight with jealousy relaxes at her admission. "He was always supportive of my dance career even after I went through a rough spot, and I was accepted into an academy in California where I can train to be a dance teacher."

"That's really cool, Serenity. You must be so excited."

"I am," she replies, smiling sadly.

"But why are you telling me this?"

"Well, it's hard leaving him behind, and I guess I just wanted to make sure that you're serious about him. I know I've been a bitch to you, and for what it's worth, I'm sorry about your laptop and for what I said about your mom at the bonfire."

She seems sincere enough, like she's just asking me to take care of Lincoln.

My thoughts wander back to Halloween night when I saw the vulnerable expression on her face as she stared at him.

"He's a big boy," I say with a faint smile. "And I'm not his girlfriend—I don't even know if we're friends."

But I want to be.

"Fair point," she concedes, "but he needs people to love him —and Trey, too. They've been basically rich latchkey kids since their senior years of high school. Did you know that Link's mom left them? Took a job in New York and just never came back."

I frown and shake my head.

"And John is around now, but he basically abandoned Link and Trey for his job for two years."

The familiarity of their situation sends a shiver through my body. *We're all just discarded kids trying to survive.*

"Link told me about your fight. Do you know why he was watching *Romeo + Juliet*?"

I shake my head. "I'm guessing it wasn't just because of the badass soundtrack and fancy gun fights."

Serenity's lip twitches with amusement before her expression turns serious. "It was his mom's favorite movie, and he still watches it on her birthday every year."

"Gosh, I didn't know," I say quietly. "We've all lost parents, huh? It seems the boys and I have more in common than I thought."

"Well, you did run in the same circles as kids."

That catches my interest. "What do you mean?"

"They were regulars at your parents' networking shindigs. I was always jealous that they got to go and I didn't, but my parents weren't part of that circle."

Link ignored my question when I asked. Trey made it seem like he didn't remember. Did he lie? Does that mean that Link knew who I was all along?

"Anyway, I need to get back to studying. I'll see you around." I nod, still lost in my own head when Serenity pauses and levels me with a hard stare. "Just so you know, this doesn't make us friends or anything."

I raise my hands in a placating gesture. "I wouldn't dream of it. By all means, continue your reign as the school bitch."

She almost smiles again. Almost.

I watch her walk away before my gaze falls to the books and papers scattered around me, but I can't bring myself to continue studying. Serenity's words bounce around in my head.

You did run in the same circles as kids.

My emotions war with each other because even though he kept this from me, we really do have similar trauma. When I think about Link's mom just up and leaving, I'm not sure which end result is more depressing—abandonment or suicide.

Is the permanence of death better than knowing your mom is still out there somewhere living her life without you?

The thought makes my heart ache for both of them.

I stand, throw on my sweatshirt, and shove my belongings into my backpack. I head for the elevator, take it down to the foyer, and push out of the double doors into the cold November night, hugging myself against the chill that immediately seeps into my bones.

It's almost midnight, and I have every intention of going

back to my dorm room, but I'm not surprised when I stop in front of the guys' building, the wolf statue at the entrance staring down at me with cold, feral eyes. I shiver.

They're probably asleep, I reason as I shuffle my feet, debating whether to go inside. *What will I even say?*

The trees creak and groan as the icy wind kicks up. My spider-sense tingles as if there's a Marvel villain lurking in the shadows.

"What're you doing?" A deep, smooth voice cuts through the darkness, and I jump, a scream escaping my lips.

I spin around, fear clawing at my chest.

Two large figures approach, but the streetlamp behind them keeps their faces in shadow. I slide my keys between my fingers and make a fist, ready to throw a punch.

"Whoa, chill, Sunshine."

"Lincoln." I almost collapse as hot relief floods my limbs. "You scared me half to death."

As they come closer, I realize that Trey is the second figure.

Great.

I flush, feeling like a complete loser for overreacting, and I fumble to put my keys back into my hoodie pocket.

They watch me for a moment as I stand there awkwardly, and I try to think up a logical reason as to why I'm loitering out here in the cold at midnight. Then they glance at each other with mirrored smiles before they burst into full-on belly laughs. I would have relished the sound if I weren't so embarrassed.

These assholes.

I turn away, but a large, warm hand lands on my wrist, pulling me backward. I stumble and run face-first into Link's hard chest.

Ow. Rubbing my nose, I glare up at him, then over at Trey for good measure.

"Don't be like that. I'm sorry," Lincoln says between chuckles. "Your stance and expression were just priceless, little warrior."

"Seriously." Trey grins. "Were you going to stab us with your keys? So feisty."

"Maybe if you guys weren't creeping around in the middle of the night—"

"Whoa, whoa," Trey interrupts. "You're out here creeping, too."

"Yeah, are you going to tell us why you're here?" Lincoln asks, raising an eyebrow.

They're standing on either side of me now, and I swear I can feel the heat from their bodies, despite the chilly night air. The sexual tension between the three of us is off the charts. My stomach rolls nervously as I look between them. I'm suddenly not so sure I'm ready to talk to them about anything.

"Spill it, Bennett," Trey says, his autumn-brown eyes searching mine.

Sighing, I look over at Link. "I ran into Serenity tonight." An emotional lump forms in my throat as I think about what I want to say. I look up at Lincoln and steel myself. "She told me how your mom left and your dad checked out. She told me about your mom's birthday. Why didn't you tell me? It made me sad." I take a breath and finger a strand of my hair. "I just... I know how that feels, to be abandoned, and I thought maybe..." My thoughts are getting jumbled in my head as I ramble. "And she also said you guys knew me from Brighton, but I don't remember you at all, and...I guess I just wanted to talk."

I brace myself for Link's indifference, denial, disdain, or the angry bully from the bonfire.

Instead, his expression softens as he stares down at me, and it makes me feel a little too vulnerable.

"I'm sorry," I say, trying to step away. "This was a stupid idea."

"No," he says firmly, once again pulling me back. I raise my eyebrows in surprise but don't protest.

"But it's freezing out here, so let's go inside."

Link slides an arm over my shoulders, causing butterflies to riot in my stomach, and the feeling only intensifies when I feel Trey's hand against my lower back as he falls in step beside us. Their delicious scents mingle together like fire and ice, enveloping my senses.

We don't talk as they lead me up to their suite, but it's a companionable silence. Sandwiched between them, a warm feeling tugs at my heart, but it's spoiled by a stab of guilt. I never considered that I'd want them both. It never seemed to matter before because they've always been so nonchalant, but something's different now.

When we reach their door, I stop abruptly, and the guys look down at me in surprise. I feel my face getting hot as I step away from them, my arms going around myself protectively.

"Look," I start. "I know you're both used to *different* girls."

Trey's gaze darkens. "What do you mean by 'different'?"

"You know, experienced girls." *I sound ridiculous.*

Lincoln's lips curve up, fighting a smile. "Slutty girls?"

I wince, knowing it's an assumption of mine based on rumors, and it's not a very feminist view to have of other women.

It's also not entirely what I meant.

"No. Well, maybe a little." I press my fingers to the bridge of my nose, trying to collect my thoughts. "I just mean, you guys have fooled around with a lot of girls who know what they're doing, and despite the few experiences I've had with you both separately and…together, that's not me."

They watch me intently while I flounder with what can only be described as word vomit. But for some reason, I can't stop.

"I don't let guys I've hardly talked to finger me at parties. I don't let my boss eat me out at work while I make out with his best friend. Hell, I've only ever slept with two people." I take a deep breath. "And I certainly don't want to come between two best friends or string anyone along because, let's face it, love triangles are the worst. I mean, look at *Gone with the Wind*, *Pretty in Pink*, *Star Wars*, *Twilight*."

They stare at me like I've grown two heads.

"Well," I continue. "I guess *Star Wars* doesn't count since, spoiler alert, Luke finds out Leia is his sister. And as far as supernatural love triangles go, *Twilight* is pretty weak compared to *The Vampire Diaries*—but I can't compare them because then I've crossed into TV. And you don't even want to get me started on TV love triangles."

"Stop." Lincoln's authoritative voice cuts through my rambling, and my eyes snap up to his slate-gray ones. "One—whether your actions match this perception of yourself is irrelevant, and frankly, if you enjoyed it, you should own what you've done. We don't think less of you, so why should you? Two—bros before hoes."

I almost burst out laughing.

"And three," he continues, stepping close so we're inches apart, "in order to have a love triangle, you need to be in love."

For some reason, his last comment stings, but I force a smile. "Fair enough."

"Come inside and stop overthinking shit, Bennett," Trey says, ruffling my hair like I'm a damn puppy. So I do.

CHAPTER TWENTY-FIVE

LINCOLN

*W*hat did Serenity say to her? Did she tell her about that stupid cat?

That girl has never had a big mouth when it comes to me, but what if her jealousy of Charlie pushed her into telling one of my secrets?

Obviously, my fucked-up family situation came up, and I'm a little surprised by Charlie's reaction. No one but Trey has had much empathy for the plight of this poor rich boy. Even Serenity grew impatient with me. But she grew up with her selfish bitch of a mother, so I can't blame her for not understanding what it was like to have lost one who cared. My mother was everything—a confidant, a best friend, and the one person who I thought would never leave.

I'm pretty sure Charlie doesn't know *why* my mom left—I never even told Seren that.

Am I ready for that conversation?

There was a reason that I didn't even tell Trey until the other night. Ellen's death was a pretty high-profile news story, and leaking rumors about a dead woman is in poor taste, no matter how much I hated her. Not to mention, it would destroy my father's reputation. I'm a bitter asshole, sure, but no need to fracture our relationship further.

I'm really not sure how Charlie would react to the information that her mom tore my family apart and made me into this cynical, uncaring prick. I'm not ready to tell her because then I would have to tell her how I used her—took her virginity—all in the name of misplaced hate.

I watch as she takes off her Converse and moves to sit on the couch, staring out through our balcony doors into the darkness beyond campus. Her brow furrows, making a worry line that I want to smooth away with my thumb. I sit down in the armchair across from Charlie to be on the safe side. I don't trust myself with her. Ever since our encounter in the theater, some measure of control I had around her slipped, and I haven't been able to rein it back in.

Trey opens the fridge and grabs a beer, cracking it open and taking a swig before heading over to the bar. I smile slightly as he pours me a whisky neat and mixes a whisky Diet for Charlie. Trey knows I don't drink much beer, but he also knows Charlie's drink of choice. For putting on the front of a stereotypical fuck boy, he's actually pretty thoughtful. Hell, despite his shitty upbringing, Trey has proven himself time and again to be protective of those he loves and loyal to a fault.

"Thank you," Charlie says quietly, accepting the drink from Trey. When he heads back to the kitchen, she looks at me, and her eyebrows lower.

I have to force myself not to smile because the spark that lights inside her when I push her buttons lights everything inside me too, but in an unexpectedly good way. No one ever challenges me, and I like that she does. She doesn't treat me like I'm broken.

"I know this shouldn't bother me, but it does," Charlie starts haltingly. "I don't remember either of you from when I was younger, and I feel like I should because apparently you both used to come to my house all the time." Her small fingers run through her wavy hair anxiously, making it a sexy, tousled mess as it falls around her face. "So you knew who I was at the bonfire. How long have you hated me, Link?"

Trey starts to talk from the kitchen, pausing his search for snacks, but she silences him with a glare. "Don't even get me started on you. You implied you didn't remember when I asked you this exact question the other night at the theater."

"Cut him some slack," I say with a smirk. "He was blitzed for most of high school, so he was telling the truth. Marcus and Sebastian were cool guys. So yeah, we spent a lot of time in your pool house."

Charlie rolls her eyes and glances at Trey. Then she folds her legs beneath her and places her hands in her lap as her rich green eyes come back to me. "Do you remember me?" she asks coldly.

It's a loaded question because of course I do.

Despite how we may have felt about our parents as children, it's undeniable that money was their top priority—and Martin Conners was one of the wealthiest property investors in the business. I was dragged to countless parties and meetings so our dads could rub elbows. But Charlotte Bennett wasn't more than a rich man's quirky daughter until *that* night—the night I took her virginity. But that admission is locked down. I might want to ravage every inch of Charlie's body, but that doesn't mean I'll divulge an unforgivable secret.

I swipe my finger along my bottom lip absently as I consider my answer.

"Yes, I remember you," I say finally. Trey raises his eyebrows, probably wondering if I'm smitten enough to spill my damn guts. I'm not. "You were the little girl playing dress-up at her daddy's parties."

The comment comes out more condescending than I mean it to, but what can I say? Old habits die hard.

Charlie narrows her eyes at me. "I was *not* playing dress up," she says defensively. "Matt and I were together, and I felt like I needed to support him. He didn't want to hang out with the other kids—he was more interested in the adult talk." She lowers her eyes. "We were supposed to get married someday," she says quietly, as if she's ashamed.

Matt.

I feel my body tense. Just his name on her full lips fills me with undeniable rage.

Trey sits down on the couch next to Charlie, his hands reaching out to rest on her knees. She angles herself toward him.

"We've seen you around campus with that asshole since the night of the party," he bites out. "Care to tell us the story?"

Charlie looks up, shaking her head. "You two are such stalkers," she says with a faint smile. "I'm shocked you guys haven't frightened him off with all the big dick energy you throw around."

Surprisingly, the idea of us keeping tabs on her doesn't seem to phase her a bit.

"Don't think I didn't try," I say darkly.

Charlie looks over at me in confusion. "What?"

"The Monday after our party, I went to Chancellor Edwards, but the douche is on the hockey team, and he's apparently very good…."

"*Very* good," Charlie confirms.

"So she won't kick him out unless he actually violates school policies or breaks a law." My mouth twists in disgust. "Apparently, an Evans telling her Matt's a first-class prick isn't enough."

I haven't told anyone else about the rape rumor yet. I'm still looking into whether it's legit, and conveniently, the girl who accused Matt has already transferred schools.

"Wow." Charlie laughs and the sound seems to lighten the whole room. "You did that for me?"

I stare at her. "I think you know the answer to that."

"So are you going to tell us what happened, or do we need to beat it out of him?" I ask, cracking my knuckles. Honestly, I have no idea why this girl isn't terrified of me.

Charlie bites her bottom lip. "It's personal and humiliating."

Trey inches closer, his thumbs moving softly over her knees. She closes her eyes and sighs. His gesture clearly relaxes Charlie, but her response comes across as so sensual, I have to rein in my dirty thoughts before my dick gets any ideas.

She still hesitates, looking over at me. "We didn't come here to talk about me, Link." My name on her lips twists something inside me, but I ignore the feeling. "And as much as it bothers me that you knew me from Brighton and never mentioned it, that's my petty issue, and it pales in comparison to your mom leaving. I know what it's like to lose your family."

"Look, Sunshine," I say, running my hands through my hair. "It was two years ago."

"But that doesn't make it less real or less painful," she interrupts.

"No, that's true." I drop my eyes because talking about it fills me with so much resentment, and I'm tired of offloading my damage on her. "My dad cheated on my mom," I say quickly. "And after we caught them, she left." I squeeze my hands into fists, still refusing to look at Charlie. "I kept thinking that she'd get over it—that she loved me enough to come back. But she didn't. And one day, I walked downstairs and found their divorce papers taped to the fridge like it was a damn grocery list."

I open my hands, flexing my fingers as I force the tension out of my body, and finally look up at Charlie.

Her empathetic frown tugs at my heart uncomfortably, and I force a cavalier smile. "But we all deal with these things differently, right? I know you vent through your writing. I can tell by the short stories you've shared in class. I can tell by the way you scribble in your notebook while you glare at me." She flushes, and I smirk. "Well, it turns out that I vent by shutting people out and being a rude asshole.

Because of your mom.

Before I realize what I'm doing, I stand and approach the couch, sitting down on Charlie's other side. I reach out, my hand pushing a strand of hair behind her ear. Her lips part as she stares at me, like she doesn't understand my actions. I hardly understand them. "While I appreciate that you're worried about me, I'm okay now."

Because of you.

Her gaze searches my face, and when she seems satisfied I'm being truthful, she nods.

"Now," I say, changing the subject, "tell us about Matt so I know whether I need to break his face again."

"Fine. But no face breaking, boss," she says sternly. "No matter what I tell you."

I don't say anything.

"Promise me," she insists, giving me a gentle shove for emphasis.

I sigh. "All right, whatever. I promise."

She directs a skeptical look my way before continuing. "Matt and I were pretty much inseparable from a pretty young age. We met at a neighborhood park one day, and from then on, I'd wait for him there because Matt's dad wasn't a nice person, and he needed a friend." She pauses, her eyes glassy, and I picture little empath Charlie protecting that psychopath. "I was smitten with him by the time I was twelve."

Matt's father was intent on doing business with my stepfather, so they came around our house a lot. When Matt and I were teenagers, our dad's went in together to buy the Macy's building in Seattle."

"The one that closed a few years ago?" I ask.

She nods. "They were supposed to purchase it through my stepdad's company and keep Macy's up and running. Matt's dad was supposed to become a partner. But at the last minute, the deal fell through, and it was sold to another interested party. They lost a $586-million sale."

I give a low whistle. "That deal would have pretty much guaranteed their family wouldn't go bankrupt."

Charlie frowns. "What do you mean? The Johnsons are old money."

"Were," I correct. "I looked into it, and Matt's here on a hockey scholarship because his family is broke."

Charlie raises her eyebrows. "Wow, I had no idea. Yeah, then I guess that was smart of his dad. I bet he was pissed at losing all that money."

Trey strokes Charlie's thigh, and I see her shiver. "So what happened?" he asks quietly. "I assume he didn't break up with you over his father's business loss."

"Well, after that day, Matt started acting strange. He was stand-offish and intentionally caused fights. Then, one night just before our senior year started, I walked into my room and found Matt fucking some girl on my bed." Tears trickle down Charlie's cheeks.

She takes a deep breath and sniffs. "I don't miss him one bit, and I have no regrets, but the feeling of betrayal is always sharp when I think about that night."

I see Trey's hands tighten on Charlie's legs. He's pissed. I'm pissed. My anger runs hot, but then she looks at me, her eyes red and shining with hurt and betrayal, and the need to comfort her wins. I cup her face, my thumbs wiping away the tears. I dip my head down so we're eye to eye, her panicked breath fanning over my face.

I lean forward, pressing a chaste kiss to her mouth. I taste the salty sharpness of her grief on my tongue. She responds tentatively to my touch, and I close my eyes, reveling in the feeling of her soft lips moving slowly against mine.

Reluctantly, I pull away. "If he ever hurts you again, I—" I lock eyes with Trey's fierce, determined gaze—"*we* will kill him."

And I mean it.

CHAPTER TWENTY-SIX

CHARLIE

*T*rey's touch is soothing on my legs, and I can still feel Lincoln's lips on mine even after he leans back, his eyes still locked on me.

I'm suddenly aware of how close they are, and I take a long pull from my drink. I wince, feeling the alcohol burn down my throat.

"Is there any Diet Pepsi in this?" I croak.

Trey laughs, and the sound does stupid things to my insides. I take another drink, finishing it off in one gulp.

"Whoa, slow down, Bennett." Trey's fingers skim feather-light touches over my jeans. "We're not trying to get you drunk."

I shake the glass at him, with a smile. I can already feel warmth spreading through my limbs. "More, please?"

He raises an eyebrow but takes my glass and walks over to the bar to refill it. I look back at Lincoln, who's watching me with narrowed eyes.

"Maybe we should call it a night," he says, glancing at the clock.

It's past 1 a.m. I know he's right, but I'm not interested in going back to my dorm. It's nice being here. With someone. With them.

Lincoln moves to stand, but I grab his hand.

"No. Please," I say. His dark hair falls over his forehead as he looks down at me, and I have the sudden urge to touch the soft strands. I can feel Trey's gaze from across the room, and my cheeks heat. "I'm not ready to go back. I want to stay."

"Oh…kay," Lincoln says, staring at where our hands connect.

I pull away from him.

"Sorry." My face is on fire. I have no idea why I did that, but I feel like an idiot.

They probably think I'm a clingy weirdo.

Lincoln chuckles. "We don't think you're a weirdo, Sunshine."

Dear God. Did I say that out loud?

Lincoln sits back down. "If you want to stay, all you have to do is ask." His voice is deep and husky. I feel Trey sit down on my other side, sliding the fresh drink into my hand. I shiver involuntarily, though I'm not sure if it's from the cold glass or being wedged between them.

I take a sip. This one definitely has less alcohol in it, which is probably a good thing because I swear I'm getting loopy off the first one. Trey's large fingers trace patterns along my skin, leaving trails of fire in their wake. I close my eyes and release a shuttered breath.

When I open my eyes, Lincoln's face is inches from my own. I place my glass on the coffee table, and I can't stop myself this time—I reach out, pushing the hair from his forehead. He makes a growling sound as my fingers weave into his thick strands. My eyes snap up, looking into his. They're practically black, his pupils dilated with lust.

Trey's hands drop to my waist and slide under my shirt, skimming along my stomach. I swallow a moan. I can already feel the dampness in my panties.

Lincoln hesitates only a second before pressing his lips to mine. The kiss is tentative at first but quickly escalates to urgent and needy. It's not as desperate as it was in the theater. This kiss says things he and I can't say—emotions we aren't willing to accept. It makes me dizzy and breathless, and I'm free-falling. But for once, I welcome it. I let go of all my control because I feel completely safe. I slide my tongue between Lincoln's lips to tangle with his, and he moans softly. Trey's hands inch my sweatshirt up, and I break my kiss with Lincoln so Trey can pull it over my head, leaving me in my jeans and bra.

I pull Link's face back to mine hungrily, and Trey moves my hair to one side and drops soft kisses on my neck and shoulder.

Holy shit. It's happening again.

I feel like I should stop this. Sharing them—it's not right. But I don't feel guilt like I thought I would. Instead I just allow myself to exist in this moment—to want them both.

I rise up on my knees, crawling into Lincoln's lap as I grind my pussy against him shamelessly. He pushes back against me, groaning at the contact, his hands grabbing my ass to pull me even closer.

"Shit," he growls.

Trey chuckles before flicking open the clasp on my bra and pulling the straps from my shoulders. He cups one of my breasts in his large hands, pinching my nipple. Hard. The jolt of pain makes my pussy tingle, and I break my kiss with Lincoln, gasping for air. Trey's stubble scrapes against my sensitive skin as he leans in and takes one of my aching, hardened nipples into his warm mouth.

Lincoln starts to bite and kiss along my jaw. His hands slide beneath the waistband of my jeans, moving around my hips to rub my clit through my damp panties.

"Fuck," I breathe, already feeling a euphoric ache building between my legs.

"You're so wet," Lincoln purrs appreciatively. "Is this what you want, Charlie? Both of us? Together?"

Despite the books I've read, the idea of sex with multiple guys hasn't really crossed my mind. I figured guys didn't actually want to see each other's dicks, and a real threesome would probably involve a lot of accidental...dick bumping.

That would be hot. I giggle involuntarily.

Trey pauses his sucking. "What're you thinking about?"

"I, uh..." But the words are caught in my throat when Lincoln's thick, long fingers slide between my folds and into my pussy.

I can't believe this is happening.

I stand so Trey can peel off my jeans, while I stare at the bulge in Link's gray sweats. The outline of his huge cock is tented against the soft material, and a dark wet spot is already visible where his precum has soaked through. Lincoln goes to move from the couch, but I push down on his shoulder.

"Wait." I want to sound confident and strong, but nerves are rioting in my stomach. He looks up at me with raised brows. "Sit back."

Trey stops to watch our exchange.

Lincoln complies, repositioning himself with a wicked gleam in his eye. I lick my lips. I want his cock in my mouth, and he knows it.

I pull down his joggers and boxers with trembling fingers. I might not be very experienced at sex, but I've given my share of blowjobs—and I'm good at it. I've just never been as eager as I am now. I want to see Lincoln Evans—this boy obsessed with control—fall apart because of me.

The thought steadies my hands, and I give his cock a firm stoke. Then I lean forward, lapping up the large bead of precum on his tip. His head falls back, and he lets out a loud groan. The salty taste explodes on my tongue, making my mouth water, and

I wrap my lips around him, my tongue sliding along his velvety soft skin.

"Fuck, Charlie," he breathes.

I give him a long suck before I pull off with a pop and smirk up at him. I spit into my hand and pump it up and down his length. I feel movement next to me and glance over. Trey is watching us with his pants half off, his bronze eyes hooded while he slowly strokes himself. It's the first time I've seen his cock up close in all its veiny glory, and I can't say I'm disappointed.

Honestly, watching him touch himself while I get Link off is the hottest thing I've ever seen.

I smile and turn back to Lincoln, leaning in to take him back into my mouth. He's so big—much larger than Matt was—and I worry I might choke as I take him farther and farther down my throat. More precum fills my mouth, and I hum in pleasure, the vibration eliciting all kinds of animalistic noises from Lincoln's throat. I love it.

Trey is still rapt, his hand stroking his dick with long, languid movements. Link's gaze locks with Trey's, and the connection I see between them is pure lust-fueled fire. Trey clearly likes what he sees, and Lincoln doesn't mind a damn bit, and I'm so here for it.

I relax my throat, taking him deeper, licking him like a damn lollipop. I reach up, gently massaging Link's balls, and then I run a finger along his taint and tease it between his cheeks.

Lincoln's fingers tangle in my hair. His hips move as he starts to lose control, fucking my mouth. I gag and my eyes water, but as I watch the mounting ecstasy on Lincoln's face, I want more. I hear Trey moan in appreciation, and I see his hand shuttling faster along his dick.

The warm rush of arousal drips down my leg. I feel like I could come, and I'm not even being touched.

Lincoln's cock thickens as his thrusts become less

controlled. "Fuck, baby, I'm about to come," he pants, fisting my hair. Then he grunts as he unloads into my mouth. I swallow it down eagerly, savoring the salty-sweet mixture.

I continue to suck Lincoln gently while his cock softens in my mouth. Then I stand, straddle his lap, and press my mouth to his, sliding my tongue between his soft lips so he can taste himself. He grasps my face possessively, and he returns the kiss, taking everything I'm giving him in a slow, sensual dance of our tongues.

"God damn, you're good at that," he breathes finally as we break apart.

I hear Trey's deep, throaty chuckle. We both turn to look at him, and he's still sitting next to us, his hard length in his hand.

"Your turn," Link whispers in my ear. "Fuck him."

I look into his eyes. I expect to see jealousy warring with lust, but I don't. I place my hands against his cheeks, running my fingers through his stubble.

"Are you sure?" I ask quietly.

"Sunshine, you're already dripping all over my cock right now," he growls. "I want you to fuck him. Now."

Lincoln's demanding tone sends a thrill of arousal straight to my core, and I climb off of him and crawl into Trey's lap.

CHAPTER TWENTY-SEVEN

TREY

My cock is aching as I watch Charlie kiss Lincoln. That was, by far, the hottest blow job I have ever seen, and it wasn't even on me. Seeing Charlie with her cheeks hollowed out, sucking my best friend into oblivion was intense, to say the least. The way they moved together, so in sync, was mesmerizing to watch. If I were any other guy, I might be jealous. But I can see their connection—and it's much stronger than either of them will admit.

I feel like a damn sap, but she's so fucking beautiful with her dark hair tousled and her cheeks flushed.

She moves to crawl toward me, but Lincoln stops her with a hand on her hip. She looks back in question as his fingers hook the edges of her panties, pulling them off her legs in one fluid motion. She turns back to me, straddling my lap and sliding the heat of her soaking-wet pussy along my cock.

Holy fuck, that feels amazing.

My eyes roll back into my head, and something between a whimper and a groan escapes my lips. "Bennett, I want you so fucking bad."

"Take whatever you want, big man. I'm yours."

I kiss her hungrily, and she fights me for dominance, our teeth clashing and biting. She continues to grind against me, our bodies sliding against each other with delicious friction. I can already feel my balls tightening as pings of pleasure zip down my spine.

"Don't you dare fucking come until you're inside her," Lincoln growls.

Charlie laughs. I open my eyes and look over her shoulder at him. He's watching us with hunger, his hand on his cock, which is already starting to harden again.

"Bend her over," he demands, his gray eyes practically black with arousal.

"So bossy," I mutter with a smile, grabbing Charlie's hips and lifting her off my lap so she's on all fours on the couch, giving Lincoln a view of her tight pink pussy.

"So perfect," he breathes.

I'm inclined to agree as I move behind her so that Link and I are side by side. I run my hands along the soft skin of her back, watching goosebumps rise. She shivers when my hands reach her perfect ass. I stare at her plump cheeks, then smack one roughly with the palm of my hand before I soothe the mark I just made with my tongue.

Charlie gasps, then buries her face in the couch.

I raise an eyebrow. "Does our good girl like it a little rough?"

She looks back at me, biting her lip and narrowing her eyes. "I swear to God, Trey. Put your dick in me before I combust."

I can't help but laugh. I look over at Lincoln. "Tell me what to do, boss," I say, using Charlie's pet name for him.

His eyes blaze at the invitation, and I know I've found his kink. "I want you to eat her out. Lick her from her pussy to her asshole," he says with a throaty whisper.

I comply eagerly, no stranger to ass play. I spread her cheeks to get better access as I lean over and run my tongue through her warm flesh, lapping first at her clit before moving on to thrust it into her pussy.

She bucks against my face, whimpering, "Trey, ugh, that feels so fucking good. Shit."

I start licking her frantically as I pull my tongue all the way up to her puckered hole.

"Fuck," she moans.

I can hear Link's breath hitch as he watches her writhe. My cock is so hard it's pulsing, and I feel like I could explode.

"Finger her while you eat her ass," he says.

And I do, holding myself up with one hand while my other runs around her waist to find her clit. I rub it, slowly at first, as I continue to tongue her, marveling at the mewling sounds coming from her mouth. Her whole body is shaking beneath me, and I start to move my fingers faster.

"Don't let her come yet," Lincoln says, breathing heavily. Charlie lets out a growl of frustration and I smile. I pause, my eyes coming up to meet Link's. He's completely blissed out, his chest rising and falling, and he's stroking his cock furiously. I can see every vein spiraling along his shaft, and precum is oozing from his tip. I push down the sudden urge to lick it off.

"Lincoln," Charlie begs, looking over at him, "enough edging. Please let him fuck me."

His gray eyes move from her flushed face to mine, settling on my mouth where I'm sure he can see Charlie's arousal glistening on my lips.

"Fuck her," he says through clenched teeth.

I get to my knees and grab Charlie's hips roughly, my fingers digging into her skin, and she pushes herself back against me.

"God, Trey, I need to feel your cock inside me. Now."

I push into her roughly, stretching her wide, and we both moan loudly. Her pussy is so warm and tight that I'm losing my mind trying not to come too quickly.

"Fuckfuckfuck." I've never felt anything so incredible, the pleasure ripping through my veins like heroin.

Charlie white-knuckles the couch as I pound into her over and over, unable to restrain myself. My thrusts become erratic and uneven as I feel my orgasm climbing. "Fuck, babe, I'm going to come."

"Holy shit," she practically screams, and her pussy spasms around me as she orgasms. At the same time, I hear a long, deep moan leave Lincoln's throat. I look over, and he's right beside me, gripping his engorged cock over Charlie's body as he comes, string after string of white semen covering her ass and back.

I come right behind them, feeling the world tilt beneath me as I push deep into Charlie's pussy, my cock twitching, filling her up. Marking her. And then we all collapse into a sweaty, exhausted heap.

I lie still for a moment, trying to catch my breath. Charlie is beneath me, and Lincoln's cum is a sticky mess between us. Lincoln is lying on his side on the couch next to us, his large hand gripping my arm as if he needs to ground himself. I roll slightly toward him, moving some of my weight off Charlie so I'm not crushing her, and I lay my head on his bicep. He doesn't seem to mind.

"Shit," he breathes.

"Agreed," Charlie says, pushing herself up so she can roll over and look at us. My eyes meet her forest-green ones as she brushes her tangled hair from her forehead. A smile lights her face and makes my heart ache, and I rub my chest involuntarily. She looks so fucking happy.

Then she kisses me softly, her mouth moving slowly against mine. Her coconut-vanilla scent tickles my senses, mixing with the smell of sex, and it's an inebriating combination. My head spins as I get lost in her, and when she finally pulls away, I'm breathless.

Then she leans over, locking eyes with Lincoln before kissing him tenderly, and I watch him come apart in the same way. His bewildered expression would have been funny if I didn't know exactly how he felt.

"Can I take a shower before I go back?" Charlie asks.

Link and I glance at each other before nodding silently like idiots.

I drag my eyes down Charlie's body as she stands, taking in the swell of her tits and her flat stomach, and I stop at her perfect pussy. I can see my cum dripping down her thigh.

So hot.

Without thinking I push the warm liquid back up into her.

"That's better," I mumble with a satisfied grin. "Mine."

Charlie gapes at me for a moment before she bursts out laughing, and I start chuckling too. Lincoln's body shakes next to mine as we all deteriorate into a fit of delirious laughter. Warmth spreads through every inch of my body, and I can honestly say I haven't felt this happy in a long time.

"Are you blushing?" I ask Link after Charlie disappears down the hall toward the bathroom.

His cheeks and the tips of his ears are pink.

"No, asshole," he scoffs, shoving my shoulder. "But I can't say I'm used to sitting with you in our living room with our dicks hanging out."

I glance down. "Fair point."

We grab our clothes and turn away from each other to dress, though after what just happened, I'm not sure why we suddenly care about modesty.

We're just sitting back down to crack open some beers when Charlie reappears. She's back in her jeans and hoodie, and her dark hair, damp from her shower, is twisted into a makeshift braid over one shoulder.

She approaches us hesitantly, her eyes bouncing between us, but, as adorable as it is, I'm done with her shyness, so I grab her hand and pull her roughly onto the couch. She laughs in surprise but nestles her small body between us.

"I honestly didn't know if you guys would be comfortable doing more stuff...together," she says after a moment. "But that was amazing."

Lincoln shrugs. "We're pretty comfortable with each other when it comes to sex," he says casually.

Charlie's eyes widen, and I pinch the bridge of my nose, knowing what she's about to ask.

"So you guys *have* shared a girl before?" She fidgets with the end of her braid, twisting it anxiously around her finger.

I smile because her voice has an edge to it that reeks of jealousy.

"We, uhh...not exactly," Lincoln starts.

"We had a threesome once last year," I say, before taking a long swig of my beer.

Charlie's mouth falls open, but she closes it quickly. "With who? Please don't say Serenity."

Lincoln and I choke on our drinks "What? No," I croak, clearing my throat. "She's firmly in the like-a-sister zone."

"So then who?" she asks, raising an eyebrow.

I look over at Lincoln, wondering if he's comfortable with me sharing the story. He holds my gaze a moment before giving me a hesitant nod.

I raise my brows. *Are you sure?*

He nods again, so I shrug, looking back at Charlie. "It wasn't a girl."

Charlie frowns in confusion. "What? So like, an older woman?"

I laugh. "No, it was a guy."

Her eyes widen, flaring with interest and desire. I'm not sure what reaction I was expecting, but it wasn't that.

"What?!" she exclaims, practically bouncing. She clutches Lincoln's thigh almost possessively while turning her attention to my face, her expression begging for more information. "Aren't you both straight?"

Lincoln chuckles.

"Well, yeah, so first you should probably know I'm bi."

Charlie's eyes light up. "I had no idea. You have such a..."

"Slutty reputation?" I finish with a smirk.

Charlie flushes. "I'm sorry. That's judgy of me."

I take the hand twisting her braid and link my fingers through hers. Our hands feel good together. "It's okay," I say, smiling. "I know my rep, and it doesn't bother me. I've had my share of both guys and girls, but guys just tend to keep their mouths shut about sex, especially if they aren't out."

"Makes sense," Charlie says slowly, nodding her head. "But you're straight, right, Link?"

He nods, smiling faintly. "Pretty straight, yes."

"So how did you end up in a male-male sexcapade with this guy?" she asks, trying not to laugh.

"He was high and horny as fuck," I say, smiling widely.

Lincoln rolls his eyes. "I was *not* that high."

"Not really helping your case, dude," I laugh. "Anyway, we were at a party back home for the weekend. I have a fuck buddy who I call sometimes—we've been hooking up off and on since he came out in high school. He's a cool guy, and he's always had a huge crush on Lincoln."

"What?" Lincoln sputters. "He has not!"

Charlie snorts with laughter.

"Yes, he has," I say. "Why do you think he used to come to our house so often?"

"To fuck you, obviously," he says, gritting his teeth.

"So the threesome," Charlie cuts in, holding back a grin.

"Right, so I meet my buddy at this party, and we start messing around in an empty bedroom. We're pretty much undressed when Lincoln busts in, stoned out of his mind, and sits down on the bed next to us."

I smile over at Lincoln, who's squirming next to me uncomfortably. "So my friend and I stop our…activities, trying to decide what he wants, and Link looks over and suddenly notices we're half naked and that he probably interrupted something."

I snicker as I think back on that night. Charlie is leaning forward, hanging on my every word.

"He doesn't say anything, so we just went back to what we were doing, but Lincoln's watching us go at it. Finally, he looks at my friend, who was already giving him some serious come-fuck-me eyes, and Lincoln straight-up starts rambling on about how he's horny as hell, and he just turned down a pathetic excuse for a blow job by some sorority chick with a limp tongue. So he says he'd like one from my buddy because he's got to be an expert at sucking dick."

I try to hold my laughter as I talk because Lincoln is staring daggers at me. "And so we're just staring at him with our dicks out and our mouths open in shock, and he kind of shrugs and goes, 'What? I'm stressed as fuck and need release. Now.' And I kid you not, I have never seen a dude drop to his knees so fast in my life," I say grinning widely.

Charlie is shaking with laughter.

"We all went lust-crazy after that," I continue. "Lincoln got a blowjob, and I wasn't about to stop what I was doing, so I fucked my buddy while he did it. When it was done, we all agreed never to tell anyone." I shrug. "I honestly don't know how the rumor about sharing a chick got started though, but he was definitely no chick."

Lincoln scoffs. "That would be Lisa."

I raise an eyebrow. "Serenity's little minion?"

"Yeah, she started that rumor when I turned her down at the bonfire," he says with a shrug. "Guess I just never set the record straight." He leans forward, his mouth inches from Charlie's. "But for the record, no *other* slutty threesomes happened."

She smirks at him, leaning forward to press her lips against his in a brief but hot kiss. "I think your guy threesome sounds hot," she says after pulling away with a heated look. Lincoln raises his eyebrows.

"Why am I not surprised?" I feel my dick thickening again at the thought and try to subtly adjust myself.

Lincoln glances at me. "Why do you say that?"

"Bennett here told me all about her male-male book collection," I say, winking.

Her cheeks flush slightly, but she doesn't deny it. "I like what I like," she says with a confident smile. "Male-male romances are next level—especially if they have lots of hatred and angst."

Link meets my eyes as if asking if I'd want that, too. And I nod because my best friend is hot as hell, and I trust him. The smile he gives me in return is almost shy and very un-Lincoln-like, but he finally seems completely open to the idea.

Thank fuck.

"Okay, it's super weird when you guys talk without actually talking," Charlie says, looking between us before stifling a yawn. Her eyes look heavy, like she's about to pass out.

She stands. "I guess I should head back."

We both stand with her, but I place a hand on her waist before she can walk to the door.

"When is your first class tomorrow, Bennett?" I ask.

"It's at ten. Why?"

"Maybe you could stay," I say softly.

Lincoln nods, grabbing her hand. "Yeah, it's cold outside and late. Stay." He runs a finger along her jaw. She leans into his touch and stares back.

Jesus, the way she's looking up at him is giving me all the feels.

"Okay, sure," she whispers finally.

Lincoln and I follow her down the hall. We don't need to talk about the sleeping situation. After tonight, I think we just know neither one of us is giving her up, so why fight it? We walk into Lincoln's room and strip down to our boxers. I look at Charlie, who watches appreciatively from the foot of the bed. I smile, tossing her the T-shirt I just took off.

"You can sleep in this," I say. "And there's extra tooth brushes under the sink in the bathroom."

Before long, we've all collapsed into the soft king-size bed, Charlie nestled between us. My fingers graze her hip, and I slide my hand over her stomach as she wiggles her back closer to my chest, sighing contentedly. Listening to the sound of her and Lincoln breathing, I drift off to sleep.

CHAPTER TWENTY-EIGHT

CHARLIE

I awake to rain slapping against Lincoln's window and roll onto my back. The sound makes my heart hammer. I glance between the guys—they're still fast asleep. I take a deep breath and close my eyes, trying to relax, but the sound of water dripping onto the metal gutter outside vibrates through my brain.

Drip, drip, drip.

Shit.

My stomach twists, and I curl into a ball, pulling my arms over my face.

You're okay. You're with Trey and Link. You're okay.

I hear her in my head—she's singing "The Middle" by Jimmie Eat World, her voice a gentle hum in my ears.

"It just takes some time, little girl, you're in the middle of the ride. Everything, everything will be just fine...."

But the tune doesn't seem to drown out the dripping. It's so loud. Then she's not singing anymore. I see her pale, limp hand dangling out of the tub of crimson water. Blood runs down her wrist in rivulets, trickling onto the tiled floor.

The sound of it—*drip, drip, drip*—is all I hear.

"Charlie."

It's Trey's voice, but it's far away and muffled.

"One-hundred, ninety-nine, ninety-eight…" I mumble. My heart is beating so hard it hurts. *Why won't she wake up?* "Mom. Please." A sob rips from my throat.

Drip, drip, drip.

"Ninety-one, ninety, eighty-nine…"

"Charlie!" They're saying my name together now, and strong, warm hands are shaking me.

"I'm sorry, Seb. I'm sorry, Marcus."

I'm trembling.

"Everything, everything will be all right…."

"Charlie, sweetheart, come back to us." Trey's voice is gentle and soothing, and suddenly I can feel the cotton of Link's bed sheets against my skin. And his fingers are tracing up and down my arm, while Trey's callused hands cup my cheeks.

I open my eyes, staring into Trey's warm brown ones. They're full of fear and concern. "Baby, we're here," he whispers.

Tears soak into the pillow as another sob shakes my body. I press my face to his chest and cry as the panic attack subsides, and his arms wrap around me. Lincoln presses his body against my back, cocooning me against his warm skin. Their heartbeats falling in unison with mine are measured and comforting. Finally, I take a shuddering breath and pull back, feeling embarrassed.

I sit up and press my back to the headboard, the sheet pooling around my waist. I rub the moisture from my eyes, straining to see in the darkness. I can still hear the rain, but it's not as loud.

"What happened, Sunshine?" Link pushes himself up.

"Panic attack," I whisper. I clear my throat, and I'm not sure they hear me.

Trey sits up, frowning. "You don't have to tell us if you don't want to." His words are low and quiet between us. I consider hiding it like I always did from Seb, but knowing they can't see my face gives me courage.

"I dreamed of the day I found my mom." Link's muscles stiffen.

"She cut her wrists, and I was the one who found her."

"Is that when you started having panic attacks?" Trey's voice is soft.

"Sort of. They started after Matt cheated on me and got worse after my mom died. But my stepdad leaving was when they got really bad."

"What do you mean he left?" Link asks.

"I came home from school one day, and he was just...gone." My voice breaks. "He didn't leave anything except the stuff in my room and enough food for a week or two."

The guys scoot closer to me, bare thighs brushing my skin, their body heat mingling with mine. But they stay silent, and I continue.

"I was alone for a year," I continue. "I couldn't afford the tuition here even on a scholarship after I graduated, so I worked at the old video store on Fourth for six months, saving what I could."

"Jesus..." Link's voice is raspy with pain. "I'm so sorry."

I swear I hear guilt in his tone, an emotion I was sure the Lincoln I've gotten to know didn't feel.

"I ate cereal for almost every meal because it was cheap, and I never got tired of it. I bought Lucky Charms, Fruity Pebbles, and Fruit Loops because of the rainbow hues—my life was so gray; I wanted colors. Sometimes, I went to local parties or the bookstore just to be around people. I was so lonely."

Trey leans his head on my shoulder. "Where the heck were your brothers during all this?" I feel his words vibrate against my body. He sounds angry.

"I never told them," I say. "By the time Martin left, Seb was already in Vancouver living his dream with Marcus. I didn't have the heart to tell them their dad was a piece of shit."

We all sit in silence, listening to the rain outside, which has retreated to light sprinkles against the glass. After a few minutes, I hear Link snoring softly and smile. I nudge him with my elbow, and Trey lifts his head as I slide back beneath the covers.

"Let's go back to sleep," I say, yawning. I'm out within seconds.

CHAPTER TWENTY-NINE

CHARLIE

*S*omething's buzzing.

I look around sleepily, confused at first until I remember last night. My heart rate kicks up thinking about how hot the guys were together with me.

Together. With. Me.

I hear the buzzing again and realize it's probably my phone.

Trey's head is nestled against my shoulder, his blond hair tickling my neck, and he has one arm wrapped possessively around my waist.

Lincoln is facing me, his mouth practically touching mine as we lie there. His relaxed face is boyish in the soft morning light. My heart squeezes at the sight of him looking so peaceful. He always seems so closed-off and guarded, like he's waiting for the world to betray him, though lately it seems like something is different. I thought he hated me at first, but now, especially after last night, I can't really believe that anymore.

I wiggle a bit, trying to move from beneath Trey's heavy arm while disentangling Link's leg from mine, and I finally manage to slide free. I don't know if it's conscious or not, but once I'm out of the bed, Trey rolls closer to Lincoln so they're practically spooning.

So cute.

I pad over to my discarded jeans and grab my phone from the pocket, checking the screen. I have five text messages from Fiona, and I realize with a quiet groan that I was supposed to meet her for coffee before our history class so we could study. It's already nine.

I text her back, telling her I'll be there in five, and start pulling on my pants.

"Going somewhere?" Lincoln rumbles, causing my heart to race as surprise prickles my senses.

I turn, but my legs, which are only halfway into my jeans, twist together, and I fall onto my butt.

"Oof" is all I can say. *Real smooth, Charlie.*

I smile guiltily at the guys, who're staring down at me. They're stupidly sexy right now.

Trey clutches his chest dramatically. "Were you about to try to ghost me again, Bennett?" His voice is rough from sleep.

"Not intentionally," I laugh as I finish wiggling into my pants. "I completely forgot I told Fi I would study with her this morning." I throw off Trey's shirt before realizing I'm naked underneath.

"Shit." I drop to my knees to search for my bra, which I find under the bed.

When I stand, a strong arm wraps around my waist. I squeal in alarm as I'm tugged back onto the bed and against Trey's hard, warm chest.

"You're such a caveman," I say with a smile.

His hands immediately slide up my body to cup my breasts, and his mouth drops to my neck, biting roughly.

The sensation sends electricity to my pussy. I moan involuntarily, closing my eyes. "I really need to go."

"Maybe we're not ready for you to leave yet," Lincoln purrs.

I open my eyes, locking onto his gray irises, which are stormy with lust. He leans forward and hooks his fingers onto the waistband of my jeans, which are still unbuttoned and pulls them off in one swift motion before I can protest.

And just like that, I'm completely bare and at their mercy.

Trey is still holding me tightly from behind. I can't really move, and the feeling of helplessness turns me on even more for some reason. Trey's heart is pounding against my back, and he's grinding his hardening cock against my ass. Arousal is already starting to run down my leg, making an obvious wet spot on the gray sheets beneath me as I twist and squirm in his grasp.

"Go ahead. Fight me, baby," Trey rasps. "It makes me so fucking hard."

Holy shit.

Link's hands move to my thighs, spreading me wide. I'm shaking with need as his fingers inch closer to my aching core. He grazes my pussy lips with a light touch before sinking two fingers inside, moving them around slowly.

"Fuck, Lincoln." I push back against Trey's dick as I try to thrust into Lincoln's hand.

Trey makes a low groaning sound and kisses my shoulder while he pinches and rubs my nipples.

I whimper when Lincoln pulls his fingers free, and I feel like I'm having an out-of-body experience when he brings them to his lips and sucks them clean like I'm the most delicious thing he's ever tasted.

"Holy shit, that's hot," Trey mutters.

I swallow, wide-eyed, and nod in agreement as I watch Lincoln crawl forward, his hands falling to either side of Trey's thighs, which are caging my hips, and kisses me hard. My head spins as his tongue swirls with mine, and I taste myself on his soft lips. I want to grab him and pull him closer. I want to feel his stubble rough against my fingertips and his sweaty, hard body pushed against mine. I want us to be so close we're practically the same person, and I whimper with desire as I pull against Trey's strong grasp.

When Lincoln pulls away, I'm trembling and completely breathless. "Tease," I complain.

He chuckles and then lowers his face to my pussy, and I practically buck out of Trey's grip as Lincoln slides his tongue through my folds and closes his warm mouth over my clit, sucking and biting.

"Oh my God," I pant.

Hot pleasure builds in my stomach and shoots down my legs and up my spine, lighting up my entire body.

Trey grinds harder against my back, and I can feel his sticky, warm precum dripping into my ass crack.

"Link," I moan, looking down at him.

Every nerve in my body is raw and spots are floating before my eyes as I approach the brink of an orgasm. He's sucking and biting more frantically, and his fingers sink deep into me. He starts sliding them in and out with strong, measured thrusts.

"Fuck, I'm going to come."

"Then come for me, Sunshine," Lincoln says, the words vibrating around my clit.

Trey grunts behind me, his body jerking, and warm cum splashes against my back, dripping down my body, and I lose control, coming so hard I black out for a moment.

Trey collapses back, taking me with him, and Link sits on his knees, his face wet with my arousal. He grins smugly, and I can't help it, I start giggling.

"Okay, for real," I say between laughs. "I need to go."

"Wait," Trey says, pushing me up and climbing off the bed. He runs to the bathroom, and I hear the water running before he comes back in with a warm washcloth, then gently wipes his cum from my back.

"Trey, did you...?" Lincoln starts, raising his eyebrows.

"Uh, yeah. I did. It was...unexpected." Trey sounds almost sheepish. "Sorry about that."

I cover my mouth to hide a smile. I let him finish cleaning me off before I throw on my clothes and grab my backpack and phone.

I look over at Link and Trey as I turn to leave, suddenly feeling a bit awkward as questions run through my head.

Are the three of us some sort of weird throuple? Do I kiss them goodbye?

When neither guy moves from the bed, I smile shyly and give a small wave. "So, see you guys around?" The statement sounds more like a question. *That was lame.*

"You know it," Trey says with a sexy grin.

Lincoln just stares at me with those unreadable gray eyes.

I leave their dorm and head down the elevator. I wonder nervously what kind of crazy-ass situation I just got myself into while I run across campus, pulling my tangled hair into a ponytail as I go.

I covertly sniff my sweatshirt, wondering if I smell like sex.

Fiona is totally going to know.

It's a blustery morning, and gusts of wind tear at my clothes and hair, and fat drops of rain are starting to fall, splashing coldly against my cheeks and forehead.

I push through the gate leading out to Main Street and run the couple blocks to the coffee shop. When I enter, I spot Fiona sitting at a table with a textbook open and a large coffee cup sitting next to her half empty. She looks up at me as I approach, raising her eyebrows as she takes in my disheveled appearance.

"You look like hell," she says with a smirk.

"I'm so sorry," I say, trying to catch my breath. "I forgot to set an alarm. I think we still have time to do the flash cards if you want."

I sit down across from her, unzipping my backpack and

pulling out my history notebook. I slap it onto the table and start to open it when her hand slams down on the cover.

I look up at her, startled. Her emerald eyes are narrowed like she's trying to figure something out. Then they widen.

Shit.

"You didn't go home last night," she whisper-hisses.

"Uhm, what makes you think that?" I ask, biting my lip. I'm not sure what I should actually tell her, but I also don't want to lie to my friend.

"You're wearing the same clothes you were in when you left to go to the library," she says, looking at me deadpan.

I look down at my outfit, wincing. "Yeah, I guess I am."

"And your hair is in a ponytail."

"So?"

"You hate ponytails. You say they make you look like Paul Revere."

"Well, they do."

"That probably means your hair was messy and you didn't have time to do anything else with it." Her eyes light up and she leans forward. "You're hiding just-fucked hair! Oh my God, you were with one of the guys!"

"Shhh!" I resist the urge to press my hand over her mouth. I glance around to make sure no one is looking at us. "Don't say that so loud."

She's stares at me, her eyes huge and full of questions.

I shift nervously. "We should probably start studying."

"Screw that. Don't change the subject." She drops my notebook back into my bag. "Tell me *everything.*"

Maybe not everything, but I'll give her something, I think.

I take a breath, deciding what I should say. "Fine," I sigh. "I had a weird conversation with Serenity in the library last night."

"Go on...."

I nod hesitantly. "Promise you'll keep this to yourself?"

She nods back solemnly.

"Well, she admitted that Link and Trey and I probably crossed paths at my dad's business parties. And then she told me that Link's mom left and never came back, and John pretty much ignored him for two years."

Fiona looks thoughtful. "Aww, poor Lincoln—no wonder the guy is such an Eeyore."

Outside the coffee shop, the wind picks up, pelting a mix of hail and rain at the window, and I shiver as I stare at the roiling clouds.

"Anyway," I continue, trying not to smile at her comment, "the issues with his mom felt so similar to my own parental issues. I just had this overwhelming empathic reaction, and somehow, I ended up at Lincoln and Trey's dorm at like midnight."

"And then?" Fiona waggles her eyebrows at me suggestively.

I roll my eyes. "And then I made an idiot of myself when they caught me loitering outside their dorm like some sort of stalker." I lower my voice. "But yes, they invited me up, and yes, we talked about stuff. And then, yes, one thing led to another and somehow we all did...stuff."

"Stuff? All I get is 'stuff'? No details?" Fi says with an exaggerated pout.

"Yes, that's all you get."

"Wait...we? It was with *both* of them?"

"Erm, yeah. It was." I look down, my face feeling hot. I'm not really embarrassed by what we did, but I know it's not conventional, and I don't really want my friend to think I'm the slut of Whitmore U.

"Hey, Charlie, no judgment here," Fiona says, reading my mind like usual. I look up at her in relief. "Just, like I said before—guard your heart. Those boys are natural heartbreakers."

I sigh. "Believe me, I know. I didn't really mean for it to happen, and I care about them both. I don't even know if it means anything or changes anything. We didn't really get to chat about it before I left."

"Well, that's a complicated mess then, huh?" Fiona's lips curl into a small smile.

"No kidding."

My phone lights up on the table with a text message, and I see the time. "Shit, we should go to class," I say, standing up.

Fiona agrees, and we gather our stuff, pull up our hoods, and run out into the storm.

CHAPTER THIRTY

CHARLIE

$\mathcal{T}$he weeks leading up to Thanksgiving are busy, to say the least. Dr. Jackson selected Lincoln to organize our final project since John has stepped back from the theater, and I think he secretly loves the power because he begrudgingly accepted the role but then spent the entire hour of class telling the other students that their screenplay ideas were garbage like some sort of holier-than-thou director.

He didn't say anything about our project thankfully because I'm stuck halfway through my second draft now that my muse is slipping away–broody Lincoln was fueling all kinds of inspiration for my screenplay, but now that the three of us are in this undefined relationship of sorts, that passion has fizzled. Not that I'm complaining. I like orgasms more than him bullying me, but still, bliss, whether it's temporary or not, is not good for my writing career.

Serenity mentioned that the university make light of a rape accusation against Matt. I had Fiona ask around, but the rumor seems to have stopped dead in its tracks, so either it wasn't true or it was well covered up. I suspect the board wants to keep Matt here because the hockey team is a huge cash cow for the university. The guys are worried about me, and I get it, but I often wonder if their feelings come from Matt being an ex who hurt me or from an intuition that he's actually a predator. Either way, Matt has been showing up a lot lately, begging me to have coffee or lunch with him. And while he does make me uncomfortable, I'm not sure why because he's honestly been pretty nice every time I've turned him down.

The guys are in no hurry to define our relationship, but they've been more than happy to push the boundaries of whatever this is between us.

Trey has pulled me into every secluded corner of this university to do all kinds of wicked things to my body. He's cornered me in the library and empty classrooms and janitor closets. I always tell myself I need to stop. Every time I do more with him, I lose more of my heart. But I can't resist his stupidly hot face, especially when he looks at me from beneath that flop of golden-blond hair.

Lincoln, on the other hand, is way more cautious than Trey's overtly sexual nature. Yes, we have private moments together in their dorm, and he's certainly not shy in the bedroom, but I think our connection is causing him big feelings, and sometimes, I see fear in his eyes in the midst of sweet moments.

When he gets overwhelmed, Link throws himself into the theater. He doesn't talk much about what happened between him and John, but I get the impression that giving Link the theater was a peace offering between them, and Link is so passionate about the place, carefully selecting movies and curating old movie posters. He even replaced all the plain poster displays with neon-lit frames. Honestly, the place has a magical, cinematic vibe that reminds me of theaters from the eighties and nineties, when going to the movies was an epic Friday night adventure.

Little gestures seem to be Link's way of opening up. Last week, he finally let me screen one of the movies with him. And despite us being alone in that big, dark theater as we shared the armrest like a couple of awkward teenagers, we just enjoyed the movie. Neither of us acted on the sexual tension between us until we got home and practically mauled Trey.

Then, the other day, I came back to my dorm to find a package at my door with a note attached.

Don't say I didn't do my research. -L

I tore open the wrapping and found a special-edition copy of one of my favorite male-male romance books about two best friends (one straight and one gay) who eventually get together after a delicious amount of angst and turmoil. The entire book was littered with colorful tabs where Lincoln had made notes and underlined quotes.

He actually read this, I thought as I flipped through it, smiling to myself. I read the note again.

Does that mean he'd be open to doing more intimate stuff with Trey?

After that, I went to the library to try to get some reading done, but all I could think about was Lincoln and Trey kissing and jerking each other off, and before I knew it, I was squirming uncomfortably in my seat, and I had to get up and walk around to clear my head.

As if he could sense my thoughts, a strong hand grabbed mine and yanked me roughly down one of the aisles. I gasped, but I knew Link immediately from the woodsy scent, and I let him lead me to a dark corner. He pinned me against the brick wall, his intense gaze stripping me bare right down to my soul.

"We need to talk," he said, his voice deep and oh-so-sexy.

The smell of old book bindings mixed with his minty breath was completely intoxicating, and I threw myself at him, my mouth pressing to his. I think my impulsivity surprised him because he stiffened a moment before his body relaxed, and his hands grasped my ass and lifted me off the ground. I wrapped my legs around him and relished the heat of his touch.

Link's dick was rock hard, pressing firmly against my aching, soaking-wet pussy, and I was already losing my mind in a haze of pleasure as I whimpered into his mouth, grinding myself against him. He made a strangled noise in the back of his throat and finally pulled his mouth from mine. He continued holding me tightly, and we stared at each other, panting, still so close our noses grazed.

"I didn't bring you here to fuck you, Sunshine," he ground out, his voice raspy with lust, his grip on my thighs white hot and iron tight.

"I know," I replied. "I'm sorry. I missed you." I winced after I said it because I sounded so stupid and needy, but his metallic-gray eyes softened.

"I know" was all he said. *Han Solo arrogance at its best.* Then he sighed and put me down, leaning over to place one hand next to my head against the wall, his broody mask falling into place. "I think Trey and I are leaving tonight to head back home for Thanksgiving. We just wanted you to know since you have a late class."

I swallowed and nodded, trying not to feel disappointed as I averted my gaze. I figured they were probably going back to be with Lincoln's dad for the holiday, but I think a part of me was hoping they would stay. Being alone during the holiday has been the norm since my stepdad left, and my stepbrothers were always so busy with the pub.

"Thanks for telling me," I said, managing to keep my voice neutral.

Link's other hand came up, his fingers gripping my chin so I was forced to turn my head back to him. Then he kissed me hard before he left me alone in the stacks feeling like his dirty little secret.

Knowing they were leaving, I managed to track Trey down in the cafeteria, and he insisted on a quickie in the employee stairwell between the second and third floor—our most public rendezvous yet. He tugged my yoga pants down, pulled out his dick, and fucked me from behind, his hands rough on my hips as he slammed into my body over and over. It was ridiculously hot.

And that was that.

Most people left yesterday, including Fi, and now campus is pretty empty. Seb and Marcus asked if I wanted to come visit with them in Vancouver over the break, but since they're living in Canada, we'd already had our version of Thanksgiving in October, so I figured I would just stay and get more homework done and try to enjoy the peace and quiet. But now that Thanksgiving is here, I feel a little down.

I also finally started using the university gym. I used to play tennis and work out a lot when I was in high school, but that stopped after all the shit that happened. I'm just stepping out of the locker room when I turn into the hallway and run directly into a hard chest. One of my AirPods flies from my ear skittering across the hardwood floor.

"Gosh, I'm sorry," I mutter, moving to step around the person to retrieve the ear bud. A large hand clamps into my wrist, stopping my movements. I look up, realizing the person I ran into is Matt.

His palm on my arm is cold and clammy, and his grip is tight, almost possessive. The feel of it sends a shiver through my body—and not the good kind.

Despite the way he's holding me, his expression is friendly. I pull away, and he hesitates before releasing me.

I take a step back. "Hi, Matt," I say warily, still managing a tolerant smile.

Something about him still makes me so uneasy, and I can't

put my finger on what it is. I've been telling myself I'm still having lingering feelings of hurt and betrayal.

"Hello, beautiful," he says, running a hand through his short-cropped hair.

"Please don't call me that." I bend down to collect my AirPod.

"Why not? It's true." His smile falters like I've hurt his feelings. "I didn't expect to see you on campus. I thought you'd be home with your family."

"I decided to catch up on school stuff and make some extra money," I say vaguely, not wanting to give him any insight into my personal life. I certainly don't want him to know the part he played in my emotional spiral.

"You're working? Where?"

Fuck. I don't want to tell him, but he could probably find out pretty easily if he asked around. Not many of us work at the theater, and it's become a popular hangout, so a lot of people know Fiona and me just from seeing us there.

"The little movie theater on Main," I say hesitantly.

"Wow, that's cool. You always did love movies."

I hate that he still knows me. It's like he's holding some part of me hostage. It almost feels like a violation.

I don't want him to know me anymore. I want them *to know me.*

I try to push the guys out of my thoughts, but as I stare up at Matt, my nerves pick up. I'm alone here. If something goes sideways, Lincoln isn't going to come to my defense with fists flying; Trey isn't going to wrap me in his arms and soothe away my panic.

It's just me.

My heart rate kicks up at the thought, but I steel myself against the feeling. *I'm okay. I survived on my own for months.*

"When do you work next? I'll stop in for a movie," he says, oblivious to my inner turmoil.

"Umm, tonight. But aren't you going to see your dad for Thanksgiving?"

Something akin to anger flashes in his eyes. "We don't talk anymore."

"I'm sorry, Matt," I say awkwardly, but I can't say it's a bad thing. Even though I never saw it happen, I know Matt's relationship with his father was abusive, both mentally and physically, so despite how I feel about Matt, I'm happy for him.

"It's fine. You didn't know," he says with a shrug.

I edge around him. "Okay, well, I need to get back and change and do some homework before my shift."

"Sure. Maybe I'll see you tonight."

"Sure, maybe," I reply and practically sprint out of the double doors and across campus.

THE MOVIE THEATER IS DEAD. There's a couple making out in the back of auditorium three, and a group of professors came in for the last showing of *Top Gun* drunk off their asses—they walked through the door singing the worst rendition of "Danger Zone" I'd ever heard. Damon and I exchanged amused glances after we sold them their tickets, and they stumbled away giggling.

We're just starting to close up for the evening, working in companionable silence while he cleans and I count the till, when we hear a knock on the glass. I look up and see Matt standing outside the door waving at me with a smile on his face. My stomach does an uncomfortable dip.

Damon looks up, too, and then glances at me. "You know that guy?"

"Uh, yeah. An old friend."

Something about my tone must sound anxious because Damon gives me a serious look and adjusts the glasses on the bridge of his nose. "Do you want me to chase him off? I can pretend to be your manager and say you're busy."

I smile at him. "You just want to be manager for the night," I say, elbowing him teasingly.

The poor kid is broke and has been gunning for the assistant manager position that John mentioned a few weeks ago.

Damon smiles back at me, and we both turn when Matt knocks again, waving his hands in a 'what the fuck' gesture. I roll my eyes and look back at Damon. "Just, stay nearby while I see what he wants. I don't really want to be alone with him."

"Sure, of course," Damon looks like he wants to ask me about Matt, but he doesn't say anything else. Instead, he places a hand on my shoulder, giving me a gentle squeeze, and aims a hard look at Matt before returning to his closing duties.

I walk over to the door, turn the lock, and step back to let him into the lobby. I don't really want him to hang around, but I also feel bad making him stand out in the cold.

"What's up, Matt?"

"I guess I'm too late for a movie, huh?" he says with a faint smile.

"Yeah, unless you want to see the end of one."

He seems like he wants to come farther inside, but when I don't move, he leans back against the door, propping one of his dirty shoes against the glass.

"I just wanted to see you," he says. I notice his hands are shaking, and he quickly sticks them in his jacket pockets. "Can we hang out tonight? I'll buy you a coffee."

"I don't know," I say nervously, biting my lip. I hate the way his eyes track the movement.

"C'mon." He smiles in a way that used to induce butterflies but now just sends chills cascading through my body. "It's just coffee. I promise. We won't even stay out late."

When I hesitate again, he places a hand on my bicep. I look across the street, where I can see the bright coffee shop windows illuminating the wet sidewalk. There's several occupied tables.

It's a public place. What could he do? Plus, the thought of just going back to my dorm all alone right now sounds depressing.

"Okay," I say, shrugging away from him and fingering the end of my braid.

Matt frowns at the gesture before he realizes what I said.

"Really?" he asks eagerly.

"Yeah. Just give me about twenty minutes to finish closing up, and I'll meet you over there."

"Great." He gives me a wink before walking back out into the night.

Damon gives me a dubious look. "Coffee, huh? Does Lincoln know?"

I meet his dark blue eyes, amused. "Why would Lincoln care?"

Damon looks away quickly, the tips of his ears flushing pink.

"Damon," I say, lowering my voice sternly. "What aren't you telling me?"

"Well, you know how you guys are...whatever you guys are."

I'm not surprised he's noticed the tension between me and Link—the kid is super perceptive, preferring to observe rather than interact just like I do—and honestly, I doubt I hide my fucked-up, undefined relationship well.

I huff out a laugh and resume counting my till. "I have no idea what Lincoln and I are," I admit. "But he doesn't control whether I have coffee with someone or not."

"Well, of course not," Damon says. "That's not really what I meant. Lincoln is..."

"An asshole?"

Damon snorts a laugh. "Well, okay, that's fair. But he's also super possessive, and I know he hates that guy."

I stop midcount and look up at him. "How do you know he hates Matt?"

"I've seen him around here before, though I didn't know you knew him," Damon says with a shrug. "And when he tried to come in, Lincoln stopped him and got all alpha male in his face in the lobby."

My eyes widen. "When was this?"

"Maybe a few weeks ago, just after Halloween," he says thoughtfully.

"Then what happened?"

"I didn't hear what they said because their voices were all low and growly, but then Lincoln kind of pushed him, and he looked super pissed, but then he just turned and left," Damon says, shrugging. He gives an exaggerated shiver. "Honestly, though, that guy gives me the creeps—kind of a hot serial killer vibe."

I jump as one of the auditorium doors swings open, and the make-out couple walks out, their arms wrapped around each other's waists.

"Have a nice night," I say to them before I finish my counting and turn back to Damon. "Well, don't worry. It's just coffee. And while you're right, I doubt Lincoln would approve, he's not here right now, and he's only the boss of me while I'm working."

Damon shakes his head and smiles. "Your funeral if he does find out.

I LOCK the door and watch Damon disappear down the street. He made me promise to call him if Matt tried anything, and I told him I would. He's a nice guy, and I feel a little less anxious knowing someone is looking out for me.

The icy wind cuts through my clothes, and even though the distance to the coffee shop is short, I still put up my hood and run across the street, skipping around puddles to avoid soaking my boots.

I rush through the doors, savoring the whoosh of coffee-scented air that hits my face as I enter. I pull down my hood, glancing around before I notice Matt sitting in a booth in the corner. I walk to the counter, order a mocha, and then turn to watch him while I wait.

He's staring at something on his phone, and he hasn't noticed me yet.

He looks like a regular college guy, sporting a gray Whitmore U hoodie with matching sweatpants. His face is all hard lines and angles—he's obviously lost weight and gained muscle. His almost-black hair is longish, and it falls over his dark brows into his eyes. I'd probably find him attractive if I didn't know him.

I think of his eyes that night, so uncaring—no remorse or guilt. But maybe I remember it wrong. I was so distraught. Maybe he just made a mistake and he really does just want forgiveness. I wouldn't date him again, but I'm not above giving him a second chance.

Everyone deserves a second chance, right?

"Mocha for Charlie." The barista's voice pulls me from my revelry, and I take the drink from her, smiling.

I glance over again at Matt. He's waving in my direction, so I take a deep breath and walk over to the table.

"Hey, Matt," I say, setting down my coffee and throwing my backpack into the booth.

"Hi." He gives me a sexy smile, but it makes my stomach ache.

"So what's been going on?" He leans forward. "Tell me how school's been going."

"It's great here," I say, thankful that he's starting with small talk. "I think I'm doing pretty well in my classes, and I'm in the middle of applying for an editing internship with Rosewood in New York next summer.

"Sounds cool." His eyes narrow, but his tone sounds bored.

"I guess I've even made a few friends, too."

"Friends?" he says, tilting his head to the side. It's creepy the

215

way he moves, like he's one of those raptors from *Jurassic Park*—calculating and lethal. "You mean like Lincoln Evans and Trey Walker?"

Hearing their names fall from his lips immediately makes me bristle, but I swallow it down. "They're not who I was referring to, but I suppose you could say we're sort of friends," I reply tightly.

"You should watch yourself around those two," he says darkly.

His tone irritates me. "I think you've given me less of a reason to trust you than they have," I snap, glaring at him.

Anger flares in his eyes before he schools his expression. Then his face falls, and something close to regret shadows his features. "Low blow." He places his hand over his heart like I've wounded him.

I hope it hurts, asshole.

"But it's a fair thing to say," he continues. That comment surprises me. He sighs. "I know you said you're over it, but let me just talk this time. You don't even have to give me a response. Just listen."

I nod.

"I had a lapse in judgment," he starts. "We'd been together for so long, and I'd never been with anyone else. I guess I just wasn't mature enough to be in a serious relationship that young, and I fucked up. And, Charlie, I'm so fucking sorry. I don't expect you to forget, but I'm hoping you'll believe me when I say that I regret it. I regret hurting you."

I twist the end of my braid, somewhat stunned by his words because they make complete sense, and in the back of my mind, I wonder if he's just telling what he thinks I want to hear.

His eyes fall to my hands. "But obviously you don't completely believe me. That's fine. I just wanted you to listen."

"Why do you think I don't believe you?" I ask.

He tips his chin at me. "You fidget like that when you're

anxious. It's the second time you've done it tonight. I make you anxious."

"You do," I admit.

"How do I fix that?" he asks, his dark brows pulling together.

"I'm not sure you can." He drops his eyes, seemingly disappointed. "But," I say, watching as he glances back up at me. "I guess hanging out now and then is okay."

The corner of his mouth tips up in a small smile, and he sighs with relief. We sit for a few minutes as we sip on our coffees before he finally clears his throat.

"So the movie theater, huh? Do you get to, like, run the projectors?"

I nod. "I do. It's a fun job. Everything is pretty dated so we use a lot of old equipment, but I think that makes it more interesting."

My phone buzzes on the table, and I glance down, seeing Lincoln's name on the notification screen. My stomach does a little leap of excitement.

"Sorry, one second," I say to Matt. I pick it up and read the text.

LINCOLN

Call me.

I frown, my heart pounding in my chest. *Why would he want me to call him unless something's wrong?*

I look up at Matt, who's watching me intently. "Is everything okay?" he asks.

"Yeah, my friend is just having boyfriend trouble," I lie, hoping he can't read me like he used to. "I'll be right back."

I jump up and walk outside so I'm sure Matt can't overhear my conversation before I hit the button to call Lincoln. He answers immediately.

"Sunshine," he says, the timbre in his voice eliciting goosebumps down my arms. He sounds unhappy.

"What's wrong?" I ask, trying to keep the panic from my voice.

"What's wrong?" he parrots. His tone suggests I should know exactly what's going through his mind. "What's wrong is you're having coffee with *that prick.*"

My mouth drops open, and anger radiates through my chest. "And how would you know that? Is Damon your little spy now?"

"I called him to see how closing went and it just...came up," he says defensively.

"Uh-huh." My voice rises. "Well, last I checked, you're not my keeper, Link, so I can have coffee with whoever I want."

"Anyone but him, sure."

"Anyone. Period," I grind out through clenched teeth.

"Charlie, he's not a nice guy. He's dangerous."

My heart stutters when I hear my first name on his lips.

Even though I can't see his face, his voice is thick with emotions. I don't know what to do with this new side of him. I can handle him being an emotionally distant asshole and even a lust-driven idiot. But the vulnerability saturating his voice is bleeding me dry.

"Link," I say softly as I listen to his uneven breaths through the phone. "I'm fine. We're in a public coffee shop."

"I know," he says just as softly, and then he's so quiet that for a panicked moment, I look at my phone screen to see if he hung up. But then I hear him take a deep breath, and when he speaks again, he sounds more like himself. "Trey keeps telling me to trust you, and I do, so I won't come running back to campus like the obsessed asshole you think I am and use Matt Johnson's face as a punching bag."

"I appreciate that." My voice is heavy with sarcasm. "It's surprisingly good advice—you should listen to him."

He grunts doubtfully. "But we're going to talk about this when we get back. I'm not going to lie—the thought of you with other guys makes me rage, but you with Matt? Makes me down-right murderous."

"And why is that, Link?" I ask, not caring that I'm pushing his buttons.

"You know why," he snaps.

"Actually, I don't. Now I'm going back to my coffee date." I emphasize the word "date" to antagonize him just a little more.

"Charlie." Link's voice laced with warning.

"See you Sunday," I say sweetly before ending the call with a satisfied smirk. Then I power down my phone so he can't call me back and walk back into the coffee shop.

Matt and I talk for another hour until the employees start putting up chairs. We leave, walking out onto Main Street and making our way back to campus. I can feel his hand grazing the small of my back as we walk, and I fight the urge to walk faster so he can't touch me. I stop in the middle of the quad, not wanting Matt to know which dorm I'm in.

"Are you sure you don't want me to walk you to your place?" Matt asks. "It's pretty late."

"No, that's okay," I say. "I'm going to swing by the dining hall for a late-night snack before I head back."

He nods, seeming to accept my explanation. Then he steps forward, leaning in for a hug, but I step back. He raises his hands in a placating gesture. "Can't blame a guy for trying," he says with a wink.

I spin on my heel, about to run in the other direction, when his voice stops me. "Oh, and Charlie? I really would suggest staying away from Lincoln and Trey. You never know what guys like that actually want from a girl like you—I'd hate for your relationship with them to cause you...problems." Then he turns and leaves, walking toward the Elk Building, where all the athletes room.

CHAPTER THIRTY-ONE

CHARLIE

*a*s I enter the dining hall, I grab my phone from my pocket, curious about what time it is. Then I remember that I turned it off after I talked with Link outside the coffee shop. I hit the button to power it back on and glance around. This time of night, all that's open are some self-serve cereal stations and several vending machines.

A few students dot the long rows of tables, most of them with laptops or books open, shoveling cereal into their mouths. I walk over and grab a bowl and a small carton of milk from the mini-fridge. I yawn, fill the bowl with Lucky Charms and walk over to a table, throwing down my backpack and taking off my coat.

I consider doing something productive like writing, but I'm suddenly so tired. Adrenaline was humming through my blood the whole time I was with Matt, so now that I feel safe, I'm just drained. At the same time, I don't want to go back to my dorm. I know deep down what I want.

I pick up my phone and wince. I have nine unread messages, one from Trey and eight from Lincoln. I feel a twinge of guilt when I think about the way I reacted. For a long time, Seb was the only person who really cared enough to check in, and because I was so set on sparing his feelings, I learned to deflect and avoid questions and situations that might have made him think I wasn't okay. I'm not used to anyone else caring, and it feels strange.

I open Link's messages, and have to swallow the lump in my throat. He's definitely angry, maybe even hurt.

LINCOLN

Did you seriously just hang up on me?

Call me back. We're not done.

I'm serious, Charlie.

For fuck's sake.

Are you really going to ignore me?

Fine. Enjoy your date with that prick.

Just be safe.

Never mind. We're headed back.

I stare at his last text.
They aren't really coming back tonight, right?
I decide not to respond and open Trey's message instead.

TREY

Bennett, that wasn't nice. You don't play fair.
Text me when you turn your phone back on.

Is he okay? He said you're coming back.

The three dots indicating Trey's reply pop up on my screen, but they're blurry as I stare at them, and I realize I'm crying. I sniff and glance around, but no one seems to be looking at me.

Why the heck am I crying, I ask myself.

If I'm being honest, I miss them, which is stupid since they only left a day ago. I wipe my eyes angrily.

> **TREY**
> He's okay.

> I'm sorry. I didn't mean to upset him. He's just such an infuriating bastard.

> **TREY**
> You're telling me. I've been sitting here listening to him rant off every bad thing that probably happened to you. He was so paranoid it made me paranoid. You've really gotten under his skin.

My stomach flutters as I read Trey's reply, and a small smile curves my lips.

> And what about you? Have I gotten under your skin, too?

The dots appear and disappear a few times before Trey's response lights up my screen.

> **TREY**
> Baby, you've had me since the night of our first house party. I couldn't stay away even if I wanted to.

My stomach does a full flip, an unexpected ache blooming in my chest. The three of us are very different, but we're all damaged goods—victims of selfish parents and shitty circumstances—maybe that's why we work. Most people want to fix them, to fix me, but maybe we don't need to be fixed. Maybe we just need to be loved as we are.

As usual, I feel better after talking with Trey. He's not here with me, but even his simple texts somehow soothe my mood, like my own personal light in the darkness.

So are you guys actually coming back?

I wait for his reply, but when he doesn't answer, I get up and trudge back to my dorm room, my heart heavy. When I enter my room, I realize I'm not alone.

I cry out in surprise as I'm tugged into the darkened space. The door slams closed and someone spins me around, pinning me against it roughly. A hand slams into the wall beside my head.

My backpack falls from my limp fingers as I stare up into Lincoln's face, his gray eyes darker than usual, like gunmetal. They churn with rage, hurt, and a heavy dose of lust. He's panting hard, his breath coasting over my skin, the heady scent of mint and vodka permeating my senses.

"Are you drunk?" I ask. "Tell me you didn't drive."

"Actually, I drove," Trey says, and I look over Link's shoulder to find him lounging in my desk chair, spinning around like a little kid. Then Trey stops, turns on my desk light, and steeples his fingers, staring at me in earnest like Nick Fury in all his mysterious glory. He's seen one too many Marvel movies.

"I might've had a drink," Link growls. "You drive me crazy."

I still, my breath hitching as I turn my gaze back to him, and I want so desperately to touch him, but I'm not certain how he'll react. I lick my lips nervously, and Link follows the movement, his eyes dilating. His other hand, which still clutches mine tightly, feels like fire burning my skin.

"Tell me about your *date*," he grits out, his voice dangerously low.

I take a shaky breath. "We talked for an hour in the coffee shop, and then he walked me back to the quad."

"Did he try anything?"

"No."

"Did you want him to?" His features darken while he waits for my answer.

"No."

"You hung up on me. You turned off your phone."

"You pissed me off."

Trey chuckles, and Link closes his eyes, clearly trying to regulate a veritable storm of emotions.

I raise a shaky hand and cup his cheek, my thumb gently rubbing against his stubble. "You don't have to hide who you are or what you're feeling, Link. Not from me. I'm not afraid of you."

His eyes snap open, and I'm taken aback by the anguish I see in their depths. "I'm a controlling asshole."

"I'm used to it."

"You deserve better."

"So do you."

"Agree to disagree?"

Our faces are so close, our lips are touching when we speak, and the tension between us is thick. I feel like my body's vibrating.

Trey clears his throat. Lincoln turns to glare at him.

"You guys didn't have to drop everything for me," I say quietly.

Lincoln moves to sit on my bed and pulls me into his lap, his arms a possessive band around my waist.

Trey walks over and Link and I scoot closer to the headboard, making room for Trey at the foot of the tiny twin bed.

"We missed you," Trey says huskily. He cups my face in his large hands. The warm ambient light brings out the gold in his eyes and hair. "But we can leave if you want."

"No, it's okay," I say quickly.

"Your dorm is so small," Link says, looking around.

I roll my eyes at his rich-boy tone. "Not all of us can afford the penthouse. Have you guys never seen my dorm?"

Lincoln stiffens against me, and I look back at him. His eyes are fixed on my pillow, or more specifically, the stuffed cat next to my pillow.

I flush. "That's Ani, my stuffed cat." I elbow him in the stomach playfully. "You're not going to make fun of me for having a toy, are you? You have Ninja Turtles action figures in your kitchen cupboards."

"She may have a point," Trey mutters.

Link picks up the cat, running his hands through her faux fur, a smile playing on his lips.

"What?" I ask, staring at his amused expression.

"Nothing." He turns back to me, and his eyes are hungry again. My stomach flips when his fingers graze my neck, and I feel his erection hardening against my back.

Then Trey leans forward and presses his lips firmly to mine. When I open my mouth, allowing him access, he sighs happily.

My head spins as Link kisses my neck, his teeth nibbling and biting. His fingers inch under my shirt, pulling at the hem, and I break apart from Trey, allowing Link to pull the material over my head.

Trey's eyes lock with Lincoln's, the look communicating something. Then Trey stands, walks over to my desk, and turns off the light.

Link turns and wedges his body between my legs so that I'm looking up at him. He stands on his knees, fingering the button on his jeans with intent, but curiously, his hands are shaking. I reach for him, pushing his fingers gently to the side to help. Once Link's pants are off, I sense more than see him pull off his shirt. The room is so dark, I can hardly make out his silhouette. Then he leans over me, his body a warm, heavy heat against my skin.

I hear Trey's movements close by as he removes his clothing as well. Then the bed dips as he sits beside us in the small space, his hands tangling in my hair, but he seems to be letting Link control the situation. Trey's cock bobs close to my head, and he starts to pull on it in slow, languid strokes.

I moan when Lincoln grinds his dick against my pussy, our underwear the only thing separating us from complete skin-on-skin contact. Lincoln and I have never had sex, but I get the impression that he wants to now, and I know I certainly do. Being in the near pitch-blackness like this, it's an oddly familiar feeling. I've only experienced it with one other person—a nameless, faceless stranger I surrendered to and who somehow erased all my pain, if only for a little while.

The moment we're in overlaps with that memory, and it whisks me back.

TWO YEARS AGO...

"I want you," I breathe. "Please." And I grab his ass, pulling him closer to my aching cunt. His cock slides through my folds, his warm, sticky precum mixing with my arousal and creating delicious friction against my clit. Then I feel the head of his dick slide lower, lining up with my entrance.

I want him to fill me until I can't breathe.

Part of me is wondering if I'll regret it—giving my virginity to this strange boy with the magic lips and deep, sexy voice. There's an edge of tension to him, and he's been barely holding back, his hands playing my body with both gentle touches and rough possession—and surprisingly, I'm here for both. In fact, I know I've been pushing him. I want to feel him lose control so I can forget the shitty state of my life. And even though I don't know this person at all, my gut tells me he's safe—I can trust him.

Then he thrusts into me in one needy go. His cock feels impossibly huge as it enters me, burning its way into my body. I gasp, clinging to his shoulders as my nails bite his skin. The pain brings tears to my eyes, but I close my lids tightly and will them away, focusing on the warm, comforting heat of our flesh pressed together.

Despite the hungry way he entered me, he stills once our hips meet, allowing my body to adjust to him. His hand on my throat squeezes tighter, but the sensation doesn't evoke panic. Instead it grounds me, and I breathe in deeply.

Then he starts to move, pulling out almost completely before thrusting in, each movement taking him deeper inside me. I'm so wet, my arousal soaks into the comforter, and the burning sensation of being stretched is replaced by white-hot pleasure. I moan loudly, no longer self-conscious or afraid.

"Fuck," he pants as he thrusts back into me at the same time I utter, "More."

I can feel him shaking like he's trying to hold back. Like he doesn't want this to end. And I don't either.

His hand moves from my throat, skimming over one of my breasts and pinching my nipple. The pain mixed with pleasure pings through my body, lighting me up, and I grind my clit against his pelvis every time he pushes back into me.

I feel the moment when his control slips, and I bury my face in the crook of his neck, tasting his sweat, savoring how powerful it makes me feel knowing I did this to him.

His breaths quicken, becoming ragged, and the pulse in his neck flutters rapidly against his skin. His free hand grips me tightly, bruising my flesh, marking me.

I nip at the large tendon in his neck, and something between a moan and a growl escapes his lips.

"I..." Whatever he was going to say is lost as he slides back into me, hot and slick, and I clench around him as the most potent orgasm I've ever experienced tears through my body. I feel the jerk of his cock as he comes with a strangled cry. He pushes deep into me and holds himself there as he empties into the condom.

He collapses on top of me, but quickly rolls off so he's not dead weight. I blink into the stifling darkness. The only sound is our rhythmic breathing as we both lie there, speechless, boneless. The cool breeze from the open balcony door flitters across my overheated skin, soothing me like gentle fingers.

We're still touching, his arm pressed firmly against mine, and the sensation comforts me as my eyes drift closed and I sink into the first dreamless sleep I've had since my mother died—no voices or visions—just blissful nothingness.

"I CAN'T DO THIS." Lincoln's deep voice breaks through my memory, and my eyes refocus on his face.

Trey's hand stops mid stroke.

"What?" I go still.

We're frozen on my bed, his strong forearms still resting on either side of my shoulders and his warm breath tickling my swollen lips.

"I can't...I don't want to do this." Link rolls off me, his movements sluggish and defeated.

I can't help the feelings of shame and rejection that saturates my body, twisting my heart painfully. I cover my traitorous eyes with one arm, willing myself not to cry. It's an unwanted emotional response, and I swallow it down, knowing if it were me telling him no, I would want him to respect my wishes.

I clear my throat before I respond, praying my voice won't crack. "Did I do something wrong?"

I feel him turn his head in my direction, but I don't look.

Link stands abruptly, the bed shaking with the movement, and around my arms, I see the light come on.

"Where are you going?" Trey's voice sounds as hurt as I feel.

I can hear the rustle of clothing and then the sound of my dorm room door opening.

"I'm sorry. I need some air." Then Lincoln is gone.

I still refuse to uncover my face.

Trey stands and puts his boxers on before sitting down beside me on the bed and gently pulling my arms down. I stare at him, hating the tears that trickle down my face.

He pulls me up and against him, and I melt into his embrace, letting his warmth comfort me until the lump in my throat eases.

"It's not you, baby," Trey whispers. "Having sex is a big step for him."

I almost laugh. "I seriously doubt that Lincoln Evans has ever had problems with sex."

"Meaningless sex, sure. But you're important, and it scares him."

I swallow, wishing I could believe his words.

CHAPTER THIRTY-TWO

LINCOLN

I feel like the world's biggest asshole as I storm down the hallway from Charlie's dorm room and practically punch the elevator's call button to take me to the foyer.

I glance back. *Is she going to follow me?* If she does, I won't be able to stop myself. My cock is still painfully hard.

I feel so damn guilty.

I should have told her about that night before everything got this far. But fuck, how can I sleep with her now with this huge lie hanging over my head?

You already fucked her; you took her virginity and then left.

The elevator is taking its sweet time. I growl angrily, hitting the call button again before scrubbing a hand over my face and then practically running for the stairwell instead. As I jog down the stairs, the airs is too hot, and I feel like I'm suffocating.

I burst through the exit door, collapsing against the Raven Building's rough brick wall. I breathe deeply, letting the winter chill saturate my body.

Trey and I talked about this in the car on our way back from Brighton—me fucking her again. I thought I could do it but the way she wanted me was like *that* night all over again.

That unexpected, perfect, fucked-up night when I took her virginity, and she took my goddamn soul.

She still has it.

Ever since I had sex with her, I've only been able to fuck girls in the dark. I never wanted to see their faces because they weren't her.

I release a shaky breath and start walking back to my dorm.

I know what I want now. I want us all together. I like us together. She needs Trey, Trey needs her, and I need both of them more than I care to admit.

It feels like there's a lead weight on my chest. I want to give her every part of me, but I'm so fucking scared to lose her when she finds out all of my truths.

As if in response to my chaotic thoughts, the wind gusts, and I shove my hands in my pockets, hunching over against the icy blast that cuts through my clothes.

TREY

After Link left, I tucked Charlie in and promised her that we'd talk tomorrow. I tried to reiterate that Lincoln's reaction wasn't her fault, but she seemed doubtful.

Unfortunately, I've been waiting for something to trigger him. Link tends to panic and act out when life gets heavy. When Serenity confessed her love to him last year, he broke up with her and then went on a drinking binge that rivaled my greatest hits. But ever since Allie left us, he sees potential relationships as just another opportunity for someone to abandon him, so I figured this was coming as I watched him soften from Charlie's bully to her lover.

When I enter our dorm, I find him lying on the living room

floor next to an empty bottle of whisky, his arms and legs splayed out like a kid making a snow angel. His stares up blankly while quietly singing "Little Star" from *Romeo + Juliet*.

"Whoa, buddy, you okay?" I walk over and sit next to him.

He glances at me, the life returning to his stoney eyes. He smiles sadly but looks grateful to see me. Then, like he used to do when he had nightmares, he scoots close to me and lays his head in my lap. I run my fingers through his dark hair.

"Why couldn't I do it?" His breath reeks of alcohol.

"Do what?" I ask carefully.

A fat tear gathers in the corner of one eye and trickles down his cheek. "You were there. Charlie wanted me, and I said no."

"And why did you do that?" I ask softly.

When he looks at me, the pain in Link's eyes makes my heart ache. Even when his mom left, he opted for quiet resentment and anger. There wasn't a single tear in sight.

"It's just...I finally know what I want. I want her. And I know I've fucked it up before it even really began. How can I let Charlie in when she doesn't know everything? That her mom shredded my family, so I stalked her, hated her by default, and I intentionally took her virginity, for fuck's sake. All for something she had no control over. I was such a selfish prick, and she'll never forgive me for it."

"How do you know unless you tell her?"

"I'm not ready. I'm too much of a coward." He swallows, his Adam's apple bobbing with the movement. "But I can't lose her."

"If you push her away again, you'll lose her either way."

He nods mutely. "I know."

We sit in silence for a while, and he starts singing "Little Star" again. I hum along, still running my fingers through his hair.

"Trey?" he says finally, his gaze connecting with mine.

"Yeah?"

"Will you sleep with me in my room tonight?"

"Sure, buddy," I say, and I help him up, and we head to bed.

CHAPTER THIRTY-THREE

LINCOLN

*C*harlie and I have come to an understanding. I told her I was sorry the day after my asshole moment on Thanksgiving night, but I wasn't ready to talk about my issues, and she was certainly more forgiving than I deserved. I'm feeling extra guilty about the whole thing after Charlie's panic attack with us. Her mom was clearly very important to her, and despite how I feel about Ellen Conner, I don't want to damage Charlie's memory of her mother.

As the Christmas holiday approaches, the three of us are practically inseparable—so much so that rumors are starting to spread about the nature of our relationship, but she either doesn't notice (which is doubtful since Fiona is the queen of sniffing out gossip) or she doesn't care. We all sit together during meals now—and I do mean all of us. Serenity and Charlie seem to have called a truce of sorts, so while they don't acknowledge each other much, they at least seem civil.

I've also put a lot of energy into organizing Dr. Jackson's final project, which has kept my mind busy. I connected the theater students with our English/film class so that they can start going over scripts, and I've been working with the film tech geeks to get all the recording equipment we need to actually film the student shorts. The whole thing has been more fun than I expected.

With finals coming up, my afternoons with Trey and Charlie are spent studying in the library, sprawled over beanbags like normal college students. Charlie laughs a lot, and so do I for once. And honestly, I'm soaking up the idea that maybe this is what my life should be like and could be like—though that line of thought always leads me back to the shit I've been keeping from Charlie.

I've decided that I need to talk to my dad about everything. As painful as it is, I never asked him about his side of the story, and I feel like it might give me some closure and the courage to actually confess to Charlie. Plus, I'm hoping it'll help me to start to forgive him.

Today is a rare snow day in the Pacific Northwest, and Charlie manages to drag me from my comfort zone (but what else is new), showing up at our door adorned in a fuzzy green toque with a ridiculously big gray ball on the top and matching fuzzy mittens, her smile wide and infectious and her cheeks still rosy from the snow-laden air. She's fucking breathtaking.

"You look like a child," I say smirking as I pull on one of the long pigtails peeking from under her hat. She looks up at me, scowling, her forest eyes full of mock offense.

"I do not." She gives me her best pout, and my heart unexpectedly flips in my chest. She shoves me back into the living room. "Now go get Trey and get dressed so we can play in the snow."

I look down at her booted feet. "You're dripping onto my floor."

"You're such a grouch." She says and goes to push me again, but I catch her wrist, holding her in place. Her face is inches from mine, and I can feel her warm breath on my face.

Charlie leans forward and kisses me, her soft lips still cold from the outside air. I suppress a moan and swipe my tongue into her mouth, deepening the kiss.

Just then, an ice-cold jolt zips up my back and through my nerves like a full-body shock, and I jump away from her, yelping in surprise.

Charlie doubles over laughing.

"You play dirty," I say, rubbing warmth back into my skin and giving her a dark look, but I can feel the smile tugging my lips. She lunges toward me with her ungloved hand.

"Don't you dare touch me again," I practically shriek, dodging her grasp and vaulting over the couch to put something between us.

"What the hell is going on?" Trey walks into the kitchen, rubbing his eyes sleepily. He glances between us, and I look over at him in outrage.

"Our girlfriend just ambushed me with her cold, undead hands."

And then I freeze when I realize what I just said. We all do.

I look over at Charlie, who's regarding me with raised eyebrows, and then back to Trey, who's suppressing a laugh behind his hand.

Well, this is awkward.

I clear my throat and do what I do best—ignore the elephant in the room.

"What are you waiting for?" I say to Trey. "Get your hot ass dressed so we can properly retaliate."

I turn back to Charlie, who seems to have recovered from my verbal slip and is now regarding me with an evil grin as I eye my coat hanging behind the door.

Channeling my peewee football days, I fake left and then go right, darting around the couch. I grab my coat from the hook and wrap it around myself triumphantly. "Can't get me now, can you?"

Then I lunge for Charlie, going for a tackle. She giggles and ducks out of my reach before tearing off out the door and down the hallway, her boots slapping against the floors.

I slide on my boots, tying the laces tightly. Trey is shaking his head with an amused look on his face while he drinks OJ straight from the container like the Neanderthal he is.

"What?" I ask, standing.

"Well, one, you said my ass is hot—so thanks for that." He winks, and I feel my ears heat because that *did* slip out. "And two, it's just good to have you back, Link." He smiles affectionately. "I missed you, buddy." He puts the juice away, and walks back to his room to dress.

In a few minutes, we both head outside and into the falling snow, but naturally, we only last a few minutes before Trey starts whining that he's cold, so we bring the poor baby back inside. I'm walking backward, talking to Trey about our politics test, when I run directly into Charlie, who's stopped short at our front door. She's staring down at a large manila envelope that wasn't there when we left, and when I look closer, I see her name scrolled across it in large red letters.

Trey looks around me and frowns. "What's that?"

"I'm not sure." She picks it up and tears it open and pulls out some photos. My blood starts to boil when I see them: Charlie and Trey fucking against a tree in the cemetery; Charlie and I making out in the library; the three of us standing on this very spot—Trey is kissing Charlie, while I cup her ass, ushering her into our dorm.

Charlie's hands start shaking.

I snatch the pictures. "What the fuck?"

"Whoever took these has been following you for months." Trey grabs the photo of them. "This is from Halloween." His jaw ticks.

She looks in the envelope and pauses before pulling out a folded piece of paper.

I bet Rosewood Publishing would love to know what a little slut you are.

"Rosewood Publishing?"

She looks up at me, her eyes glassy with fear. "I'm applying to intern there this summer. I suspect that they wouldn't want to be associated with a sex scandal." Her voice is full of shame, and I hate that our relationship is stirring those emotions.

I tuck the internship information into the back of my brain to bring up later because why didn't she tell us about this? The idea that she'd leave this coast for months makes my stomach twist, and I don't really understand the reaction. But at the same time with all the secrets I have, can I really be mad?

"Do we know who would do this?" Trey interrupts my thoughts, taking the letter from Charlie and studying the messy script. "Because I plan on pounding his face in."

"You and me both," I mutter darkly.

Charlie glances between us. "It looks like Matt's handwriting," she says softly, and my brain detonates.

"I knew it! I knew that asshole was bad news, Charlie."

"He's been so nice..."

I take her face between my hands and dip my head to hers. "Please, Sunshine. You beautiful, stupid, way-too-nice girl. Stay. Away. From. Him."

Despite how I feel inside, I try to keep the bossy asshole out of my tone because I know it just raises her hackles.

She nods, the soft skin of her cheeks rubbing against my palms.

I pull her body against mine and hug her tightly, pressing my chin to the top of her head. Trey sighs behind me and squeezes my shoulder, giving me a look that says we're going to find and kill that bastard.

CHAPTER THIRTY-FOUR

CHARLIE

*W*inter break is days away, and for once, I'm not dreading the holiday time. Even though Marcus and I are still on the outs, I'm excited to see my stepbrothers. I'm not as excited to spend it at our childhood home—memories of that house are a mixed bag at best—but it's the first time since Martin left that we'll be together over Christmas. Ever since Seb graduated high school, he and Marcus would plan and host a holiday event at the pub, but this year, they decided to close up shop. Of course, that also means I have to finally explain the empty house when they get there, but I suppose I couldn't hide their dad's actions forever.

We haven't been able to track down Matt because the hockey team has been out of town for two away games in a row. It's been making the guys crazy, but since we can't actually prove the blackmail was him, there's not much we can do other than be more vigilant about how openly affectionate we are, which Trey is terrible at doing. The guy *has* to be touching one of us at all times.

Lincoln and Trey will be in Brighton for the break too, so I'm hoping to spend a couple nights with them. Hopefully, I can get a few meaningful conversations out of Link to see where we stand.

As far as Trey is concerned, I've come to the unfortunate conclusion that I'm falling for him pretty hard. I say unfortunate because I know this isn't his MO, and eventually he'll get bored with me and move on.

Nothing gold can stay, I think, and then realize I've probably been studying too hard if I'm quoting Robert Frost in my everyday life.

Regardless of what we may or may not be, Trey and Link have become my friends (with benefits), and I have a hard time imagining my life without them.

We're gathered on Link's bed, sifting through Netflix movies on Trey's fancy laptop. The boys are sitting with their backs to the headboard, and I'm lying diagonally with my head in Trey's lap and my feet across Link's legs.

We scroll past *Titanic*, and Trey side-eyes me with a smirk.

I flush and shake my head. "I promise I won't make you guys watch anything romantic."

"Romance is okay sometimes," Link says with a shrug.

"Oh yeah?" I say with raised brows.

"Depends on your definition of romantic, I guess," Link clarifies. "Give me your ideal romance movie."

I shrug. "I don't know." I feel self-conscious under their curious gazes.

"Okay, okay, try this then," Trey interrupts. "Most romantic movie line of all time?"

I smile. "That's easy. *The Empire Strikes Back*."

The guys stare at me in silence.

"Hold up," Trey says finally, his warm eyes twinkling with mirth. "Your favorite romantic line is Leia's 'I love you' to Han's 'I know'?"

"Yes?" I don't know why it comes out as a question. "C'mon, it's Harrison Ford after you've been watching him for two movies with his flirty half smirk and those tight pants…"

"He's old enough to be your grandfather," Trey deadpans.

"*Not* when I watch *Star Wars*. Han's character is forever in his twenties, and let's face it, he and Leia have a feisty enemies-to-lovers vibe. Their banter is top-notch."

"Wow," Link says, chuckling. "This is not a conversation I thought we'd ever have with a girl. *The Empire Strikes Back* through a romance lens? Unreal."

"Were you expecting something from *The Notebook*?" I ask with a raised brow.

"C'mon, Sunshine. There's a ton of stereotypical romance quotes that girls swoon over," Link says with a shrug.

"Such as…?" I challenge.

And like movie nerds they are, the assholes start spouting off movie lines shamelessly, each of them mimicking the respective character voices.

Trey: "'You complete me.'"

Link: "'You've bewitched me, body and soul.'"

Trey: "'The greatest thing you'll ever learn is just to love, and be loved in return.'"

Link: "'I would rather share one lifetime with you than face all the ages of this world alone.'"

"'I wish I knew how to quit you,'" Trey finishes with a grin.

"*Brokeback Mountain*. Good one," Link snarks, and they grin at each other knowingly.

"For fuck's sake," I mutter. "I'm impressed—except with Trey's British accent. That was awful."

Link laughs, the sound melting my insides like it always does, and I relax between the guys, letting them hash out which movie we should watch because I honestly don't care as long as we're together. Sometimes, I feel like they flirt with each other as much as they do with me, and it gives me all the butterflies. And despite the fact that our relationship remains undefined, everything feels so perfect, and in the back of my head, I wonder if it's just too good to be true.

"Are you sure you don't want to come home with me?" I ask Fiona again as I sit on her fluffy purple duvet, watching her pack.

Fiona's roommate, Catherine, glances over at me from where she's studying at her desk and rolls her eyes. "I offered the same thing, but the girl is stubborn."

"She's my mom," Fi says, smiling sadly. "I'm giving her one more chance to prove she's not a complete piece of shit. Worst case, if things go sideways, I'll just leave and come back here."

Fiona's visit with her mom over Thanksgiving was a train wreck. Apparently, Fi's mom and her new rich boyfriend went on a drinking binge, and she walked in on them fucking on the kitchen counter. Then to make matters worse, her mom was too hungover the next day to cook, so Fi had to lie to her extended family and order take out.

"Fair enough," I say, knowing even after everything my mom did, if she were still alive, I'd probably be giving her another chance too. "But promise you'll call me if you head back, and I'll come back, too. I can't stand the thought of you bumming around campus over Christmas by yourself."

"Fine," Fiona concedes, though I'm not sure I believe her.

"Well, I'm going head out." I put on Link's Whitmore U hoodie and shiver when I catch a whiff of his woodsy scent. "I want to get some writing done before Trey and Link finish their last final."

"You know you're done with school stuff, right? Your last final was yesterday."

I pick up my backpack off the floor. "I don't just write for school, you know."

"Ugh, right, right. My bestie, the great American novelist," she teases, tossing a scrunchie at me. Then she stops, eyeing me critically as I go to leave. "I know you insist you're not dating Trey or Lincoln...or both of them, whatever. But you sure have been wearing a lot of their clothing lately."

I glance at Catherine, who's suddenly watching me very intently. I clear my throat. "I'm leaving," I say, ignoring Fiona's shit-eating grin.

"And don't think I didn't see you sniff that hoodie like a creeper when you put it on!" she calls out as I close the door.

I frown, wondering if Catherine will gossip about that little interaction later. Now that we suspect that Matt has entered full stalker mode, interactions like that make me nervous. Not that I care about my reputation that much, but I do care about the internship.

I take the elevator down and walk out into the lobby. The rain is pummeling the windows, and I sigh as I put up my hood and tuck my long hair into it.

I actually own a raincoat, I think. *I suppose I should use it sometime.*

I sprint across the quad, heading for the humanities building, the heavy books in my backpack making my strides clumsy and uneven. With my head down, all I see are my green rain boots as I skip over muddy patches in the grass. I accidentally step into a deep puddle and stumble forward.

I cry out as I lose my balance, but a strong hand steadies me, halting my descent. I blink up through the raindrops coating my eyelashes and see Matt's blue eyes staring down at me. My stomach twists with dread. He's wearing a black raincoat with the hood pulled up, and it gives me ominous vibes like I'm staring at the red-eyed Matt from my nightmares. His gaze scans my soaking-wet body, and he frowns when he pauses on my oversized hoodie.

"Where are you going?" he asks, his voice as cold as the freezing downpour.

I yank my hand free, and I continue running toward the library, sighing with relief when I step into the warm foyer, my wet boots squeaking obnoxiously on the floor.

I hear Matt's heavy footsteps behind me, and the thrill of fear makes me dizzy as I turn to see him entering as well, shaking water from his coat.

"Don't you own a raincoat?" he snaps, staring disdainfully at my wet clothing. "And whose hoodie is that?" He has a sharp look in his eyes bordering on jealousy and rage.

I ignore his question, swallowing hard as I do my best to glare confidently at him, but my insides feel like mush. "I need to go study," I say, backing up.

"Didn't you finish your last final yesterday?"

I freeze. Foreboding prickles the back of my neck and sends a shiver through my whole body. "How did you know that?"

He smiles. "Did you like my gift? I really missed seeing your O face."

I know I should be afraid, but his words are infuriating. "Too bad I faked it with you."

Matt's eyes narrow dangerously.

Suddenly, a heavy arm falls across my shoulders, the familiar mix of apples and cinnamon tickling my nose and soothing my nerves. I relax into Trey's warm hold.

"What's going on?" he asks, glancing down at me before his eyes shift back to Matt, pinning him with a murderous glare. Neither one of us answers, and Matt stares darkly at the way Trey's thumb is tracing circles on my shoulder.

I look around. "Where's Link?"

"He and Brantley are just talking with our politics prof," Trey says, still watching Matt closely. But as if on cue, I feel Link before I see him. He steps up beside me, and tension radiates off him in waves.

"You have a lot of nerve, Johnson," Link growls, taking a step toward him.

I grab his arm, stopping him in his tracks. "Not here, Link," I plead.

Matt smiles widely. "Better listen to your little whore if you don't want me to ruin her life."

This time, Trey lurches forward, and I grab his hand, intertwining our fingers tightly.

"Back off, Matt," Trey practically spits. "Come near Charlie again and—"

"And what?" Matt sneers, taking a menacing step forward. The guys are in good shape, but I have to admit that Matt's hockey build is intimidating. "You can't touch me at this school, and you know it."

"Why are you doing this?" I ask him angrily, blinking back tears.

"I just want everyone to know what a little slut you are, just like your mother," he smirks. "You're certainly making the task easy." Then he bends down, leveling his eyes with mine. "I suggest you drop these two douchebags if you want to preserve your precious reputation." Then Matt straightens.

Frustration floods my chest as I watch him stalk away. His words play on repeat in my head. The way he spoke about my mom makes me angry, but a strange sadness settles in my chest as well because after all the years we spent together, he never really knew me at all. My reputation is irrelevant, but losing that internship over this? It would crush me.

"He's right, you know." Link says. "We can't do shit." He sounds frustrated.

"What if we file a harassment complaint with the police?" Trey asks.

"I don't think we can prove it's him who sent the photos." I fidget with my hair. "We'd have to record him threatening me or get him to admit it through texts. That'll be hard to do but not impossible, I guess." I stare at Link and Trey meaningfully. "But you guys *can't* pick a fight with him. We have to find another way."

"And what if he actually hurts you?" Link huffs. "I think maybe getting the jump on him is justified, babe."

"Violence is never the answer. You're such an alpha male sometimes," I say with a resigned sigh.

Trey snorts a laugh, his fingers relaxing in my grip. "Sometimes?"

Lincoln gives a small smile, the tension in his body easing. "It's part of my charm."

We walk toward the library entrance, and I glance at Link. "I'm not sure charming is a word I'd use to describe you."

"What do you mean? I can be charming." Lincoln frowns. "How would you describe me?"

I tap my chin thoughtfully as we sit down at a table near the front of the building. "Moody, confusing, definitely possessive..."

"A picky eater, and doesn't play well with others...," Trey cuts in.

Link glares at his friend. "Okay, asshole, I'm not a toddler."

"I would add grouchy," I say with a giggle.

Link's dark stare turns to me as Trey barks a laugh, earning a scowl from some nearby students. Link sets up his laptop and pointedly ignores us, though I see the smile playing on his full lips.

I pull out my notebook, trying to act normal, but underneath our banter, the tension from our encounter with Matt hangs heavy, and a sense of helplessness washes over me when I realize that Matt was right: he's untouchable, and I'm not. Working as an editor in New York has been my dream for a long time. Can I sacrifice everything I've worked toward to be with Trey and Link, or more importantly, should I? Anxiety swirls in the pit of my stomach when the answers elude me.

CHAPTER THIRTY-FIVE

TREY

"So Charlie said she's coming to your place tonight?" Link asks for the millionth time. We're back in Brighton for Christmas, and we made plans to see Charlie later. "You have no chill. Maybe we should have waited a couple of days. Don't we seem kind of desperate or something?"

"Okay, one, we're not in high school, Link, so I could care less about seeming desperate. And, two, why wouldn't I invite her? I mean, it's an empty house, and we are fucking her pretty regularly."

He gives me a dark look and flops onto his bed. "Technically, you're the only one fucking her right now."

"Right," I say, raising an eyebrow at him. "Why is that again?"

"You know why," he says. "I want to talk this shit out with my dad, so he better get his ass home soon."

I lie down on the bed next to him, staring up at the little glow-in-the-dark stars on his ceiling—the only reminder of our childhood in his now boring-ass gray and navy bedroom. "Should I be offended you're all about asking dear old dad advice, but you haven't bothered to ask me what I think you should do?"

"I know what you'll say," he says, turning his head to look at me. His eyes are sad—two pebbles lost in a turbulent gray sea.

"And what's that?" I ask quietly.

"That I need to just do it—tell her everything, including how I feel about her. Always the enduring optimist, you believe she'll still care about me anyway." He takes a shaky breath. "But here's the thing. I don't believe that. And other than you, no one's ever cared for me the way she does. Even my parents' love was conditional."

The truth makes my heart ache for him. My parents are shitty, selfish people, and they never loved me—I accepted that years ago. But listening to Link's voice, thick with pain, I almost wonder if it's worse to know your parents love you but only when it suits them.

"If you think that, why does your dad's opinion matter so much? Have you finally forgiven him?"

"Maybe I'm starting to." Link's quiet for a moment. "For years it seemed like my dad was trying to buy my love back, especially when he offered me the theater. It felt like a bribe—something to assuage his guilt for being a shitty father—but now the theater is a refuge when I feel overwhelmed, and I can see it as more of an apology than a bribe."

I inch a little closer so that our arms touch. "Do you remember when we were kids and I was obsessed with that Ironman action figure?"

Lincoln glances over at me, seeming confused by my change in subject, but he answers nonetheless. "You mean the Ironman *doll* you carried around everywhere?" He snickers. "I called it your emotional support Ironman."

"Hey, man, don't hate on Tony," I say with a rueful smile. "He was my idol, hiding all his emotional damage under a cool façade of sarcasm and humor."

"That *does* sound familiar," Link playfully pushes his shoulder against mine.

"Anyway, it was the last Christmas present my dad gave me before they left. I moved in with you guys the January after that. Do you remember what happened to it?"

"I remember," he says, his smile faltering. "I was pissed at you because you kicked your way through my Lego Death Star, so I took Ironman and rode my bike out to Pine Point." He swallows heavily. "And I threw him into the ocean." He frowns at the memory. "I felt fucking terrible afterwards. I still do."

"Yeah, and I was devastated when you told me. But you know what? I understood why you did it, and I loved you, so I forgave you. Sound familiar?"

"C'mon, man." He runs a hand through his hair. "This isn't two kids fighting over stupid toys."

"He wasn't a stupid toy to me, Link." I say quietly. "I was ten, and he was all I had left of my father. You were just more important to me than anything else, especially that piece of shit." I sigh heavily. "I feel like I've gotten to know Charlie pretty fucking well over the last few months, probably better than anyone but you. And the way her eyes light up when she talks about you—I know she hasn't said it, but she loves you, dude. So much." I huff a small laugh. "I'd be jealous if it was anyone but you. She needs you, Lincoln, and you sure as hell need her. So yeah, you're right, I believe she'll forgive you. I mean, someone in this little throuple we have going on has to be the optimistic one, right?"

"Ugh, gross," Link says, giving me a mean side-eye. "Don't call it that."

I chuckle.

We lie in silence for a while before his head tilts to the side to rest against mine. He clears his throat.

"Trey…"

"Yeah?" I turn my face toward him, and my breath catches at the proximity of our lips—they're practically touching, his breath coasting over my cheeks. His gray eyes bore into mine, and I stay completely still, unsure of his intent.

"I'm not very good at expressing myself like you are, but I hope you know how much you mean to me." His voice is a low rumble, and I try to force my cock from responding to his proximity, but his body heat and the woodsy smell of his skin are doing weird things to my insides.

"I know, Link." My voice sounds gruff. I nod as I say it, our lips brushing with the movement, and my heart starts pounding. Link's gaze bounces between my eyes and my mouth, and my exhale stutters when he presses his mouth gently against mine.

I close my eyes, letting him lead as his soft lips slide against mine. It's not aggressive and possessive like he often kisses Charlie —it's hesitant and sweet, like he's not sure it should be happening in the first place—but it makes me crave more. I push myself up, leaning over him to get a better angle, and I place one hand on his cheek, gently scratching Link's stubble with the tips of my fingers.

He groans and pulls back, and we break apart, staring at each other in shock, panting quietly. I glance down at the evident bulge in his sweats. I mean, obviously, I knew that Link was cool sharing Charlie, and I even think he's considered fooling around with me while she watches. But last I checked, he was still straight.

"I'm sorry," he mutters, but he doesn't move, and the blush that rises to his cheeks is a-fucking-dorable.

"For what?"

"I think I crossed a line."

"Link," I say with a gentle sigh, my thumb still grazing his cheek, "you're my best friend, and I've always respected your boundaries, but I won't lie—I have been in love with you for years. There's nothing to apologize for." His eyes widen, and he swallows. "But you are straight...right?"

"I…I don't know what I am." His dark brows furrow in confusion. "I'm not really attracted to guys, but I am attracted to you. Is that okay?"

"Of course. It's okay to love without a label, Link."

He nods hesitantly, and I lean forward, kissing him again because, goddamn, I've wanted to for so long, but I know we have other plans tonight, so I pull away before we go too far.

I sit up, looking down at him with a reassuring smile. "I'm gonna take a shower. I'll see you at dinnertime?

He nods in response as I leave his room, horny as hell.

LINCOLN

In the background, my speakers are quietly playing Coldplay's "Fix You," the lyrics making my chest ache as they seem to mock my current predicament.

I've been considering my complex feelings for Trey ever since we started sharing Charlie. I don't regret kissing him, but in that moment, I felt like a teenager again, the fear of rejection lurking heavily in the back of my mind.

I really need to tell Charlie the truth.

For once in my life, I want to do better, be better—because of them—and ironically doing the right thing might be the reason Charlie leaves me. And I can't say if I'd survive that loss. As much as I hate to admit it, Charlie's been under my skin since I caught sight of her at my friend's party years ago— maybe even before then. I think back to my memories of little Charlotte Bennett, a diligent shadow at her stepfather's side through every party. And Matt was always there with her, schmoozing to be part of the boys' club from a young age. I swallow the anger crawling up my throat as I realize how much of her life that sweet, naïve girl gave to that prick.

The first time I saw her, I was thirteen, so she must've been ten or eleven.

TEN YEARS AGO...

I walk into the Conners' home reluctantly that evening. It's winter break, and the last place I want to be is bumping elbows with my dad's stupid-rich contacts, but apparently, thirteen is the magic age when I have to start learning about the family business. It's all boring as hell if you ask me. If this is my future, count me out. And to make matters worse, Trey is at home sick—the lucky bastard—so I'm stuck at this hoity-toity party all by myself.

I'm standing at the bar, trying to snag a glass of champagne unnoticed when I see two kids close to my age across the room. The girl looks younger, and she's scrawny—all elbows and knees—in a little pink lace dress that looks out of place with her disheveled wavy brown hair. There's a dark-haired boy at her side who's mostly forgettable, but the way his hand grips the skirt of the girl's dress almost possessively, so tightly his knuckles are white, makes me instantly dislike him. My eyes drift back to the girl, and I hold back a smile when I notice she's wearing sparkly silver Converse—no doubt, a scandal at a party like this.

I give up my ploy to steal alcohol and walk over to where my parents are chatting with a small group. "Who's that girl?" I ask my dad, tilting my head in her direction.

"Oh, that's Martin's stepdaughter, Charlotte," my dad replies before continuing his conversation.

A woman standing next to my dad looks over at Charlotte scornfully. She lowers her voice slightly before speaking. "Poor Martin

Conner got stuck with that disgrace of a girl. Honestly, did she even brush her hair?" The woman next to her snickers, and I glare at them both. Rich people are such judgey assholes sometimes.

I'm still watching Charlotte as she shifts from foot to foot, smiling politely. She looks as bored as I feel, and I consider rescuing her from the monotony of it all, but something about the boy at her side makes me uncomfortable, so I reluctantly stay put. I start feeling itchy and hot in the starchy clothing my mom made me wear, so I release the top button on my shirt and roll up my sleeves to get some sort of relief.

"Hey, you're Lincoln, right?" I turn around to see a brown-haired boy with big blue eyes standing behind me smiling.

"Uh, yeah, that's me," I say slowly.

"I'm Sebastian," he says. "Do you want to get out of here? My friends and I are hanging out in our pool house." He pulls me by the sleeve away and looks around as if he doesn't want to be overheard. "I nicked a bottle of whisky," he whispers.

"Absolutely," I say with a grin. "Lead the way."

I THINK something about that little girl must've stayed in my head from that day on. For years, we went to parties at her family's estate, and every time, my eyes would seek Charlie out before I snuck away with the rest of the delinquents. I don't know why I did it. We never spoke, even after I left her that stuffed cat. And I never really thought about how strange it was until recently. But maybe subconsciously, I knew I needed her even back then.

I blink as a noise downstairs rouses me from memory lane, and I realize it's probably my dad. Nerves settle in my stomach. I'm still so angry at my mom for leaving. But the anger I felt towards my dad is waning, and I'm finally ready to talk about what happened.

I walk downstairs and into the kitchen, finding my dad just

sitting down to eat a sandwich. I glance at the clock over the stove, realizing with surprise it's closer to dinnertime than I thought. He looks up when I enter, and gives me a smile.

"Hey, kid." I grunt in response. "Make yourself some dinner," he says, nodding at the ingredients still laid out on the counter. He looks tired, dark circles evident below his deep blue eyes, and his clothes are rumpled like he slept in them.

"Thanks, but I'm waiting on Trey to eat." I frown. "How long have you been home?"

"Not long. But you know me—nervous flier—so I haven't eaten since I left London this morning." He eyes the sandwich with something akin to love, and I almost smile. "I've been dreaming about this ham sandwich since I landed a couple hours ago." He takes a large bite with a half moan, half sigh.

"Jesus, Dad. Buy it a drink first," I say sarcastically.

"Funny," he says, looking back up at me.

"How was your trip? You look wrecked."

"It was stressful. International investments are a whole different animal, and I have a lot to learn."

"I'm glad you came back in time for Christmas." I rub the back of my head awkwardly.

My dad's expression softens. "I think I need to make up for some lost time, don't you?"

I nod and swallow the lump in my throat.

"So, what're you boys up to tonight?"

"Nothing really. Just going to stop by Trey's house for a bit." I scrub a hand through my hair. I don't go into any more detail, and he just shrugs with a nod, used to my standoffish bullshit. Trey's parents are never home, so we go there when we're in Brighton for a little extra privacy. When we were younger, it was to get wasted or do drugs, but now it's so we can fuck around with our girl in peace. Times change, I guess.

Planning on a late night, I walk over to the coffee machine

and start a fresh pot before turning back to my dad. Even though our relationship has become tolerable over the last few months, it's still not where it was before my mom left. I'm not sure it'll ever get back there.

"Dad, I need to talk to you…about Mom."

My heart thunders in my chest. *Why am I so nervous?*

His gaze meets mine, his brows raised in surprise. "I want to know how it happened. I want to know why you cheated with Ellen Conner."

He puts down his sandwich and finishes chewing as he studies me. At first, I think he's going to tell me no, but finally he clears his throat.

"Okay," he says, his voice rough with emotion. "As you've heard before, your mother and I were best friends from the time we were kids," he starts, and I nod, remembering the stories they told me about how they were inseparable as children. "And it just made sense that after high school we'd get married. I loved her very much, and I still do despite everything, but we were never *in love*—she didn't complete me."

I scoff. "Life isn't *Jerry Maguire*, Dad."

"No," he says firmly. "It's not. But hear me out." I nod that he should continue. "Our relationship was comfortable, but it was never passionate—no love story for the ages—as you just pointed out. But I was okay with that. Until I met Ellen. We resisted each other for a long time—years, actually. We both had families and obligations, not to mention Martin and I had done business together. When we finally did get together, it was my fault."

He rests his head in his hands for a moment, and when he looks up again, his eyes are red and glassy. "I'm good at shutting out emotions until I'm not, and it takes something catastrophic to break my resolve. Ellen was that catastrophe, chipping away at my metaphorical walls until the day they just broke."

That sounds familiar.

Charlie cracked my emotionless exterior as easily as you'd crack open a beer when no one else could even come close.

"We went about everything the wrong way because we were ashamed and scared. Instead of talking with your mom, I went behind her back. It's no wonder she left the way she did. We used to tell each other everything, and I betrayed her trust spectacularly—unforgivably." He blows out a shaky break. "I lost everything after that night. Your mother, you, Ellen…"

My dad's face crumples, and for once, I see him. It's the same paralyzing fear I have when I think about telling Charlie my truths. I could lose everything. But his words still twist my heart painfully.

"You didn't have to lose me," I say, frustration making my voice crack. "I was right here, Dad. And I needed you!"

"I know, kid. That was my fault. I shut down, especially after Ellen…" He takes a deep breath, not willing to bring up her fate. "I have no excuses, and you didn't deserve that." He stands, comes around the counter, and faces me. "You may look like me," he says quietly, "but you have your mother's eyes, and I just couldn't bear to see you day in and day out—not without seeing her—so I left. And I'm so sorry, Link."

I stare at him, hot tears stinging the backs of my eyes. Then he hugs me. I stiffen at the unexpected contact, but then the little boy in me who just misses his parents takes over, and I relax, pressing my face into his shoulder with a choked sob.

My dad's hand presses to the back of my head, and we stay like that for several minutes, both of us coming to terms with our long-repressed emotions. I finally pull back and look away, rubbing moisture from my face.

"Not that I mind having this long overdue conversation with you, Link. But why is this coming up now?"

I look down at my bare feet. "I made a mistake, and I think it's going to hurt someone I…love."

"Is this about Charlie?"

I look up at him. "How did you…"

He chuckles. "I've been around you two at the theater enough to see how you both look at each other. Though I have to say, son, I think Trey has his eye on her, too."

I bark a laugh. "You have no idea."

"Is it complicated because she's Ellen's daughter?"

"It was…" I debate whether I should tell him the whole sordid story, but my dad speaks up before I can really answer.

"Look, Link, you don't have to tell me what happened. All I know is since you met that girl, you've been happy—anyone with eyes can see that. My biggest mistake was being a coward. I should have been honest with your mom about my feelings for her and for Ellen from the start. And Ellen should have done the same with Martin. But sometimes adults fuck up. The best advice I can give you is to tell the truth." He gives me a sad smile, and for the first time since I caught him and Ellen in his office that day, my heart aches for him. "Worst case, you lose her. But if you don't tell her, that will probably happen anyway. The difference is whether or not your honesty makes you redeemable."

"What if I'm the villain in this story?" I ask quietly.

"Even some of the worst villains have atoned for their sins. Look at Darth Vader, Loki, Boromir, the *T. rex* from *Jurassic Park*."

My lips twitch with amusement. "Nerd," I say, shoving him playfully. He smiles, but mine falters. "I don't think I deserve redemption, Dad."

"That's not up to you. That's Charlie's choice to make. And if it means you'll finally find peace, I hope you accept her forgiveness and move on. You deserve to be happy."

"Thanks. I'm glad we could finally talk."

"Any time, kid."

I walk over to the coffee pot and pour two cups of coffee before I turn to head upstairs.

"You're seeing her tonight, huh?" my dad asks.

I look back, nodding, and then I walk back to my bedroom, anxiety and fear churning my stomach because I'm going to tell Charlie everything.

CHAPTER THIRTY-SIX

CHARLIE

*D*owntown Brighton is bustling with nightlife as I drive through on my way to Lincoln and Trey's neighborhood. The crowd is mostly college students who are home for winter break or high school students with fake IDs, if I had to guess. The streets are brightly lit with strings of colorful lights, and several blocks away, the town's large Christmas tree twinkles merrily in the center of Waypoint Park.

Brighton isn't very large, so as I leave downtown behind, I turn onto a quieter side road within a few minutes. Streetlights illuminate an impressive collection of large houses all with winding driveways and wrought-iron fencing. Clearly, these people have money.

I pull up to a locked gate, but it buzzes open right away, so I'm guessing the boys saw me coming, and I continue up the driveway to park in front of one of three garage doors. I sit in my car for a minute, staring at the house, my nerves chipping away at my confidence. But then the front door opens, and Trey leans against the doorframe, all long legs and a sexy smile on his full lips. Butterflies chase away any anxious thoughts because this beautiful boy is inexplicably into me, and I'm so here for it.

I open my door as he approaches the car with a cocky swagger. "C'mon in, Bennett," he drawls, reaching out his large hand and linking our fingers together. The warmth where our skin touches infuses my whole body, and I step closer as we walk inside together, breathing him in.

I look around as he leads me through the house and down a long flight of stairs. "Are your parents home?" I ask.

"Not a chance," he says. "My parents hardly ever venture back stateside, even for the holidays, so we come here when we want...privacy."

"Oh." The way he says the word "privacy" has my pussy heating up and clenching like the horny bitch she is, and I'm suddenly more than ready to move on to the next step with Trey and Link—if we're all on the same page, that is.

I stop when we reach the bottom of the steps, my mouth dropping open. The room opens up into a mini-theater. A few rows of couch-like seats face a literal stage outfitted with fancy light fixtures and state-of-the-art speakers. A white projection screen hovers just in front of the stage. A long, low table sits in front of the first row of seats, stocked with a large bowl of popcorn and various snacks and drinks.

"This is incredible." I release Trey's hand and run over to one of the couches so I can sink into the plush material.

He chuckles and sits beside me, pulling me onto his lap. "Yeah, when your mom is a rich stage actor, this is what the media room looks like."

I look up at him, getting lost in the whisky brown of his eyes, and his lips fall to mine. The kiss is slow and gentle, and I savor the taste of him, moaning into his mouth as I feel his cock harden against my ass.

I change positions, straddling his legs, and he pulls me closer, his fingers tangling in my hair, deepening the kiss until my head is spinning. My panties are already damp as I start to grind against Trey's hardness, making him groan. "Fuck, Bennett..."

"Get a room."

I jump, breaking my kiss with Trey. I look back at Lincoln as he walks toward us, a smile tugging at his lips. He looks delicious in his dark jeans and a gray Henley, the material of the sleeves tight around his biceps.

"Cockblocker," Trey mutters as I climb off of him and stand, turning toward Link. He stops, cocking an eyebrow at me. It's only been about a day since I saw them at school, but I'm seriously craving them both.

I close the distance between me and Link, my arms circling his slim waist as I bury my face in his chest, inhaling his intoxicating sandalwood scent. He hesitates as if surprised by the hug, but then his strong arms wrap around my body, crushing us so close together I can hear his rapid heartbeat. It's not a friendly embrace —it's intimate, and it breeds tension that has my body shaking with the need to escalate it into something more sensual, but I hold back. My cheeks heat as I feel his dick thickening against my stomach, and he finally pulls away with a resigned sigh.

Link sits down heavily on the couch, pulling me down between him and Trey. Then they both slide away from me so we aren't touching as if some distance between us can defuse the sexual tension in the air.

"Should we watch a movie?" Link asks, picking up the remote. Trey and I both nod. "Any preferences?"

"Oh no," I say, pursing my lips, "I'm not doing this again. Last time, it took us ages to decide what to watch. Why don't you choose since you're the cinephile."

Lincoln shrugs and starts shuffling through an outrageously large selection of films, finally deciding on *Scott Pilgrim vs. the World*. I settle between the boys, leaning my head on Trey's shoulder and tucking my feet under Link's warm thigh.

We're only up to Ramona's second evil ex, who I had completely forgotten was played by Chris Evans, when Trey's phone starts to buzz. He glances at it, rolling his eyes.

"It's my parents. They like to call around the holidays—it's the one time of year they pretend to actually give a shit."

I sit up from my cozy spot against Trey, and Lincoln pauses the movie, then throws an arm around my shoulders so I have a new warm body to lean against. Not that I'm complaining. I take a long pull of my Diet Pepsi.

"Hey, Ma," Trey answers, putting her on speaker phone.

"Atreyu, darling, Merry Christmas." I choke on my drink, almost spitting it into Link's lap, and cover my mouth quickly. Link snickers and pats my back. Trey's eyes narrow at me.

"Atreyu?" I mouth.

"What was that? Do you have friends over?"

"It's just Lincoln, Ma. We're watching a movie."

"Oh, that's nice." She sounds like the world's snobbiest snob, and I wrinkle my nose at the emotionless way she talks to her son. "Your father is here."

"Hello, son," he says, sounding distracted. "I hope school is going well."

"Sure, Dad, straight As."

I raise my eyebrows because I know that's a bald-faced lie. Trey just shrugs. He clearly wants the call over with, which makes me sad.

"Good, good," his dad murmurs.

"I was just cast as Lady Macbeth," his mom says, sounding smug. "We'll be doing a run in the Globe Theater in London."

"That's great, Ma," Trey says, his voice strained with fake excitement.

"I just wanted you to know because I didn't want you to expect us home during the summer this year."

"Oh, okay."

"Anyway, have a lovely holiday, dear."

"Thanks, you too." The smile on Trey's face is tight, even though she can't see him. Then the line goes dead.

We sit in awkward silence for a beat before Trey glances at me. "Well, that was depressing."

"Always is," Link mumbles, his brow lowering in frustration as he watches his friend.

"Wait, wait…" I say. "Is no one going to address the fact that your full name is *Atreyu*? As in the character from *The Never-Ending Story*?" My eyes bounce between them. "How did I not know this?"

Lincoln chuckles, and Trey rolls his eyes. "Yeah, yeah. It's not like I made it public knowledge after high school. My parents were Gen X nerds just like yours. Most people had forgotten until my senior year of high school when *Stranger Things* made it popular again."

"I love it."

His eyebrows draw together in confusion. "What?"

"Well, that movie is a cult classic, so I think it's a cool name," I say with a grin. "My parents almost named me Buttercup."

"What?" Link and Trey say together.

"Like you said, Gen X nerds," I snark with a grin. "*The Princess Bride* was my mom's favorite movie."

"That would have been dope," Link smiles. "But I'd probably have to call you Princess instead of Sunshine."

I wrinkle my nose. "I like Sunshine better."

After that, we settle back down to watch the movie, and I'm almost asleep by the time the credits roll.

"Bennett?" Trey says softly, running his fingers along my jaw.

"Mhmm." I don't want to move. Trey's deep chuckle makes my insides tingle. I sit up reluctantly and stretch my muscles. "It's pretty late…," I start, hoping they will ask me to stay. I glance at Link. He's rubbing his hands on his jeans and when I study his face, his bottom lip is pulled between his teeth.

"What's going on?" I ask him with a frown.

"I need to talk to you." Link's voice is serious and subdued.

My stomach twists with dread as I take in his grave expression and his stormy gray eyes. I glance at Trey, thinking he might leave and give us privacy, but he moves closer to my back as if to steady me.

"I don't really know how to start this conversation, so I'm just going to say it."

"Okay…"

"I know who your mom was sleeping with," he starts, licking his lips. "It was my dad. Ellen was the other woman." As much as Link is trying to keep the vehemence from his voice, it seeps out of his tone as he says my mother's name.

I frown in confusion. "Your dad? John?"

Then I think about what Serenity told me, and the similarities of our family drama fall into place like some sort of fucked-up puzzle.

"Okay," I say slowly, "that's not so bad. I knew my mom cheated. Are you about to tell me that we're long-lost siblings?" I quip, but the joke falls flat when neither of them responds.

"There's more," he says, and his tone is laced with regret and remorse. "I was so angry and hurt by everything that followed— my mom leaving, my dad shutting down. I loved my family. We weren't perfect, but somehow we weren't like the other rich families in this town. We didn't let money run our lives, or at least that's what I thought as a kid. And when I was ten, my best friend came to live with us and became like my brother."

I nod since I know most of this story already.

Lincoln clears his throat and sits up straighter. "So in the aftermath, I blamed your mom for the fallout, to the point where anger was the only emotion I had left. And you fell onto my radar—her only daughter. You became the collateral damage."

"So how long *have* you hated me? You never even talked to

me until this year, Link." I hate how small and weak my voice sounds, but the notion that he bullied me ever since we connected at Whitmore U over trauma that we both experienced is beyond frustrating.

He shakes his head sadly. "We met before this year."

I stare at him in confusion while he continues. "Like I said, I knew a little about you because I'd seen you over the years at Martin's parties, but I wanted to know more personal stuff, you know? Brighton is a small town, so it wasn't hard to get information, and I learned everything I could. I thought I could hurt you to get to her."

My eyes widen as my brain goes to a million very dark places. "What? Like you hired a hitman?" I ask in a horrified whisper.

"Huh? No, *no*," he says quickly. "Not hurt you physically—I'm not a sociopath—but I hated you so much, and I was intent on doing some severe emotional damage. I didn't really know you, so I made a lot of assumptions, mostly that you must be as selfish and heartless as your mother—she raised you, after all. That was enough justification in my fucked-up head."

My eyes fill with tears. My mom wasn't a saint, but I still loved her. She was kind and supportive, and she always made me feel invincible, and losing that feeling when she died was what really broke me. Not Matt's betrayal or my step dad abandoning me. It was the loss of my mom, first and foremost.

I wrap my arms around myself as Link's words echo in my head. *Selfish and heartless.*

"But then your mom…died." My blurry eyes snap up to him. "And it threw fuel on an already raging fire. I felt like"— his voice catches, and he takes a deep breath—"I felt like she took the easy way out."

I flinch but stay quiet.

"So, I started following you, and one night, you went to a party in our part of town. I don't really know what my plan was

—I just wanted to hurt you. You walked into that dark room that night upset and perfectly vulnerable."

My mouth drops open as the memory comes back to me—the night I fucked a stranger in the inky-black darkness of that rich boy's bedroom.

Only, we didn't fuck. We connected on another level—or I thought we did—through stolen kisses and needy touches, and mind-bending pleasure.

And it wasn't a stranger.

It was Lincoln.

Lincoln. Fucking. Evans.

My stomach bottoms out. I stand up and back away from Lincoln as the realization of what he's saying crashes through my thoughts, twisting and breaking the narrative of that night like a car wreck I can't unsee.

Link's eyes are desperate and scared. "It started as a hate fuck, but it didn't end that way. As soon as we were together, I felt it, and I know you felt it, too. Somehow, between our first kiss and our last orgasm, I fell for you. Hard."

I shake my head, his words shredding what's left of my heart into a bloody mess. "But you left." My voice cracks as tears burn my eyes. "I woke up and you were gone."

"I know. I'm so fucking sorry. I was scared. I hadn't felt anything but anger in so long—until you—and I didn't know how to handle it so I ran."

I look at Trey, who's watching the whole exchange with a pained expression. "And you knew about this?"

"I…" He glances at Link and then back at me. "Not until this year after Halloween."

"Halloween? That was months ago…." My eyes flicker back to Lincoln. "Did you read my screenplay?" I ask him quietly as I lose the battle to hold back my tears. I just don't care anymore though. My heart hurts, and I want him to understand why.

He frowns. "Yeah, I started to read it. But what…"

"The story is a glimpse into my future, or the future I thought I always wanted anyway—a girl who moves to New York to escape her broken family life and work in the publishing industry. But she runs into the one person who's either her worst nightmare or the love of her life—the boy who took her virginity when she was at her most vulnerable and then ran."

"I haven't gotten to the part about the guy yet. Is that about me?" He sounds dazed, his voice small like a little boy's.

"I didn't know it when I wrote the screenplay, but yes, I guess it is." I take a step toward him and sit back down, clasping his hands in mine. "Look, you saved me. You pulled me from rock bottom before I even hit the ground, and the memory of that night kept me going until the day I got my acceptance letter to Whitmore U."

I'm shaking as I continue. "But this whole time, you knew it was me? And you were still cruel. You did your damnedest to make me feel small, and you pushed me away. You were punishing a ghost by hurting a real person with real feelings. You could have told me back then and avoided all of this..."

"All of this what?" he asks, his voice breaking.

"Heartbreak." I can barely say the word.

"I get it," Lincoln says. "I used to be able to shut away every one of these goddamn feelings, but you've ruined that. You've fucking ruined it. Now I feel everything, and I hate it."

"You hate what you feel for me?"

"No," he says, running his hands through his hair in frustration. "That's not what I meant. But I hate that you're so important to me—that you've always been so important to me. What happens when you leave me? When you leave us?"

Silence fills the room as we stare at each other. He has so much fear and anger in his eyes. From behind me, I hear Trey take a shaky breath. I sit back slowly and glance between them.

"You're going to get that internship," Link says, his voice low. "Because you're fucking smart and a damn good writer."

"But that's just for the summer—" Trey starts.

"Is it? Because the version of Charlie in her screenplay goes to NYU."

I stare at him sadly. "I don't know what my plans are, Link. Are you asking me if I applied to transfer to New York? Yes, I did, okay? I did it at the start of the year before either of you were even on my radar. My stepdad abandoned me, and my brothers have their own lives. I wanted to get the hell out of here because I. Had. Nothing."

I suddenly feel exhausted, the emotional turmoil inside me is so heavy. "What do you want from me?"

"He wants you to stay," Trey says quietly, and we both look over at him. His eyes are downcast, and his sunny demeanor is dimmed, like our argument is eclipsing his usual optimism. "He wants you to stay here with us because no one's ever loved us enough to stay."

And damn, if my heart doesn't shatter—because they want something I can't give them right now. Lincoln's face falls, screwing up in pain.

"I'm sorry," I whisper, but it seems to echo loudly in the big room. "I wish I could give you that, but I don't know my plans yet—we're still new, and you're both you—the campus fuckboys." They flinch when I say it, and I regret the word choice but push on anyway. "We haven't even had a conversation about commitment between the three of us, let alone what it might mean for our futures."

I stand. Trey looks hurt, and I feel the panic attack rising in my chest, gripping my heart like a vise. "I need to go."

And then I turn and run.

"Charlie!" Trey calls, but I don't care. They aren't my safe place to land—not right now.

I run up the stairs, and my hands hit the front door, pushing it open, and I scramble to my car, throwing myself into the driver's seat.

I stare at the steering wheel with wide eyes, my hands shaking so bad that I'm not sure I should drive. But I can't stay here, so I start up the car and leave, and somehow, find my way home without causing an accident.

I stumble to the house and collapse on the front steps, the chill from the concrete seeping through my pants and into my skin. I pull out my phone and text Fiona, and then I wait there, oblivious to the cold, and hope that I didn't just make a huge mistake.

CHAPTER THIRTY-SEVEN

CHARLIE

*F*iona and I are traveling north to Vancouver.

Last night, Fi came to Brighton and stayed with me so that I wouldn't be alone in my misery. Thankfully, her hometown of Clearbrook isn't far from mine, so it was a quick drive over, and it's still a couple of days until Christmas, so she opted to stay with me for another night in Vancouver before heading back to her mom's house.

We snuggled in my bed all night and watched *Die Hard*, my favorite Christmas movie, and *Home Alone*, her favorite Christmas movie, and talked intermittently about the fight I had with the guys. She agreed that I needed a break, so I called Sebastian and suggested we spend the holidays at their place in Vancouver instead of in Brighton like we'd originally planned. Seb was hesitant at first, but Marcus, always the workaholic, was more than happy to stay, so Seb begrudgingly agreed.

It was for the best anyway. Had my stepbrothers come home, they would have seen the empty house, and I would have had to finally admit that their dad abandoned me. I'm not sure I'm ready for that conversation yet.

I-5 is beautiful today, framed by light coastal fog on one side and snowy mountain peaks on the other. The weather is clear and cold, the winter wind whipping across the highway so fast that I sometimes feel it tug at my little car as I drive.

I glance over at Fiona, grateful for her company. Her heated seat is on "high" and she's clutching a large coffee. Her auburn hair is piled high on her head in a messy bun, and she's wearing an oversized hoodie, yoga pants, and large round sunglasses like a hungover movie star.

I still feel terrible about my argument with Trey and Lincoln, and my feelings for them are warring with my desire to move on to another city where I can work toward a real career and escape the shadow of my mom's suicide. Not to mention, the idea of being as far away from Matt as possible is very appealing. The last few months have made me realize that I stayed with him for the wrong reasons—companionship and security—and being with Link and Trey is unconventional and chaotic and so, so addictive. I'm not sure I can live without it. I'm not sure I want to.

"So will we see moose?" Fiona interrupts my thoughts, and I glance at her before I burst out laughing.

"What?"

"Aren't there a lot of moose in Canada?" she asks, giving me a shit-eating grin.

I elbow her and roll my eyes.

I slow as we approach the border crossing, but it's early enough that the line isn't too long. Once we're in Canada, we cross the Fraser River and the highway transitions to Oak Street as I drive toward the heart of my favorite city.

First things first, we drop off our bags at the hotel. Then we spend the morning exploring Stanley Park.

Seb and Marcus live in a two-bedroom apartment a few blocks from there, and they put Fi and me up in our hotel for the night, which is not cheap—nothing in the city is.

We stroll arm in arm down Robson Street, making several

turns before we find ourselves in a cute neighborhood where the streets are lined with old apartment complexes and small manicured lawns.

"Your brothers live here?" Fiona asks, looking around. "What adorable little apartments!"

"They actually live there," I say pointing up ahead to some high-rises at the end of the block.

Fi raises her eyebrows. "Shit, that place looks expensive."

I nod. "It is."

"So, wait," she says, stopping as we reach the lobby door. "Why are you at Whitmore on a scholarship if your family is loaded? You have like ten items of clothing to your name."

I bite my lip, deciding what I should tell her.

"Spill," she says flatly.

"Seb and Marcus don't know that I don't have money," I say hesitantly. She looks confused for a moment. "They're my step-brothers," I explain, "and their dad, Martin, left us after my mom's death. He chose to...exclude me from the family finances."

"Wait," Fi says. "You're grieving from your mom's death, and he cuts you off? What. A. Douche."

"Look, you can't say anything. I know the situation seems shitty, but you don't know everything that happened. And Seb already worries about me—I don't want to stress him out any more." I reach out my mitten-clad hand and grab hers. "Please?"

"Yeah, yeah," she grumbles. "I won't tell."

"Thank you," I say, smiling with relief. "Now let's go inside before I freeze my tits off."

I hit the button to my stepbrothers' flat, and we huddle together while we wait for a response.

"Hey, little sister." Sebastian's voice is muffled static. "C'mon up." There's a loud buzz and the door clicks. I grab the handle, and we shuffle gratefully into the warm lobby. The space is lit up with wall-to-wall windows and is tastefully decorated with small trees and modern gray and black furniture. We enter the elevator and ride it up to the sixteenth floor. Then we walk to the end of a long hallway to a corner unit, and I knock.

Seb opens the door, and my face splits with a grin before I throw myself into his arms.

"It's good to see you, kid," he says, laughing and hugging me back. He smells like spicy cologne and beer, and I breathe him in, feeling completely at home again. My throat clogs with emotion, and I pull back, rubbing furiously at my eyes.

"You okay?" he asks, looking down at me with a frown.

"Yes," I say, clearing my throat. "Just really happy to see you."

"And this must be Fiona," he says, looking over my shoulder.

"Oh! Sorry!" I turn toward Fi. "Yes, this is my bestie from school, Fiona Flowers."

I'm surprised by the silence behind me, and my mouth drops open when I turn to see my friend standing shyly in the doorway, her cheeks a deep shade of crimson as she fusses with her hair.

Seb puts out his hand. "It's really nice to meet you," he says. "I'm Sebastian."

Fiona stares at him before her eyes drop to his hand, then travel back up to his face.

"Fi?" I ask, fighting a smile. I have literally never seen this girl flustered before.

"Uh-huh," she says distractedly, reaching out quickly to shake his hand.

Seb chuckles and leads us into the apartment. Fi stops me with a firm hand on my arm, letting my brother walk farther ahead of us. "You *did not* say your brother was so hot," she whisper-hisses. "I'm dressed like one of those basic suburban moms heading to the school drop-off."

"So sorry," I say, rolling my eyes. "I don't generally rate my *brother* on the hot-guy scale."

"Uh, he's like a twelve out of ten?"

I smile at her. "Don't be weird. You look pretty. You always do." I pry her fingers from my arm.

"Hrmph," she responds, and we continue walking.

The hallway opens up into a bright kitchen that's furnished with sleek black appliances and gray sandstone countertops, and a simple living room with two plush couches and a huge flat-screen TV. Fiona's breath catches as walks over to the large window wall looking out over the calm blue waters of English Bay.

"This is fucking beautiful." She looks back at me with wide eyes.

Seb smiles. "It is an impressive view," he agrees. "Can I get you ladies something to drink?"

"Do you have any lagers?" I ask, scrunching my nose at Seb's IPA.

"Even better!" Seb opens the fridge and pulls out a bottle with a blue label that I recognize immediately.

"You have Granville Island winter ale? What a good brother."

"Your favorite," he says with a grin.

"You're drinking beer?" Fiona asks, her eyebrows rising in surprise.

I shrug. "I don't drink it much, but this one tops my list," I say, opening it eagerly with a loud crack.

"What about you, Fiona? I'm guessing you're more of a liquor girl."

"Bingo," she says with a flirty wink. I roll my eyes. "Bathroom?" Fi asks.

"Right down the hall, first door on your left," Seb replies as he walks over to the bar and pulls out a bottle of gin and some lime juice. He opens a tonic water and mixes it with the gin. When he's done, he places the drink on the counter next to my beer.

"So, I'm a twelve, huh?" Seb says, smothering a smile with his hand.

"Ugh, you heard that?"

"Yeah, turns out I'm not deaf," he says with a laugh.

"Don't let it go to your head," I say. "But I hope that didn't make you uncomfortable."

"Nah. She's actually pretty cute." His eyes wander toward the hallway where Fiona disappeared.

I pause with my beer halfway to my lips and stare at him, deadpan. "Don't even think about seducing my friend. I mean it, Seb."

Seb throws up his hands. "Relax, kid. I'm just playing," he says with a wink.

We both stop talking when we hear the bathroom door open. Seb picks up the glass and hands it to Fi when she reenters the kitchen.

"I hope you like gin and tonic," he says with a smile.

"Love it." Fiona returns the smile, and I sigh, as I realize I'll be spending the entire night trying to prevent a hook up.

IT'S WELL past sunset when Seb, Fiona, and I walk to the pub to meet up with Marcus for dinner and drinks. Downtown Vancouver is lit with warm twinkling lights and bustling with people. Car horns, revving engines, and the odd siren make a cacophony that's music to my ears. I love the life of the city—it's one of the reasons why I'm considering a move to New York permanently.

We approach the pub, and I look up at the red fluorescent sign reading "Brothers' Beer & Bourbon"; we affectionately call it the "BB&B" for short. Marcus named the place with the forethought that he and Sebastian would run it together, and I suppose I should feel excluded. But they've been talking about this place since they were boys playing restaurant in our parents' basement. I never wanted to step on that dream, and I was so proud when they made it a reality.

The rich smell of burgers and french fries assails my nostrils as we enter. The pub has a classic Pacific Northwest feel with its mismatched wood panel walls and a large stone fireplace. Booths edge out the restaurant, and the main floor is dotted with two- and four-top tables. A classic bar backed by shelves of liquor bottles is packed with chatting and laughing patrons. Like a lot of businesses in Vancouver, the walls double as a local art gallery, adorned with paintings of Vancouver Island, photos of the Capilano Suspension Bridge, and various Native American pieces.

Seb waves at the hostess as we enter. She smiles and winks at him. I glance at Fi, and we roll our eyes.

Guys and their stupid charm.

The three of us weave through the crowd toward a secluded room at the back of the pub.

"Wow," Fiona says as we sit at the empty table. "This place is so cool."

Sebastian closes the sliding door, shutting out the pub's naturally chaotic atmosphere.

"And you both *own* it?" she asks for the third time, as if not convinced by the conversation we just had on the way over.

Seb smiles widely. "Yes, though Marcus's business smarts really got it up and running," he says. "If he hadn't given it a good foundation, it wouldn't have been this successful."

We settle in and order drinks, and I let myself enjoy my whisky as Sebastian and Fiona chat away. I stare at my phone, suddenly wishing that one of the guys would text me. I haven't heard anything since I left last night, and the memory of the hurt on their faces makes my heart ache. Not to mention that I just miss them. I always miss them. When I lived alone after Martin left, I started craving people, even if they were just in my general proximity, and that need has never fully gone away. But with Trey and Link? It's a hundred times stronger, and that scares me.

"About time you visited," a deep familiar voice says from behind me.

I stand and turn, smiling cautiously at Marcus as he enters the room, rolling up his shirt sleeves. He looks tired, and his dark brown hair is tousled like he's been running his hands through it obsessively.

He opens his arms, and I step into his hug, closing my eyes at the somewhat awkward embrace. Our relationship has been beyond strained, so I revel in the brief physical contact before he releases me with a tight smile.

"This is my friend, Fiona." My tone is cheerful as I try to hide the sudden onslaught of anxiety I feel around my oldest brother. As they shake hands politely, I take a deep breath and sit back down, knocking back the rest of my drink in one go. Seb frowns at me, but I ignore his disapproval, tapping my empty glass with my fingernails until the waiter brings me another.

The evening moves along smoothly as we have more drinks, appetizers, and then dinner. I'm so thankful I brought Fiona along—her outgoing personality carries the conversation effortlessly. By the time I pop the last french fry into my mouth, I feel the warm buzz of alcohol humming through my veins. I touch my nose experimentally. It feels...numb. I touch it again.

"Uh-oh." Fi narrows her eyes at me. "You may have had enough, babe."

I look over, my finger still pressed firmly to my nose. "What? Why?"

"Is your nose numb?" she asks. Seb and Marcus glance at each other in confusion. Fi looks over at them and then back at me. "Have you never been drunk with your brothers before?"

"Erm, nope." I shake my head. Sebastian's eyes widen as he studies me. "Don't look at me like that," I say. Then I look over at Fiona. "The bigger one doesn't even know I drink," I whisper to her.

Marcus's eyes narrow.

"Adorable." Fi leans close to me. "You know you're not really whispering, right? They can hear you."

I glance over at Seb and Marcus. They're both still staring.

"I drink sometimes," I announce matter-of-factly to Marcus. "But don't worry; I'm cutting myself off before I say something stupid."

"You can tell because her nose goes numb," Fiona explains with a wink.

"Right," Seb says, holding back a laugh. Marcus looks a little less amused, so I choose to ignore him, focusing on my funner brother. *Wait, funner isn't a word.*

"How's school going?" Sebastian asks, changing the subject.

"School is…okay," I say cagily, studying the ice at the bottom of my glass. "I applied to an internship in New York." I frown as a wave of sadness chokes my throat.

Seb looks at Fi, as if my less intoxicated friend will betray me.

"You need to tell them," Fiona says.

Traitor.

"Tell us what?" Marcus asks, taking a long pull of his beer.

I stare at Fiona, staying stubbornly silent, and she sighs. "Charlie just had a fight with her boyfriends."

"Boyfriends?" Marcus and Seb ask together, and Seb holds up a hand. "As in plural?"

"They are *not* my boyfriends," I blurt before clapping a hand over my mouth.

"Label or not, it's serious, and you know it," Fiona places a hand on mine when I start to fidget with my hair.

"There's really not much to tell," I say.

"No," Marcus interrupts, "I want to hear more."

"Me, too" Seb chimes in. "What's going on, and when did this start?"

"Er, it started in September, sort of," I say, my voice weirdly high and squeaky. "But we really started messing around after Halloween."

And then I start to ramble as I recount my experiences with Link and Trey, leading up to the fight last night, though I do leave out the more sordid details. They are my brothers, after all.

"Wait, so there's drinking *and* sex?" Marcus clarifies.

I nod solemnly.

"She *is* an adult now," Seb says quietly in my defense.

"Fair. But she's still our little sister, so it's not an easy sell."

I pause, looking back and forth between them. "Can I finish?"

"Jesus, there's more?" Seb mutters.

"Trey is a reputed fuck boy, and Lincoln is definitely emotionally damaged, and I have no idea what they really want from me, other than they apparently don't want me to leave, but it's not like I can stay and work at the theater forever—that's Link's prerogative, not mine." I tap my chin in thought. "That place really makes him happy," I murmur sadly, feeling like our future trajectories are splintering apart even more.

"You have a job, too?" Marcus asks.

"Fi and I work at the local movie theater. Lincoln's dad owns it, so Lincoln runs it because rich kids get whatever they want." I glance up at my brothers. "No offense."

"None taken," Seb murmurs.

"So anyway…yeah," I say awkwardly.

My brothers sit there in silence, as if in shock. I giggle.

Finally, Seb clears his throat. "Uhm, anything else?"

I consider mentioning Matt and his creepy antics, but I don't want to worry them, so I blurt the first thing that pops into my head.

"Oh, and I punched this girl in the face after she spilled her waffles on the laptop Mom gave me. It was intentional—definitely on purpose." I choke on the last word, looking up at Seb and Marcus as the memory of that day overwhelms me again. I really miss that laptop.

My brothers' faces are out of focus for some reason. *Why is everything blurry?*

"She literally ruined my MacBook with my favorite breakfast treat." I put a hand to my mouth to stifle a sob.

"For fuck's sake," Marcus says. At the same time as Seb says, "You decked a girl?"

Fat, hot tears run down my cheeks, and Fiona's hand squeezes my leg under the table. I take a deep breath, wipe my face with the palms of my hands, and force a smile.

"Yes, I broke her nose. But she and I are cool now." I shrug as if I didn't just have an alcohol-induced meltdown.

"Wait, whoa, time out," Seb says, making a T with his hands. "Lincoln and Trey? As in Lincoln Evans and Trey Walker?"

"Yeah," I say, sniffing. "Why?"

Marcus looks at Seb. "The smart-mouth boy and the moody kid who spent all their time smoking weed in the pool house with the other rich dickheads?"

"You shouldn't talk," Seb says with a laugh. "You were one of those dickheads."

Marcus grins. "Only sometimes."

"I always suspected that Lincoln had a thing for you," Seb says, frowning.

My head snaps up. "What?"

"He used to ask about you, and he watched you a lot when he thought no one noticed," Seb says with a shrug. Then he smiles softly. "I thought he was jealous of Matt the way he stared daggers at him. And he gave you Ani, of course."

"He gave me…" My head spins.

"Who's Ani?" Fiona asks.

"This little stuffed cat that Lincoln brought Charlie after Anakin ran off." He glances at Marcus. "Remember that? You and Lizzy were arguing, and she locked you out of your own bedroom," he says with a wide grin. "So we were sitting in the hallway on the floor when Lincoln snuck into Charlie's room that night."

I stare at him, at a complete loss for words, and my stomach bursts with butterflies. I never could figure out who left Ani, but I was so grateful nonetheless.

"Yeah, I remember," Marcus replies. "It was creepy."

"C'mon, grumpy bear. The kid was smitten. It was sweet."

"Smitten? He's obviously been obsessing over her forever," Marcus grumbles.

"Okay, wait, who's Anakin?" Fiona asks. "I'm so confused."

"My cat," I say.

"You named your cat after a Sith? You're the cutest nerd ever," Fi laughs.

"Actually, Anakin was a Jedi. He wasn't a Sith until he became Vader," I point out.

"I think we're getting off topic here," Seb says. Then he looks at me, his expression more serious. "We FaceTime you all the time. Why didn't you ever mention any of this?"

I hold up a finger. "Well, one, I wasn't drunk. And, two, I don't like to worry you, Seb. You treat me like I'm going to break any second." I look over at Marcus. "Three, *you* hate me now, so I figure you don't care either way."

Marcus's face falls. "I don't hate you, Charlie," he says quietly. "I just..."

"It's fine." I hold up my hand. "Turns out I'm not an innocent, fragile doll like you both always thought I was. I walked in on my boyfriend fucking someone else. I watched my mom bleed out onto our expensive bathroom tiles. And then my stepdad, who was supposed to take care of me, walked out and left me with nothing—literally nothing—no money, hardly any food, and no fucking furniture." I can hear the wobble in my voice, but I refuse to cry again.

"Wait, what?" Seb says, standing.

Marcus's hands have balled into fists, and he's shaking.

"That escalated quickly," Fiona says, her eyes wide.

"Yeah, and guess what?" I'm practically yelling. "I survived. I fought depression and pushed through every anxiety attack. I spent every night in the house *we* grew up in all alone, remembering what it was like to be a happy, normal family. I graduated high school. I got a scholarship so that I could still have a fucking future now that I'm not the heir to a goddamn fortune." I blink back tears. If I don't leave soon, I'll completely lose it. "I even applied to New York University to get the hell away from here."

Fiona's mouth drops open, and I realize belatedly that she didn't know that tidbit of information.

"We didn't know about Dad...." Marcus looks angry and sad.

They both do.

I lean over, placing my hands flat on the table. "I never told you," I say quietly. "You both still have a father, and I didn't want to break our family any more than I already have." I grab my coat and purse from the back of my chair and walk from the room, through the pub, and out into the cold winter night.

DESPITE MY INEBRIATED STATE, I still manage to wander back to my stepbrothers' apartment unscathed. Of course, I don't have a key, but some nice couple took pity on me and let me into the lobby.

Canadians are so polite, I muse as I ride the elevator up to the sixteenth floor.

I walk down the hallway and pause outside their apartment.

Realizing I'll just have to wait, I slide down the door until my butt hits the floor and pull my legs to my chest.

My phone has been buzzing nonstop with texts from Seb and Fiona, but I've been ignoring them. They probably aren't far behind me anyway, and I'm suddenly so embarrassed about my outburst.

Stupid drunk Charlie strikes again.

The tears I've been holding back hit me with full force, and I put my forehead on my knees and cry.

My phone buzzes again, and I pick it up angrily about to silence my texts altogether, when I see Trey's name on the screen.

TREY

We need to talk. Please come over.

I wipe my eyes and nose and stare at the message, knowing I shouldn't respond. I'm definitely too drunk and should wait until morning, but...

"Fuck it," I mutter. "This night can't get much worse."

I'm sorry, Trey. I need more time. I'm in Vancouver with my brothers. I don't know when I'll be back.

I turn off my phone screen just as I hear the elevator door ding open. Fiona breaks into a run when she spots me on the floor and hauls me up by my forearms.

"What the fuck, walking home alone at night." Her nails press into my skin. "You are a hot, drunk girl. And you're so small. Some psycho could have stolen you and put you right in his pocket! You're a murder podcast waiting to happen!"

I burst out laughing. "Stolen me?"

"You know, kidnapped!" Fi eyes fill with tears.

"Hey, Fi," I say gently. "I'm okay."

She nods, looking me up and down as if for reassurance. My

phone lights up with a text, and she pauses. "Oh my God, is that a message from Trey? Have you been drunk texting?"

I ignore her question as Seb and Marcus approach, eyeing me warily. I flush, looking down. Seb doesn't say anything as he places his phone against the door. It blinks green and clicks open.

"Let's go back to the hotel," I say to Fiona, not wanting to rehash any of the night's events.

She looks over at my stepbrothers. "Thank you for dinner."

"Of course," Seb replies as we stand in the doorway awkwardly.

"Charlie, wait…" A pair of strong arms pull me into a bone-crushing hug. I look up in surprise, realizing it's Marcus. And he's crying. "I'm so sorry, kid," he says, his voice shaking.

It's the first time I've ever seen him cry. Ever. Even at my mom's funeral.

"It's okay, Marcus," I whisper.

"No," he says firmly, stepping back. "It's not. You're my little sister, and ever since you came into our lives when you were a tiny, sassy three-year-old, I swore I would protect you." He takes a deep breath. "I didn't do that. I dumped all my anger and resentment on you like a petulant teenager." He pushes his finger under my chin, raising my gaze to his. "But what happened to our family was not your fault. Do you hear me? Our parents fucked up. Both of them. They're adults. That's not on you. *We*," he says, pointing between me and Seb, "are still a family."

He hugs me again, pulling me close.

My fingers dig into his shirt as I press my face against his chest. "I missed you so much," I whisper. "I thought I had lost you."

"Never," he says fiercely.

"Aww, you guys," Seb interrupts. "This is so cute."

"Fuck off, asshole," Marcus says, but I can hear the smile in his voice, and he opens one arm, bringing Seb into the hug.

"We love you, little sis," Seb whispers.

"I love you both, too," I say. And for the first time in the last twenty-four hours, I feel a little lighter.

CHAPTER THIRTY-EIGHT

TREY

*T*he two-week winter break felt like the longest break in the history of school breaks. Link and I have *not* been handling the separation from Charlie well. At all. We started out drinking ourselves stupid and neither of us was interested in reining in the other. We even tried to buy some cocaine, but Lincoln was disgusted by the condition of the dealer's house, so we chickened out before we could make the sale. It was a weird forty-eight hours considering Link's aversion to substance abuse. But after two days of bingeing, John got fed up with our shit and made us go back to campus to work instead.

So Link and I have been practically living at the theater, and when we do go back to our dorm, we've been watching an eclectic mix of movie marathons to pass the time—my personal favorite was the Estevez Festivez (a term Link borrowed from an episode of *Cougar Town*), when we watched *The Outsiders, The Breakfast Club, Young Guns, St. Elmo's Fire,* and *The Mighty Ducks.*

Regardless of our relatively self-destructive ways, we both agreed that this relationship we have with Charlie is special because, one, we're actually referring to it as a relationship, and, two, we didn't even think about fucking around, which is normally my go-to when shit hits the fan. It wasn't even on our radar.

I'm anxious because today I'll see her again, and I want her back. No question.

"You're going to grovel, aren't you?" Link asks as he leans in the bathroom doorway and watches me fuss with my hair, an amused smile touching his lips.

"Tell me you won't," I challenge, raising an eyebrow. "It wasn't fair to ask her to stay."

"I know. But I'm not ready. Everything that happened that night was basically my fault, and as usual, you got stuck in the crossfire of my bullshit." He sighs and runs a hand through his hair, the dark circles under his eyes proof that he hasn't slept much.

I turn toward him. "Yes, you fucked up, but we're not 'us' without you. If you need more time, take it. Just don't let the martyr in you push her so far away that you guys can't find a way back to each other." I give him a pleading look. "I honestly don't think my heart can take it."

Link's steel eyes soften, and he blinks a few times like he's fighting with his emotions. "I think I love her," he says quietly, and I can't stop the chuckle that leaves my throat.

"I think I knew that before you did, Link." I walk past him into my bedroom and sit down to put my socks on, and he follows, sitting down beside me.

"So what if she decides to leave?"

I let out a sigh. "Then I guess we will figure out how to go with her." I glance at him, and I can see the veiled fear behind his usual calm façade. "She's not like our parents. I know how often we've been burned in the abandonment department, believe me. But if she leaves for New York, she's doing it for a dream—something she's wanted for a while—and if we make her choose, she'll just resent us. Let's go against the gender norm and follow the girl for once."

Link relaxes a bit, his head coming to rest on my shoulder. In general, I've always been the affectionate one, but lately, Lincoln's been very touchy. It's a big step for my emotionally closed-off best friend, and it gives me all kinds of feels. Plus, he smells really good.

"I guess I can find another old theater to open somewhere on the East Coast."

I turn and kiss the top of his head, smiling against his hair. "I think it's something to consider if it comes down to it."

He nods absently, and we stand, heading to the living room to put on our coats and shoes.

"You know you still have to work with her on your film project, right?"

He sighs. "I know." He looks over at me as he zips up his jacket. "I finally finished reading her screenplay last night; it's really good." He smiles sadly. "That night was important to her too. I wish I'd told her sooner."

We grab our bags and walk out into the hallway to wait for the elevator. "You and me both, buddy, but we'll fix it."

He looks dubious, and I know it'll be much harder for him than for me because he has to forgive himself first.

CHARLIE

Being back from winter break feels like I'm starting school all over again—I'm so nervous for some reason. I spent my time away gallivanting around Vancouver with Sebastian and Marcus, and it was actually just what I needed to clear my head.

My decisions about whether to go to New York for just the summer versus picking up my life and leaving are still up in the air until the spring. But my applications are submitted, and my stepbrothers assured me that they were proud of me no matter what I choose, though Marcus did give me a very stern (and unnecessary) lecture on making life decisions based on my feelings for what he called "stupid boys." I appreciate the thought behind it, nonetheless.

Mornings in January are consistently in the low thirties. White frost clings to the grass and trees, sparkling in the sunshine, and as I trudge across campus, my breath escapes my lips in large white puffs.

I stop short when I see Trey pacing in front of the humanities building. I smile to myself as I approach him, my stomach fluttering. The boy is a work of art in the morning sunlight, all golden highlights and rosy cheeks. He looks like he's talking to himself, but he pauses when he spots me, grinning boyishly, his sienna eyes wide and bright.

"Hey, golden boy. You okay?"

"That depends on whether I can kiss you or not."

I step closer so that I have to look up at him, and suddenly the cold air seems to dissipate. "You can always kiss me."

His eyes flash with need, and he grabs my scarf, yanking me forward so hard that I stumble into him, and he presses his mouth to mine eagerly. Our lips slide together, his tongue tangling with mine until everything around us is fuzzy.

"Get a room," Brantley snarks as he walks by, and I pull back, panting, while Trey flips Brantley off. His gaze falls to mine, and he takes my hand and pulls me toward the Wolf Building.

"Trey, no. I have class."

"Your fancy-schmancy English-slash-film class or whatever?"

I roll my eyes and laugh. "Yes."

"Link just left from there; it's canceled this week."

"Oh."

Just the mention of his name makes my stomach twist. I've been thinking about what Sebastian said about Lincoln's obsession with me for all these years. When I brought it up one night, Seb admitted that he had started coming with his parents to our parties when he was thirteen—the idea that he was this silent stalker in my life for years should probably unnerve me, but it's so Lincoln-like that my stupid brain just found it endearing.

Once we get up to their dorm, Trey strips me out of my coat and drags me to his room, closing the door with his foot and practically throwing me onto the bed. I try to sit up to face him, but Trey steps between my legs and then crawls up my body, his strong forearms caging me to the mattress, his breath mingling with mine. My pussy is tingling and already uncomfortably wet as I stare at him. I bring up one hand and tangle it in his hair, the strands soft between my fingers.

"So I know we need to talk, but—"

"Yes, please. Talk later," I interrupt, digging my nails into his skin as I pull him down by his neck, so that our mouths slam together. We claw at each other like horny teenagers, tearing at each other's clothing until we're stripped completely naked.

Trey licks and bites down my body, leaving bruises everywhere in his enthusiasm to taste every inch of me, and the tiny stings of pain have me writhing and moaning as my clit throbs between my legs.

"Trey," I pant, already losing my mind. "Touch me."

He chuckles and kneels on the floor at the foot of the bed, placing my thighs over his shoulders. Then, he watches my face as he presses his thumb to my clit and rubs it slowly.

"Shit," I hiss, bucking my hips. "Stop teasing me. Please. It's been too long since I orgasmed."

"You're just so perfect right now, spread out just for me, begging me like a good girl."

His words alone heighten the ache in my pussy, and I arch my back off the bed impatiently. This time, he doesn't disappoint and lowers his mouth to my clit, sucking it into his mouth. My legs tighten around his head as I clutch the sheets to maintain some sort of grip on reality as everything tilts.

"I'm not going to last, baby," I breathe.

"You're so wet." His words vibrate deliciously against my skin, and I feel myself teetering. He teases my entrance with two thick fingers, and then pushes them inside me roughly. "Come for me."

And I do, the orgasm rocking through my body with unexpected force.

I fall back on the bed, completely limp. "Holy shit, I missed this," I murmur.

Trey crawls up next to me and pulls us under the covers, his face nuzzling the side of my neck as we lie there, and even though I can still feel his hard cock, warm against my thigh, he seems content to snuggle—for the moment at least.

"When's your next class?"

"I have hours. You?" His voice is muffled against my skin.

"Same."

"Perfect."

Trey tangles his legs with mine, and I fall asleep quickly with his hair tickling my cheek.

I don't doze for long, and when I wake up, blinking away the euphoric haze in my brain, I find myself staring at Link's door across the hall, sadness tugging at my chest.

Trey stirs under my weight and kisses the top of my head.

"Is it time to talk?" He swallows, his Adam's apple bobbing as he looks at me, his expression almost pained.

"I suppose so," I say with a frown. "Is this the part when you tell me you're finally bored with me?"

"Bored with you?"

I smile sadly, fighting the lump in my throat. "C'mon, Trey.

We both know you aren't a serious relationship kind of guy. I'm honestly impressed we got this far." I take a deep breath. "And I don't know where I'm going to end up yet. But I don't want this to end yet either."

"That works for me."

"What about Link?"

"Link wants that, too. He just needs a little time to sort through his feelings."

"He doesn't hate me?"

"I don't think he ever hated you, baby. But big emotions are hard for him. He's been pretty closed off his whole life—he's certainly never been in a meaningful relationship."

"And you have?" I ask with a smile, nudging his side playfully.

"No, but for the most part, I've never had any problem telling people how I feel."

Trey's long finger traces the side of my jaw and rests under my chin, lifting my gaze to his. His mouth presses softly to mine, and I lean into the kiss, our lips moving against each other. It's sweet and full of so many unspoken emotions, and it leaves me breathless.

I pull back, and we stare at each other. He's so beautiful, his eyes a warm amber in the soft ambient light. His messy blond hair has grown longer in the months since I've known him, and it falls over his forehead, nearly hiding his brows.

He still looks troubled. "Is that what you think?" he asks finally, his brow furrowing. "That I'm going to get bored? Find another warm body to fuck?" He looks so offended at the thought, I almost laugh. Then he sits up, taking my hands so I follow him until we're facing each other on the bed. I feel vulnerable as I sit there completely naked, but the intense expression on Trey's face is so distracting that my self-conscious impulse to cover up is momentarily forgotten.

"I know Link and I are two sides of a very different coin on the surface. He's broody and handsome and so broken. Hell, he's a pain in the ass, but we both know he's worth it. But I'm broken, too, and that's why we've always worked—we understand each other's pain."

"Trey..." I start.

"No, please just let me say this before I lose my nerve." I nod, squeezing his hands. "I joke about it, but over the years, I've literally drowned my pain in a lot of vices—drugs, alcohol, sex— I've done it all. When I was sixteen, I almost overdosed on cocaine. I thought if I got close enough to death, my parents might come home. But they didn't. They sent a get-well card to the hospital, and I dealt with so much guilt because my actions scared the shit out of Lincoln and his parents. I quit with the hard drugs after that, and dove dick first into sex."

I've never seen Trey look so serious. He's always the bright light to my and Link's darkness, so the gravity in his voice and expression is unnerving.

"So you're right," he continues. "I've slept with a lot of people indiscriminately, and I never hid that fact. Some rumors were exaggerated, but some were true. I didn't care." He brings my hand to his mouth to kiss my fingertips gently. "But I haven't looked at another girl—or guy—since the night you walked into our party and stole my fucking heart."

My breath catches at his words.

"When I'm with you, Charlie, I feel like I can do anything, be anything. You make me want to be a better person. And it's not just me. You make Link a better person, and that alone had me falling for you way faster than I ever expected because I love him. And I love you. So fucking much. And yeah, I never expected to share either of you, but here we are." His eyes redden and he clears his throat. "You're mine. Do you understand? You're it for me, baby. But we're not whole without Link.

You and him are cut from the same cloth, and he gives you something I can't. That fucking kills me. But I understand, and I'll always choose you. *We'll* always choose you."

I kiss him—forcefully, passionately—pushing my hands against his chest until we both fall to the bed. I taste the salty tang of tears, and I have no idea if they're his or mine.

Then I pull back, our ragged breathing and pounding heart beats filling the silence in the room.

"I love you, too," I whisper.

His eyes are wide and wild as they search mine, and then his lips crash onto mine, his hands holding my face like he never wants to let go. His bare cock rocks against my clit, the skin silky smooth and hot as it slides against my wet folds. I moan into his mouth, my pussy already aching for him.

"Trey," I pant. "Fuck me. Now."

He doesn't disappoint, his hooded eyes perusing my body with unfiltered lust. He thrusts inside me with one strong movement, filling me to the brim and holding himself so deep it feels like he might split me in half. He stills, panting, our sweat mingling. He buries his face in my neck, biting and licking.

I whimper and growl, shifting my hips, wanting him to move, and he chuckles against my skin. "Baby, if I start thrusting now, I *will* lose my cool, and I won't be gentle as I fuck you into oblivion."

"Do it," I practically growl, digging my nails into his back, marking him. "Fuck me like you mean it."

With a roar, Trey pulls back and lets go, driving his cock into me, as promised, with brutal force. I scream out, pleasure radiating from my core and through every inch of my body as each of his frenzied thrusts push me closer and closer to the edge.

"Come for me, Charlie. Come all over my dick."

Wave after wave of my orgasm crashes over me, the aftershocks blacking out my vision as my pussy spasms and clenches around Trey's cock.

"Fuuuccckkk," he groans, his hands fisting the sheets on either side of my body as he chases his own release, his dick pulsing inside me.

And then we both collapse.

It wasn't what I'd call love making, but it was perfect.

CHAPTER THIRTY-NINE

CHARLIE

*W*ith the semester in full swing, I've been pretty busy between school, Trey, and the theater. Lincoln and I have resigned ourselves to the fact that we can't really avoid each other—we're in the same classes, part of the same friend group, and we work together—so my life is just a delightful mix of awkwardness as February passes. We talked right after Trey and I made up, but he just reiterated that he needed a bit more time to sort out his feelings. Self-loathing is his specialty, and right now, he's got it in spades. I have noticed him genuinely smiling more with other people. It makes me both happy and sad, and honestly a little jealous. *That used to be my smile.*

Matt seems to enjoy that Lincoln and I aren't talking, which doesn't really surprise me. He's not, however, happy that Trey and I are still close. He didn't take the bait when I sent him a few antagonizing text messages, but none of use like the idea of provoking him in person, so I've been extra vigilant about avoiding Matt around campus. However, as I'm walking through the hall on my way to the cafeteria, a strong arm pulls me into a storage closet. At first, I assume it's Trey, but the hand is clammy and the person's scent is all wrong. My heart hammers with fear as the light above me flickers on and I look into Matt's pale blue eyes.

"What's your damage, Matt?" I growl.

His grip hurts and I pull against it. He releases my arm, but his hand squeezes my throat, and he pushes me against the shelving, the sharp edges digging into my back. Fear slithers through my stomach as I try to gauge his intentions.

"My damage? *My damage* is that Trey Walker is still sniffing around you like a horny dog. I told you to stop acting like a little slut." His grip tightens until I can barely get in tiny sips of air. Then, he lets go, and I fall back, gasping.

"What are you going to do?" I pant. "Rape me like you did that girl?"

He grits his teeth, and it occurs to me that I probably shouldn't push him, but I hate feeling like a victim. I was under his thumb for years, and I refuse to let him make me feel small anymore.

"Either stop fucking him or the pictures will go to Rosewood, Charlie. I fucking mean it."

I raise my chin, glaring at him with more courage than I actually feel. "Then send them. I'd rather be slut-shamed than allow you to manipulate me." Then I duck under his arm and open the door, slamming it behind me. It catches on his foot as he tries to chase me into the hallway.

I round the corner and run into Fiona coming the other direction.

"Whoa, you okay, babe?" she asks, eyeing the expression on my face.

I look back as Matt turns the corner, looking as cool as a fucking cucumber like he didn't just try to choke me.

"Is he bothering you?" Fiona glares at Matt.

I haven't told her about the pictures, so she doesn't see him as any more than my creepy ex-boyfriend, but I don't want to get her involved in my drama.

"No, it's fine," I say quickly. "He just had a question. Let's go get some pizza."

Fiona nods, watching Matt over my shoulder with narrowed eyes. As we walk away, I shiver, feeling his gaze like a knife to my back.

Matt's threat echoes in my head. It's frustrating how hard it is to actually catch someone incriminating themselves. *How do people in the movies always have their phones ready to record?*

The aromatic cheesy smell of pizza fills my nostrils as we enter the cavernous dining hall, and my stomach rumbles loudly.

"Down, boy," Fiona says with a giggle, giving me the side eye, and I elbow her playfully. "It's a shame that Matt is ruining hockey for us this year. It's such a hot sport to watch."

I roll my eyes as I grab a few slices of pizza from the buffet. We walk through the line and scan our phones to check out.

"You just want to watch Brantley grunt on the ice with a bunch of other guys. Honestly, Fi, just admit that you like him."

"Wow, you're grumpy when you're hungry," Fi says, snickering as we take a seat at our normal table. Trey looks up as we join them.

"Oh yeah, she can be a hangry bitch," Trey comments, and I give him a dark look. "See?"

Link is at the other end of the table, suddenly very interested in doing homework while he scarfs down his pizza.

I sigh, my appetite fading.

"Three-day weekend coming up," Brantley says, popping a piece of pepperoni into his mouth. "Everyone have epic plans?"

"Link and I are going to Brighton," Trey says with a shrug. "Some high school buddies are going to be around."

"Right on. What about you two?" Brantley asks, giving Fiona a wink. She rolls her eyes. Ever since we all started sitting together in the dining hall, Brantley has been trying extra hard to get into her pants, and she's been trying extra hard to put him in his place.

"Well, my mom was actually a decent person over Christmas, so I'm helping her move into a rehab center," she says matter-of-factly, as if that's a normal thing to do for a parent.

"Jesus…," Brantley mutters.

"I'll be in Brighton, too," I say, and Link looks over, his eyes hopeful for the first time since that December night. My lips part as we stare at each other, and the world blurs around us for just a moment.

God, I feel like I'm in a Taylor Swift song.

"Then, I guess we'll see you there," Trey says, snapping my brain back to the present. His smile drips sex. Link stays quiet and looks back down at his book with a pained expression.

"Sure," I say, giving Trey an encouraging, albeit fake, smile.

"For fuck's sake, you two just need to fuck and make up," Brantley says, his eyes bouncing between me and Link. "It's truly painful to watch you both pretend to ignore each other."

Lincoln looks up at Brantley sharply and slams his book closed, then stuffs it into his backpack. "See you guys later," he grinds out through clenched teeth. He stands and storms out of the dining hall.

I sigh, watching him leave. Even angry he looks so fucking hot, especially walking away.

Brantley looks over at me apologetically. "Sorry."

I shrug. "You're not wrong."

"Did I hear you two talking about hockey when you walked up?" Trey asks, changing the subject.

"Oh, uhh…" I glance at Fi and then smirk at Brantley.

Fiona gives me a warning look. "We just saw Matt in the hall, and I was commenting that it's too bad that prick ruined hockey for us this year," Fi says smoothly before I can tease her anymore about Brantley.

Trey stiffens. "You were with Matt?"

I cringe. "He was just asking me which movies we're showing right now. No biggie."

Trey looks at me doubtfully.

Brantley looks confused. "What's your beef with Johnson, anyway?"

"He's my ex," I mumble.

Brantley snorts a laugh. "Well, you dodged a bullet with that one."

"I agree. But what do you mean?"

"Well, I'm sure you heard about the girl that accused him of rape earlier this year."

"Yeah, but the school board dismissed it, right?"

"They did, but two other girls have been talking about him, too—they're just afraid to come forward now. Mason and I tried to talk to Coach about it last week, but he said it was just rumors." Brantley blows out a breath. "Honestly, I want to get to the Frozen Four as much as anyone on the team, but Johnson gives me the creeps. And, he's gotten so aggressive at practice. He's losing his shit at everyone. He cross-checked a poor freshman right into the wall yesterday. It's a huge bummer."

I glance at Trey, and he looks worried.

"I wish I had known he was your ex, Charlie. Why am I always the last one to know these things?" Brantley complains.

Trey raises an eyebrow. "Maybe because you're this school's Gossip Girl?"

"Your sarcasm is hurtful, bro," he says, clutching his chest.

Trey just shrugs and turns to me protectively, pressing his lips firmly to mine. His tongue immediately begs for entry, and I kiss him back eagerly, the buzz of the dining hall fading away as I lose myself in him.

"Ugh, gag," Fiona says. "You two are nauseating."

Trey pulls back and throws his arm around me, tugging me close. "Don't be jealous, Flowers. It's not a good look."

"Ha! Really funny, Walker," she says, rolling her eyes. "The only thing I'm jealous of is all the dick Charlie gets these days—I could use a good dicking."

"For fuck's sake, Fi," I murmur, a warm blush flooding my cheeks.

Finished with our meals, we all rise from the table and head out of the dining hall.

"I can help with that," Brantley says with a wide grin.

"In your dreams, Michaels," Fi calls over her shoulder.

"She has no idea," he whispers so only Trey and I can hear, and I smile because it's nice to feel like a normal college student for once.

CHAPTER FORTY

LINCOLN

I can't get Charlie out of my head. I'm ready to talk to her; I just don't know what to say. Instead, I've done the only thing I can do to stay sane—I've been stalking her. But not like I used to. I don't want her to see me this time. I just want to know she's safe and happy. So I started charming her best friend so I could keep tabs on her.

I take the stairs after I enter the Raven Building, careful to avoid the elevator so I don't run into Charlie, and I peek around the door before slinking down the hallway to Flowers's dorm room.

I knock, and it takes Flowers only a second before she answers. I give my her best friendly smile.

"Ugh, Lincoln, c'mon, you're killing me." She looks around the hallway and then hauls me into her room by the front of my shirt.

"Nice to see you, too, Flowers," I say dryly, smoothing invisible wrinkles from the front of my hoodie.

"You can't just show up here," she says, placing her hands on her hips. "Charlie could come by any minute. We're about to go hang out with…"

"With who?" I ask.

"None of your business," she sasses.

"Flowers...," I warn, giving her a stern look.

She sighs, running a hand through her auburn hair. "Fine, we're meeting Serenity, okay?"

I lower my brows. "Seren? Are you guys friends now?"

"Maybe? She asked us to get coffee." Flowers shrugs. "I think she's reaching out because it turns out that those plastic girls that follow her around aren't actually her friends."

"Shocking," I reply sarcastically. "I told her years ago that Lisa was fake as hell."

Flowers huffs. "I'm still not sure I trust her after how she treated Charlie at the start of the year."

I look away, rubbing the back of my neck. "Honestly, that's probably my fault. She's my friend, and I think my mean-boy attitude brought out her inner Regina George."

She laughs. "Fair point. I guess Charlie gave you a second chance too. She's way too nice for the shitty people in this world." Her phone buzzes, and she holds it up, reading the text.

CHARLIE

You ready?

Flowers gives me a hard glare and then pulls her phone back and turns for privacy, but I'm so much taller than her, I can still see the screen over her shoulder.

Give me ten minutes. Hair crisis, plus I need to take out the trash.

Flowers snickers at her reply, and I roll my eyes. "Really? Am I supposed to be the trash in this scenario? I'm wounded," I snark.

She glances back at me, giving me a solid smack in the abs, and actually turns away from me to finish the text conversation.

"She'll be here in ten minutes, Evans. Time for you to go."

"Fine, but you'll text me if you guys go out somewhere tonight?"

"Sure, whatever." Flowers sighs and looks up at me meaningfully. "She's not happy without you, Link, and she's not better off. I suggest you stop being a martyr."

I run my hand through my hair, resisting the urge to tug at it in frustration. "You're not the first person to give me unsolicited advice about this." Annoyance sparks in my chest when I think about Brantley's comment at lunch today.

"And I'm sure I won't be the last. But the difference between me and Brantley is I actually know Charlie, so I would hope my advice carries more weight."

I eye her pleading expression, knowing she's probably right.

"Why don't you talk to Trey about this, anyway? He's your best friend, and he's arguably closer to Charlie than I am."

"He already knows everything—we're on the same page about where we want to be. I'm just trying to work through some guilt."

"Charlie told me some of it, but do you care to elaborate?"

"Not really. But I fucked up, and it's hard for me to accept that I'm deserving of love, as lame as that sounds."

Flowers steps closer, her eyes softening. "I give you a lot of shit, Evans, but you really have a soft, gooey center, don't you?"

I give her a dark look. "Only for Trey and Charlie. Don't tell anyone though. I have a reputation to uphold."

Flowers giggles. "God, the hold she has on you two. I hope I can pussy-whip two guys someday—especially stubborn assholes like you and Trey. Frankly, it's impressive."

I give her a deadpan look.

There's a quick knock, and then Flowers's door flies open. We jump apart reflexively, looking guilty as shit despite our innocent rendezvous.

"Sorry, Fi, I know you said ten minutes, but the dining hall was out of..." Charlie's eyes narrow when she sees me standing there.

Every muscle in my body tightens, screaming at me to run, but I stand my ground.

Confusion clouds Charlie's features. "Link, what're you doing here?" Then her eyes widen, and I swear their color darkens from meadow green to haunted forest black. "Wait, are you two..."

Flowers and I glance at each other, and then we simultaneously understand what she's inferring, and we step apart, as if distance itself can exonerate us.

"No!"

"Ew!"

I glare at Flowers. "Ew? Really?"

"What? You're not my type."

"I'm sorry? Tall, dark, and fuckably handsome isn't your type?"

"More like, I don't fuck guys in love with my best friend."

"Okay, fine. Fair point," I concede. And then I wince when I realize what I implied.

I turn to stare at Charlie. Her pink lips are parted, and they're a stark contrast with her skin, which is sheet white as she gazes at me. I glance down and see she's wearing my gray Whitmore U hoodie, and a tickle of what can only be described as butterflies erupts in my stomach. Her dark hair is pulled back into two long braids, and my fingers twitch with the urge to pull on them playfully. She looks like she's holding her breath, and I wonder if she's about to have a panic attack.

"Sunshine? Are you okay?"

She takes a shuddering breath and blinks rapidly as she looks away. I get the distinct impression she's fighting tears, and it shreds my already bloodied heart just a little more.

She clears her throat. "I'm okay," she says quietly before looking at Flowers, who gives her a warm smile. "I'm sorry,"

Charlie says. "You both just looked so guilty, so I thought maybe..."

"It's okay," Flowers says. "I totally get it." She walks forward and loops her arm through Charlie's. "C'mon, girl. Lincoln was just leaving, *right?*"

Then she leads Charlie out of the room before I can respond, glaring at me darkly over her shoulder.

CHARLIE

Fiona and I walk in silence while I try to make sense of what just happened, the scene from a moment ago running through my head on a loop more repetitive than Daft Punk lyrics.

"Did Link just admit he loves me?" I blurt. "Wait, never mind, don't answer that." I shake my head. "Why was he at your dorm, Fi?"

We hunch together against the cold as we shuffle toward the gate to Main Street, our breath escaping our lips in hazy puffs.

Fiona bites her lip, considering her answer.

"Don't bullshit me," I warn.

She sighs. "He was checking up on you."

"Checking up on me?"

"Yes, the adorable little stalker has been grilling me for information ever since winter break."

I stop, causing Fi to stumble as our arms are still linked. "You're a double agent?"

"I guess? Sort of?"

"Why?"

She pulls me back into motion. "Do you really need to ask?"

"What did you tell him?" I ask apprehensively, remembering when I called her on New Year's Eve well before the ball dropped. She came back up to Vancouver and found Sebastian and me wasted after I'd polished off Marcus's fancy vodka. You'd think I would've been a crying mess in that state, but I was angry, and I just wanted someone else to understand why. So I told Fi *everything* that night. *Every. Smutty. Detail.* Then I passed out.

"I only answered his questions, Charlie. He wanted to know what you were up to, your mental state, that you're safe. He's just worried, I think. And I couldn't tell him no—not when I knew it was because he cared," she says with a sad smile.

I nod as we approach the coffee shop. Serenity is standing outside, bouncing from one Ugg to the other and blowing into her purple mittens.

"Hey," I say as we walk up. Her long blonde hair is tangled around her shoulders in loose curls, and her cheeks and nose are pink from the cold. "You okay?" She opens her mouth, but I hold my hand up quickly. "Actually, let's go in and get some warm drinks first."

We walk inside the coffee shop, and I shiver when I look over at the booth where I sat with Matt. It seems like forever ago now. I realize that it was a mistake to let him back into my life at all. I knew something was off with him, and when I consider it, I think I knew even before he cheated. I was just too scared to leave until he forced my hand.

After ordering drinks, we sit at one of the round tables by the window.

Serenity looks down at her coffee, then up again. "I know I don't deserve your friendship—from either of you—but I don't have a lot of girlfriends anymore." She gives a small smile and pushes a lock of hair behind her ear. "Lincoln is pretty patient with me—we've been friends forever—but I think he's tired of being my only real confidant."

"Not that I don't want to be your friend, Seren, but aren't you leaving soon?" I ask.

307

"I am at the end of the year, but I like you, Charlie. Despite the fact that I'm in love with one of your boyfriends and was a straight-up bitch to you when we met, you've still shown me kindness. And to be honest, I've never seen Link and Trey this happy. At least not since we were kids." She scrunches her nose and gives me an apologetic look. "I'm just lonely, and I was hoping you guys would want to hang out."

Fiona glances at me, and I smile. Then she looks back at Serenity with a smirk. "You must have a lot of dirt on the boys."

Serenity laughs. "I could probably tell you a few stories."

I give her a serious look. "But can you tell me why Link's so scared? I know he wants to be with me and Trey." I stumble over the sentence because I keep waiting to see judgment when I refer to the three of us being together, but Serenity's ice-blue eyes shine with empathy.

"I assume I can trust you both won't say anything if I tell you something personal," she starts haltingly.

We both nod.

Serenity takes a deep breath. "I went to a really dark place in high school. My mom is a perfectionist and she wanted me to be perfect, too. As a ballet dancer, I was under a lot of pressure, and I…." Her breath catches in her throat, and she looks up at the ceiling before she pushes on. "I started throwing up to keep my weight low. I felt like it was the only thing in my life I could control." Her eyes are glassy and her voice trembles. "It got really bad, and one night Link saved me. He found me passed out on my bathroom floor and called 9-1-1. I was so malnourished, my heart was barely beating." She wrings her hands together anxiously. "He was so angry at my mother that he threatened to call Child Protective Services—I was only 17. My mom pulled back after that, and I kept dancing, but less competitively, and I started to love it again like I did when I was a little girl."

I stare at her in shock. "I'm so sorry."

"Shit," Fi whispers. "That's heavy."

Serenity swallows thickly, and her brows furrow as if she's struggling to say more. "I just want you to understand that Lincoln Evans comes across as a black knight sometimes, but he was my white knight once. He loves hard, but he doesn't think he deserves love in return. And we both know that's not true."

I nod slowly. "I've seen glimpses of that."

"When Allie left, he was crushed—he loved her so much, and they were so alike. She and John were huge movie nerds, and I think that's why the theater reflects so much of his personality —his passion for movies is all he has left of his mom."

My heart aches. I hate that my mom was part of his heartbreak, but maybe we were meant to be part of each other's lives to help each other heal.

"Thank you, Seren. You sharing all this means a lot."

Serenity smiles, her face lighting up in a genuine way I've never seen. "Have you been to the Mexican place up the street? Happy hour starts soon, and they have the best margs."

Fiona grins and claps her hands. "Hell yes. Welcome to the family, bitch."

CHAPTER FORTY-ONE

CHARLIE

*J*t's Sunday night, and I'm home for the long weekend. I step out onto the curb, thanking my Uber driver. Trey texted me to arrive at nine, and I'm an hour late, but I hate being on time for things like this. Somehow, I'm always the first person to arrive and then I sit there awkwardly until other people show up.

The air is chilly—cold and crisp with a gentle salty sea breeze that carries the sound of laughter up and down the streets. I cross at the crosswalk, stepping to the side to avoid the cigarette smoke from the couple in front of me.

The Beaver is a local favorite. It's an old brick building on the corner of Maple Avenue. The sign over the door features a grinning beaver with cartoonishly large buck teeth clutching a beer mug overflowing with foam. There are several neon alcohol signs in the windows, some of them flickering obnoxiously as I approach. The prep-school townies call it a dive bar, but that doesn't keep anyone away. And really, it's pretty nice. Turns out rich kids are poor judges of character. Who knew?

It's weird being able to enter legally. I came here all the time when I was in high school, tagging along with Seb and his buddies, but I have yet to show my face as a legit twenty-one-year-old. I walk in and spot a large, grumpy looking guy with a shaved head standing in the entryway checking IDs, and I smile.

"Hey Gus," I say, just as he finishes scrutinizing a group of girls dressed in the skimpiest outfits I've ever seen—a bachelorette party from the looks of it. I shiver just looking at their bare arms and legs.

Don't they know it's still winter?

"Charlie!" Gus bellows, causing one of the girls to jump and glance back. His intimidating demeanor softens as his deep brown eyes meet mine. Gus has been security at The Beaver for years, and he's a serious hard-ass most of the time, but he always looked the other way when it came to our group of friends—probably because we were pretty low-key trouble makers for underage drinkers.

He grabs my shoulders and pulls me in for a bear hug that has the air whooshing from my lungs, and then he pushes me back at arms length and looks me up and down with a wide grin. "It's been too long, honey. You look beautiful. Finally here as an actual adult?" he asks with a wink.

I step back, laughing, and dig out my wallet, handing him my driver license. "Sure am," I say.

"Wow, twenty-one, huh?" he says, looking at the photo and then back up at me. "Time flies." I hear an annoyed huff behind me and glance back to see the line we're holding up with our friendly reunion.

"I should get inside," I say, waving apologetically at the group behind me.

Gus gives them a measured glare over my shoulder, and they fall quiet. I bite back a giggle. "Come see me later when things slow down, and we'll catch up, got it?" he says, handing me back my ID. I take it from him with a nod.

"Sure thing, Gus."

I breathe a sigh of relief at the rush of warm air skating over

311

my skin as I enter the bar. I look around. Not much has changed, but they did replace the awful blue carpets with dark hardwoods, so the place looks a little less divey.

The walls are an electric jumble of knickknacks, metal signs, and local sports memorabilia—the town high school crests displayed proudly alongside Seahawks, Mariners, Kraken, and Sounders gear. There's a wood burning stone fireplace lit on one wall, surrounded by comfy overstuffed leather chairs, and the bar itself is situated along the right side of the room. Tall tables dot the middle of the space, and in the back room, I can hear the loud clack of pool balls and the twerp of old school arcade games.

I don't immediately see Trey or Lincoln, but I got the text earlier from Trey saying when they arrived, so I assume they're in the back.

Nerves riot in my stomach as I consider again whether coming out tonight was a good idea. Whatever is between Lincoln, Trey, and me is pretty unconventional, and we aren't at Whitmore right now. When I'm there, I have friends, a job, and I feel like myself—a whole person. But in Brighton, I'm nobody worth remembering. I'm Matt's ex, Sebastian and Marcus's kid sister, the daughter of a dead woman.

From what Seb told me and from what Link and Trey have shared, they were two years ahead of me and went to Washington Prep, which happens to be Brighton Prep's cross-town rival. But those beautiful boys were somebodies in this town, and I have no doubt that our popularity statuses would have been vastly different had we actually crossed paths in high school.

I walk over to the bar and order my usual drink. The bartender is younger—probably in her late twenties—with pretty green eyes and short dirty-blonde hair. She smiles at me as she makes my drink. "Are you home for the three-day weekend?" she asks, filling a glass with some ice.

I nod. "Home from Whitmore U."

"You look familiar," she says, using the nozzle to spray my Diet Pepsi. Then her smile widens as her eyes light up with recognition. "You're Marcus Conner's little sister."

I smile politely, inwardly cringing at the way everyone seems to know everyone in a small town like this. It's impossible to stay anonymous, which is pretty much my life goal, if I'm being honest.

"Yup," I say.

"I graduated with Marcus. What's he up to these days?"

"He owns a pub in Vancouver, actually," I reply, my eyes still searching for a familiar face to rescue me from this small talk.

"No shit," she says. "Good for him." She sets my drink down in front of me.

Just then, I spot Trey from the other room, a perfectly tanned hand running through his mess of golden locks while he laughs with someone I can't see.

"Sorry, I see my friends." I look back at the bartender apologetically.

"No worries," she says. "Tell Marcus that Trisha says hello."

"Will do," I say before walking toward the back room. I step around the doorframe as subtly as possible to take in the scene, and I'm glad I do because I didn't expect to see so many people. Some I recognize from Brighton Prep, though no one I knew that well, but I assume the others must've gone to Washington Prep.

I take a large gulp of my drink, and wince when the whisky burns down my throat.

Wow, thanks Trisha, I think. *Is there any actual Pepsi in this?*

But that's probably a good thing as the alcohol immediately starts to quiet the anxiety in my gut. I take another generous sip.

Trey is standing at one of the tall tables in the corner, looking delicious in a blue flannel button-up, dark jeans, and brown boots. He's leaning forward across the table, his shirt sleeves rolled up showing off those beautiful veiny forearms, and his head is cocked to one side causing his blond hair to tumble sexily across his forehead. A small smile plays across his full lips as he listens intently to the person across from him, who happens to be the third hottest guy in this room—and I say third hottest because I know Link is lurking here somewhere even though I haven't spotted him yet.

I study the stranger. He's tall and muscular but lean, with hair so blond it's practically silver in contrast with Trey's golden locks. He has high cheekbones and bright turquoise eyes, the color of some tropical paradise. I stiffen when I notice his pale hand resting casually on Trey's wrist, and my eyes bounce between them as I as icy shock slides under my skin.

This is probably threesome guy.

Something unpleasant that feels suspiciously like jealousy curls in my stomach as I stare at them, which is ridiculous. I didn't feel like this when Trey told me their story, but I suppose it's more real putting a face to the guy who Trey fucked while he sucked Link's cock.

And such a breathtaking face at that, the ugly voice in my head notes.

I take a deep breath and push away my spiraling thoughts.

I blink and continue to scan the room and finally spot Lincoln. He holds a pool cue in one hand and a little square of blue chalk in the other while he chats with Serenity and two other girls.

Fan-fucking-tastic.

I steel myself to enter what I am sure is going to be social suicide and go to take another drink when I realize there's nothing in my glass but ice.

TREY

"I'm telling you, dude, I have never seen so many out-and-proud gays in my life. Seattle is my vibe," Jeremy says with a wink, leaning closer to me so I can hear him over the breathy croon of Soundgarden's "Black Hole Sun." He smells like vodka and something fruity, and I eye his drink, which is almost the same shade of blue as his eyes. "You should come visit sometime, and I'll take you to some bars on Cap Hill—really hook you up."

I snicker. "I dunno, man," I say. "I'm not really into hookups anymore."

Jeremy's eyes widen and he takes a dramatic step back, his hand falling from my wrist. "Who are you and what have you done with Trey Walker?"

"Shut up, asshole," I reply with a glare.

He chuckles. "This girl must be something." He pauses, tapping his chin thoughtfully. "I always thought you'd settle down with a guy, but I guess I can't be right about everything."

I swallow heavily at his words because I honestly thought that too. Guys were always a fun hook up—so aggressive, especially the closeted ones. They were a challenge. But girls were always an average lay to me, as bad as that sounds. Until Charlie. We've been messing around for months now, and I still can't get enough of those flushed cheeks and the way she moans when I push her over the edge into an orgasm. It's so fucking addictive. I feel my dick thickening and quickly redirect my thoughts before I get a damn boner in the middle of the bar.

What's weirder still, beyond the physical stuff, I still want her around all the time—she's kind and ridiculously smart, and she cares so fucking much about me and Lincoln. We've only had each other for years, but Charlie is the first person who actually *sees* us. She knows all the shit we've been through and all the messed up stuff we've done, and she loves us both despite our flaws, sometimes even because of them.

I clear my throat, looking over at Jeremy. "Who said anything about settling down?" It's a weak, bullshit reply, and he sees right through me.

"Trey, we've been friends a long time, and you've been a slut for most of that time," he says, looking at me steadily.

I huff a laugh. "What's your point?"

"You've never had that look on your face when you talk about a girl."

I snort. "You've only heard me talk about her tonight."

He raises an eyebrow. "You were thinking about her just now. Don't deny it."

I take a long swig of my beer. Jeremy was a pretty solid friend in high school, and it feels good to talk about this thing Charlie and I have. Of course, I didn't mention to him that Link is equally fucked over Charlie Bennett, but I suspect that won't be a secret for long after tonight.

"That's what I thought," he says with a knowing smile. Then Jeremy pauses as his eyes catch on someone behind me. "Oh, who's this little lost kitty?"

I glance back and see Charlie standing against the wall, shifting from foot to foot as she clutches her glass in a white-knuckled grip. Her brown hair falls over her shoulders in soft waves and her creamy cheeks are flushed while she scans the room. Her full lips are turned down in a slight frown, and I can't help but grin because she might be all laughs and smiles with us these days, but that serious little pout is what drew Link and I to her to begin with.

"That's Charlie," I murmur to Jeremy.

"Well, well, what an adorable resting bitch face."

I chuckle. "Yeah, that we can agree on."

She turns her head, and her dark forest eyes collide with mine. I give her a wink and lift my chin, beckoning her over. Her lips lift slightly at the corners, and she pushes herself off the wall and heads our way.

I watch her eyes flick to Link, her frown deepening. He's been flirting up a storm with Seren and her friends for the past hour. Seriously, some of those girls have hearts in their eyes and must have soaking wet panties to match. I don't think he realizes he's doing it. Despite his attempt on the way here to fall into his usual moody persona, he's different now, and the more he drinks, the more his guard slips. My heart swells to see it because I feel like I'm looking at that charming, funny, smart-mouthed boy from our past.

My phone buzzes in my pocket, and I pull it out, glancing down at the text.

LINCOLN
Stop looking at me like that.

Like what?

Okay, I know exactly what he's talking about, but he's fun to fuck with.

LINCOLN
Like you're in love with me. People are going to get ideas.

Ideas? Like I've seen your huge dick, and I liked it? Not to mention, you're a fantastic kisser.

We seem to look up at the same time and our gazes lock. I give him a wink, and he rolls his eyes at me before looking back down at his phone.

LINCOLN
Fuck off.

I love you, too, buddy.

He's happy, which makes me happy. Of course, Charlie

seeing that side of him with anyone but us is probably a recipe for disaster. Not that I think she's a particularly jealous person, but she's insecure and cautious with her heart for obvious reasons—*Matt, you fucking dick.*

"Hey Bennett," I drawl as she approaches our table. "Nice of you to finally make it." She shoots me a glare and sticks out her tongue. I grin, and my fingers are dying to pull her against me and kiss the hell out of her hot little immature mouth. But I resist. For now.

"So feisty," Jeremy says with a smirk.

Charlie's gaze snaps up to his, and I see uncertainty flash in her eyes.

Smart girl, I think, realizing she's already figured out exactly who Jeremy is.

"This is Jeremy," I say, waving a hand in his direction. "This is Charlie." I give him a steady look. "Be nice."

He scoffs. "Trey, I'm always nice."

"Hi," Charlie says haltingly, as she puts her coat down on the chair next to me. Her small fingers tap the table in rhythm to the music, slowing as the song changes over to Collective Soul's "The World I Know." "I've heard a lot about you."

Jeremy raises one perfect silver eyebrow. "Have you now?"

Her eyes flick to mine and then over to Link before her cheeks redden slightly. The look was so quick most people probably wouldn't have noticed, but Jeremy's nothing if not perceptive. He smiles wickedly and looks over at me with raised brows.

"Interesting," he says quietly.

I sigh. *That's going to bite me in the ass later.*

Charlie takes a long pull of her drink and eyes Jeremy before stepping closer to me, her body language stiff and possessive, and I can't hide my smile because it reminds me of the way Link moves around her when he's jealous—like he's stalking some sort of prey. And fuck if it's not the cutest thing I've ever seen. A strange warm feeling flutters my stomach, and I realize this must be what butterflies feel like.

That's a first.

One of Charlie's hands starts to move like she wants to touch me, but then she seems to realize what she's doing and stops, dropping it to her side.

Jeremy's grin widens with understanding, and he raises his hands. "Don't worry, kitty," he says, his ocean eyes dancing with mirth when her brow furrows in confusion at his nickname. "I'm not interested in this one. He's all yours."

She relaxes and glances at me guiltily. I take a slow drink of my beer and give her a wink.

"So you guys went to high school together, huh?" She smiles shyly. "Tell me what Trey was like."

Jeremy's eyes light up, and I groan. "Oh, I've got some stories for you."

LINCOLN

I felt her the moment she entered the room, her eyes burning into me like they were tunneling right into my soul, but I refuse to acknowledge her. My control has been slipping all night, and I feel like I'm finally barely holding onto my old grumpy self by my fingertips, and if I let us share that loaded look across the room, it'll be all over. I'll push her against the wall, lift her into my arms, and claim her as mine for everyone to see—and I won't be able to stop. Despite the distance I've tried to keep, I can't cling to the darkness anymore. She lights parts of me I didn't even know still existed.

She's sunshine personified. My sunshine.

Whether she's around me or not, I find myself smiling more.

Laughing more. Just enjoying my life like a normal twenty-something.

I flex my fingers around the pool cue clutched to my chest and watch Serenity as she considers the balls on the table.

"Why suddenly so tense?" she asks with a small smile. "Your girl just arrived."

"She's not my girl." I flick her playfully on the nose.

It's not a lie. She's not.

But she will be. Our girl.

Seren gives me a "yeah right" look and lines up a shot, hitting her third stripe in a row into the corner pocket.

"How did I not know you're a pool shark?" I murmur.

"Because you've been too deep in your own damage to see anyone else around you," she says, not unkindly, but at the same time, *ouch.* "And don't change the subject. Tell me why you're still fighting this?"

I take a breath and glance around. Allison and Margo have been eyeing me like fresh meat all night, but Serenity's been keeping them in check, for the most part, and they seem distracted now that more people have shown up.

"Since when are you on Charlie's side?"

She shrugs. "We're friends now, I think. And as much as it fucking kills me, she's good for you," she says with a sour smile.

I know this has to be hard for her. She's been in love with me our whole lives, and even after I could finally see it, I took advantage of her feelings for years, and the guilt sits heavily in my gut.

"And you didn't answer my question," she says pointedly, finally missing a shot.

I glance across the room, relieved when I see Charlie has joined Trey and Jeremy at their table. Trey catches my eye and gives me a slight nod. My body relaxes some, and I take a drink of my whisky, letting the sweetness burn down my throat.

I look back into Serenity's ice-blue eyes. "I fucked up."

"And you don't think she'll forgive you?" Seren sounds doubtful, and I concede a small smile.

"She already has from what I can tell, but she's giving me space to deal with my own doubts."

Seren's gaze burns with curiosity, but to my shock, she doesn't ask me my secret. She watches as I line up my shot, hitting the white ball with a bit too much force. The solid ball I was aiming for goes wide, bouncing off the side of the felt and clacking into another cluster of balls, dropping a stripe into the pocket.

I wince.

Serenity smirks. "So you're avoiding her?" she asks.

"I was," I say with a sigh. "Trey invited her tonight, but I think I'm ready to talk about everything."

Serenity glances in Charlie's direction, and I follow her gaze. Jeremy is talking animatedly with his hands, and Charlie is giggling, the straw to her drink resting against her perfect lips.

Her eyes flick this way, and I look away quickly.

"I talked to her, you know," Serenity says. I almost don't hear her over the music and laughter filling the room.

I play dumb because this isn't news to me. "When?"

"It was a couple weeks before Thanksgiving break, I think. I wasn't planning on talking to her, but I was in the library one night..."

"I'm sorry, you were *where*?" I interrupt with a shit-eating grin.

She flips me off. "Funny. Anyway, I saw her sitting at a table by herself, and she looked...lost and a bit frustrated, so I approached her against my better judgment."

I remember the night in question well. My eyes wander back over to Trey and Charlie, as memories from that perfect night replay in my head. My dick hardens just thinking about how hot it was to have them both—together. I think I'm ready to take it farther now, with both of them.

"I told her about California, and we kind of called a truce. Then a few days ago, I met with her and Fiona for some drinks. They're really nice people," she admits guiltily. "And we were pretty mean."

"Yeah," I run my hands through my hair. "Tell me about it."

"I'm not even going to ask why you hated Charlie so much, but I'm glad she's around now."

"So what else did you tell her?" I ask, taking a long sip of my drink.

"I told her about how you threatened to call CPS on my mom—how you saved me. I just wanted her to see that despite all the walls you put up to keep us out, underneath you are a good person." Her eyes soften. "And you deserve to be loved."

A lump forms in my throat, and I swallow it roughly. "That was uncharacteristically kind of you." I smirk to hide my emotions and tug on her hair, and she swats my hand away. Then she leans over the pool table. "Eight ball, right corner pocket," she says before sinking it smoothly.

I roll my eyes. "Okay, you win, Seren."

"Rematch?" She asks with an evil grin.

I lean my pool cue against the wall and shake my head. "No way."

This time when I look at Charlie, we lock eyes, and I swear my heart stops. I harden my gaze, trying to push down every emotion threatening to rush to the surface of my skin. Just then a large hand lands on my shoulder, breaking our eye contact. I look over at Jason, my high school buddy, who asks if I want to join him outside for a smoke break. I haven't smoked in a long time, but I suddenly feel itchy and uncomfortable, like the room is closing in on me. So I nod and follow him to the back exit.

I place my hand against the door, but I can't help but I glance back as I do. Charlie's green eyes are tracking my movements, and they look a bit glazed over like she's drunk—or getting there, anyway. But worse, they're shining with obvious anger and hurt. Then, like the masochist I am, I keep my face carefully neutral and turn away.

CHARLIE

I'm kind of drunk. I'm also pathetic, I've decided as I stare dejectedly at my reflection in the bathroom mirror, gripping the edges of the sink tightly. I know I need to stop drinking now, or I'll do or say something stupid. I squeeze my eyes closed and take a deep breath before stepping back into the crowded space.

I walk back toward where Trey and Jeremy are laughing with some girls from my high school. Before I went to the bathroom, they were talking my ear off about how they were in love with Seb in high school, and I had to stop my eyes from rolling to the back of my head because *of course* they were.

I stop next to Trey but don't join the conversation. Instead, I drop against the wall with a huff, staring over at Link again like a petulant child.

Yup. Definitely drunk.

I hate that Lincoln is making me feel this way.

I knew coming here was a bad idea.

I miss my Link—the soft side of him where he's considerate and funny and sometimes even adorable, which is not a word I would have used to describe Lincoln Evans just a few months ago.

But here in Brighton, surrounded by his old high school buddies and swooning fangirls, I've faded back into the background, a blip in his peripheral vision, as he moves around the room chatting and laughing. I feel like nothing. And I'm not going to lie, it fucking hurts. I even saw him smoking when I went to the bathroom. I've never seen him smoke. It's like this

323

Lincoln is some stranger, and everything that happened back at Whitmore before winter break was some alternate timeline.

"Except there's no Infinity Stones to fix this fucking mess," I grumble.

"And who exactly do you want to snap out of existence?" Jeremy asks, his voice laced with amusement.

I look over quickly. "You're a quiet walker," I slur, eyeing him warily. "Like a ninja."

"You're a loud talker," he says, raising an eyebrow.

"Touché," I say with a shrug and glare at Lincoln.

"If looks could kill. Do you want to talk about it?"

My eyes fall to Trey, who seems content in his conversation. "Not really." I look around for a drink.

Jeremy nudges a glass of water toward me. "You'll thank me in the morning."

I take it and swallow a few gulps, trying to clear my head. *I'm so pathetic.*

"You're not pathetic, sweetie. You're in love."

"I'm also apparently unaware I'm talking out loud," I mumble. But I don't deny what he says. "I thought I was in love once before, but…"

"But?" Jeremy urges me gently.

"But I wasn't. I get it now." I squint at him skeptically. "Shouldn't you be chewing me out for loving them both? You and Trey seem close. I thought you would be pissed at me if you knew."

He barks a laugh. "I understand wanting them both better than anyone," he says, giving me a wicked grin. I blush. "But being a gay guy, I also understand that love is love. And those boys? They love each other deeply—have for a long time. And they clearly love you too. If that works for you three, why should anyone judge?"

"You're wrong. Trey loves me, but I'm not sure Link is capable of the kind of love I need from him." I hate how my voice cracks. "I want to be what he needs but I don't think he needs me."

My own words rip through my body like knives, shredding my heart to bits, and I blink back tears.

"There's a lot of 'needs' in that statement," he says softly. "What about what you both *want?*"

I look over at Jeremy, taking in his silver hair, teal eyes, and pale skin. He's looking at me like he's trying to figure something out.

"You're very pretty, you know," I tell him earnestly.

He smiles. "You're not so bad yourself, kitty."

I glance at my phone and realize it's almost midnight. I feel so defeated, and I just want to go home and drown in my own misery. I move over to the table and grab my coat. Trey looks up as I do, his brow furrowing.

"Are you leaving?"

"Yeah," I say. "Sorry, Trey. I'm just really tired."

Tears prick the backs of my eyes again, and I don't want to lose my composure in this bar full of laughing strangers. Then the song flips to Fuel's "Shimmer," and fuck if I don't feel my bottom lip start to quiver. I turn, my coat clenched tightly in my hand, and run to the front door.

"Bennett!" I hear Trey's voice behind me, but I ignore him, breathing in the rush of icy air that hits my lungs as I step outside onto the sidewalk. I take out my phone and pull up the Uber app, cursing when I see that prices are sky-high and the wait is several minutes. I sit on the curb, put my coat to my face, and let myself cry.

TREY

"Bennett!" I call after her, doing my best to follow her without causing too many heads to turn.

Honestly, I was hoping Link would finally give in and break all this tension between them. *But she broke instead*, I think as she takes off across the room.

A large hand catches my arm, halting my progress.

"What's going on?" Lincoln asks.

"I'm not sure," I say. "She just took off. But I'm going after her."

He sighs. "This is my fault."

"Yeah, it is," I say, and he flinches. I put my hand over his, pausing for a moment before pushing him away from my arm. "Just...let me go to her. I'll smooth it over."

He nods tightly. "I'll fix it soon. I promise."

I turn, walking into the main part of the bar, and nod to Gus as I run out the front door. The chill in the air cuts right through my flannel shirt, and I hug my arms around myself, searching for Charlie.

I don't have to look far. She's a few feet away, sitting on the curb with her face pressed into the coat on her knees. Her shoulders are shaking gently, and I know she's crying. My heart aches at the sight.

I approach her slowly, sitting down beside her. "Charlie," I say, pausing when her posture stiffens. "Are you okay?"

She looks away, rubbing her cheeks with the heel of her hands. "Fine." Her voice shakes. "Just too much to drink, I guess." When she looks at me, her eyes are red, and I can still see tears clinging to her lashes.

I sigh. "Don't give up on him, Charlie. Please. I know it doesn't seem like it, but he's trying—he's ready to talk."

Her green eyes darken with anger. "I'm so tired of everyone telling me that—defending his shitty behavior. I know you want me to save him, Trey, but I can't do it anymore." She takes a deep breath. "I'm not enough," she says quietly. "I wish I was."

"Just talk to him," I plead. "I know he wants to fix this just as bad as you do."

She stares at me, and for a minute, I think she considers my words, but then her eyes soften sadly, and she shakes her head. "I don't think I can," she whispers. "This—" she gestures at her chest "—hurts too damn much." Her lip quivers as she meets my gaze. "I feel like his dirty secret right now, and I can't...I won't wait around for him to decide whether I'm worth it or whether he's worth it." She sighs heavily. "Just let me go home. My Uber will be here any minute."

I nod mutely, pulling her into my side and kissing the top of her head. "Get some rest, Bennett."

Then I go to stand and walk back inside, a cold feeling of dread pooling in my stomach.

CHARLIE

Footfalls scuff on the pavement, and I sniff, rubbing more moisture from my eyes.

"Trey, I said I'm okay. Please just go."

"Not Trey," says a deep voice.

I stiffen, looking up at Matt Johnson.

He towers over me, and the streetlight to his back makes him more shadow than man. "I thought that was you."

I look at my phone to see where my Uber is. *Shit. Five more minutes.*

"What a nice little argument that was," he says, his tone thick with malice.

I consider going back inside to wait, but he's standing

between me and the door. "Did you follow me to Brighton? Can't you just leave me alone? What is it you want, Matt?" I ask, feigning confidence that I don't feel.

He crouches down to my level, his sharp features coming into focus. "I wasn't stalking you, Charlie baby. I just happened to be over at the diner having a bite when I saw you come out. You look upset." He sounds almost gleeful. "Guess you took my advice and dumped those losers."

Anger flushes my cheeks as I gaze back at him. "Leave me alone, Matt. Really."

"I'm actually going home, too. Can we share an Uber?"

"What? Are you stupid?" His look darkens. "You literally blackmailed me and then tried to choke me in a custodial closet, and you want me to just *share* a ride with you?"

"It was for your own good," he snaps, and I flinch involuntarily.

He sits down beside me, and I scoot away from him. He smells like Patchouli and beer, and it makes my stomach churn.

A text from Lincoln pops up on my phone. I swipe it up, not bothering to read it, and hold down the button to turn off my phone before shoving it angrily into my pocket.

"Here," he says, handing me a bottle of water. "You can probably use this more than me."

I look at the bottle warily.

"Relax" he says, rolling his eyes. "I just got it from the convenience store across the street." I don't trust him, but it looks like a sealed bottle. "For fuck's sake," he says. Reaching into his pocket, he pulls out a receipt and waves it in my face. "Did you need proof that I just bought it?"

I snatch the water from him, twisting off the cap and taking a long swallow of the cold liquid.

"I'm not sharing a ride with you," I say, scooting farther away.

He stiffens but doesn't move, and we sit in silence until a

white Toyota Camry pulls up to the curb. I'm annoyed that it took closer to ten minutes for the guy to arrive. I stand and the ground tilts under my feet.

"Shit," I mutter, throwing my hands up for balance as Matt catches my bicep.

Maybe I'm more drunk than I thought.

His touch makes my skin crawl, and I try to snatch my arm away from him. "Back off," I growl, but my words are slurring.

When I move to step into the car, everything spins, and I almost fall again. Matt opens the door and pushes me inside.

"Charlie?" the Uber driver asks.

"That's me," Matt says. "Sorry, my girlfriend had a bit too much to drink."

Alarm bells start going off in my head.

"She better not puke in here," the Uber driver says, watching me from the rearview mirror.

"Nah, man, I think she's okay."

"S'not bffriend," I slur.

Something's seriously wrong. My mouth won't work right. Everything is coming out slow. My body is getting heavier.

"It's okay, baby," Matt says with a cruel smirk. "We're going home now so I can take care of you."

Panic blooms in my stomach as he leans over to press a hard, wet kiss against my mouth.

But I can't stop it. My arms aren't working, and I can't talk.

A tear leaks from the corner of my eye as the car starts to move. The window is cold against my overheated cheek.

Then everything goes black.

CHAPTER FORTY-TWO

CHARLIE

*W*hat the hell is happening? My consciousness drifts in and out of darkness, like I'm trying to keep myself above water. My head pounds painfully with each rapid beat of my heart. My stomach is churning.

This must be a nightmare, I think as something hot and wet slithers against my breast.

I want to push whatever it is away, but my arms are heavy like lead. My eyes drift open, and I blink the bleariness away, trying to focus. There's a dead weight on my legs and scratchy sheets beneath my back.

Where am I?

I'm disoriented and confused, like my head is full of cotton.

My surroundings start to slide into focus, and a chill ripples through my body when I recognize the room around me, and the pair of blue eyes rising to meet mine with a sinister smile.

This isn't a dream.

The heavy weight is Matt's body covering mine, and his lips glisten with saliva. My stomach rolls violently when I realize the warm feeling was him licking one of my bare nipples. I try to buck him off, to fight him, but my limbs are sluggish and clumsy. Nothing seems to work right.

"Ahh, there you are," he drawls, and the deep gravel of his voice sends a stab of panic through my chest. "Just in time for me to finally take that little pussy, just like I always wanted."

"No, please," I manage to murmur, and I feel hot tears flood my eyes.

"What's wrong, Charlie baby?"

My mouth starts to water as bile rises in my throat. I swallow thickly. "Please stop, Matt," I say, but I know he won't. His pupils are blown into huge black holes, and the look behind his eyes is all unhinged lust. Something is moving against my bare stomach, and I look down, my neck stiff and achy. Matt is completely naked, his hand pulling on his bare cock furiously. Another tear slides down my cheek. I hate that I'm crying in front of him, but I'm so fucking scared.

He lets go of his dick, and his fingers hook the edge of my panties, ripping them away. I wince as the fabric goes taut against the skin of my hip before it tears at the seam, leaving me completely naked. My heart feels like it might burst, it's beating so hard, and the edges of my vision darken.

Terror washes through my veins like ice water as Matt's finger teases my pussy entrance, and my body finally starts to fight back as adrenaline takes over. My legs are locked tightly in place by his bare thighs, but I raise my fists, pummeling his chest.

"You drugged me, you asshole," I sob, using all my strength to hit him.

He bares his teeth at me as he's forced to bring up his arms to protect his face. One of his hands catches my wrist, pinning my arm above my head. The position overextends it painfully, and my strength starts to wane. His other hand shoots out, his open palm connecting with my lip, and pain explodes across my face, the metallic tang of blood hitting my tongue.

Futile rage vibrates through my body. "I guess the rumors were true; you are a rapist," I sneer before spitting blood and saliva into his face.

His eyes blaze with anger, and as I stare back at him defiantly, I have the fleeting thought that he might actually kill me.

"You little bitch," he growls, his warm breath huffing in my face. "This pussy was supposed to be mine." He pushes his hard length forcefully against my belly, sticky precum warm against my chilled skin. Bile starts crawling up my throat again. "You ruin everything, just like your stepfather and your whore mother."

My brow furrows in confusion, and he smiles at my reaction.

Then, before I can process what he's telling me, his fingers enter me with a rough stabbing motion. The intrusion burns, and I gasp, my eyes wet with tears. I squeeze my eyelids shut, not wanting him to get off on my pain.

"Oh, you didn't know that your mother was a slut? Why don't you ask Seb about it? He saw what happened that night," he says as he twists his fingers inside me. "It's shocking that he didn't tell you, considering how disgustingly close you two are. Or maybe he's the one who took your virginity. Is incest one of your kinks?"

My eyes open in anger, and my muscles tense as I try to push him away. "You're sick," I say, forcing my voice to sound strong and steady.

He laughs, the sound grating on my already frayed nerves like nails on a chalkboard. "You have no idea," he says.

Matt's gaze is so empty, so devoid of emotion, and it's the first time I realize that he's a complete sociopath. Then he removes his fingers and aligns his bare cock with my entrance.

I tense, bracing for what's about to come.

Fear, anger, and the bitter taste of shame overwhelm me. My skin feels too tight, and my mouth floods with saliva again. This time, I can't stop the wave of nausea rolling through my stomach, and I turn my head and vomit violently onto Matt's arm and bed, choking and sputtering because of the awkward angle.

He jumps away from me, his face crumpling in outrage and disgust, and I instinctively curl in on myself, squeezing my eyes shut and stifling a sob. I feel the mattress dip as he stands, and he's yelling something, his voice harsh and angry, but I can't hear him anymore. My ears are buzzing, and I'm shaking so hard that my teeth are chattering.

A door slams, but it sounds far away. Everything seems far away, and I drift into darkness again.

THE COLD IS what wakes me. It feels like death seeping into my bones.

My mouth tastes like stale vomit, and I raise a shaky hand to my eyes, wiping away the crusty salt from my dried tears.

I roll over slowly, half expecting to see Matt standing in the shadows, ready to finish what he started, but the room is empty. I push myself up and look around. Vomit is drying next to me on the comforter, and I see the stringy white remnant of Matt's precum smeared along my stomach. I grab a handful of sheets at my side and wipe it away with disgust. I fight against my racing heart as a panic attack threatens to incapacitate me.

"You can fall apart later," I mutter to myself, knowing I need to get out of here.

Somewhere safe.

My eyes scan the room, and I spot my clothes in a pile next to the bed. My body still feels weak as I pull myself up and rifle through my coat. I fall to my knees with relief when I find my phone in the pocket untouched and power it on.

The screen takes forever to come to life, and I stare at the door the entire time, waiting for Matt to come storming back into the room.

If he finds me again, he'll kill me. The thought sends more tendrils of panic through my gut, and I take a deep breath to calm myself.

Lincoln knew. He didn't trust Matt from the start. He wanted me to stay away from him.

Why didn't I listen? I'm naïve. This is my fault. I need to leave.

I fumble to put on my clothes. My underwear is a lost cause, and I can't find my bra, but I pull on my jeans and shirt with numb fingers. I push my feet into my Converse, not bothering to tie them, then stumble to the bedroom door.

With sweaty palms, I ease it open and peek into the dark hallway. When nothing moves, I walk as quickly as I can manage toward the stairs. I'm still woozy from the drugs in my system, so my body feels disjointed and lethargic. It's been a while since I've been in Matt's house, but everything looks the same—wealthy but dated, like their money ran out in the nineties, which is probably true.

I reach the front door without incident and look outside, breathing a sigh of relief when I see the driveway is empty.

He left.

I walk out into the February night, and as soon as my feet hit the pavement, I start to run, pushing my way through the front gate. I take off down the sidewalk and only stop when I get to the park a few blocks away, gasping and panting.

I drop down to the grass, cold dampness soaking into my jeans, and stare sadly at the quiet playground where two little kids once played tag. I kissed him for the first time on the swings. We had a picnic in the grass with wine we stole from his dad's cellar. The memories aren't bright and happy like they once were. Now they're blurry and ash gray. Tainted. This place feels haunted. I shiver.

Everything about Matt was a lie.

With trembling fingers, I unlock my phone and call for help.

LINCOLN

"She's probably asleep," Trey says, stifling a yawn.

I growl and throw down my controller. We've been home since two, and she hasn't responded to either of us. Radio. Fucking. Silence.

Trey glances at me. "Do you want to start another game?"

I shake my head.

He takes in my rigid posture as I stare at my phone again, willing her to answer. "You know you can't really be mad."

I glare at him. "Fuck, Trey. You think I don't know I caused this? It's why I didn't want her to come out tonight," I seethe. "I knew I'd fuck it up." Frustration and impatience make my body feel like it's vibrating. "I just...I want to know she's okay."

Trey told me what she said: that she didn't want to be my dirty secret, that she thinks she isn't enough.

She's wrong. She's *everything.* I just haven't told her yet.

"I should have just said fuck it and told her from the start. I waited too long. Fuck my insecurities." I look up at him, my hands pulling roughly through my hair. "What the fuck do I do? How do I fix this?"

Just then my phone vibrates and Charlie's name pops up on the screen. I slide the bar and press it to my ear.

"Charlie? Are you okay? I've been texting..." I pause when all I hear are her uneven breaths.

"Link?" Her voice is small, frightened.

"Charlie, what's wrong?" I rush out.

Trey's eyebrows raise in alarm at my tone, and I put my phone on speaker.

335

"I...please don't be mad at me." Her voice breaks, and my heart breaks right along with it.

"Hey, Sunshine," I say gently. I feel frantic inside, but I push it down. Her voice tells me she's about to fall apart, and I need to stay calm. "I'm not going to be mad. I promise. Just tell me where you are. Trey and I will come get you."

"He..." she says, her voice barely more than a whisper. "He gave me water. I thought it was sealed. But he drugged me, and..." A wrecked sob echoes through the phone. "I'm so stupid, Link, and I'm so sorry."

Rage explodes behind my eyes.

Trey is already standing, grabbing his wallet and keys, and I stand with him as we take off through the house to the garage.

"Who? Matt? I'll kill that fucker. Is he still there?" I grate out, my teeth grinding together hard enough to crack.

He's beyond dead. I'm going to murder him.

"No," she says. "He left. And I left, too. I'm at Morris Park down the road."

"We're on our way, baby," I say, trying to keep my voice strong and steady. All I want to do is scream.

Trey cranks up the car, tires squealing as we shoot out of the garage and speed down the quiet neighborhood street.

"Hurry, Link. I'm so tired," she murmurs, and then she goes quiet.

"Charlie?" Fear grips my chest. She doesn't answer and the phone beeps with a lost connection. "Fuck!" I yell, my fist hitting the dashboard.

Trey squeezes my shoulder, grounding me. "We'll get her, Link," he says. "And we'll make that fucker pay."

I nod grimly, and pinch the bridge of my nose. Guilt burns my stomach. *If I had just talked to her sooner.*

The park isn't far, and I'm already opening my door, my feet stumbling onto the sidewalk before Trey even stops the car. She's lying on the grass, seemingly asleep. Her face is pale, and her long hair is tangled. Dark mascara is smudged under her eyes and trails down one cheek, and there's dried blood clinging to a cut on her lip.

The sight of the blood on her face sends my brain into absolute caveman mode. All I can think is that he hurt her, but I try to control my rage.

She needs me first.

I drop to my knees at Charlie's side and sweep her hair away from her forehead.

"Sunshine, can you hear me?" I ask softly.

She stirs under my touch, pressing her cool cheek into my palm. "Link?" she rasps. "I'm so thirsty."

Trey's door slams and then I hear his footsteps as he runs up to us, dropping down on her other side. I look up at him. "Do you have water in your car?"

He nods.

"Why don't we get you to the car," I gently tell Charlie. "Trey says he has water there."

Her eyes dart over to Trey as if realizing he's there for the first time, and she instinctively reaches for his hand, gripping it tightly.

"Trey," she sighs, relief evident in her voice.

"I'm here, Bennett," he says softly, squeezing her back. As she gazes at him, her green eyes brighten and glisten with tears, and they fall, streaking her pale cheeks. Trey uses his thumbs to wipe away the wetness, his amber eyes full of so much pain and love, and I realize that while I spent all this time spent agonizing over my own shit, Trey has fallen so head over heels in love with this girl that it hurts my heart to watch them together.

Tendrils of jealousy thread their way through my body as I watch their intimate exchange, and I sit back from Charlie, fighting the sense of rejection and loss threatening to swallow me whole.

337

She doesn't need me. They don't need me. The selfish realization is a slap in the face.

"Let's get you someplace safe, okay?" Trey says quietly, looking at me with a frown.

I know he can see the panic in my eyes, and he gives me a warning look that tells me not to run. He knows me so well because that's all I want to do: push them both away. Run from all these emotions that are choking me. Be a coward.

Trey lifts Charlie into his arms and carries her to the car, placing her gently in the back seat. I hear her whimper as he releases her. He reaches into the front console and grabs a bottle of water, handing it to her. Then he presses a chaste kiss to Charlie's lips and says something softly before turning back to me. His stance stiffens with anger as he takes in my expression.

"Don't you fucking dare," he hisses, his voice breaking. "I have played the middleman between you two for weeks because I *know* how you feel about her. She needs you right now more than ever."

I look down, my lips flattening into a hard line. "She has you, and you're what she needs."

Trey lunges for me, and I stumble in surprise when he pushes me until my back hits a tree, the rough bark biting into the nape of my neck as his forearm presses against my throat.

He's shorter than me, but only just, and his eyes flare with rage and hurt. "You need to make a choice right now, Evans," he growls. His face is so close that our noses graze. "You can man the fuck up and accept that you're in love with her, and despite all that you've done, she still wants every damaged piece of you." He takes a shaky breath, baring his teeth. "Or you can break her heart and walk away, but understand you'll be breaking my heart too, and you *will* lose us both." His voice cracks, and his eyes redden as tears slip from the corners. "You're my best friend, and I love you, but I love her too, and I know what will happen to her if you leave. None of us can come back from that."

I swallow thickly as all the fight leaves my body and shame washes over me.

"I...I don't want to leave," I say, a sob crawling up my throat. "I want to be strong enough for you both, but I'm so fucking scared I'm not. What if I'm not enough?"

Trey's arm drops from my throat, and without his weight to steady me, my knees almost collapse. Then he's catching me, hugging me like he did the night my mom left. Like he's strong enough for the both of us.

"You are enough, Link. You always have been. You're everything. To both of us."

I let Trey hold me, burying my face into the crook of his neck as I break. All of my anger, pain, and regret drain away. And he accepts everything as I cry against his skin, cradling the back of my head, holding all my shattered pieces together. He holds me until there's nothing left and I can take a full breath. Movement over Trey's shoulder catches my eye, and I see Charlie sitting up in the car, watching us with a somber expression.

"You good?" Trey asks, his hands cupping my face to redirect my gaze. He seems satisfied with what he sees.

I clear my throat, rubbing my cheeks with my fists. "Yeah," I say roughly. "Let's get out of here. I'll drive."

CHAPTER FORTY-THREE

CHARLIE

*T*he car ride is quick, and I barely have time to register the misery I feel before we pull into the garage of an impressive mansion.

The garage itself is huge, full of fancy-looking sports cars and motorcycles, and even a boat. I stare out the window blankly after we stop until Trey's gentle hand on my elbow captures my attention.

"Charlie? Are you okay?"

I look up at him. "Where are we?"

"We're at Link's house." Trey studies me with concern, and Link turns in the driver's seat, his eyes dark and unreadable, all emotion from his earlier turmoil carefully hidden.

I don't know what to say. I'm not okay. I don't normally admit that easily, but sitting here with Trey and Lincoln watching me makes me feel raw, and I don't want to hide anymore—at least not from them.

"No," I say honestly. My voice is barely audible even in the heavy silence of the car's interior.

"Maybe we should take her to the hospital," Trey says, looking up at Lincoln.

"No," I say quickly. "I'm okay. And it won't even matter. Remember the other girls from campus? I just want to sleep. Please."

Lincoln gives a tight nod and exits the car. He opens my door, reaching in to help me out, but I involuntarily flinch back toward Trey, and I'm confused when I see the hurt on his face. Logically, I know this wasn't his fault, but the irrational drunk feelings I had at the bar have burrowed into my brain.

If you had just wanted me the way I want you, this would never have happened.

Trey's gentle hand on my back eases me out of the car and then his strong arms scoop me up effortlessly. I bury my face in the warm skin of Trey's neck, feeling his pulse against my cheek. He smells like beer and a spicy musk that's distinctly his, and I inhale it shamelessly, allowing the tension to finally leave my muscles.

I'm safe.

I hear Lincoln's footsteps follow us into the house, and I peek over Trey's shoulder at him. He meets my gaze. He looks so lost. Guilt is a sharp pain in my stomach because I feel lost too.

My lost boy. We can be lost together.

Tears prick my eyes again, and I look away first. I'm so tired of crying, but my eyes don't seem to get the memo. Everything inside me feels wrecked—splintered and sharp like broken glass —and I'm not sure how to feel whole again.

We walk up some stairs and down a hallway. Trey slows as he comes to a door and pushes it open with his hip. The room is clean and simple with gray walls, but the single light on the nightstand still gives a cozy vibe. The king-size bed is neatly made and covered in a fluffy navy duvet. Trey sets me gently onto the bed and sits beside me.

Lincoln lingers at the door, and I hate it. Half of me wants him at my side too because all three of us are stronger together. But the other half feels so angry and hurt, and those feelings are only magnified by the throbbing in my head and the ghost of Matt's rough touch that I can still feel violating my body. I shudder.

"Bathroom?" I ask, and Trey nods to a door to the right.

I pee quickly and then scrub my hands until they're red from the scalding water. Then I use some of the mouthwash next to the sink, swishing the burning blue liquid extra long to get the sour taste out of my mouth.

I reenter the bedroom and sit next to Trey, picking at my nails nervously.

"Tell me what happened." Trey's deep voice is soft and reassuring. His fingers graze my cheek, leaving a trail of warmth in their wake. The bone-deep coldness I've felt since waking up in Matt's bedroom still lingers, and I realize I'm shaking. I twist my fingers into the comforter, willing my body to relax.

I'm safe.

"Did he..." Lincoln starts, and I meet his stormy eyes from across the room.

"No," I say quickly. "Not really, anyway. I mean he wanted to...tried to...." My voice breaks, the words choking me. Link's expression darkens, and his body stiffens with rage. "I'm sorry," I stutter. "I'm not ready yet...."

Lincoln approaches. He kneels by the bed, cupping my face in his hands. Even with his hair an unruly mess and dark circles under his eyes, he's heart-stoppingly beautiful. His pale face is an open book for once, a hurricane of emotions swirling with anger and pain and so much love that I feel my heart swell as I stare at him. His breath brushes my lips, and he wipes away my tears with gentle but firm fingers.

"Sunshine," he breathes, "I'm so fucking sorry this happened. I should have been honest with you. I should have fought for you the way Trey fights for you. I should have gotten over myself so I could protect you."

I frown. "Link, you couldn't have known this would—"

"He's going to pay," he growls fiercely, and terror shudders through my body.

"You can't, Lincoln." My hands grasp his forearms as I rise to my knees in panic. "Please. He's dangerous. He'll kill you." I'm shaking again, making my voice stutter. "I can't lose you too." My eyes bounce between his as my heart pounds so violently that it's deafening in my own ears. "Please, Lincoln, swear to me. I can't...I won't. Please don't leave me. I need you. I want you."

My words dissolve into nonsense as Lincoln's strong arms pull me into his lap. He holds me tightly while I sob into the soft cotton of his T-shirt, soaking it in tears and snot, but I don't even care.

His hands stroke my hair and trace patterns on my back. I can hear the low rumble of his voice as he whispers something to Trey, and then his breath brushes against my ear. "You're okay. I'm not going anywhere, baby. I promise. Breathe, sweetheart. I've got you."

His lips brush my head and then my forehead, and I look up at him—at those rich gray eyes. Our faces are so close that our noses touch.

Somewhere, some logical part of my brain is telling me that I need to ask him point blank how he feels; I can't play this will-they-won't-they game anymore because I won't survive another heartbreak.

But then his tongue darts out and licks his bottom lip, and my body takes over. I lean forward, our lips colliding, our tongues tangling, our teeth clashing. I pour all my need and want and pain into that one kiss.

He hums in appreciation, returning the kiss hungrily, his fingers tangling in my hair and pulling me impossibly closer.

"Since the invention of the kiss there have been five kisses that

were rated the most passionate, the most pure. This one left them all behind."

I smile against Link's mouth and swallow a delirious giggle as *The Princess Bride* quote plays in my head.

"What?" He pulls back in confusion, but I growl in protest and pull his face back to mine, adjusting my position until I'm straddling his lap, his hard length pressing deliciously against my pussy.

I hear Trey chuckle nearby and then a soft click as the door closes.

When I finally pull away, Link's staring at me, his lips swollen and eyes wide with surprise. "Charlie, I don't want to push you after what you went through tonight. Plus, I still don't know if I'm ready to...I mean I *want* to..."

I press my fingers to his mouth. I crawl off his lap and stand, taking his hand.

"Link," I say patiently. "I'm not asking you to fuck me." I give him a small, sad smile. "I need a shower. And right now, I just need to forget. Please help me forget."

He studies me quietly for a moment, his face still unusually open and vulnerable. Honestly, it's a bit unnerving. But then he nods, and we walk into the large bathroom. I stop in awe as I take in the ridiculously over-the-top ensuite, which I hadn't noticed before. The dark gray and brown floor tile looks like smooth, flat river rocks. There's a huge walk-in shower in one corner next to double sinks, and a Jacuzzi tub is situated in the other corner.

"Rich people," I mutter.

Lincoln laughs. "Isn't your family rich too?"

"Yeah, but not like gold-faucets-and-shit rich."

"I don't think it's *real* gold," he says defensively.

I roll my eyes with a smile, release Link's hand, and walk toward the shower. I start to strip off my jeans and shirt, and pause when I remember I don't have any undergarments on. I look up, meeting Lincoln's hooded gaze. My eyes drop down his body. He's wearing a black t-shirt and gray sweatpants, which are tented where his cock is already hard.

Seriously. Sweatpants on guys should be illegal. I swallow hard, my pussy already tingling.

"Don't stop now, Sunshine," he says huskily, and my cheeks heat.

I realize this is the first time he's going to *really* see me naked. And here, under the warm yellow bathroom lights, shyness and insecurities tickle my stomach. I'm acutely aware that we're not in a dark projection booth or under the ambient lights in his dorm. He can see me—he can see everything.

I blow out a shaky breath and continue, pulling my shirt over my head and shimmying out of my jeans. Lincoln walks toward me, his hands falling to my hips as he pulls me close, his cock pressing firmly against my center. His mouth drops to my neck, and I feel his soft lips kiss the sensitive skin below my ear. I shiver with pleasure, letting out a quiet moan as my eyes sink closed.

"You're so fucking beautiful," he whispers between kisses as he moves along my throat, up to my jawline, and finally presses his lips to mine.

The kiss is slow at first as his tongue parts my lips and slides into my mouth, tangling with mine. I bite down on his lower lip playfully, sucking it into my mouth, and he growls in appreciation, his fingers tightening on my hips. Link's stubble grazes my face roughly, the sensation going straight to my core as moisture gathers between my legs.

I bring my hands to the back of his head, teasing the soft hairs on his neck, and I tangle my fingers into the longer strands, tugging gently.

Lincoln pulls back, and I stare at him breathlessly. He leans into the shower and turns on the warm water before reaching behind his head to pull off his shirt. My breath catches in my throat as I stare at his torso. The boy is a fucking work of art—toned arms, firm, flat pecs, and hard planes of muscle defining his abs. Dark hair trails from his belly button down the middle of the V of his waist, disappearing beneath his sweats.

"Like what you see?" Link asks with a cocky smirk.

"I guess," I say with a shrug, trying to play it off like I wasn't just staring him down like a snack.

His expression darkens dangerously, and he removes his sweats in one swift motion—*Mmm, no boxers*—and his cock springs free. My mouth waters at the sight. It's long and thick with large veins circling the shaft leading to his mushroomed tip.

He stalks forward and backs me into the shower spray. I sigh in relief as the taint of the night's events wash from my skin and spiral down the drain. Despite the aggression radiating from Link's body and the sexual tension weighing heavily between us, he's gentle and patient as he uses the body wash to clean my body. The callused pads of his fingers slip across my skin, erasing everywhere Matt touched. This bathroom is clearly Link's because by the time he's finished, the intoxicating smells of his soap and shampoo have mixed together in the steamy air.

I turn in Lincoln's embrace, looking up at him, the double shower head cascading warm water over us. He stares back, his eyes, which are normally so dark and stormy, are the lightest I've ever seen—like early dawn—and his long, dark lashes cling together as he blinks away the water dripping down his face. When I smile shyly, his lips turn up to mirror my own, and it's breathtaking to see a ray of sunshine overshadow his cloudy exterior.

I did that.

I lean forward, my lips moving softly against his in a slow, rhythmic dance as if we have a lifetime to enjoy each other, and I wish desperately that were true. His cock is a hard warm weight against my stomach, and he hums into my mouth when I press my body against it, feeling it slip and slide against my wet skin.

I grasp him in my small palm, running my thumb over his sensitive tip. He thrusts into my grip a few times, his breath hitching as I squeeze my hand around his hard length.

His arms tighten around me, his fingers digging into my ass. I smile against his mouth as I swallow a needy moan. He's so responsive to my touch, and it makes me feel powerful and wanted. But before I can take it too far, he pulls back, looking down at me with wild eyes and flushed cheeks.

"I'm making *you* forget, remember?" he rasps, and before I can respond, his hand is between my legs, his fingers pressing firmly against my clit. His lips drop to my neck, licking and kissing their way to my shoulder while he continues working me over with his magic hands. One long finger enters my pussy, followed quickly by a second, and my knees start to shake as pleasure ripples from my core through my entire body.

"Fucking hell, boss," I breathe as I clutch his shoulders for support.

His attention reaches my hard, aching nipples, and he takes one into his mouth, rolling his tongue against it before biting down just hard enough to mix my pleasure with a spark of pain.

I'm already close to coming, but I want him to come, too. I want us both to lose ourselves in this moment.

Lost together.

"Link, wait," I pant, pulling at his arm.

He looks up at me in confusion, his pupils blown wide with lust. I grab the conditioner bottle, fill my hand, then urge him back to his full height. I grab his ass with one hand to yank him close. My other hand slides eagerly along the length of his cock.

When I guide it between my thighs, he starts to protest, his body shaking. I look up at his conflicted expression. I know he wants to fuck me—it's written all over his face—but I also know something holds him back.

347

"Relax, baby," I murmur. "Do you trust me?"

"Yes," he whispers hoarsely.

I continue to guide him, and his dick slides against my clit and through my folds, the conditioner making our skin-on-skin contact positively euphoric. We both moan. I lean back against the wall, giving Link a better angle, and he seems to read my thoughts as I tighten my thighs, and he starts thrusting, every slide against my clit sending me closer and closer to a release.

Link's face is leaning over me, our mouths hovering close together as we pant, our breaths and movements becoming messier as we start to lose control. His mouth takes mine in a heated, sloppy kiss that's all saliva, growls, teeth, and tongues, and our bodies are slick and hot as we claw at each other, desperate for this heady, intimate connection to continue.

Link cries out as he comes, his cock pulsing between my legs, warm, sticky cum coating my thighs. I watch him fall apart above me, his full lips parting and his eyes glazing over as his body bucks and shakes against mine, and I follow him, coming *hard*. Ecstasy roars through my body, so intense that my vision blackens at the edges, and for a moment, all I can hear is my own heartbeat raging in my ears.

My muscles shake from holding myself up at an awkward angle, and we drop slowly to the shower floor, holding onto each other for balance. Link props his back against the tiled wall and pulls me into his lap. His hands graze my back lazily. We sit like that for a while, the warm water soaking our skin, until there's a knock on the bathroom door.

I jump at the noise, and Link's arms tighten around me instinctively.

"Did you guys drown?" Trey asks, his voice muffled. "You've been showering for a while."

"It's my turn for once. Fuck off," Lincoln replies, nuzzling his face into my neck. I laugh, leaning into his touch.

"I'll take that as a no," Trey says.

"It's practically dawn, and I'm pretty tired," I say with a yawn. "We probably should get out."

Link sighs but lets me stand. Then he turns off the shower, and we both step out and dry off, wrapping the towels around ourselves before heading back into the bedroom. Trey is laying on the bed in his boxers, staring at his phone, but he looks up as we enter, his smile widening as he sits up.

I flush under his scrutiny and walk quickly to the closet, thumbing through Lincoln's T-shirts until I find an extra-soft one.

"Just gonna steal my clothes, huh?" Link asks.

I look back at him leaning against the doorframe, an arrogant smirk on his lips, his towel sitting sinfully low on his hips.

"Oh, is that not okay?" I ask in a sweet voice. "I can ask Trey for a shirt then." I take a step like I'm going to do just that.

Link's hand blocks me from leaving. "No," he says firmly.

"That's what I thought," I say quietly with a smile as I drop the towel and tug his shirt over my head.

I walk out of the closet and sit down next to Trey on the bed, leaning my head on his shoulder and stifling a yawn. I watch with heavy eyes as Lincoln pulls on a pair of boxers, openly staring at the graceful way his muscles flex with the movement.

God, he's beautiful.

"If you two are done eye-fucking me, maybe we can all get some sleep," Link grumbles as he approaches us.

I glance over at Trey, snickering when I see him watching his best friend with the same approving, lustful look.

We crawl under the covers, and nestled between them, I quickly fall fast asleep.

CHAPTER FORTY-FOUR

LINCOLN

*C*harlie is tangled between me and Trey, her soft hair tickling my arm. She never put on any underwear after last night's shower, so her warm bare ass is pressed firmly against my morning wood. Or would it be afternoon wood?

Her forehead rests against Trey's chest, and their legs are intertwined. Between the three of us, the body heat under the covers is almost stifling, but it's also comforting. I've spent so many nights alone over the past several years that waking up this way—with the two people I love most pressed close—is addicting.

I reluctantly slide out from under the covers, easing myself slowly away from Charlie so that I don't wake her, and head to the bathroom to rinse off with a cold shower, hoping the cool water will defuse my impressive boner.

Can't really run into Daddy Dearest with this thing, I think.

Afterward, I dry off, brush my teeth, and leave the bathroom to dress. I pull on a fresh pair of boxers, some sweats, and a T-shirt. As I walk out of my closet, I pause when I see Trey sitting up, rubbing his eyes. His blond hair is an unkempt mess.

"Hey," he says quietly, squinting at me. "You good?"

"Yeah." I run my hand through my damp hair. "I'm just gonna go make us some coffee." I sigh and look down at Charlie. She's still fast asleep, her breathing soft and even. "Take care of our girl?"

Our girl.

"Always," Trey says with a sleepy smile, laying back down and pulling her gently against his body.

CHARLIE

I can't move. His hands against my skin are cold and clammy, and he's touching me everywhere, pawing at my breasts and stomach. His handsome face, which I once adored as a girl, is like a foggy memory, and as much as I squint or close my eyes, I can't see that boy anymore. What I see now is twisted, and it fills me with fear.

I want to fight. I want to run. But my head lolls to the side. Hot tears run down my cheeks and onto the bed. I'm helpless to stop this.

"Charlie..."

"No, stop," I rasp.

I can't breathe. He's so heavy on top of me.

"Charlie!"

I wake with a sharp gasp, pulling air into my lungs as the fingers of panic start to loosen their hold on my throat. I look around wildly and realize I'm safe in Lincoln's bedroom.

"Charlie, shhh." Trey's deep voice grounds me. "You're okay."

"Sorry," I mutter. "Bad dream."

His arms tighten around me, and I relax into his embrace, taking a long moment to breathe him in until my limbs stop shaking. Then I look around. Golden fingers of afternoon sunlight filter through the parted curtains, casting dancing shadows on the floor.

"What time is it?" I ask, rubbing my eyes.

"Just past one," Trey says, tracing his fingers down my arm. "We were up pretty late. Do you have someplace to be? Will Seb and Marcus be worried?"

I shake my head slowly. "No, they're still in Vancouver, so I had the house to myself." I turn in his arms and look up into his warm chestnut eyes. "Where's Link?"

"He went to make us coffee."

Just then, the door opens and Link enters, balancing three coffee mugs in his hands. He pauses, something in his gaze unsure and vulnerable. I sit up, reaching for one of the mugs with a tentative smile, but Lincoln's expression remains cautious.

"Thank you," I murmur, breathing in the rich aroma.

Trey takes the other offered cup as Link sits onto the bed, and we all lean against the headboard and sip in contented silence. My thigh is touching Link's, and my cheek is pressed against the soft warm skin of Trey's shoulder. I feel so safe and loved, and it's a relief after weeks apart from Link, followed by last night's events. Just thinking about Matt makes my stomach churn.

After a few moments of quiet, Link turns to me, his granite gaze hesitant. "You don't have to talk about it if you don't want to," he starts haltingly, "but if you do want to, we're here. No judgment."

I swallow heavily, and nod, feeling stronger than I did last night, but even as I start to speak, my vision blurs, and I feel moisture clinging to my lashes.

"When I woke up in Matt's room, he was naked, and he was trying to force himself on me." My tears feel too hot as they trickle down my face, but I know I have to say it out loud. I want to face it because I'm so angry that I let it happen—in the fifteen years I've known Matt, I wasn't strong enough or smart enough to see him for the true monster he is. "He said he wanted to fuck me like he should have when we were together, and he was angry about the bad blood between his dad and Martin. He called my mom a whore. Do you think he knew about the affair?"

"I'm not sure how he'd know, considering what your stepdad did to keep it under wraps. It was probably just a dig to get a rise out of you," Link says, his voice low and dangerous.

I take a deep breath, and Trey reaches out to grasp my hand, interlocking our fingers.

"I was angry too. I called him a rapist, and he slapped me." I touch my sore lip. Trey's fingers tighten around mine, and I hear a low growl from Lincoln, but I refuse to meet his eyes again. "I shouldn't have provoked him," I say softly.

"Bennett," Trey says, grasping my chin so our eyes meet. "This isn't your fault. Do you hear me? He's a twisted fuck who tried to rape you. None of this is your fault."

My chin wobbles, and I bite my lip, wincing when my teeth graze the cut. But I nod because deep down I know he's right.

"He used his fingers, and then..." I consider whether to mention what Matt said about Seb, but decide against it. It's a conversation I want to have with my brother first. "He tried to rape me."

"What made him stop?"

"Well, I started to slap him, but I couldn't get him off me—I was still so weak. Then when he tried to enter me, I...".

"You...," Trey murmurs.

I look between them, my cheeks flaming. I'm not sure why I'm so embarrassed to tell them, but I am. "I...I puked."

They both still.

Link raises his eyebrows and glances at Trey over my head, a smile tugging at one side of his lips. Trey covers his mouth.

"What?" I ask just as they both start laughing uncontrollably

"You puked on the fucker?" Trey's body shakes against mine.

The sound makes my heart flutter, but I try my best to look annoyed.

"Well, sort of. On him. On his bed." I try not to grin as I watch them collapse against the headboard, holding their sides like a pair of little boys snickering over a fart joke.

"I'm sorry," Link holds up his hand as he gasps for air. "We're not laughing at what happened."

"No, absolutely not. But just the thought of you hurling on him. It's fucking hilarious," Trey says between chuckles.

I sigh. "You guys are such boys sometimes."

"Right," Link clears his throat and schools his features. "So then what?"

"Well, he just left, and I was still halfway drugged and coming down off adrenaline, so I passed out. When I woke up, he was still gone."

Trey looks genuinely relieved. "Thank God for that gag reflex of yours."

I nod, biting my lip and looking down, my smile fading. "I meant what I said last night though. I know what he did makes you angry. I'm angry too. But you can't go after him. Either of you. I saw the look in his eyes. He's legit crazy." I wipe another tear from my face and grit my teeth, hating that I feel so weak and helpless.

"We can't promise that," Link says quietly. "He hurt you. He tried to rape you. It's not okay." Link runs his fingers along my jaw and dips his head to meet my gaze. "He doesn't get to get away with hurting you, Charlotte. Do you understand?"

My full name on his lips causes the ticklish flutter in my heart to stammer in earnest, and I impulsively press my mouth to his, hoping I can somehow convey all the emotions crashing through my body with that one gesture.

Behind me, Trey exhales heavily.

Link pulls back. "You keep kissing me like that and you'll

start something Trey and I will most definitely finish," he warns, digging his half chub against my thigh.

I press another kiss to his velvet lips, smiling against them with wicked intent, when my phone pings with a text.

"Hold that thought." I pull away and reach over Link to grab my phone from the nightstand. My hand intentionally brushes over his cock, causing him to growl and eye me darkly.

FIONA

> Hey babe. Are you gone all weekend? I had to come back to campus. I tried to move my mom into the rehab place but it all went wrong.

"Fuck." I hit the Call button next to her name. Link and Trey exchange a worried glance.

"Hello?" Fi answers, her voice cracking.

"Fi, what happened?"

"Her fucking boyfriend convinced her not to go. He gave her drugs. I found them on the couch passed out in their own vomit." A sob catches in her throat. "I tried to make her go, but she just got pissed at me, saying all this hateful shit about how I think I'm better than her because I go to a big, fancy school."

"Oh, honey," I say softly.

"I'm sorry," she sobs. "I didn't know who else to call."

"Shhh, it's okay. I'll come back. Are you on campus now?"

"I just got back," she sniffles. "I'm sitting in my car because Catherine has a scrunchie on the door, so she's fucking someone in there."

"Jesus, Fi, I feel like this might be an okay time to interrupt."

"Charlie, I am *not* a cockblocker," she says indignantly. She sounds a little more like herself, and I hold back a snicker.

"I'm going home to get my stuff now, okay? Then I'll drive back to campus. Stay with me tonight." Trey's hand on my arm causes me to look up. "One sec, Fi." I press the Mute button.

355

"We'll all go back tonight," Trey says. "She can stay in my room. You can stay there with her if you need to."

"Are you guys sure?" I glance at Link, who nods, and then back to Trey.

"Of course," Trey scoffs. "Bennett, your bed is tiny. You'll both be more comfortable at our place."

I smile gratefully at them and unmute my phone. "Fi? The guys are coming back with me. We'll all stay with them tonight."

"Really?" she asks, her voice thick with gratitude.

"Yeah, it's totally cool."

"Please stay with us, Flowers!" Trey says loudly over my shoulder.

I push him away, rolling my eyes, but Fi giggles into the phone. "Okay," she says.

"See you soon," I say, hanging up. I look between the guys. "That was really nice of you both."

Link throws his arm around my shoulders and kisses my forehead. "She's your best friend. She's always welcome."

My heart.

"Are you going to tell her what happened?" Trey asks quietly, and I shake my head.

"No, I don't think so. She has enough to stress about right now." I go to stand and realize I'm wearing nothing but Link's shirt. "Crap, no underwear. Wearing just my jeans should be super fun."

"No, wait. I gotcha!" Trey jumps up from the bed and leaves the room. I look over at Link in confusion, and he just shrugs, but his eyes crinkle like something's funny.

Trey comes running back, several colorful scraps of fabric in his hands. "What's your style? I've got a thong here and bikini style. Hmm, oh shit, these are crotchless—probably don't want those." He tosses them aside.

I stare at him in horror. "Why do you have women's underwear?" Then my eyes widen. "Wait, are you offering me discarded underwear from your booty calls?!"

Lincoln loses his mind for the second time today, doubling over with laughter at my outburst. I glare at him, then cross my arms over my chest and turn my shocked gaze back to Trey.

He runs a hand through his golden locks, looking confused. "What?"

"I'm not wearing someone's used underwear, Atreyu Walker."

"Oh shit, she full-named you." Link says between laughs.

No!" Trey shakes his head adamantly. "These are brand new. I just have a collection of new underwear just in case..."

"In case of what?" I ask, raising an eyebrow.

"In case things with a girl get...spicy," he says haltingly, his cheeks flushing. It's the first time I've ever seen Trey flustered, and I have to say, it's adorable. "Girl underwear rips so easily...." He looks down at the underwear in his hand like an embarrassed child.

"For fuck's sake. Give me the bikini ones."

Trey perks up then, his smile returning as he hands me the lacy hot-pink panties.

I glance over at Link, who looks slightly disappointed.

"What?" I ask, my eyes narrowing.

"I was just hoping you'd pick the thong. I bet your ass would look sexy as hell in it."

I roll my eyes but still blush at the comment. I glance at Trey. "Fine, give me those, too."

Trey and Link look at each other and grin.

Boys.

I grab my jeans and shirt off the floor, then pick up Link's hoodie, which is draped over his desk chair, and pull it over my head.

"I need to go grab my stuff from my place, and then I'll meet you guys back on campus."

The guys exchange a look.

"I'm coming with you," Trey says. "Just give me five minutes to get ready."

"It's fine, Trey. I don't need an escort." But he's already gone back to his room to get dressed.

"Like hell we're going to let you go anywhere by yourself until we find Matt," Link says, standing up and stepping into my space. He backs me against the wall and cages me in with his large hands on either side of my head. I feel the heat of his body infusing mine as he stares down at me with those gravestone eyes.

I sigh as I realize that fighting them on this is probably a losing battle.

"You're mine now," he growls. "And no one will ever fucking touch you again—besides Trey," he amends. "Do you understand?"

I know I should probably object—toxic masculinity and all that—but the possession in his voice goes straight to my pussy, and all I can do is lick my lips and nod compliantly. His eyes track the movement, and I duck under his arms, moving to the door before we start mauling each other again.

"I'm just going to wait downstairs," I say breathlessly, squirming at the wetness now coating my brand-new panties.

"Sure," Link says with a knowing smirk, and I practically run out of the room.

CHAPTER FORTY-FIVE

CHARLIE

*W*e all pile into Lincoln's Range Rover, and he drives Trey and me over to my place so we can take my car back to campus. I'm surprised to see Seb's black Lexus in the driveway when we pull up. We walk up the steps and through the front door.

"That you, kiddo?" Seb calls.

"Yes," I answer as I walk into the kitchen.

"Sorry, I know I said I wasn't coming back over the long weekend, but I had to make a last-minute run to Seattle, so I thought I'd stop on the way…." He turns and sees me standing there flanked by Link and Trey. His expression darkens. "What're *they* doing here," he growls.

"We're going back to campus together," I say like I wasn't just bawling my eyes out over these two the last time I saw Seb. His jaw ticks as he stares at them, his blue eyes darkening dangerously. "Take it easy, Seb," I say quickly. "We're okay now."

"Yeah? Because the last time I saw you, you were crying so hard you could hardly breathe."

The memory of one of our drunken nights over winter break comes back to me with alarming clarity. I flush and glance at Link and see a flash of guilt before he schools his expression.

"Actually, there's something I need to talk to you about," I say with a heavy swallow. Seb stares at me steadily and finally nods. He sits down at the kitchen island and waves his hand as an invitation for the rest of us to sit as well.

I scoot the chair back and sit. "I'm going to tell you something that happened last night, but I don't want you to freak out."

Seb tenses.

"Bennett," Trey murmurs. "He's your brother, so I don't think that's a fair ask."

Seb looks over at him curiously, and I sigh and start my story again.

For some reason, every time I tell it, it gets a little easier, as if it happened to someone else, and I wonder if it's my body's way of protecting itself.

Seb takes it about as well as I expect, his face flushing red with anger as he stands from his chair so quickly it topples to the tiled floor with a clatter.

"I'm going to *kill* that fucker!" he roars, and I glance at Link and Trey, who give me an I-told-you-so look.

"I'm okay, Seb. Really. But I have to ask—Matt said seemed to know about Mom's affair. He called her a slut and said you knew something about that night. Do you know what he was talking about?"

Seb's face drains of color, and his eyes drop to the counter, where he clutches the edge with white knuckles.

"Seb, what's he talking about?" I repeat.

He gives me a pleading look. "He wasn't talking about your mom's affair. It's about the night he cheated on you," Seb chokes out.

"I mean, I know you saw it, too. You went in after me."

"But I know who it was with."

360

I stiffen, my eyes widening in shock. Seb's eyes are glassy and red, like he's on the verge of tears.

"Who?" I whisper.

"It was…your mom."

My legs go weak, but Trey catches my elbow. "But my mom was in love with Link's dad. She wouldn't have done that."

Seb glances between me and Link in confusion and frowns. "What're you talking about?"

"My dad was the one having an affair with Charlie's mom," Link says, his deep voice carefully neutral, and I appreciate the effort he makes, considering the resentment he still feels toward my mom.

Seb's eyebrows disappear beneath the sweep of dark hair over his forehead.

"It's just…" My voice sounds strangled. "I knew my mom was a cheater—we all did—but I thought it was because she was in love with John. Why would she sleep with Matt? My…my boyfriend? That's so wrong."

"I don't think it was like that," Seb says quietly. "When I confronted him, your mom was on the bed crying. I don't think it was consensual."

My mouth explodes with saliva as bile crawls up my throat, and I lunge for the hallway bathroom, the door slamming against the wall as I enter. My knees hit the cold floor painfully as I fall in front of the toilet just in time to vomit. I flush and sit there with my head in my hands, sweating and shaking. A light hand on my back makes me flinch.

"Okay, baby?" Trey asks gently. He kneels next to me, tracing gentle patterns on my back.

I nod, giving him a tight smile, and take his hand to stand. I stumble to the sink and rinse out my mouth, then walk back into the kitchen. Seb and Link abruptly stop talking.

"I'm sorry," Seb says. "I should have told you…" He takes a deep breath. "After you ran out that night, I went into your room. Matt was finishing up, and your mom was on the bed trying to cover herself with a sheet. I…I just stood there in complete shock. The guy was my best friend since grade school."

Empathy tears at my chest as I listen, and I realize Seb probably felt the same keen sense of betrayal I did that night.

He swallows. "Then I hit him. I was so angry at what he did to you and what it looked like with your mom. We got into it, throwing punches, and then he was just lying on the floor, gasping and laughing like a maniac. He said he had to do it because my dad deserved to be punished for ruining his life." He frowns in disgust. "I think he raped your mom out of some sick sense of vengeance. You were just his collateral damage."

I feel Link stiffen next to me, and I place a reassuring hand on his thigh. But at the same time, my mind is reeling. "He blamed my stepdad for the failed business deal, so he raped my mom," I mumble. "He's been crazy all along." My head drops into my hands. Then I look up. "Did you talk to my mom about it? Why didn't she go to the police?"

Seb smiles sadly. "I tried to get her to report him, but she refused. She was scared." He frowns at the memory. "I went to his house the next day, and I confronted Matt's dad, hoping that the guy had some shred of decency, but he threatened me and our family—said Matt had video evidence that would play his word against hers, and he was seventeen when it happened, so he'd say *she* raped *him*."

"He was seventeen?" Link asks incredulously, and he and Trey look over at me in confusion.

I swallow heavily. "He was younger than me by almost a year and half because he skipped a grade in middle school. He was sort of a genius. His birthday fell in the fall, so, yeah, he wasn't eighteen during that party."

"Wow," Trey says, with a whistle. "The guy is an even bigger tool than I thought."

"That's an understatement," Seb mutters. "He obviously got it from his dad. I always knew that the guy had a temper, but he put Matt in the hospital after I confronted him—almost beat him to death."

"I had no idea since I stopped talking to him after that night." I frown.

Seb nods. "And in the end, Ellen took the threat seriously—I couldn't make her turn him in."

"And then my mom killed herself," I say as I start to shake again. "Do you think it was because of the rape? Was it Matt's fault?"

Seb reaches across the counter and takes my hand, squeezing it. "Maybe. Maybe not. She'd also lost John and then her family. A lot of things might have been the tipping point," he says gently. "I wish we knew the answer. I know you miss her. I miss her too."

I rub my eyes, holding my fingers there as I breathe. I'm so tired of crying, of looking at my life through a distorted lens of tears. It's exhausting.

"Why didn't you tell me?" I ask, staring into Seb's crystal-blue eyes. He shrugs, looking away as if my gaze overwhelms him. "I wanted to tell you, but I was processing it too. And I was so frustrated with Ellen for not coming forward. And then when she committed suicide, it just seemed cruel to mention it. I thought it would just make a bad situation worse." His expression darkens. "But if I had known he'd be back in your life, I would have told you. I feel like it's my fault—I knew he was a predator, but I never said anything, and then you were the next victim."

"That we know of," Trey says quietly, and I shiver.

Seb straightens up. "How long has this been going on?"

Trey grimaces and glances at me, and I nod, giving him permission to explain. "A few girls accused him of rape in the

363

last couple months, but the guy is a hockey prodigy at Whitmore, so the accusations were dismissed."

"Fuck," Seb mutters.

"He started hanging around me and acting strange, and then he blackmailed me with photos of us doing...stuff." I flush because I am talking to my brother, after all. "He said he'd send the pictures to Rosewood if I didn't stop seeing them. I just thought he was trying to ruin my chances at that internship. I didn't really know he was dangerous until he choked me in the closet just before the winter break though."

"He did what?!" Link growls at the same time that Trey says, "Are you kidding me, Bennett?"

I wince. "I'm sorry. I didn't want to worry you, and I handled it..."

They both look seriously pissed.

Seb pinches the bridge of nose before dropping his hand to the counter and looking at me apologetically. "I almost said something when you talked to your friend about him that day at the hockey arena, but I didn't want to worry you, and at that point, we didn't even know that you guys would cross paths. This was my fault."

"No, it wasn't," I say firmly. "He's a sociopath, and I was naïve about the whole situation."

"Regardless, where's the asshole now?" Seb growls, looking between Trey and Link.

"We don't know," Trey says with a frustrated sigh. "Link contacted his dad's private investigator this morning, hoping to find him, but Matt hasn't been back home or to campus since it happened." Seb frowns.

"You guys contacted a PI?" I ask uneasily.

"I know you think he's dangerous, Sunshine," Link says through gritted teeth, "but you're not safe until we locate the fucker and put him in his place. He can't hurt you like that and get away with it."

"I don't want to bring Marcus into this yet because I'm not sure adding more overprotective males to the situation is wise, but I may see if I can make an excuse to use some of our security guys to give you some extra protection. I assume at least one of you will be with her at all times?" Seb adds pointedly, talking over my head.

"Whoa, whoa, c'mon," I protest. "Do I really need an escort *and* security?"

"Yes," they all say in unison.

I roll my eyes.

"Fine, but I want someone watching Fi, too. I wouldn't put it past Matt to target her to get back at me."

WE LEAVE the house and head back to campus. Link has been acting a little off ever since we talked to Seb, so I opted to ride with him to try to talk while Trey drives my car, but he's been tight-lipped.

"You're overthinking something."

He side-eyes me and shrugs. "It's what I do," he says, his voice flat.

"Care to tell me what it is?"

"No," he says, matter-of-factly.

Stubborn asshole. I sigh and pull out my phone to text Fiona.

> We're about five minutes away.

FIONA

> Can't wait to see you. I'm waiting in the Wolf Building's common area.

> See you soon.

FIONA

> Ciao.

"Is Flowers okay?" Link asks, glancing over at me as he makes the final turn toward the Whitmore U parking lot. I made him stop at a gas station on the way so I could buy a healthy stash of Twizzlers, chips, and Cherry Coke.

"Hard to tell over text, but she seems better," I say, wringing my hands together.

I'm worried about her. Ever since she knocked on my door last fall, she's been the clear sky to my cloudy day, so it's hard to see her hurting. Nothing should stifle her spirit.

We get out of the car and wait on Trey as he parks next to us, then digs my duffle bag out of the trunk.

"Jesus, what's in here?" Trey grumbles. "Feels like I'm carrying all of Lincoln's emotional damage in one little bag."

Link narrows his eyes.

"Books," I say with a grin.

"How many books do you really need for three days?"

"That's kind of a stupid question, don't you think?"

"Right," Trey drawls sarcastically, hefting the bag.

Today is warmer, a balmy fifty degrees, but the clouds have settled overhead, thick and mottled gray. Rain is definitely on the way. Now that spring temperatures are warming the ground, tulips and daffodils are just starting to sprout, small splashes of green against the rich brown dirt of the flowerbeds we pass on our way to the Wolf Building.

I spot Fi on one of the overstuffed couches in the common area as soon as we enter. Her auburn hair is piled in a messy bun on her head, and she's sporting yoga pants, a pink Whitmore U hoodie, and fluffy gray slippers. Her AirPods are in and her freckled nose is scrunched in disgust while she stares at her phone. Our eyes meet when she looks up, and she pulls out one of her earbuds and runs over, throwing her arms around me.

"Mmm, you smell delicious—like vanilla and Charlie," she hums, breathing me in.

"You sound like Trey and Link," I laugh, wrapping my arms around her small body. Trey chuckles behind me.

"They have good taste," she says around a sniffle, pulling back with a forced smile.

I frown at her watery eyes. "I'm sorry about your mom." Fi gathers her belongings and we all walk toward the elevator. "I know you really wanted to get her into rehab."

Fi sighs heavily as we approach the boys' suite. "I did, but I've resigned myself to the fact that she's never going to change. I really thought she could do it for me, but it turns out I wasn't enough."

"Well, take it from me, we're all about found family, and you're part of ours now, Flowers," Lincoln says with a rare smile, placing his hand on her shoulder. "Trust me, it's better than the real thing."

Fiona's mouth falls open as she stares up at him and then glances at me. "Who the heck is this guy and what happened to the irritable asshole we all know and love?"

Trey and I snort a laugh. Link just rolls his eyes and flips us off as he walks down the hallway toward his room.

"There he is," Fi says with a giggle.

Fi and I settle in for the afternoon in Trey's bedroom, bingeing Netflix and junk food.

"Do you want to talk about what happened?" I ask as we sit nestled together, my laptop perched on my knees. I'm not going to lie, we're engulfed in Trey's scent right now, and I have to keep myself from sniffing his pillow like a creep.

"No, I'm good now. You can't force addicts to change and all that—and my mom is a stubborn bitch."

"You offered her as much support and help as you could. You're a good daughter. I hope she realizes that someday."

"Someday...," Fi murmurs wistfully.

"Our happy-ever-after is someday away, right?" I swallow. "That's what I used to tell myself when I was living alone after my mom died. I was so close to rock bottom, but I knew someday everything would be okay. It's really what kept me going back then."

"Someday away. I like that." She leans into my shoulder, her floral scent filling my nostrils as tendrils of her hair tickle my cheek.

I'm still hesitant to tell her about what happened with Matt, but it's like she has a sixth sense about everything.

"So," she starts, sitting up and turning to me, "tell me what happened with you this weekend? Something's on your mind. Spill."

I give her a sideways look, but ultimately, I tell her everything about Sunday night—even how Link and I made up.

"Shit," she says, her eyes welling with unshed tears.

"Yeah."

"I could kill that bastard myself," Fi says fiercely, and I can't help the laugh bubbling up my throat.

"Get in line. Between you, Trey, Link, and Seb, I think I'm well protected. Matt practically has a bounty on his head at this point, so hopefully he just stays away."

"What about hockey, though? I think the school will notice when he just doesn't show up for the next practice or game."

I shrug. "Don't know. Don't care."

We decide to start up our show marathon again, and we only stop when Link orders Chinese food. Trey grabs a round of beers, and we all sit around the living room enjoying dinner.

I glance at the three of them digging into the little white cardboard boxes with their chopsticks, then I stand and walk to the kitchen, grabbing a fork discreetly from the drawer before sliding back onto the couch.

"Do you not know how to use chopsticks?" Fi asks with a smirk.

I freeze as Trey and Link's heads snap up and all three of

them stare at me while I shovel a huge forkful of sweet-and-sour chicken into my mouth.

"Uhhh, frmmmgmgm," I say around the mouthful, turning what's probably a bright shade of pink.

Trey snickers. "So ladylike."

I glare at him and swallow my food. "I said, my mom didn't know how either, so I just never learned."

"Child abuse at its finest," Trey says with a snort.

"Yeah, this needs to be rectified STAT." Link grabs the extra set of chopsticks from the coffee table.

We spend the next hour laughing as Fi and the boys try to teach me to eat with chopsticks, finally resorting to rubber-banding them together.

For a while, we all forget our drama.

There's no psychopath ex-boyfriend, no addict mother, no emotional baggage to manage. We're just four friends hanging out.

And, damn, it feels good.

CHAPTER FORTY-SIX

LINCOLN

*E*verything is quiet. Too quiet.

I can hear my thoughts blaring in my head while I stare at the ceiling. I didn't sleep much last night. It's 6:30 a.m., and the sun is just beginning to brighten the corners of the sky with a soft blush.

Trey is asleep nestled into my side, his breath slow and even. He has one arm thrown above his head, and his golden hair is an artful morning mess across his forehead and the pillow. We forgot to close my curtains last night, so the predawn light flooding the room isn't helping my insomnia, but at least I can appreciate its beauty now—just another way Charlie has changed me for the better. The little things matter again.

But I can't shake Sebastian's words from yesterday. *"I think he raped your mom out of some sick sense of vengeance. You were just his collateral damage."*

How am I any different? Didn't I plan to hurt Charlie because I was so angry at Ellen? Yeah, it wasn't rape. But emotional damage is still damage.

The guilt and shame almost choke me as I compare my

motives to Matt's, and I still can't shake the feeling that I don't deserve her.

I'm also haunted by Trey's accusatory eyes when I tried to run after we found Charlie in the park. I felt the hurt and potential loss lurking there all the way to my bones—to my soul.

I mean something to her. *To them.*

I always hated the selfless martyr trope in movies and books —deciding *for* someone that they're better off without you—but now I understand the dilemma.

Would they really be better off? Wouldn't leaving be just as damaging? But how do I live with myself knowing my motives were no better than a sociopath's sick intentions?

The thought causes nausea to roll through my stomach and climb up my throat. I swallow quickly and ease myself out of the bed so I don't wake Trey. I grab some workout clothes from my closet and slip into the bathroom to change. Then I head to the living room and lace on my sneakers, hoping an early run will clear my head and settle my nerves.

I take the stairs down and open the door, reveling in the cool morning air brushing over my overheated skin. I glance at the sky—dark, ominous clouds are moving in from the east, eating up the pale blue expanse in their path. I trek across campus, the cold dew quickly soaking into my runners. Once I make it through the gate to Main Street, I start to run, and I don't look back.

TREY

I wake up alone, dull gray daylight filling Lincoln's bedroom. The sheets are twisted and tangled around my body. I roll out of the mess, stretching until I feel my muscles protest, and then slide out of bed. I pull on some of Link's loose basketball shorts and walk out into the hallway, my eyes narrowing at the quiet that greets me.

My gaze flicks to my room. The door is open, and I can see from where I stand that my room is empty.

Did the girls go out alone?

Link seems to be gone too, so maybe they all went somewhere together.

I walk into my room, grumbling about people who don't leave notes and dig out a T-shirt and a hoodie and then slide on my sneakers and head downstairs. I figure they probably went to the dining hall for breakfast.

The sky is an angry roiling mess of gunmetal-gray clouds. It looks as if the heavens could open up at any second, so I up my pace to a jog, not keen on getting caught in a downpour. I push through the dining hall doors and scan the tables, my eyes catching on a familiar shock of auburn hair.

Charlie sits next to Flowers, their heads resting together as they watch something on her laptop. Charlie pauses to take a large bite of Lucky Charms and then nudges Flowers' arm before they both break out in laughter. It's nice to see them so happy, but at the same time, Lincoln is still MIA.

I stride toward the table with purpose, bending down when I reach Charlie to speak quietly into her ear. "Bennett, you and Flowers shouldn't be out here alone." My whisper comes out low and menacing.

She startles and looks back at me guiltily. When her head turns, we're so close that our mouths brush, and I can't help the wicked smile that ghosts across my lips.

"You guys were still asleep, and we were hungry," she says, her tone sassy like a teenager who just broke all the rules but doesn't give a fuck. But she can't pull that on me—I've been that teenager.

I look over at Flowers's curious gaze and turn on my classic

Trey Walker charm. "I'm going to borrow this one for just a few minutes." Then I pull Charlie to her feet. Her forest-green eyes dilate, and she doesn't resist. I smirk because I know my bossy side turns her on.

I drag her through the double doors and around the side of the building. It's not particularly cold, but the air is heavy.

"Trey," she whines as I press her back against the rough bricks, pinning her with my hands on either side of her head.

"I thought we all agreed you wouldn't go wandering around alone right now," I growl.

She licks her lips and smiles. "I'm not alone." Her voice takes on an innocent lilt as she bats her lashes at me. "Fiona is with me."

What a brat.

"Oh yeah?" I say, raising an eyebrow. "And not to be sexist, but what do you two plan on doing if your crazy ex shows up? Hmm? He's a hockey player. He's twice your size."

"Fi is freakishly strong," she mutters like a smartass.

"Uh-huh." I lean in closer until we're breathing each other's air.

She looks back at me, her eyes hooded, and leans forward, her mouth sealing over mine, and I lean into the kiss, pressing my hard length against her as we grind against each other. Everything fades around us as our tongues twist together and our teeth bite and nibble.

Cold drops of rain bring me out of my lust-induced haze, and we look up at the sky in dismay. The earthy smell of petrichor wafts through the air, filling my nostrils as water pitter-patters onto the concrete pathways. "Where's Link anyway?" I ask, trying to will my boner down. It's ridiculously obvious in these thin shorts.

"I don't know." She scrunches her face when a fat raindrop falls onto her nose. "I thought he was still asleep with you when we left."

I smile slightly and wipe away the moisture from her face. "Well, he was gone when I woke up."

"He probably just went to the gym," she says, taking my hand. "Let's go back inside. I'm going to punish you if my Lucky Charms are soggy."

"Let's hope they're mush then. What're we talking about? Spanking? Choking? Because I'm flexible. Figuratively and literally," I say, wagging my eyebrows at her.

Charlie laughs out loud, smacking my abs. "You're an idiot."

We walk back into the dining hall just as the rain begins to fall in earnest.

CHARLIE

Breakfast blends into brunch and more friends start showing up as the morning turns to noon. Brantley's eyes light up when he spots us in the dining hall, and Damon's happy to sit and pick my brain about movie theater stuff.

"I think everything went really smoothly over the long weekend," Damon gushes, pushing his glasses up his nose with a grin. "I can't believe John and Lincoln let me run it for three whole days by myself. Pretty sure I got the assistant manager position in the bag."

I smile at his enthusiasm. "Are you going to stick around for the summer then?" I remember Link wanted someone during the slower season.

"Yeah, I'm taking summer classes since my parents are traveling, and I could really use the extra money for my books next year, so it would be awesome if I got it."

"Well, I suspect you're already the top candidate, but I'll talk to Link if you want," I say.

His eyes widen. "Really? That would be so great!"

"Sure," I say with a wink.

"Speaking of..." Damon gives me a sly grin. "You and Lincoln seem to be talking again."

"You could say that." I glance down at my phone because he still hasn't answered my texts this morning. I'm not necessarily worried, but it's weird for him to just disappear like that. Normally radio silence is my move.

Fiona asks Damon a question, and I take the opportunity to lean toward Trey, putting my mouth close to his ear so no one else overhears me.

"Have you heard from Link yet?"

His hand, which has been possessively clutching my thigh under the table squeezes, and he shakes his head. I can tell he's worried too; his muscles are tense.

"Looks like the rain is letting up a little. Might be time to make a break for it," Brantley says, looking out of one of the cathedral-like windows. Everyone agrees, packing up and muttering about doing homework before classes.

"Do you want to come with us back to the guys' dorm?" I ask Fi as I pick up my dirty dishes.

"No, I think I'm okay now," she says with a smile. "Thanks for the girl's night."

"Anytime."

"I'll just walk your way to get my stuff."

I nod as we step outside, the damp, misty air clinging to my skin as we walk toward the boys' dorms. I glance over at the Elk Building, which looms over a grove of newly budding maples like a black obelisk. I know Matt's not in there right now, but a chill ripples through my body, nonetheless. I don't understand how he can just disappear, and based on all the photos he took of me before, the thought that he might be lurking nearby, watching, is always in the back of my mind.

I slow as we approach the Wolf Building. Lincoln is sitting

on one of the benches nearby with his head in his hands. He's soaking wet, and the muscles in his shoulders are rigid with tension. Trey and I glance at each other, and he gives me a small nod.

"Someone should walk Fi home," I say.

"I'll walk her," Brantley says, his lips curving in a charming smile.

Fi follows my gaze, spots Link, and then looks back at me and nods, for once not arguing with Brantley's gesture. Trey gives my hand one more squeeze and drops it, and the three of them continue into the building while I walk over to Link.

I don't say anything when I sit. I just reach out a hand, running my fingers over the warm ridges of his shoulder muscles. He's wearing joggers and a sleeveless T-shirt, which clings wetly to every curve of his body. He doesn't react to my touch other than I notice some of the tension leaving his body.

"Lincoln," I say quietly. "Are you okay?"

He shakes his head, wet strands sticking to his forehead. He has to be freezing, but I don't see any goosebumps.

"What's going on, boss?" I ask, scooting closer and running my hands into his damp, dark hair. The wind starts to pick up, stray raindrops dotting my hoodie.

At first, I think Link's not going to answer, but he finally sighs and sits up straight, looking over at me. His eyes are the same tumultuous gray as the storm swirling above us.

"The day my mom left was the last day I allowed myself to feel anything other than anger, and even that was heavily repressed. Until you." His voice is low and raspy and his gaze holds so much pain. "First that night at the Washington Prep party, and then again here, when I spotted you across the bonfire."

"The way you glared at me. I was sure you hated me."

"I never hated you," he says, blowing out a weary breath. "I hated your mom, and you were part of her. I hated Matt because he wasn't right for you—you were with him all those years, and it should have been me. And I hated the way you made me feel. The way you've always made me feel. When you're around, I completely lose control. Fear, pain, guilt, lust…love—I just feel it all in its rawest form all the time. I had spent two years carefully building this emotional wall, and you just chipped away at it on a daily basis with a look, a touch, a few words. Even just your presence affected me."

I frown. "I did all that?"

He swallows, his Adam's apple bobbing, and he nods. "Trey thinks it's because we're so similar—that we've always needed each other to be whole, like two pieces of a puzzle." I see his fists clench and unclench like he's barely keeping himself in check.

I think back to Trey's words. *"You and him are cut from the same cloth, and he gives you something I can't."*

"He's right," I say simply.

"But I don't want him to be right," Link shouts, standing abruptly.

A student rushing by to escape the weather startles at his outburst, but continues to stumble along.

Link's words slap me in the face. "What're you saying?" The rain is falling in steady sheets now, quickly soaking me through, and my teeth start to chatter.

"You deserve better," he spits, and his response sends whitehot anger licking under my skin.

"Cut the I'm-not-good-enough crap, Evans," I yell, standing and pushing my waterlogged hair from my eyes. "You don't get to decide what *I* deserve."

"You don't understand!"

"Then help me understand!"

"Matt and I are the same."

"What're you talking about?" I ask, shaking my head. "That's bullshit."

"How is what I did for the sake of vengeance any different than what he did to you?"

"Well, for one, you didn't try to rape me," I say matter-of-factly.

He flinches and stares at me miserably. I take a few steps forward so I have to peer up into his face. His eyes are red, and rain clings to his dark lashes and falls in rivulets down his pale cheeks. He's looks otherworldly and so fucking beautiful.

"Maybe I didn't try to physically hurt you," he begins, his breath warm against my chilled skin. "But my intent was to wreck you—to break you to pieces until there was nothing left in your heart but ash. Because that's how I felt when my mom left."

"But you didn't, Link," I say, begging him to understand. "You made a choice. And that's the difference."

His eyes look wild as he stares back at me. It's if he can't keep up with his own thoughts. "But what if I hadn't made that choice? What if I did that and then you killed yourself just like your mom, what if—"

"Baby, stop," I plead. "I wouldn't have—"

"No, no," he stutters, talking over me. His hands clutch my cheeks. "It would have been my fault. That's why I ran that night at the party, Charlie. I saw it all flash before my eyes, and it broke my fucking heart because it turns out I love you. My feelings were so certain. So powerful. So overwhelming. It terrified me. I couldn't admit it then, but I can now. I love you."

My mouth falls open, and my tears feel too hot as they slip from my eyes.

"I was always drawn to you," he says, his thumbs grazing over my cheeks. "I would watch you when we were kids at your parents' parties, too chicken to say anything. You were just ten the first time I noticed you, this spunky little girl with the sparkly Chucks." His mouth twitches at the corner, and I almost smile.

"Lincoln, listen to me," I say firmly, wiping water and tears from my eyes. "You and Matt are not the same. Yes, your intentions were shitty, but guess what? We all have those moments, but it's the choices we make afterward that ultimately decide what kind of people we are. And you? You're the best kind of person—to me at least. You make me whole. You make Trey whole. You're everything to us, Lincoln, and I love you too. So fucking much."

His eyes bounce between mine frantically, and his grip on my face tightens. "I'm so fucked-up."

"We're all fucked-up, baby. But that's what makes us human."

He kisses me then, and my head spins. Every one of my senses heightens as our lips, slippery with the soft taste of rain, collide. The earthy smells of trees, grass, and soil mingle with Lincoln's distinct sandalwood scent in a heady, addictive mix, pushing me past rational thought. I press my body against his, feeling his already-hard cock pressing against my core. He responds immediately, pulling us impossibly closer and lifting me off the ground. I wrap my legs around his waist. He stumbles, but we don't break our kiss as he walks us backward until I feel the rough bark of my favorite oak tree push into my skin.

My hands are everywhere—in his hair, squeezing his biceps, reaching for the impressive bulge in his thin, wet joggers. He groans when I grip his length, thrusting his hips toward me, and I increase the pressure and give another firm pull.

"Fuck," he breathes, pulling back.

I remove my hand reluctantly and place it on his hip. Our foreheads press together as we catch our breath, both of us shaking with so much pent-up lust that it's almost painful.

"I hate that I didn't find you years ago, Link. But when we locked eyes at the bonfire, I was a goner. You have my full attention, baby, and I never want to look away. You're it for me. End of story. Don't ever doubt us again."

"So bossy," Link says with a chuckle before he leans in and kisses me softly. "Never. I'll never doubt us again. Promise."

His words ignite a fire in my veins. "Your room," I breathe. "I need you to fuck me. Right now."

Link drops me so fast, an embarrassing shriek leaves my lips and his hand crushes mine as he yanks me toward the Wolf Building. We're both laughing as we enter, our wet runners squeaking on the smooth foyer floors. A few people look at us curiously as we stagger to the elevator. I've never felt this with him—light and free—as if we're in the final moments of some nineties romcom with our happily-ever-after in sight.

As soon as the door opens, I push Link roughly inside, and we collapse against the wall, kissing sloppily as we paw at each other, all kinds of obscene noises falling from our lips.

"Shit, Sunshine," Link pants. "If you keep this up, I'm going to blow my load before we even get to the good stuff."

I laugh, stepping back as the elevator door opens, and we practically run to his dorm room, which Trey thankfully left unlocked. Link yanks my hoodie over my head before the door even clicks closed and tosses it across the room, where it lands with a wet plop.

We're both eager to strip, but our clothes, as soaking wet as they are, are much harder to remove than normal, and we end up stumbling around as we try to peel the soggy garments from our bodies. Link's sweats twist over his feet, and he falls back- ward, landing on the ground with a loud "Oof." And, being graceful as always, I trip over his legs, my arms windmilling as I land against his hard chest.

A fit of giggles shakes my body, followed by Lincoln's deep laughter, and that's how Trey finds us when he steps out his room—wet, half-naked, laughing messes on the living room floor.

"What the actual fuck is happening?" he mutters, which just

triggers me further until I'm laughing so hard my abs hurt and I can hardly breathe.

Lincoln kicks his sweats the rest of the way off and stands up, scooping me off the ground with him. "We're just gonna go fuck," he says with a smirk as he cradles me to his chest.

"Aw, can I come?" Trey whines as we disappear down the hallway.

"Hurry up," Link yells, and I laugh as Trey starts pulling clothing off, leaving a trail down the hall.

CHAPTER FORTY-SEVEN

LINCOLN

*W*e're both in our underwear by the time we get to my bedroom, and Trey shuts the door, giving me a knowing grin.

Charlie cries out in surprise when I turn and toss her onto my bed so hard that she bounces before I lean over her, my body spreading her legs, which she instinctively wraps around my waist. I stare down at her a moment, her green eyes bright and molten as she stares back.

The tips of her fingers feather along my back and down my spine, leaving trails of ticklish heat. An involuntary shiver of pleasure wracks my whole body. That simple touch shouldn't affect me so much, but my cock is already rock hard and aching, precum soaking the front of my boxers.

I tangle my fingers in her long damp hair and lower my mouth to hers, running my tongue along the seam of her lips. She opens immediately, her tongue soft and needy against mine, little whimpers escaping her throat. Kissing someone has never felt this way—like an addiction that will never be sated. It's making my head spin, my control slip, and for once, I embrace the chaos wholeheartedly.

Trey joins us on my bed, but instead of jumping into the fray, he sits back against the headboard and watches, he's already shimmied out of his boxers, and his hand falls onto his hard cock. I meet his gaze for a moment, and he nods, understanding exactly what I want. This is the first time I've fucked Charlie since that night two years ago.

My hands run down her body, skimming along her jaw and neck until I reach the curve of her breasts. I slide my eager fingers under the silky material of her bra. Charlie immediately pushes herself into my waiting hands.

She's so responsive. So mine. So *ours.*

I tease her nipples until she makes a needy huff, and then she reaches around, unhooking her bra with a flick of her fingers.

"So impatient," I purr.

"Touch me, Link," she begs, her breath coming out in hot little pants.

"And bossy, too." She practically growls in response. "That's the only time tonight you give the orders, got it?" I say darkly.

Her pupils are blown, the green a tiny ring barely visible in the dim light. She bites her lip and nods, and I give her a wicked smile before bringing my mouth to the hardened bud of her right nipple, pulling it into my mouth and sucking and biting, and then I give the same attention to her left.

She moans as I kiss and lick down her body, worshiping every inch of her like I've done in my dirtiest fantasies. The only welcome difference is Trey sprawled out to my left, squirming and tugging on his cock like he can't get enough of the show.

I know now that I was stupid to resist this. To resist us.

It was always going to be us.

Always.

The taste of her soft skin is wholly intoxicating, and she trembles and bucks against my hand when I skim my fingers over her panties, which are already damp with arousal.

"Look at me," I demand, waiting for her eyes to meet mine before I pull off her underwear and lick her from taint to slit.

"Shit," she almost yells, and I give her a devilish grin and crawl up her body, offering her one of my fingers. Her eyes narrow, but she takes it into her mouth, swirling her tongue around it.

"That's it. Make it nice and sloppy. Good girl."

She watches with a lust-drunk, hooded gaze as I reposition myself between her thighs.

"Do you trust me?"

"Yes, always," she breathes, making my cold heart do a flop in my chest.

So I grab a pillow, placing it under her curvy hips before I spread her legs wider and push her ass cheeks apart. She gasps as I carefully slide my finger, slick with her saliva, past the tight ring of her asshole. I ease it slowly up to the first knuckle and then the second and finally the third.

"We need to loosen you up, baby, if you want us both at the same time." I smile, glancing at Trey as I say it, and his eyes roll back in his head, a moan escaping his full lips.

Charlie's pink, pouty mouth drops open and her eyes widen. When she starts pushing back against my hand, I slide another finger into her hot, wet pussy, thoroughly coating it with her arousal, and then slowly slide it into her ass with the first one. Then I scissor them open, stretching her tight little hole wide.

"That feels amazing," Charlie pants, and then what can only be described as mewling sounds escapes her lips when I put gentle but firm pressure on her clit with my thumb, my touch teasing.

"God, you're fucking perfect," I murmur as I watch her.

She's spread out before me, completely naked and squirming, and she's so responsive to my touch. Trey is gripping the base of his cock, panting, his forehead damp with sweat, like he's trying not to come too quickly.

My cock is pulsing in my boxers, and I feel like I could come from just the sight of Charlie at my mercy and Trey wrecked to my side. "Are you ready for me, Sunshine?" I ask, removing my fingers from her ass.

"Please," she whimpers. "I need you inside me."

I remove my boxers, my cock slapping against my stomach like we're in a filthy porno, and Charlie licks her lips as she stares at it—also like a filthy porno.

I crawl up her body, my mouth meeting hers in a blistering kiss that quickly turns sloppy and animalistic. The metallic taste of blood mixes with the taste of *her*, and I can't hold back any longer. This kissing alone will be the death of me.

I line up the head of my dick with her pussy, and when I ease my way inside, it's exactly like I remember but a thousand times wetter and hotter and tighter because this time it's bare.

"Fuuuck." I seat myself inside her completely at the same time she cries out, her nails biting into my shoulders. I still, willing myself to breathe so that I don't blow my load because fuck, she feels good, and I never want it to end.

I drop my forehead to hers, and our sweat and breath mingle as we stare at each other. Her eyes are so fucking tender, my heart squeezes in this foreign, but not unwelcome way.

"I love you so fucking much." Then I pause because I'm shocked that something so intimate just escaped my lips during sex.

Her mouth ticks up in amusement as she watches me, her gaze a mix of trust and love and so many other emotions I thought I would never share with another person.

Ever.

I was so wrong—and now I'll never be able to live without this.

I start to move, achingly slow at first.

"Faster, boss, or I might die," she says, groaning as I pick up my pace.

"Amen to that," Trey mutters.

I pull all the way out and then slam back in. Her pussy grips my cock perfectly, and our bodies meld each time I thrust.

Charlie trembles, and I watch in awe as she starts to succumb to pleasure, letting go.

Our movements become more frenzied as our orgasms build, and I can feel the tingle move from the base of my spine, and my balls start to tighten.

"I'm close," I pant. But she's already there, crying out as her pussy clenches and pulses around my cock, sending me tumbling off the edge of bliss with her. Her body milks me dry as wave after intense wave crashes through my body, drowning me, blurring my vision. I bury my face in her neck as I hear Trey's strangled cry in unison with Charlie's.

We both go completely boneless, and I breathe her in—a heady mix of vanilla and sweat and sex.

After taking a moment for my blissed-out brain to return to normal, I pull my softening cock out of her. Trey is relaxed, his eyes closed, ropes of cum all over his abs and chest.

I slip into the bathroom, returning with a warm washcloth so I can clean them both up. Trey peeks open one eye as I wipe the mess off his skin and then I move on to my cum dripping from Charlie's pussy. Trey slides down, resting his head on the pillow, and Charlie lays her head sleepily on his shoulder, watching me as I toss the wet washcloth into my hamper.

She gives me a lazy smile.

"Who are you, Lincoln Evans?" She grabs my hand and pulls me down on her other side. They both look content, and I fucking did that.

"Do you want to take a shower?" I ask.

She shakes her head. "Too tired."

Trey turns on his side, one arm circling Charlie's stomach as he curls his body against hers and buries his face in her hair. I pull the comforter over all of us, lying on my back as she snuggles into my side, her cheek resting against my peck, right over my heart.

"Your heartbeat is so fast," she whispers. "Are you okay?"

"It beats for you" is all I say, but I have no idea if she hears. Her gentle, even breath against my skin tells me she's already asleep.

Good thing too; that was cheesy as hell.

But I smile because for the first time in a very long time, I regret nothing.

CHAPTER FORTY-EIGHT

CHARLIE

*T*he next two weeks feel so *normal* and perfect—almost too perfect, so I assume something bad is about to happen.

Our English/film project has been taking up a lot of our time. Link is organizing the logistics with the theater while I edit my screenplay for the thousandth time. We start filming the short next week, so I want to make sure I'm ready to email it to Liv and Gavin, the two film students who Link reluctantly said would "do" as actors to bring my words to life. I feel bad for them because I think Link's going to be a brutal director—especially since my story is just as personal for him as it is for me. Trey assured me that he'd be around just to make sure Link wasn't overbearing, but he said it with a sexy wink, which just made me fantasize about us punishing Link for bad behavior.

Now, the three of us are gathered in a quiet section of the library. Link and Trey are distracting beyond measure while I'm trying to concentrate.

"It needs more sex, Sunshine," Link says, smirking cockily at a paragraph in my screenplay where I describe my fingers tracing his torso in embarrassing detail.

I roll my eyes and throw my pen at him, which he catches deftly.

Showoff.

"It's a school project, Link, not soft-core porn, so I don't think there should be vivid descriptions of your big cock and my wet pussy," I say, my tone heavy with sarcasm.

"Jesus, when you say 'cock' and 'pussy' like that, it makes me want to do filthy things to you." He gives me a hooded look and blatantly adjusts his cock. "Also, you should use something besides 'big' to describe my dick—that's way too generic." His lips tug up in a smile that makes my heart do backflips.

Trey drops his book onto his lap in frustration. "You guys are going to give me a serious boner in the fucking library if you don't stop. Can't you work on something that doesn't involve smut?"

I hide a smile and ignore him, quickly typing 'big' into a Thesaurus search. "Maybe 'colossal,' 'vast,' 'hulking'?" I giggle, and then my eyes widen with glee as I skim the results. "Oh! What about 'a whale of a penis?'"

Trey snorts a laugh, and Link glares. "Okay, you ruined it."

I stick my tongue out at him and go back to marking my paper with my red pen.

Link sighs. "You're making a lot of work for yourself, Sunshine."

"At least my comments are helpful," I retort, raising an eyebrow at the 'more sex' comment that Link scribbled in all caps in the margin of my screenplay.

"What?" Link protests. "I stand by my criticism. Making it artsy and emotional is fine and all, but it feels like part of the story is missing. I'm serious. Think about it."

I bite my lip, giving his advice some actual thought. "I guess I can talk to Dr. Jackson about it and see if I'd be crossing a line by adding a tasteful sex scene—but I'm not asking him if we can make some poor theater major do full frontal."

"Good girl," Link says, his voice lowering to a sexy timbre as he eye-fucks me across the table. My core tingles with just those two words.

"And there it is," Trey says with a frustrated growl, lowering his book over the growing erection in his basketball shorts. "You guys are the worst."

"Is that a book in your lap, or are you just happy to see me?" Brantley says, grinning like an asshole as he walks up to our table.

Link and I snicker.

"For fuck's sake," Trey mutters.

Brantley pulls out an empty chair and flips it around, then sits down, his hazel eyes intense. "I've got some gossip for you guys." He lowers his voice and glances around.

We all look at him expectantly, and let's face it—skeptically—because it's hard to tell when to take him seriously.

"Guess who showed up at practice today? Matt-fuckhead-Johnson."

I suddenly feel like I've been dropped into a vat of ice water, freezing all my limbs and constricting the air from my lungs. I stare at Brantley with wide, frightened eyes.

The guys didn't tell Brantley exactly what Matt did to me—past or present—only that it was unforgivable, which was all he needed. He might be a bit of a clown sometimes, but Brantley's a loyal friend, and he's been acting as our eyes and ears in case someone from the hockey scene heard from Matt. But we didn't expect him to just show up.

"Coach gave him hell at practice for being MIA for the past two weeks. But we have a big game Saturday that will determine whether we make it to the Frozen Four, so he hardly got any punishment other than a verbal warning." Brantley gives a small shrug. "Matt was pretty close-lipped about the reason he was gone when anyone asked. Honestly, though, the vibe he's giving is pretty weird."

A wave of panic rises in my chest. I thought campus would be safe, that he'd be stupid to show up here, but now...

The thought of running into him, even in a public setting, terrifies me.

I don't even realize how bad I'm shaking until Link covers my hand with his and Trey's fingers gently tap my thigh under the table.

Brantley eyes me warily. "You okay, Charlie? I know he did some shit. You guys gonna tell me what it was?"

Link glances at me as if in askance.

"C'mon, the guy is my teammate, and that's a big deal. If he's that bad, I need to know."

I barely manage a nod because he's right. I don't want anyone else to get hurt because I kept my mouth shut. I didn't say anything before because we couldn't find him, but this changes everything.

"He tried to rape Charlie back during the long weekend," Link says. I shiver because he sounds murderous.

"And he hit her," Trey adds, his expression equally grim.

"Jesus," Brantley mutters. "Rumors were probably true then. How is this guy still breathing?"

"We haven't been able to find him, until now," Link says darkly. "We've had my dad's private investigator looking for the douche, but he's been in the wind."

"Why the fuck would he come back?" Brantley asks with a puzzled frown.

"I assume because he thinks he's untouchable, but we're about to mess him up."

"Lincoln..." I clutch his arm.

"I know he's dangerous, but he's outnumbered, Charlie," Trey says, his fingers falling over where my hand squeezes Link's bicep. "We'll be fine."

"Well, then I'm coming," I say resolutely, meeting their eyes.

"Bennett, you just about had a panic attack a second ago," Trey says gently.

"I'll be fine," I say, shaking my head.

Will I be fine?

I consider my feelings when I think about confronting him, but with Link and Trey by my side, the fear and panic lessen considerably. "I don't want either of you hurt or arrested. You can't just go beat him up."

"Says who?" Link and Trey echo, and Brantley laughs.

"Uh, the law. It's called assault."

"Sunshine…"

"No, I'm going to campus security first. I'll tell them what happened, and they can come with us to confront him or whatever the procedure is. I want to do it right."

"Bennett," Trey groans. "That's just going to lead a trial with your word against his, and we all know how those turn out. C'mon. He's Whitmore U's star hockey player who's about to take them to the Frozen Four, plus he's a model scholarship student who's also an affluent white guy."

"I see your point, Trey, really," I say. "But what choice do we have? We all know physical violence hasn't scared him off before. The dude is unhinged."

All three guys watch me in silence before Link sighs. "You're not going to change your mind, are you?"

"No," I say.

"Fine, we'll try it your way," he concedes reluctantly.

TURNS out my way doesn't really work like I hoped. We all agree to meet after our last class and walk over to the security office together, and when I mention it's about sexual assault, the officer on duty requests that Chancellor Edwards join us.

"We'll have to get the Brighton police involved because it

happened off campus," Chancellor Edwards explains, her brow creased with concern. "No witnesses?"

"No," I say quietly. "He drugged me at the bar, and then it happened at his house."

She glances at Brantley. "You said he came to practice today?" Brantley nods. "Okay, I'll contact BPD. They will probably be in touch with you for a statement."

"I'm sorry," I say, tugging at my lower lip with my teeth. "I know I should have said something sooner...."

"You did nothing wrong, Miss Bennett." She sighs. "But, yes, unfortunately, cases like this with little evidence other than he said-she said testimonies are rough for the victim. And I've been working on finding something on Matt because of other allegations that have come to light, but I haven't been able to pin anything on him. The girl who came forward originally won't return my calls."

"I told you about this psycho months ago," Link grinds out.

"I remember our conversation, Mr. Evans, but I couldn't just expel a student without a legitimate reason."

"Money is a good reason," he grumbles, and to her credit, Chancellor Edwards's lips give a hint of a smile.

"Either way, it's our prerogative to make our students feel safe, so at this point with four allegations under his belt, I can have security escort him off campus and fill in Coach Mitchell so he can do damage control with our communications department and find another hockey center." She looks at me with empathy. "I am on your side, Charlie; the sticky issue is that his status on the hockey team brings in a lot of money for the school, so the final decision is out of my hands if no criminal charges stick and the board votes to keep him here."

I finish up the paperwork, and we all walk to the dining hall. It's dinnertime, but my appetite is long gone, so I sit at the table and poke at my cereal with a spoon, trying to ignore the awkward silence, which is only broken when Fi and Serenity join us and Brantley fills them in on the situation.

I don't know how much Serenity knew, but probably not a lot since she frowns at me more than once, her ice-blue eyes shocked. Whatever, though. I'm happy to let other people tell the story at this point.

"Your Lucky Charms are getting soggy, baby," Trey murmurs. His arm falls over my shoulders as he tugs me against his side.

I stare at the little shapes, now bloated with milk and floating through a pinkish marshmallow deluge, and something inside me cracks. I look up at Trey through a blur of tears. "I guess they're Unlucky Charms now." My voice cracks as a sob shakes my shoulders.

No one says a damn word as I lose it, burying my face in Trey's soft blue T-shirt.

Then, Serenity breaks the silence. "Why don't we do something fun?"

She smiles at me when I lift my head from Trey's chest and wipe my nose on his shirt.

"Sorry," I mutter, eyeing the mess.

He kisses my forehead. "Anytime, Bennett."

I look over at Serenity and return her smile shyly. "Sure."

So she takes us across campus to the dance studio, leading us into the auditorium. It's a beautiful space with elegant vaulted ceilings and a huge stage with a hardwood-esque vinyl finish.

Serenity runs ahead and slips backstage to hit the lights, and the whole space flares to life.

"Take your shoes off and come up here," Serenity says with a mischievous grin as she steps from behind the curtain.

We all comply, tossing our shoes into a pile.

The floor has a springy feel as I step onto the stage with Trey and Link. "This place is amazing."

"Wait, wait, I have a surprise," Serenity says eagerly, running backstage again. She's only gone a minute before she reappears when Michael Jackson's "The Way You Make Me Feel" radiates from the sound system.

My eyes widen. "No way," I squeal. "Are you seriously letting me live out all my *Center Stage* fantasies?"

"You know it." Serenity snatches my hands, and we spin around. I'm certainly not as graceful as Serenity, but with her leading, it almost feels like I'm dancing with some semblance of rhythm.

Before long, everyone is dancing but Link, who leans against a prop in the corner and watches while Trey swings me around. But let's face it, no one thought Lincoln Evans would actually dance—it would ruin his image. He eventually takes over the music, and we try to imitate every dance movie soundtrack he throws at us—*Flashdance, Pitch Perfect, Footloose, Save the Last Dance.* Then Fi and Brantley try to recreate the *Dirty Dancing* finale, grinding against each other obscenely.

"Jesus, those two need to get a room," Serenity says around a giggle as we watch them gyrate. But she's right—their chemistry is off the charts. As the song fades out, Lincoln plays Genuwine's "Pony," looking back at us with a smirk, and Brantley and Trey take the cue perfectly in a poor attempt at imitating Channing Tatum's moves from *Magic Mike*, which is pretty much just them stripping.

Serenity and I whistle and yell, and Fi opens her purse and starts tossing dollar bills onto the stage. Then Trey starts shoving them down his boxer briefs, which causes the three of us to collapse in a fit of laughter. Even Lincoln laughs, shaking his head in disbelief, and I suddenly feel an overwhelming amount of love for my friends. We may not be blood, but they're my family now.

By midnight, we're all sitting with our feet dangling at the edge of the stage, sweaty and exhausted. My stomach is sore from laughing.

"Thank you, Seren." I lean over to look at her. She pushes her blonde hair from her eyes and smiles. "You're going to make a really awesome dance teacher someday, and we'll miss you when you leave."

Serenity blushes, looking down for a second before meeting my eyes. "Thank you, Charlie. I'll miss you guys, too."

"Who has the longest arms?" Fi says suddenly, glancing around. All three guys stick their arms out, and Fi hands her phone to Lincoln. "Think you can take a selfie of all of us?"

He nods, and we all huddle together, leaning in different directions to get the best angle before we all cheese for the camera.

"Perfect," Fi says, swiping her phone closed. "I'll text it to you guys."

Everyone parts ways as we walk back to our various dorm rooms, and after all the emotional stress plus our dance party, I'm practically dead on my feet. My phone buzzes just as we reach the guys' room, and I click on the message, smiling when I see the photo Fi sent.

Brantley has his tongue out and Fi looks completely disgusted. Serenity is smiling like the beauty queen she is. I'm grinning from ear to ear, my green eyes bright. I'm sitting next to Trey, who's looking down at me with so much love, while Link is on my other side with his signature sexy half-smile. We all look disheveled, but also so fucking happy.

Fi's right. It's perfect.

CHAPTER FORTY-NINE

CHARLIE

*T*oday is *the* day and the theater is a madhouse— swarming with film and English majors trying to prep for their final projects. Lincoln has been slinking around with a clipboard and his usual resting dick face, barking orders —all these people in his safe space make him grumpy.

Against my better judgment, I pulled him into the manager's office, locked the door, and gave him a quick blow job because I just wanted him to relax. His attitude has been scaring the shit out of the poor technical theater students who have been hard at work getting a modern projector to work alongside our old-school tech. He was a bit more agreeable after that.

I got my acceptance letters this week—one came Monday and one Tuesday—and I haven't told Trey or Link, mostly because they're under enough stress as it is worrying about Matt and dealing with finals.

And speaking of Matt, ever since he was escorted off campus, John's PI has been tailing him, and he assured us the guy has hardly left his dad's house in Brighton. Seb was happy with that bit of knowledge, so he called off Marcus's security guys; however, Marcus started asking questions when he saw their overtime hours on his payroll, and so we had to tell him about Matt. He was furious, of course, because every male in my life wants to solve my problems with guns blazing like they're John McClane. Excuse me while I roll my eyes, but also feel overwhelmingly loved. Sebastian and Marcus are actually in town now to see my screenplay in action, which is making me extra nervous.

The streetlights outside are just starting to flicker on when I see Liv and Gavin walking up, and I wave as they walk inside.

"Hey," I say, smiling. "Are you guys nervous?"

"Nah," Gavin says nonchalantly, but Liv rolls her eyes and elbows him.

"Yes, he is. We both are. He's been stressing over it all week."

"I'm nervous too, but I think it'll be great," I say, trying to exude confidence that I don't feel.

Out of the corner of my eye, I see Damon (the new assistant manager) stumbling out of the back room juggling cups and popcorn tubs. We make eye contact, and he smiles tightly when sees me.

"I think I'm needed. I'll see you guys inside?" I walk over to grab some cups before Damon drops them.

"Thanks. It's been way busier than I thought it would be." Damon wipes the sweat from his forehead with the back of his arm. "But you must be excited."

I shrug. "I've always had a bit of imposter syndrome when it comes to my writing, so this whole thing is kind of nerve-racking and surreal."

Suddenly I'm hit from behind, and a small pair of arms practically lifts me off the ground in a hug. "You're gonna be famous after this!" Fiona squeals.

"God, you scared me." I grab her wrists, which are still wrapped around my waist while trying to calm my racing heart.

"Oh geez," Trey says as he enters the lobby with Link, skirting around small groups of people entering the auditorium.

"You're not letting Fi into our throuple, are you? It's going to get too crowded, and I don't like her like that."

Fi gives me a sly wink, and her hand slides to my ass. Link and Trey's eyes widen as they follow the movement.

I can't help laughing as I pull from her grasp. "Not a chance."

I notice Sebastian and Marcus walk in, and I run toward them, throwing myself at Seb. He laughs when he catches me and swings me around, and I almost knock over Marcus, who steps back, trying not to smile.

"There are a lot of people here," Marcus remarks.

I shrug. "Dr. Jackson has been promoting the project nonstop. He wants to make it an annual thing—the crossover between Film, English, and Theater departments has been really successful. And Link organized the whole thing with the theater as a venue, so it's kind of a big deal."

Seb glances over at Lincoln and they lock eyes like they're sizing each other up, but to my surprise, it's Marcus who makes the first move.

He leans forward, extending his hand, which Lincoln shakes. "It's been a while, Lincoln. Nice job with this place. It looks great." Then he smiles at Trey and puts up his fist. Trey grins and bumps his fist against Marcus's. "Good to see you again, bro."

Seb snickers and leans close to my ear. "They used to get stoned together. A. Lot."

I notice that the lobby is emptying quickly.

"Should we go in?" Link asks. "Serenity and Brantley are already inside, and I saw Dr. Jackson sitting up front with a bunch of other faculty."

I nod, swallowing my nerves, and we all walk through the doors just as the lights are starting to dim.

EACH FILM IS ONLY about twenty minutes, but they're all so well done. Whitmore U may be a lawless school for rich kids, but damn if they aren't talented.

I clutch Link's hand when our film flickers onto the screen, the title, *Hand Me Down*, fading in. He interlaces our fingers, giving me a cocksure smile, and Trey's arm wraps around the back of my seat, his fingers grazing my shoulder. My anxiety settles, and we watch the movie unfold.

The story I wrote isn't autobiographical by any means, but it certainly reflects my loss, my abandonment, and my drive to escape a bad situation, and Liv plays the part beautifully—a girl who's treated as everyone's hand-me-down, including the mysterious boy who took her virginity.

And Gavin exudes Lincoln's arrogance and swagger to the point where Trey and I start giggling at the similarities in their mannerisms. Link tries to act annoyed, but I can see the smile tugging at the corner of his lip.

The piece is just a snippet of a larger story that I plan to publish someday, so it ends following an emotional scene between Liv and Gavin as she realizes that the boy who broke her heart all those years ago is the same person putting it back together.

I blow out a breath as the credits roll, feeling infinitely lighter now that the screening is finished. The room ripples with applause.

I lean over, my lips going to Link's ear. "We made a movie, baby," I whisper, and he smiles at my words, turning to kiss my mouth softly.

"Damn straight," he murmurs.

The lights come on, and Dr. Jackson steps up front. "We're just going to have a five-minute intermission. The next and final film is a bit longer than the others, so use the bathroom and grab your snacks while you can."

"I'm going to go swap out the reels," Link says, going to stand, but I put my hand on his wrist.

"I'll do it; I need a breath of air anyway."

He nods and scoots into my seat after I edge down the aisle so he can chat with our friends.

In the lobby and turn the corner quickly, not wanting anyone to stop me. I feel gross and sweaty from sitting in the stuffy theater, and I suspect I may need to dig the deodorant from my purse before I go back in.

I walk up to the projection area and pull out the reel of short films from the projector, replacing it with the longer piece, and queue it up, scheduling it to start in five minutes.

A rattling noise echoes behind me, and I turn to peer into the darkness. Nothing moves in the shadows, and all I can make out are the tall silhouettes of the other film towers.

I shrug and then turn around.

Something heavy crashes into the back of my skull. The pain is sharp and sudden and then everything goes black.

WHEN I COME TO, the first thing I register is the rough carpet against my cheek and hands. I blink open my eyes, squinting in the dim light. My head throbs with every beat of my heart, and there's something wet and sticky on my hair, and when I touch it, blood coats my shaky fingers, the tangy metallic scent hitting my nostrils and making me gag.

Someone hit me, I realize.

I look around in panic. I'm still upstairs in the theater, but I'm on the ground between two film towers. I brush dirt and bits of film mylar from my clothing and skin as I try to stand. But my vision blackens at the edges as I get to my feet, and everything tilts. I collapse onto my knees, gasping for air.

"Feeling a bit woozy, are you?" says a cold, detached voice.

I turn, staring wide-eyed at Matt, who's sitting on the building table with his legs swinging casually back and forth.

"How...how did you get in here?" I try to keep my voice steady as I stare at him in disbelief. *Am I having a nightmare?*

"I knew tonight would be chaotic—so in classic movie villain form, I snuck in while everyone was distracted with this garbage. I've been watching you when I can—though eluding the PI has been a pain in my ass—and you went to the fucking chancellor. Really, Charlie? That was a stupid move."

He jumps down from the table, his eyes flashing with anger, and panic seizes my chest when I notice the dull glint off the gun held loosely in his right hand. He comes to stand before me, grabbing my shirt sleeve and pulling me roughly to my feet. I try to focus on him as the room twists and turns around me, and I swallow a wave of nausea.

He smiles emotionlessly. "You got me kicked off the hockey team and put on probation from university..." He sneers as he says the words. "It's not like I could stalk you there, so I hang out here a lot and wait. I watch lots of movies, you know? But you haven't been working much either, which has been frustrating for me."

He gestures to the window behind me overlooking Auditorium 2. "I watched *The Breakfast Club* a few days ago."

He taps the barrel of the gun against his chin thoughtfully. "It's funny, we watched it all those times when we were kids, and I always thought Bender was so cool, but when I saw it again, I realized I relate more to the jock, Andrew—always trying to please his dad. He can't think for himself, and he hurts people and takes risks because that's what he's pressured into doing."

He pulls me forward and pushes me into the chair next to the building table, his eyes unfocused as he talks.

Despite the fear rippling through my body, his words touch a place of empathy as I remember Seb telling me how his dad almost killed him. I saw the bruises on his body when we'd fool around when we were teenagers, but he got so angry when I tried to talk about it. As we got older, Matt seemed to get along better with his dad, so I stopped worrying, but until the day I walked in on him cheating, I always had a nagging feeling that I should have said something, done something, to stop it.

"Is that because your dad pressured you too, Matt?" I ask quietly, hoping that if I can distract him long enough, I can find a way out of this. I have no idea how long I was unconscious, but the film I queued up earlier still seems to be showing, so the guys have to be wondering why I'm not back at this point.

Matt looks at me, his eyes sharp again. "He wanted me to marry you someday, actually. Not because he liked you, but because he thought I might be able to get my hands on your inheritance."

"Lovely," I snark.

"But I messed it up when I avenged him—he didn't appreciate my gesture and didn't like that there were witnesses, and he put me in the hospital when he found out. Did you know that? I almost died." His eyes grow distant for a moment. "I wish I had died."

"So that's why you did it? You raped my mom because our parents lost their stupid business deal." The words fall out of my mouth with an accusatory tone, and I instantly regret them. Matt surges toward me, the gun aimed at me. His hand shakes as he dips his head to meet my eyes.

"That *stupid* business deal was my family's windfall. So yeah, what better way to punish your stepdad's failure than fucking his wife. I recorded it, you know. So that I could show him what a whore she was." My jaw tightens, anger at his words battling against fear as he continues waving the gun in my face. "You just ruined the show when you walked in."

"You were fucking her in my bedroom, Matt," I hiss. "Didn't you think that might be a bad place for it to happen."

403

"I thought it was poetic. Two sluts in one bed—like mother, like daughter."

"Except I never fucked you," I bite out.

"No, but you've been fucking *them*."

I see movement over Matt's shoulder, and I do my best not to focus on it. Someone is at the top of the stairs just out of sight. Hope twists through the pain and fear.

"You were mine until you opened your legs for not one, but two little rich kids." His voice is tight and clipped as his knuckles whiten around the gun. "Guess you always did like to fuck around with broken boys, as if you could fix us. But, let's face it, you're just as fucked-up as we are."

"Trey and Link are nothing like you," I growl.

As I say it, muffled applause erupts below us, and Matt glances at the auditorium window. "Show's over," he sneers, and aims the gun at me. "And after I kill you, I swear I'll kill them, too."

I hear the faint sounds of sirens in the distance, and Matt stiffens, his eyes growing wild just as Seb steps from around the corner, lunging for the gun.

I scream as I watch them fight for control of the weapon. I'm frozen on the spot until a hand twists into my fingers and yanks me toward the stairs. Lincoln pushes me gently against the wall, cradling my face in his hands as he inspects me, his gray eyes teetering between fear and rage as he takes in the blood on my neck that's now seeping into my white shirt.

"Are you hurt?" he rasps, but all I can think about is Seb fighting for the gun, and I snap.

I push Link out of the way, and he's so surprised, he actually stumbles.

"Charlie!" Link shouts as I duck under his arms, my brother's name tearing from my throat like a damn battle cry. Seb and Matt are rolling on the ground, fists flying. I look around frantically for the gun, but he pulls me backward.

404

"Link! I don't see the gun." My voice rises in panic.

Just then, Trey comes pounding up the stairs, and Lincoln shoves me at him. I trip over my own feet, but Trey catches me when I fall into his hard chest.

"Get her the fuck away from here," Lincoln orders, and Trey nods grimly.

"No!" I scream, pulling against Trey's grip. He hauls me back as I start to struggle—kicking and punching him. "Let me go, Trey." But he picks me up like I weigh nothing and tosses me over his shoulder. "Trey, please," I sob, tears blurring everything around me, helplessness clogging my throat.

A loud pop echoes from above us, followed by a guttural cry, and we both freeze before Trey quickens his pace down the stairs, his long legs taking me farther and farther away from my brother and Link.

I can't breathe. The thought of losing either of them is unthinkable, and the panic surging through my body is so strong, it's debilitating.

We make it into the lobby, and Trey drops us to the ground, his breath coming in ragged gulps.

"You have to let me go back," I plead. "We have to help them."

Trey's grip on me tightens, and I know it's a losing battle. All the fight leaves me.

Blue and red lights flash around us, bouncing off the walls and circling the room like some sort of fucked-up disco ball.

I bury myself against Trey, crawling into his lap as my body shakes with my sobs.

"Shhh, Bennett, it's okay," he whispers. "It's going to be okay."

For once, Trey's voice can't calm me because nothing about this is okay.

If Seb or Link is hurt—or worse—I won't come back from that. Nothing will ever be okay again.

LINCOLN

Once Charlie is safe with Trey, I turn to Sebastian and Matt struggling on the ground. They grunt and curse as they roll around, knocking into furniture and upending stacks of film canisters.

Sebastian is big, but Matt's a hockey player, and even though he's a center, he's still built like a human wall.

I scan the scene, finally spotting the gun just out of Matt's reach under one of the projectors.

Just then, Matt rolls over Sebastian, straddling his waist. He fists the front of Seb's shirt and lays into him with a solid punch to the mouth. Blood pours down Seb's chin.

"Still can't beat me in a fight, huh, Sebastian?"

Sebastian sneers at him and spits blood. "Fuck off, Matt," he growls.

I step forward, grabbing both of Matt's arms, and he cries out when I cinch them together behind his back until they're close to popping from their sockets.

"The gun," I pant, pointing with my chin as my muscles strain to hold Matt still while he thrashes against my grip.

Sebastian wiggles from underneath Matt's body and crawls for the gun, grabbing it and pointing it at the asshole's face.

"Stop moving, fucker," Sebastian he bares his teeth, now red with blood.

Matt stops his struggle, staring up at Sebastian with murderous intent. I allow my arms, which are shaking and burning from holding him in place, to relax as I let go and lean back.

I look up at Sebastian, unsure what to do next.

"As much as I'd like you to shoot this asshole, I assume we should wait for the cops."

Sebastian's hand is shaking on the trigger, and I eye him warily, curious if he'll do it. But Matt makes the decision for us. He kicks his leg with surprising agility, his foot catching Sebastian's ankle. He goes down, and the sound of the gun as it fires is deafening.

My ears ring, and pain reverberates through my body.

A ragged cry rips my throat raw as I look down in shock at the blood blooming across the gray material of my dress shirt.

I barely register Sebastian hitting Matt across the back of his head before the world starts to tilt, my vision swimming in and out of focus.

My back meets the ground hard, knocking the breath from my lungs.

Sebastian drops to my side, panting. "Shit. Stay with me, buddy. She'll kill me if you die. Stay with me, Lincoln."

I can barely hear him over the ringing noise.

I don't doubt he's right, and the thought of causing Charlie more pain makes my gut twist. Then Sebastian applies pressure to my shoulder and the darkness takes me away.

CHARLIE

Trey is here. Marcus is here. Seb is here. *Where's Link?*

Apparently, the theater was evacuated as soon as Sebastian and Lincoln figured out what was going on. The cops and paramedics arrived after Trey and I made it downstairs, and a nice woman named Rita has been fussing over my head wound while I sit in the back of an ambulance, asking me a million questions as she carefully wraps gauze around my temple. Everyone looks worried, and Rita keeps telling the guys I'm in shock and may have a concussion.

Two unconscious people were brought down, but the other paramedic wouldn't let me see them. I assume one is Matt and the other is Link, but no one pulled out one of those black body bags like you see in movies, so I have to assume they're both still breathing.

In the back of my head, I'm screaming. There's a wall there that's holding back my pain and grief because I know that as soon as that emotional dam ruptures, I may not survive.

I feel so cold, and every once in a while, a tear trickles down my cheek, startling me with its heat.

My stepbrothers and Trey have all taken turns trying to talk to me, but I hate the gentle voices they use, like I'm a small child, so I refuse to respond.

Yes, I understand the irony of acting childish about them treating me like a child.

"We're going to take you to the hospital," Rita says. "You'll have to stay overnight just for observation." She's the only person talking to me like an adult.

"Where's Lincoln?" I ask quietly. "Is he okay?

She looks at me steadily as if gauging how much information I can handle before sighing resolutely. My insides are unsettled as I wait for her response.

"They won't tell you?" she finally asks.

I shake my head. "They're afraid I'll have a breakdown or something."

"They love you."

"I know," I say simply. "But you don't need to protect me like they do, and that boy is half of my beating heart, so please tell me if he's okay."

She nods. "He was shot in the shoulder, and he lost a lot of blood. But I doubt the bullet did much damage. My colleague said it went through cleanly—didn't hit anything important.

Some surgery should fix him up—though please understand there's no guarantees. They've already taken him and the other guy to the hospital."

I let out a shaky, resigned breath. "Thank you."

"Of course," she says, smiling warmly. "Will you give the police a statement?"

"I want to see Link first."

She purses her lips but agrees.

Trey climbs into the back of the ambulance, and I nestle into his side, my stomach fluttering when his soft lips brush my forehead. We don't talk, but it's the first time since I woke up on the theater floor that I feel like I can breathe easier.

CHAPTER FIFTY

CHARLIE

*I*t's been six weeks since the night when Link was shot and Matt was arrested.

Matthew-fucking-Johnson was charged with aggravated assault, attempted murder, rape (thanks to Sebastian coming forward with information about my mom), and three counts of sexual assault, and he's still rotting in jail while he awaits sentencing since he certainly has no money for bail. I'm not looking forward to the trial, but if it means he can't hurt anyone else, I'd do it a million times over with zero regrets.

Trey and I have been busy taking care of Lincoln while he recovered from his shoulder wound as well as juggling school and working at the theater when we can. Even when the physical wound itself had healed, Link would have nightmares and flashbacks from that night. He was embarrassed at first, but it's hard to hide from the two people you share a bed with.

Now with school stuff finally done and Link mostly healed, I'm ready to just enjoy life, and enjoy *them*. We've talked about taking things to the next level—like a real threesome, if you will.

I know what I want to try. I've been writing about it in my notebook, which has been giving me some serious lady blue

410

balls. Even now, I flush as I stare at the filthy words I just scribbled on the page while I wait for Trey and Link in the hallway
outside their classroom to finish their last finals.

"You're blushing, Bennett," Trey drawls.

I jump guiltily, slamming the book shut as I stare up into
their beautiful faces. Trey's golden hair is a shaggy mess—he
still refuses to cut it—and I told him he'd be rivaling Chris
Hemsworth soon enough, but I love tangling my fingers in the
soft strands. His whisky eyes are sparkling with mischief as they
rake over my body, which just makes my face flush hotter. Link
is just as unfairly stunning as usual. His dark hair is controlled
chaos, artfully styled to perfection, and his expressive eyes,
which are narrowed in suspicion as he watches me, are so light
they're practically platinum. I've nicknamed them Fifty Shades
of Gray because of the way the hue changes with his moods, but
they've been light more often than not these days. His full lips
twitch in his half smirk, and I have to hide my own smile. He's
happy now, and that makes me happy.

"What're you writing?" Link asks, tipping his head at my
notebook.

"I, uhh...it's nothing." I don't know why I'm suddenly so flustered. They've had their fingers in my ass, for Christ's sake.

Trey reaches down and pulls me to my feet. He bends over,
his lips brushing my ear. Goosebumps rise along my arms.
"You're a terrible liar."

Link's arm falls over my shoulders, and we walk outside and
across the quad. It used to bother me sometimes, the looks we
get when we're affectionate—mostly glares from other girls or
guys giving rude gestures or obscene winks—but I hardly notice
them now. Love is love, and we definitely love each other, as
unconventional as our relationship may seem to other people.

"It was a sex scene, wasn't it?" Trey continues to prod.
"Charlotte Bennett, are you writing smut?"

"Fine," I concede. "I'm writing smut. I don't know if you've met my boyfriends, but they're hot, so I have *a lot* of inspiration."

"I bet they have huge dicks," Link murmurs, and I roll my eyes.

"Average," I say with a shrug.

They both stop, looking down at me with deadpan expressions, and I burst out laughing.

Link's face darkens. "We might have to punish you for that comment." Trey is already nodding in agreement, a wicked smile curving his lips.

"Oh no," I say sarcastically with a snicker. "Sounds terrible."

"Seriously though, can we read it? Trey asks as we walk into the Wolf Building and wait for the elevator. "I assume whatever you're writing is somewhat autobiographical,"

"I was hoping you'd want to actually." I bite my lip nervously. "Because now that we finally have a free night…"

They grin.

Link's eyes meet Trey's. "I call dibs on her pussy."

"Fine by me. You know I'm an ass man," Trey says with a wink.

"Really? Dibs? I'm not the front seat, and we're not thirteen." But their words still cause my pussy to tingle as I think about them both railing me at the same time.

We enter the guys' apartment and fall onto the couch. Trey snatches the notebook from my hands and flips it open while Link crowds him, leaning on his shoulder so they can both read the scenario I've been writing and rewriting for weeks.

After a few minutes, the anticipation becomes too much, and I stand up and pour myself a glass of whisky from Link's stash and stare out the large glass windows. The dark green expanse of trees stretches out as far as I can see, rising to the base of the distant mountains before they give way to white snowcaps, shimmering in the June sunshine.

I finally told them my news once Link was fully on the mend

—I got the internship this summer—it starts in July—but my application to NYU was rejected. By then, I already knew what I wanted to do, but the guys read my mind. They both assured me that we'd all be spending the summer in New York, and Link had already rented us what he called "a little apartment" over-looking Central Park. I don't even want to know how much that rent costs. So with NYU definitely off my radar, I decided to stay at Whitmore U and finish out my degree, and then I plan to apply to several publishing companies in Seattle and Vancouver so that we're not leaving the theater behind. I have no doubt they'd upend their lives for me and move across the country, but Trey and Link have so much fun running Lakeside Cinema—I'd be a monster to ask them to start over somewhere else.

I hear the book fall shut, my thoughts scattering. I let out a shaky breath and turn to face my soulmates. I was a hopeless romantic as a girl, getting lost in epic fantasy with loves that lasted forever on page, like Aragorn and Arwen. Then, I stopped believing in love for a while. I approached it with cynicism and caution. But love is different for everyone, and for me, it's Trey's calming presence, his easy smile and optimism, and his ability to hold Link and me together when everything is breaking apart. And Link? Well, he's my dark knight—fiercely loyal and protective, brutally handsome, and my other half in every way possible.

Trey and Link share a look, and I know they're thinking about what I want. It's new territory for Link at least, so while I'm hopeful they'll be down, I'm steeling myself for disappoint-ment. Something passes between them before they turn to look at me, and it blows my mind that these boys are just as in sync with each other as they are with me, like the three of us together make one person.

I put down the now-empty glass with a trembling hand.

Why am I so nervous?

A smile touches my lips as I take in their hooded looks

413

before Trey literally sweeps me off my feet and tosses me over his shoulder. Link chuckles, and my stomach flips at the sound. I'll never tire of hearing him laugh. I look up from my precarious position, watching Link reach behind his head and pull his off T-shirt in one smooth motion, letting it fall to the floor as he follows us.

Trey sets me on the bed and starts stripping his clothing off, following Link's lead. I watch with hungry eyes as I take in the show—all defined muscles and smooth skin.

"We're about to wreck you, baby girl. In the best way possible," Link says, smiling darkly.

I swallow hard.

"Please," I scoff. "I was wrecked from the first day I met you two, but I regret nothing."

Link steps out of his boxers, his cock springing free and slapping against his stomach, precum smearing across his abs. He climbs onto the bed and starts to peel the clothing from my body. Everything is already tingling, Link's rough touch setting fire to my skin as his fingers graze my body. I'm a whimpering mess by the time my panties come off. Trey joins us and unsnaps my bra with skilled fingers.

Link leans in, his mouth falling against mine, and I open for him immediately, his kiss a drug that I'll never get enough of. His lips are soft and slow at first, savoring every movement and taste. Trey's lips start at my neck and work their way down, sucking and kissing my shoulder. I moan obscenely when he takes my hardened nipple into his warm mouth, licking, sucking, and biting.

Link pulls away and kisses down my other side before pulling my other nipple to his mouth, his tongue caressing and lapping with enthusiasm. His eyes are a mixture of adoration and lust, like he's seeing me for the time all over again, and it's such a turn-on.

"You're both going to kill me," I groan, my whole body hot

and aching with arousal. Link and Trey glance at each other, sharing a smirk, and then they both pull away. I pout in disappointment, causing Trey to chuckle.

"Time to relax and enjoy the show, baby," he growls and pushes me back against the headboard.

I stare with wide eyes as Trey turns to Link, and my stomach flutters with anticipation.

They sit on their knees facing each other. They're so close that their cocks, which are standing fully erect between them, are almost touching. Link glances at me, and he looks vulnerable and unsure, an expression so out of place on his normally confident face.

"You don't have to, boss," I say quietly as I watch, and Trey nods, taking Link's chin in his hand and turning him so their gazes meet.

"You're safe here, Link," Trey says, his face so tender and serious that my heart squeezes. "If you don't want to do this or if you want to stop, I will—no questions asked."

"No, I want to," he says firmly, licking his lips.

Trey's brown eyes follow the movement, a smile tugging at his lips. "Good because I'm not gonna lie, this has been a fantasy of mine for a while."

Link raises his eyebrows but doesn't say anything as Trey reaches for him. His large hand falls to Link's hip and slides around to cup his ass, pulling him so close their cocks bump. Link gasps at the contact, but he lets Trey continue to lead.

With his other hand, Trey cradles Link's stubbled cheek, and he pulls his mouth close so they're lips are inches apart. "I'm going to kiss you now," he rumbles.

Link's nod is slight, almost imperceptible, but his chest is rising and falling with quick breaths.

Then their lips touch, sliding together.

At first Link stiffens, but as Trey's tongue moves against the seam of his mouth, he starts to relax. Their kiss is tentative and slow, Link's eyes closing as their rhythm picks up. I see Trey's knuckles whiten as his grip on Link's face tightens, and then Link's shaky hands are skimming over Trey's biceps and pushing into his hair.

It's the hottest thing I've ever seen, and the sight is making me feral.

I slide my hand down my stomach as I watch them, slipping my fingers between my folds. Arousal is smeared all over my thighs, dripping onto bed. I circle my clit, snippets of pleasure zipping up my spine.

Trey moves his hand from Link's ass and slides it around, taking his own cock and Link's into his hand. Using the precum leaking from both of them as lube, Trey gives them a solid tug.

"Holy fuck," Link moans, his head falling back as Trey continues to jack them both together. "That feels incredible."

My fingers slide into my pussy, and I can't stop the whimper that escapes my throat. They turn to look at me, both of them blissed out as Trey continues his ministrations, but the sight of me touching myself seems to set them both off.

"Holy shit, this is hot," Trey mutters, his hand picking up speed.

"Gonna come," Link says, as he falls forward and presses his face into Trey's neck, his hands clutching Trey's shoulders.

My fingers pinch and circle my clit furiously as I drink in the sight of Trey and Link lost in each other, and I can feel an orgasm burning through my veins with tremendous force.

"Me too," I gasp.

Link and I both moan loudly as we tumble off the edge simultaneously. I force my eyes open as pleasure vibrates through my body and watch as Link loses his mind too, cum erupting from the red tip of his cock and spilling over Trey's hand and onto his cock and stomach.

Link collapses in a daze with his forehead against Trey's

bicep, breathing hard while I lay in a boneless heap, my head replaying the sexiest scene I've ever witnessed in real life.

"That was...so hot," Link says finally as he falls back onto the bed next to me. "Way hotter than I expected."

"Same," I whisper.

And then we look back up at Trey who's kneeling at the foot of the bed, eyeing us hungrily while he pumps the raging erection in his hand. He crawls over my body, pressing his mouth to mine, the kiss making my head spin and reigniting a fire between my legs as his cock, sticky with precum and Link's release, presses against my aching cunt.

He moves his lips to the shell of my ear. "Spread your legs, Bennett." When I do, he sits up and runs two fingers languidly through the mess of cum on his abs. "This will *come* in handy," he says with a devilish grin.

"Dude," Link moans from beside him. "Only you would make a joke right now."

Trey just grins wider and then slides his fingers between my ass cheeks, smearing the warm liquid around my hole.

"Fucking hell," I grind out, my hips thrusting up involuntarily as one of Trey's thick fingers slides in up to the knuckle.

Trey stills. "You okay, baby?" he asks as he rotates his finger in a slow circle.

I bring my legs up so my knees almost touch my ears, giving him better access.

"More," I pant.

"Goddamn, you're beautiful," Link says, brushing hair from my forehead tenderly.

I look over at him just as Trey inserts another finger and scissors them open, stretching me wider. A string of unintelligible noises fall from my mouth as he does it, while his other hand starts to rub my clit lazily.

Link's hand falls to his dick, which is already starting to

harden again. "I can't wait for us to take both of your tight little holes," he says with a filthy smirk.

"Roll over and get on your hands and knees," Trey orders, giving my ass cheek a firm smack at the same time he pinches my clit. I yelp as the zip of pain and pleasure goes straight to my core, and I roll over, pressing my ass toward Trey shamelessly. Any shyness or vulnerability I felt before has been completely forgotten.

Trey adds a third finger.

"I feel so full already," I say, pushing back against him.

He leans over my body, and when he removes his hand, I whimper at the lost contact. "I'm about to fill you even more," he whispers, his breath fanning over my sweat-slicked skin. "Get into Lincoln's lap. Now."

I swallow at his bossy tone and look over at Link who shifts toward me. His back is against the headboard, and his hand is stroking his cock in steady pulls, which he pauses when I move to climb into his lap. I place my hands on his shoulders as I lower myself onto him, his cock achingly hot and rock hard as it slides inside me. We both moan loudly.

I tense when I feel Trey's body against my back, the head of his dick sliding between my cheeks. I want him inside me but nerves start to cut through the euphoria of the moment.

Trey seems to sense my panic. "I'm going to go slow, Bennett," he soothes as he pushes against my hole.

Link places his hands on my flushed cheeks and kisses me tenderly. "We've got you."

And somehow my body listens, and I relax, allowing the head of Trey's cock to slip past the tight ring of muscle. I grit my teeth against the initial burn, my eyes watering as he continues to ease his way in. But when he's fully seated and gives a tentative thrust, all the pain gives way to pleasure.

"Jesus, I can feel you inside her," Link groans as Trey starts to move more freely. "I need to move."

"Yes, move," I cry, dropping my head to Link's chest.

I've never felt so fucking full in my life—like I might split in two. But then they start to move together, and it's like they're completely on beat, thrusting in and out of me in perfect rhythm.

"Fucking hell, I'm not going to last long. You're so fucking tight," Trey says, his thrusts becoming harder and more frenzied, and I feel Link's hands tightening on my hips and he also picks up his pace.

Trey's voice is a rumble behind me. "Look at you taking us both so well."

I flush at his praise. It's sweaty and dirty and delicious as they pound me from both ends, and when Trey reaches around my hip to rub a thumb over my clit, I detonate, my climax ricocheting off of every nerve ending in my body. I can't help it—I scream their names.

Trey isn't far behind, crying out and grunting as his cock pulses, filling my ass with his release, and he keeps pumping until we hear Link's strangled cry, his warm cum filling my cunt, and we all collapse into a sweaty, sticky, satiated mess.

After allowing a few minutes for our heart rates to slow, Link pulls me against him, his soft cock falling from my pussy at the same time Trey gingerly pulls out as well. I feel their cum slide down my body and mingle between my thighs, but I don't have the energy to care about the mess.

"I love you," I murmur.

"I know," Trey and Link say in unison, and I feel their bodies shake on either side of me with the kind of delirious laughter that comes from endorphins and exhaustion.

"Nerds," I say, holding back my own laugh.

I snuggle between them, our bodies slotting together perfectly.

I've finally reached my someday.

ACKNOWLEDGMENTS

This story has been rolling around in my head in one form or another for a long time, and a lot of people have influenced the path it's taken over the years.

First, to Ramses—we were just kids when we met, but you inspired me in so many ways. You were my first morally gray crush, and despite your rough edges, you had the biggest heart. I miss you so fucking much every day.

To Mike—I'll never forget what it was like to feel those butterflies and the irresistible invincibility that comes with young teenage love. You made me a hopeless romantic from a young age.

To my stepbrothers Mason and Gavin who taught me that blood isn't what makes us family. I love you both a ridiculous amount.

To Corrie, Lori, and Tay who are constant proof that best friends are an unequivocal necessity in this fucked-up journey we call life—no matter how busy we get or how much time passes.

To my mom and dad who always supported my dream of being a writer, even when so many people insisted that an English degree would take me nowhere.

And to my stepmother, who embodies success in the English field, for giving me the confidence that I was indeed following the right path.

To Travis and Matt and the rest of the gang from Sehome Cinema, circa 1999-2002—working with you all was memorable to say the least, and I'll never forget the laughs, the drama, and the connections I made at that point in my life.

To Meg and Laura for being the best alpha readers ever. This book is a part of me, and you both managed to offer me advice without totally wrecking my soul in the process. Thank you for giving me the confidence to actually publish something worth reading.

To Brett, Jen, Cesar, and Cintia—thank you for being my biggest fans and preordering this book the second it was available (probably against your better judgment). You guys are my favorites, truly.

To all my professors at Coastal Carolina University—Nelljean Rice, Dan Albergotti, Sara Sanders, Ray Moye, Lee Bollinger, Randall Wells, Maggie Ivanova, Donald Millus—without you, I wouldn't be the writer I am today. Cheers!

To my editor Caroline—sometimes I swear you understood my characters better than I did, and without you, I never could have published this polished, amazing story.

To Kate with Y'all. That Graphic. for the beautiful cover—you're an amazing graphic artist, and you were so patient with me and all my newbie questions.

To my husband who encouraged me to write *Someday Away* despite the odds that it might fail spectacularly—it would never have been written if not for your unwavering support, compassion, and patience. Loving a writer is hard work. Despite my doubts, my anxiety, and my single-minded obsession, somehow you're still here. I love you, Woodchuck. Always.

And to my readers—I hope you love these characters as much as I do. Thank you for taking a chance on this book, and I'll always be grateful for your support and praise (and even your criticism).

ABOUT THE AUTHOR

Sara Elisabeth has been a writer since she was six years old when she was inspired by authors like Ursula K. LeGuin, Terry Brooks, and S. E. Hinton.

She's from the Pacific Northwest, spending most of her life with one foot in British Columbia and one foot in Washington state.

When she's not writing romance novels, Sara's certainly reading them. She's also a self-proclaimed nerd with a passion for Diet Pepsi, RPG video games, movies, and 90s alt-rock music.

Find Sara's books on Amazon or visit www.saraelisabethauthor.com.

instagram.com/saraelisabethauthor
threads.net/saraelisabethauthor
facebook.com/saraelisabethauthor
amazon.com/author/saraelisabethauthor
goodreads.com/saraelisabethauthor